The

VICTORY GARDENS
of BROOKLYN

Library of Modern Jewish Literature

Merrill Joan Gerber

The VICTORY GARDENS of BROOKLYN

A Novel

SYRACUSE UNIVERSITY PRESS

Syracuse University Press, Syracuse, New York 13244-5160
Copyright © 2007 by Merrill Joan Gerber
All Rights Reserved

First Edition 2007

07 08 09 10 11 12   6 5 4 3 2 1

The paper used in this publication meets the minimum requirements
of American National Standard of Information Sciences—Permanence
of Paper for Printed Library Materials, ANSI Z39.48-1984.∞™

Publication of this book is made possible by a grant
from the Fishman Family Foundation.

For a listing of books published and distributed by Syracuse University Press,
visit our Web site at SyracuseUniversityPress.syr.edu.

ISBN-13: 978-0-8156-0892-9   ISBN-10: 0-8156-0892-6

LIBRARY OF CONGRESS CATALOGING-IN-PUBLICATION DATA

Gerber, Merrill Joan.
The victory gardens of Brooklyn : a novel / Merrill Joan Gerber. — 1st ed.
p. cm. — (Library of modern Jewish literature)
ISBN 978-0-8156-0892-9 (pbk. : alk. paper)
1. Sisters—New York (State)—New York—Fiction.   2. Jews—New York (State)—New York—Fiction.
3. Brooklyn (New York, N.Y.)—Fiction.   4. Lower East Side (New York, N.Y.)—Fiction.
5. Immigrants—New York (State)—New York—Fiction.   6. Jewish families—Fiction.
7. Domestic fiction.   8. Jewish fiction.   I. Title.
PS3557.E664V53 2007
813'.54—dc22   2007021382

Manufactured in the United States of America

MERRILL JOAN GERBER is a prize-winning novelist and short-story writer who has published six novels—among them *The Kingdom of Brooklyn*, winner of the Ribalow Award from *Hadassah Magazine* for "the best English-language book of fiction on a Jewish theme"—as well as six volumes of short stories and three books of nonfiction. Her work has appeared in *The New Yorker, Atlantic, Mademoiselle, Redbook, Commentary, Sewanee Review, American Scholar, Southwest Review,* and elsewhere. Her story "I Don't Believe This" won an O. Henry Prize in 1986. Ms. Gerber teaches fiction writing at the California Institute of Technology.

Contents

PART ONE

The East Side, 1906–1925

1906

ONE

Ava stumbled as Mama pulled her along the empty streets. The wind stung her eyes and caught in her throat, making her gag and forcing her to bury her face in the long black hairs of Mama's fur coat. The heavy fur had a sour animal smell, but burrowing into it was better than suffocating in the wind. Mama's footsteps clattered roughly on the pavement. Ava heard the sawing of her mother's breath in the icy wind. Why were they running through the night this way? Mama had snatched her from her bed and sucked her out into the black night. Her brother, Shmuel, was guarding Uncle Hymie's store on Delancey Street, so she couldn't ask him what was happening. Although he was only twelve, he wasn't afraid to spend the night all alone as watchman because he wanted the twenty-five cents Uncle Hymie paid him.

The fur of the skunk coat rose up in Ava's nose and made her sneeze. Ava longed for her safe bed. How peaceful and still it had been there before her mother had wrenched her out of its warmth and began dragging her through the streets. Mama, who was generally calm, seemed to have lost her mind.

But all at once they stopped—so suddenly that Ava's teeth came down on her lower lip and the taste of blood flooded her mouth. Her mother dropped Ava's hand and stared at the doorway of a brownstone house. Beside the doorway was a wide, lit window, bright as a stage. And looking out the window was Papa.

He seemed to be looking right at her, but she could tell he was unable to see her. He was sitting at a table with three people: a pretty young woman with long red hair and two older people. A white cloth covered the table

3

that held a silver samovar and plates heaped with slices of honey cake and sponge cake. Sabbath candles flickered in their brass holders. Papa was sipping tea. His big hand was on the table, covering the small hand of the young woman. The older man talked and gestured. His mouth opened like a pink doughnut inside his bushy black beard. Papa whispered something to the girl; she cast her eyes down and smiled. Papa lifted her hand to his lips and kissed it.

"Pig!" Mama screamed suddenly. She began to bang on the door. "He has a wife and children, the man is a swine!"

Someone opened the door a crack, and Mama shoved it in, pulling Ava with her. Ignoring the others at the table, she cried, "What about your children, Nathan? You gamble and take food from their mouths and I have put up with it. Hymie and Rose gave us money for food when you lost all we had. But this! This!"

Mama's whole body was trembling. "Here is your baby! A witness to your sin. Can you live with that, Nathan? Your sweet baby girl?"

Mama pushed Ava toward her father; she tumbled against him, and her nose scraped against the buttons of his vest.

"Papa, please come home," Ava sobbed into the rough cloth of his jacket. But when she raised her eyes, her father would not look at her; his head was jerking from one side to the other, his handsome face wild with confusion.

"Why do you call him Nathan?" the red-haired girl cried out. "His name is Isadore!"

"What do you expect from him, the truth?" Mama shouted. "Listen! He's a married man. Whatever he's told you is a lie. He's my husband. He gambles and he cheats. If this is your daughter he's after, thank God that she's saved from him."

The red-haired girl began to cry. Papa grabbed his coat from a hook on the wall and put it on.

"Run, coward!" Mama said. "Run! Run so far I never see you again!"

The older woman was clutching her chest. The draft from the open door blew the candles out.

"Is it true?" the young woman sobbed. "Is it true, Isadore?"

But Ava's father slammed his hat on his head and rushed out the door.

"Papa!" Ava screamed. "Where are you going?"

But he was gone, a dark figure running in the street, his coat tails flapping.

"My God, my God," the older woman was crying. Mama looked at the red-haired girl. "I saved you," she said. "I couldn't save myself, but I saved you. Someday you will thank me."

TWO

"Sit down now and eat your soup!" Aunt Rose said to Ava. "Eat your bread and every bit of the crust. Here you don't get away with murder like your mother lets you."

The crust of Aunt Rose's bread was hard as steel; Ava hated the rye seeds with the bitter taste. Aunt Rose made food with too much pepper. Ava had to dilute each spoonful of soup with a drink of water.

"When is Mama coming to see me?" Ava asked. Aunt Rose was at the sink, pulling the insides out of a chicken. Yellowy yolks, veined with red and clustered like grapes, came out of the chicken in a slimy handful. Ava gagged. In her own bowl of soup were two of those eggs, hard cooked, rubbery. She knew she would have to eat them.

"She'll come when she comes," Aunt Rose said. "It isn't overnight she can earn the divorce money." She began to mumble, "That no good *momza, schvein.*" She was talking about Ava's father. Ava hated to hear it; she wanted to cover her ears with her hands. She loved Papa and missed him. He was such a handsome man, always dressed as if he were going to the most important affair in the world. She loved to think about his smooth cheeks, the marvelous smell of the cream he put in his hair to keep it wavy and smooth. When he used to lean over her in her bed, his face filling up the room, she would feel safe and loved. He would tell her stories about Vienna, where he was born. About the fancy house his family had lived in. How he could speak seven languages—and that someday he would take her there, and they would walk in the beautiful parks.

If only her mother hadn't run to that house where her father was holding that girl's hand! Then he would still be at home, coming up the steps to their apartment late at night, singing, his leather heels tapping on the linoleum. Sometimes Ava wished that the red-haired girl could be her mother instead of Rachel, her real mother. Ava would live with the girl and her own father in that apartment behind the window, and Ava would polish the beautiful silver samovar. The girl would sing to her and help her make clothes for her doll, Peggy. It seemed as if the girl, because she was so young, could be her friend. It would be nice to have a new mother for a while.

Her real mother was too impatient. When she had a few days between jobs and came to stay at Aunt Rose's, she hardly had time for Ava at all, but spent long hours huddled at the dining table with Aunt Rose, discussing serious matters. When she finally had a moment for Ava, all she wanted to know was, "Are you eating enough? Are you helping Aunt Rose with the housework?" Even so, Ava wanted to be with her mother. She had been at Aunt Rose's so many weeks! She knew better than to ask when she might be able to live at home with her mother and Shmuel again. It made Aunt Rose angry.

"The sooner the better!" her aunt would always answer. "Do you think we're made of gold that we can feed another mouth forever? Thank God we don't have Shmuel also. We take from our plates to put on yours, and what do you do? Leave the crusts! Spit the flanken in the toilet! I know, I know you do it. Do you think I'm a fool?"

Ava cut into one of the yellow eggs with her spoon. She would pretend it was a matzo ball and swallow it very fast. Now Aunt Rose was holding the chicken over the flames of the burner. "*Zzst, Zzst!*" The chicken hairs were singed off, and the sickening smell of burning feathers filled the kitchen.

"Hurry up and finish!" Aunt Rose said, seeing Ava watching her. "I want you to go down to Kaplan's and get me a herring for Hymie's breakfast."

"I thought Mama might come tonight," Ava said. She tried to hold her breath while chewing on the chicken egg in order not to taste it, in order not to think about how it grew in the slick wetness of the hen's belly, close to the purplish liver and the beating red heart. "She said she would try to come in a week."

"Babies don't know from days or weeks," Aunt Rose said. "When the babies come, your mother has to be there, ready. You don't just open a zipper and the baby comes out, you know."

"I know," Ava said.

"What do you know?" Aunt Rose said, setting the chicken in a bowl. "What do you know about how babies come?"

"I know . . . enough," Ava said. She knew her mother sat at the bedsides of screaming women and helped their infants fall into the world, slimy and wet like the chicken yolks. She knew her mother put her hands in blood, like Aunt

Rose pulling at the guts of the chicken. When Ava grew up, she would never, ever clean or cook a chicken. She would be rich and have her own cooks.

"Mama said we could go to visit Shmuel," she added. "So she must be coming soon."

"Shmuel!" Aunt Rose said. "If he were here, he would eat crusts. Would you like to change places with him? Maybe you should go to the orphanage and Shmuel should come here? Then you'd learn how to behave. There they make you eat, and if you throw up, they make you eat the vomit! Here I'm too good to you."

Ava began to gulp her soup. She tore at the bread crust till it cut her gums, chewing desperately.

"That's better," Aunt Rose said. She began to wash the dishes in the sink. "When you're done, take the dime on the counter and go down to Kaplan's. And here," she reached into a cup on the windowsill and took out a penny, "you can buy chocolate licorice with this if you hurry right back."

Ava gulped down the last of the soup. "I'm done, I'm done!" she announced. Through the window she could see pigeons on the rooftop across the alley. Liberated from the table, she felt she could almost fly, free as a bird. The food was in her; she was done with all that struggle till dinnertime.

"I'll go right now."

"Don't stop and talk to anyone!" Aunt Rose warned. "You remember what your mother said? Now go and get a schmaltz herring, tell Kaplan I want a good one, a good big one!"

Outside of Kaplan's, though, like a miracle, sitting on a pile of wire egg crates, was Ava's father.

"Papa!" she screamed. "Oh, Papa!"

"Shh, shh, Chaveleh, don't wake the dead. No, no, don't climb up on my back like a little monkey. I'll give you a big hug in a few minutes, I promise you. Just take my arm and we'll stroll around Kaplan's as if we were on the boardwalk."

Brimming with joy, Ava promenaded through Kaplan's while her father whispered, "How tall you've grown! Does your Aunt Rose roll you out with her rolling pin?"

"I hate it there," Ava said. "I hate it. She makes me eat bread crust till my gums bleed. And Uncle Hymie rubs my face with his rough cheek and smells like an old cigar."

"I'll buy you a soft *chalah*," her father said, "and you can eat only the inside, I promise you." He pointed into the glass case. "And what else would you like? Some of that? A whole whitefish? A giant salami? Or would you like sweets, my sweet girl?"

"Why don't you come home?" Ava demanded. "Then Shmuel can come out of the orphanage, and Mama won't have to plunge her arms to the elbow in blood!"

"Who told you that?" Nathan asked. "What a thing to say!"

"Aunt Rose says it every day. She says Mama has to do that until she gets enough money to buy the divorce."

Her father's face went pale; he leaned against the glass case and became silent. Ava found herself looking into the blank dead eye of a whitefish; the fish lay stretched over crushed ice in the cold cabinet.

"It's because you fell in love with a young girl," Ava said, staring at the fish. "And Aunt Rose said that isn't all."

"What do you mean?"

"She said she thinks you had another family in the old country."

"God in heaven," Nathan said. "A yenta and a liar as well."

"I don't care, Papa," Ava said. "If you would just come home . . . "

"I came to find you today to say good-bye," Nathan said abruptly. "I'm going to live in a place called Cleveland; I have business there."

"Are you taking the girl with red hair?"

"No, no, of course not. Your mother took care of that for me. The witch."

"Please don't say that," Ava begged. She could see Mama's face in her mind: the confused blue eyes, the smooth colorless skin, her hair piled high on her head. She would rather live with her mother than with Aunt Rose, but most of all she would rather live with her father.

"Your mother is a cold woman," Nathan said. "She belongs right here in this case with the other cold fish. Dead to the world."

"Can you take me with you?" Ava asked, tugging at her father's jacket. "I can cook potato *kugel*. I can make *kreplach*. Aunt Rose makes me help her with dinner every night."

Nathan lifted her up and kissed her nose. "Aah, my little Chaveleh, how I adore you. When my business goes well and I earn a lot of money, I'll come back and get you. We'll live in a big house with a great curving staircase, like I had in Vienna. You'll have an elegant doll carriage and a carved rocking horse and a big strong dog to guard you and be your friend. And every Sunday we'll walk in the park and watch the swans sail by on the lake."

"I want to come with you now, even if I can't have all those things yet."

"A blessing on your head," Nathan said. "In time it will all come to pass. What you can have now is anything in this store, anything you want. Come now and show me what I shall buy for you. Show your papa."

THREE

When Ava climbed the stairs to Aunt Rose's apartment, she held in one hand the herring wrapped in newspaper, in the other she carried a big paper bag filled with delicacies from Kaplan's: a big scoop of Indian nuts—tiny pale shells, each one containing a sweet, soft, vanilla-tasting tender kernel; a small bar of chocolate *halvah*; a golden-crusted fresh *chalah*, soft as cotton inside; and a wax-paper bag heavy with salty Greek black olives.

She would have to hide them somewhere; she knew her Aunt Rose would be full of questions about why she had taken so long. She must never tell what she knew about her father! She especially could not tell that one day soon she would go to live with him, that they would be rich, and that she would have an elegant doll carriage.

Even before this her mother had been afraid he would kidnap her. In the time Ava had lived with Aunt Rose, she was warned daily never, ever to talk to strangers in case they might be men her father had sent to capture her. Her aunt and mother never thought her father would be bold enough to come himself; they called him terrible names, *coward, pig, devil, thief*. Ava knew they didn't know him, the father she knew. If they did, they would have to love him.

She hesitated on the landing. From behind a closed door she could hear blind Mrs. Mirsky shaking her box of pearls. Aunt Rose had told her how Mr. Goldstone, the jeweler, paid Mrs. Mirsky three pennies for stringing a necklace. Sometimes Ava would sit out front in the cold winter sun with Mrs. Mirsky and watch how she did it. She would pour a bag of pearls into a black box and shake them through holes to small compartments beneath. Then, feeling with her trembling fingers, she would choose the smallest pearls to poke through her needle and let them slide down the string to the knot; then the next to smallest, until she had just the right number of pearls, each one a little larger than the last, strung to the center pearl, the biggest one of all. Sometimes she let Ava string the second half of the necklace, always checking with the tips of her fingers to be sure Ava had chosen the right-size pearl.

Now Ava rapped on her door.

"Who's there!" the old woman called out.

"Ava Shermak," Ava called.

"Chaveleh! Come in. No, wait, I'll come open the door for you." Ava heard her slowly shuffle to the door, open the lock. Was Aunt Rose also opening her door? Oh hurry, Mrs. Mirsky, she prayed. But it was too late!

"What took you so long?" Aunt Rose shouted, coming into the hall. "I was having a heart attack already, worrying." She wiped her hands on her apron. Aunt Rose's hands were always slimy with the insides of chickens or coated with dry, caked flour. Her nails were short and broken, her skin rough, her knuckles red and scaly. She reached for Ava's arm, and Ava cringed, pulling back.

Now Mrs. Mirsky was in her doorway, staring sightlessly over Ava's head. "What's the matter out here?" she said, her head wobbling on her thin neck like a turkey's.

"I had to do an errand for Mrs. Mirsky!" Ava cried, shaking loose from Aunt Rose's hand. "She asked me if I would buy her a few things at Kaplan's, and I said yes, and now I have to go in and put them in her ice box."

"Did I tell you to get me something?" Mrs. Mirsky asked, confused. Her eyes were like white marbles rolling in her old face.

"Here, give that to me!" Aunt Rose said, pulling the paper bag out of Ava's arms. "I'll put them away for you, Masha," she said to the old woman, pushing past her in the doorway. "If I let Ava do it, she'll take an hour, and I have work for her to do before dinner."

"No—!" Ava said, but Aunt Rose was already pulling out the *chalah*, the olives, the nuts, the *halvah*.

"For an old woman this food isn't good to eat," Aunt Rose said. "Nuts you can't digest. And so much salt in the olives isn't good for you. What's happening to your head, Masha? What you need is soft-boiled eggs, maybe some flanken soup—not all this *chazerai*."

Mrs. Mirsky was shuffling back into her apartment, going down the hall to the kitchen. She stopped midway and turned toward Ava. "You know, it's a nice day outside, maybe you could take me for a little walk, Chaveleh, while the sun is still warm." She had already forgotten about the food.

"I'll be happy to take you if Aunt Rose lets me," Ava said.

"Of course I'll let her," Aunt Rose said. "What do you think—that I wouldn't?" She looked menacingly at Ava. "Just come right upstairs as soon as you come in. We're going to have company for dinner."

"Who?"

"When the time comes, you'll find out," Aunt Rose said.

Ava heard her mother's voice as she came up the stairs with Mrs. Mirsky. Her heart leaped with hope—maybe this time Rachel had earned enough money and could stay home at last with Ava and her brother.

"Mama's here!" Ava said, tugging on the old woman's arm to make her move faster. It had taken so long to walk to the corner and back. Mrs. Mirsky took one step and rested for two minutes, then another step and another long rest. Ava's feet tap-danced with impatience; they wanted to run, to fly.

"Come in and eat a little something," Mrs. Mirsky offered, fumbling in the pocket of her sweater for her key. Ava imagined all the delicacies her father had bought her at Kaplan's—the *halvah*, the olives, the soft *chalah*. Then she remembered what she would have to eat at Aunt Rose's—the chicken, with its pale fatty goose-pimpled skin, its sinewy drumstick, and its shuddery-purplish liver.

"Here, let me open the door," Ava said, turning the key in the lock and urging Mrs. Mirsky inside. She knew exactly what would happen if she didn't eat dinner—but she didn't care. "Please sit down," she said to the old woman. "I'll get us something to eat." Racing into the kitchen, Ava opened the icebox and took out the olives in their oily fragrant bag. Then she cut the *halvah* up into slices and tore the *chalah* into chunks. She stuffed a small piece into her mouth, savoring the golden crust, the sweet yellow strands of bread inside. Then she sank her teeth into the shiny skin of an olive, feeling the burst of salty juice upon her tongue and then the rough hard center of the pit.

"A little tea, maybe," Mrs. Mirsky suggested from where she sat at the dining table, but Ava could only mumble an answer, so full was her mouth now, with more bread, another olive, then a great sweet chunk of *halvah*, grainy and mouth-wateringly delicious. It felt as if she were in her father's arms, being held, being hugged. She could not stop herself. She ate till she could eat no more. When she finally brought a piece of bread in for Mrs. Mirsky, the old woman had fallen asleep upon the dining table, her head cradled in her hands.

Ava ran to Aunt Rose's place, where they were already eating dinner. "This is how she eats every day," Aunt Rose said to Rachel. "She eats my heart out."

On Ava's plate was a portion of overcooked carrots, potatoes swimming in grease, and the terrible chicken. She had sat down to eat with her coat on, calculating that she could slip some food into her pockets and throw it away later, but everything was too soft, too runny, and, besides, the two women had their eyes fixed steadily upon her. Her mother looked thin and tired. Her blue eyes were pale; they looked empty. Her light brown hair was carelessly fastened with hairpins; there was a big scratch across her cheek.

"What happened?" Ava asked, reaching toward her mother's cheek.

"Never mind, don't bother your mother with silly questions," Aunt Rose said.

"A scratch from a woman in labor," Rachel said. "Let her hear," she told her sister. "Why should a child think it's all so easy? It's her lot in life, she'd better be prepared." She turned toward Ava. "A woman was having her baby. Her labor went on and on, she was in pain, she was screaming. I was leaning over to wipe her forehead when she felt a terrible tearing inside her, and she scraped her nails across my face. It wasn't her fault." Rachel shrugged. "It doesn't matter. It will heal."

" . . . and maybe leave a scar," Aunt Rose said.

"So I won't be a perfect beauty. Who is there to look at me now, anyway?" She sighed wearily.

"I was thinking . . . " Rose said. "A woman who sews for Hymie, she has a brother-in-law who was just widowed, her sister died of a stone in the stomach, he's looking for a wife."

"No," Rachel said. "Don't start that. I'm not interested. All I can think about is Nathan . . . "

"Oh—you should see Papa!" Ava cried, and then she stopped and began stuffing her mouth with chicken. But her mother had not heard.

" . . . I think about him with that girl, and I could run after him with an axe. If only I could find him."

"I heard that a neighbor's cousin saw him," Aunt Rose said.

"It could be," Rachel said. "He has to be on earth somewhere, gambling, *shtupping* his women."

"Sha, *die kinder*," Aunt Rose said.

"Better she should learn now than be taken for a fool later like her mother." Rachel sighed deeply and began once again to eat.

"You eat your food now!" Aunt Rose commanded Ava. "Food is not to play with."

"And poor Shmuel has hardly enough to eat where he is," Rachel said.

"Let me bring mine to him," Ava offered. "Please, Mama, when can we go to see him?"

"Today—no, tomorrow. As soon as I rest a little, we'll take the train, and we'll bring him a cake."

FOUR

The orphanage was in an old building that had once been a factory. Ava and Mama waited in the lobby while a woman in a gray apron went to get Shmuel. Ava held the bag containing the fragrant honey cake that Mama had baked for him late last night; although her mouth watered to taste some now, she knew it was hopeless to ask. Mama was angry at her because of all the things Aunt Rose had told her. The list of complaints was endless: how Ava did not clean the hairs from her hair brush, how she left food on her plate at every meal, how she dried dishes by holding the wet dish in her unclean hand instead of holding it properly in one end of the dish towel.

Ava glanced at her Mama's face, pale above the high white collar of her blouse. She didn't look angry; instead she looked as if she might cry. Her lips were pressed together till they were almost white, and she squeezed Ava's hand till it hurt. Ava would have liked to sit down on one of the wooden chairs, but she could not pull her hand away from Mama's grip.

The air was cold in the lobby; they stood on the cement floor, listening to ugly sounds: the clank of metal dishes, the thud of heavy things being pushed across the floor, the angry voice of an adult. Suddenly Ava heard the sound of a child screaming, and she grabbed for her mother in fright. What if Shmuel were being beaten? What if Mama decided to put her here to spare Aunt Rose all the trouble?

If she were in an orphanage, Papa would never be able to find her again. They had had to ride on a train for two hours just to get here—he would never know which train to take or which direction to take it in. At least while she was at Aunt Rose's, she could hope. Every day when she went down into the street, she could imagine that Papa would be there or might send some-one to get her and take her to him.

"They're coming," her mother whispered. The sharp crack of heels could be heard clicking down the hall. "I hope he remembers me. I haven't seen him for so many months!"

The woman in the gray apron came into view, her face set in a terrible frown. She was without Shmuel. "Your son is gone," she said. "He was here this morning and now he's gone."

For an instant, Ava hoped, almost before she realized what a bad thought it was, that she could have the honey cake for herself.

"How could that be—gone?" Mama asked the woman.

"He's done it before. He's one of the worst boys here. We have rules—we have to have rules with this many children here, and he doesn't like rules. He has disappeared before. I expect he will be back before night."

"What if he isn't?"

"Don't worry," the woman said. "But if it happens again, it will be the last time. Then back he goes to you."

"I can't take him," Rachel said. "I travel, doing my work. My sister keeps my daughter, but she can't keep Shmuel."

"That is unfortunate," the woman said. "But we can't keep him either—causing us this much trouble, day after day."

While Mama listened, tight-lipped, to complaints about Shmuel's behav-ior, Ava pulled her hand away and walked off. She wandered down a long hall and looked into a room where two women were stirring great pots of soup and cutting vegetables. One of the women glanced up and called angrily, "No visitors! Go away! Go!"

Ava ran up a metal stairway, her heart pounding, and found herself in a large room filled with cots. Every bed was carefully made up with a gray wool blanket. Where were all the orphans? Ava thanked God she wasn't an orphan, although in a way she supposed she was like one since her father had left and her mother was away so much. Staying at Aunt Rose's was terrible, but not as bad as staying at an orphanage would be. Poor Shmuel. He was a wonderful brother and she missed him so much. He used to come in from the street and give Ava a bag of jellybeans or a handful of hot roasted chestnuts, steaming and cracked open in the center, the meat of them as soft as baked potato, as sweet as Indian nuts.

"How did you buy them? Where did you get the money?" Ava would ask him, but he would only grin and tell her to enjoy the food. Aunt Rose said he had the charm of a Galitzianer and that he would come to a bad end.

Where could he be now? Ava heard the shouts of children and walked to a barred window to look out. Down in the yard she saw a dozen boys playing ball, but none of them was Shmuel. She knew she ought to go downstairs: her mother would be worried. In the hall she opened a door she thought led to the stairway, but instead she found herself in a storage room. A tall pile of boxes in the corner shook, as if someone were hiding behind them.

Frightened, Ava stepped back and reached behind her for the doorknob. A dark head popped into view and Ava gasped.

"Chaveleh!" the boy cried, and then said quietly, "It's me, it's me. Shh. Don't call out."

"Shmuel!" She threw her arms around him. He squeezed her till she could hardly breathe.

"Mama is downstairs," Ava said. "They said you disappeared. They said if they found you, they'd send you home."

"Don't worry. They always say that." He laughed; his smile was like Papa's smile, reassuring and as bright as the sun. "How is it at Aunt Rose's?" he asked. Ava made a face and shuddered.

"Soon you'll be out of there," he promised, hugging her again. "Times will get good, and we'll live in a grand house and have servants and our own horse and cart." He even sounded like her father.

"What are you doing in this room?" she asked.

"I come here to play cards with the boys. I win things. I have a whole box full of prizes I won: a knife, a gold ring, a pair of wool gloves. When I come home, I'll have lots of things for Mama and you. Or we can sell them and use the money for other things."

"Mama is downstairs! Come and see her."

"I can't take a chance," Shmuel said. "This time they might really tell her to take me with her. I couldn't risk having to live with Aunt Rose."

"But it's supposed to be terrible here. I heard that even if you vomit, they make you eat what you throw up!"

"Who said that?"

"Aunt Rose. When I don't eat all my food she says it."

"Look," he said. "You have to learn not to be such a good girl all the time. You probably believe that either you have to eat or take the punishment. But there are other ways. If you don't like your dinner, wear something to the table with a pocket. Put your crusts or whatever in the pocket and later flush it down the toilet. Or drop it behind the radiator when she's not looking and get it later and throw it away. Or don't get it! Let her wonder why it smells so funny in her house!"

"What I hate most is her tapioca pudding," Ava said. They both smiled, imagining the pudding in her pocket.

"They don't make anyone eat vomit," Shmuel said. "You don't need to worry about me. I have friends here. It's not bad. I know I'll come home and be with you soon. In the meantime I do what I can do here."

"Mama has a honey cake for you," Ava said. She rolled her eyes heavenward. "Oh, you should smell it!"

"You eat it, Chaveleh. Don't tell Mama till you're on the train that you saw me up here. Give her a big kiss from me. Tell her I'm not really causing trouble—I'm doing good things for the family."

"But she'll be so sad if she doesn't get to see you!"

"If she sees me, she'll just cry or be angry. She'll never understand what I'm doing or why I'm doing it. But I think you can understand. Come here . . ." He motioned to Ava, and she followed him to the far end of the storeroom. From behind a hissing radiator he pulled a long black sock. "Look!" he said and turned it upside down. Tumbling out upon the floor came a stream of silver coins—nickels and dimes and quarters.

"Are those yours?" Ava asked. "All of them?"

Shmuel nodded. "Maybe soon we can get our old rooms back. Or even better ones, with our own bathroom. And maybe a stove that uses gas instead of coal, so that Mama won't be bothered with ashes all the time. You just put a quarter in the meter, and the flame burns enough to cook a hundred pots of soup."

"Mama will think you stole the money, Shmuel."

"That's why we can't tell her about this. I earned most of this by doing extra chores for fellows who didn't want to do them. Some of the money I won playing cards. But Mama could never understand my taking chances; that's why you can't bring her up here to see me. You'd better go now. If you go out the front door—it's right under that window—I'll be able to see her. But promise you'll wait till you're on the train before you say you saw me."

"I promise," Ava said. "But maybe I could leave the honey cake for you, hidden outside, by a tree or something."

"There's no safe place," Shmuel said. "You just eat it and think of me."

Ava came into her brother's arms again, feeling tears in her eyes. "Oh, Shmuel, will we ever all be together again?"

"If you mean Papa too, I don't know. You know how Papa doesn't like to sit still; he likes to do new things all the time."

"Well then, just us, the three of us."

"Yes, yes! That I'm sure of. You must go now. If anyone sees you coming out of here, just say you got lost."

"Good-bye, Shmuel." They kissed again.

As Ava left the orphanage with her mother, she pretended she saw a flock of pigeons in the sky, and she pointed upward over the roof of the building. As Rachel shaded her eyes to look for the birds, Ava looked back to see Shmuel's dark curly hair in the window of the orphanage as he watched them walk away.

FIVE

"Hurry, hurry, Rachel!" Aunt Rose yelled from the upstairs window of the tenement building where she had been watching for them. "Dolly Sulberg's sister Sophie collapsed in the bakery! They need you over there. Something went wrong, she's two months early. They called Dr. Marx, but he's in the Catskill Mountains. Sophie's husband ran to Dolly's for help, and Dolly came to me because I met her in the fish market yesterday and told her you were home for a few days."

Mama pulled Ava up the stairs so fast she felt as if she were flying. "My bag is under the bed in the back room," she said. "Get it, Chaveleh, and also take the rubber gloves from over the sink. And some of Aunt Rose's towels—old ones. There are never enough towels."

"You're taking her with you?" Aunt Rose cried.

"Why not?" Rachel asked. "She can learn something."

"Life is long," Aunt Rose said. "Some miseries can wait till you get to them."

Ava knew Aunt Rose had "lost" three babies. When Ava was small, she had thought Aunt Rose had actually lost them, perhaps in the crowds on Hester Street, but now she knew they had died inside her before they were born. She knew it was probably wrong to think that the babies were better off dead than living with Aunt Rose, but in her heart she felt it was true.

Sometimes she wondered how Aunt Rose and her mother could be sisters. Mama, though very competent, was shy, never pushy; she seemed to wait for others to act before she acted. She was kind and always patient. Sometimes she seemed to Ava quite dull. Aunt Rose was just the opposite: loud, bossy, and argumentative. She was always sure she had the right answer for everything, knew the best way to solve any problem. When others made suggestions, she generally clamped her teeth shut and crossed her arms, staring across the room, tapping her foot till the others had the good sense to stop interrupting her.

Mama had told Ava that in the old country, in Poland, in the little town of Kutno where they had lived as children, Aunt Rose had always been put in charge of the household when their parents were away. Their father had been a tanner of hides and at times went on trips away from home to sell bags and belts and straps made out of leather. Even though Mama was now a grown woman with children, Aunt Rose thought she was still in charge.

"Leave Ava here with me, Rachel," she insisted. "She can peel potatoes. She can scour the bathtub. She can sweep the bathroom floor. It's full of toothpowder she's spilled. Every day I tell her: you only need to put a few grains on your fingertip, that's all you need to do the job— but no, she shakes it out by the cupful."

"I can't help it, Mama," Ava said. "A lot always comes out of the hole."

"Elbow grease is what that child needs!" Aunt Rose said. Ava looked down at her feet. Last week when Aunt Rose was ranting about Ava's needing elbow grease, Ava had gone across the hall to Mrs. Mirsky to see if she had some elbow grease they could borrow. What a laugh Aunt Rose had had with Uncle Hymie about that! He thought Ava was funny. He was always pinching her cheek and rubbing his stubbly whiskers across her face when he insisted she kiss him good night. The smell of his cigar nearly made her sick.

"I may need her help, Rose," Mama said. "Come—" she said to Ava. "Let's hurry and see if we can help the poor woman."

It was already getting dark outside. Ava was hungry. They had not had time to eat dinner after coming back from visiting Shmuel. The honey cake was still in the paper bag, upstairs. Uncle Hymie would probably find it and eat it before they got home. Mama pulled her along; things were clanking inside her medical bag. Her long skirt seemed to confine her legs and shorten her steps, but she hurried as fast as she could.

"When we get there," Mama gasped, "don't ask me a lot of questions. Just be still unless I ask you to do something."

"But what if . . . ?"

"No questions. I have no strength for questions now."

They turned into a wide street, and on the corner a man was selling sweet potatoes. Ava smelled them before she saw the little metal wagon with drawers; the fragrance was overwhelmingly sweet and comforting; for some reason sweet potatoes reminded her of her father. He had always bought her anything she wanted whenever they strolled together on the street—chestnuts or ice cream or little cakes. The vendor bent over to shake the coals in the middle drawer. In the bottom drawer were the raw potatoes; in the top drawer the baked ones, slightly blackened on the skin and pinkish gold inside, soft and delicious. Her mouth watered.

"Here we are," Mama said abruptly and pulled Ava into a doorway. The smell changed immediately to something bad—cold grease and boiled cabbage. They walked up a narrow metal stairway, the air getting thicker and less breathable as they ascended. On the second landing Mama paused before a door with the letter B on it, and knocked. Ava heard footsteps hurrying toward the door. A thin, grim-faced man opened it quickly and stood back to let them in.

"So," he said. "You are the midwife."

"Yes," Mama answered. "How long has your wife been in labor?"

The man frowned as if he were annoyed at something. "She should not be in labor," he said. "Not for two months more." He spoke in Yiddish, which Ava could understand though she could not speak it.

"We cannot hold her responsible for that," Mama said, setting down her medical bag.

"But we had tickets to hear Caruso tonight at the Metropolitan Opera House." The man seemed quite angry that his wife had spoiled his plans. Ava looked at his face and shivered. He had small eyes, closely set together on either side of a long narrow nose. His face was scarred with little pockmarks, and he had a small, neat mustache over his thin lips. He looked as if he might never have smiled in his life.

"Take me to her," Mama said. "The opera will have to wait."

They followed the man through a narrow hallway and into the small bedroom. A woman lay in bed on her back, her belly rising and heaving like a huge fish under the blankets. When she saw Rachel, she cried out. "Oh my God, my God, Help me!"

"Don't be afraid, "Mama said. "It is only pain." She touched the woman's brow. "Baby pain is nothing to fear. It is not pain from sickness."

"I am sick," the woman cried. "I know something is wrong, oh God!" She gave a weird animal-like scream. Ava stepped backwards to run away and found that she had stepped on the man's polished black shoes.

"Take care, stupid!" he said angrily in Yiddish. "Klutz!"

"You are stupid!" Ava said and went forward to stand beside her mother. She hated this man already.

"Talk to her," Mama whispered. "I will get my things ready."

Ava stepped closer and saw the sweat on the woman's brow. She searched for her hand under the sheet and took it. "Please," she said. "Don't feel so bad. It will get better. Once I had a terrible stomach ache. I couldn't be still—I had to go and lie on the floor in the bathroom. Then I had to run up and down the stairs." The woman heaved and writhed in the bed. "But then the pain stopped and I got calm. Try to remember that the pain always has to stop."

"Good girl," murmured Mama. "That's good." Ava felt her heart skip a beat. Her mother had never said "good" to her before. Suddenly the woman stopped twisting her body and lay still. She sighed and opened her eyes.

"Let me examine you now," Mama said, pulling down the blankets.

"Make him go out," the woman cried, gesturing toward her husband.

"Gladly, gladly," he said sourly and tapped down the linoleum hallway in his shiny shoes. Mama sat down on the edge of the bed and placed her hands on the woman's raised knees, gently spreading them apart. Ava thought of Aunt Rose's hands going inside a chicken, pulling out the purple heart, the yellow red-veined eggs, the mucous and slime clinging to her fingers.

A human being giving birth was nothing more than an animal, a howling, helpless animal. From the other room she heard the sounds of music, of a Victrola playing. She heard the deep, rich voice of a man singing. Mama heard it, too. She paused a moment and lifted her head.

"Men cannot face this," she said to the woman.

Ava felt a rush of sympathy for men; she was a woman and would some-day be heaving in childbirth in a bed. But she understood why men could not face it; it must remind them that they, too, were animals. The music coming from the other room was not the sound of an animal, but the sound of beauty and hope. It was not the grunt of this poor woman in pain. Ava dropped the woman's hand and rushed from the room. In the parlor she saw the record playing on the Victrola. The man was drinking a glass of tea at the table. Ava sat down with him at the table. He nodded grimly. He pushed a plate of *mandelbrot* toward her, but she shook her head. They sat together, listening to the music. When the record ended, the man stared at her. "Turn it over," he said, finally.

She didn't like to take orders, but his eyes were like dark olives, fierce and a little desperate. She stood up and did as he asked. The woman was scream-ing again, and it was better to listen to the opera singer than to the sounds of terror.

When her mother finally came out of the room, she said, "I am not trained for this. Something is seriously wrong. We must get her to the hospital."

SIX

Aunt Rose came out of the bedroom wearing her good wool skirt and her new black hat. "What are you waiting for, Rachel? You're not even combed yet."

"I told you, Rose—I don't think I'll go."

"It's an obligation, not a choice. Shivah is an obligation."

"For you it is. You're Dolly's good friend and Sophie was her sister. I don't know the family."

"You do know Dolly a little. Besides, Isaac Sauerbach you met the night poor Sophie died. You owe him to pay your respects."

"He seemed unkind to me that night," Mama said.

"He's a widower," Aunt Rose said significantly, "and we owe him this much. He paid your fee, didn't he?"

"Much good I did him," Mama said.

"Nonsense," Aunt Rose said. "Blame God. Don't blame yourself. Things can go wrong. Did I blame my doctor when I lost my babies? Did I blame Hymie? Better to blame God, curse God—get it out of your system."

"Sophie had small bones and a weak muscle that couldn't keep the baby in. It had nothing to do with God."

"So who makes muscles and bones?" Aunt Rose said practically. "Go, comb your hair and put on the black lace blouse." She motioned to Ava. "You, too. Get your coat and button your shoes."

"What does Chaveleh need to go for?" Mama asked. "It will be depressing. It's no place for a child."

"To see a woman in labor you think is all right, but to see a grieving husband isn't?"

"The first I thought would be a happy event," Rachel said. "This I know isn't."

"A child can't know only from happiness," Aunt Rose said. "We do not get only happiness in this life."

"I believe she knows that already," Mama said, looking Ava's way. Ava was playing cat's cradle with a long piece of string; she had just made an ironing board. Next she was going to make a doll's bed. She kept her concentration on the string, looping her fingers carefully into the right places.

"Well," Rachel sighed, "all right. Chaveleh, go and comb your hair. We'll go with Aunt Rose. But we'll only stay for a minute or two."

"Fine," Aunt Rose said, satisfied. "That's all you need to stay. It's the thought that counts. There won't be that much to say anyway."

The hallway of the dead woman's house had that same sour odor as it had had a few days ago. Ava thought of golden sweet potatoes to block the ugly smell from her mind. She could feel the piece of string in her pocket; she wondered if she could sneak away into an empty room and try to make a Jacob's ladder.

When she came into the apartment, the first thing she saw was the man's pointy black shoes. He sat motionless on a low chair, his knees slightly apart, a glass of tea in his hand. It seemed as if he had hardly moved since the last time Ava had seen him.

All the mirrors in the apartment were draped with sheets. The bedroom, which had been so full of pain and cries earlier in the week, was deadly still; through the open doorway Ava could see the bed, neatly made up, a crocheted bedspread pulled over it tight and white as a piece of ice. The dead woman's sister, Dolly, sat barefoot on a low stool. "I can't believe it," she moaned, raising her tear-stained face so that Aunt Rose could kiss her. "So young and so beautiful. My little sister Sophie. Gone, gone."

"Oy, oy," Aunt Rose cried, tears coming down her cheeks as well. "Who can understand such things?"

Ava glanced up and saw the man and Mama staring at one another. His face looked gray, as if he were in some deep shadow. Then she realized he had stubble on his cheeks, he had not shaved.

"I am very sorry," Mama said to him. "I feel terrible."

"That's what you said in the hospital," he answered.

"I was sorry then, also," Rachel said, bowing her head. "I tried to help her, but there are some things we cannot help."

The man shrugged. He stood up and walked to the Victrola. He placed a record on the machine, wound the handle, and lowered the needle into place.

"Isaac!" Dolly cried. "It isn't right! You don't play music when you sit shivah!" The loud tenor voice of the opera singer vibrated the glasses on the table.

"Caruso," Isaac announced proudly. He sat down and began sipping his tea.

Dolly shook her head. She looked at him as if he had lost his senses. Finally she leaped up and pulled the needle from the record. "God in heaven, Isaac. This isn't a party!"

"So . . . " he said. "If it is not a day to have a party, perhaps it is a day to work." He walked to a small alcove and pulled back a flowered curtain. Behind it stood a black sewing machine and a small chair. He sat down in front of the machine and opened one of the wooden drawers on the side. From it he took a spool of thread and began to attach it to the machine, lacing it into little holes and around thin silver hooks. Then he reached for a length of cloth that was folded on a box beside the machine and placed it under the needle. His feet, in their shiny pointed shoes began to pump the iron treadle. He rocked back and forth as he ran the material under the bobbing point of the needle.

Dolly whispered above the clicking sound, "He has been bringing work home to earn extra money for the new baby. Poor man, he hasn't any family to support now."

"He's a good man," Aunt Rose said. "He is beside himself with grief. Leave him there to sew if it's any comfort to him. Who will report him for that?"

"Report him?" Mama asked.

"To God," Dolly said. She shrugged. "To the rabbi. To whoever disapproves of such things." She began to cry again. "Oh no, my darling Sophie, how can I live without you?"

"Come," Mama said to Ava. "It's time to go."

"Say good-bye to Mr. Sauerbach," Aunt Rose reminded her. But he had pulled the little flowered curtain around himself and the machine, and was now hidden in the alcove. All they could hear was the hum and buzz of his sewing machine.

SEVEN

"Look at this!" Aunt Rose said the next day as she came in the door from shopping. She held up a pair of tickets. "Such a coincidence. Tickets to hear Caruso sing at the Metropolitan Opera House. Francine Moskowitz got them from her cousin Shermie, and her husband hates the opera. So since they won't go, Rachel, you can ask that poor sad man to go with you. Shivah will be over by then."

Mama was folding her things into a suitcase. "What are you talking about?" she said. "I am going out to find work again. I've been here too long as it is."

"Listen to me," Aunt Rose said severely. "Here are the tickets!" She waved them in Mama's face. "You will offer them to Isaac. He is a widower. He has a good job. He owns his own sewing machine—did you see it? Black with gold scrolls painted on it. A Singer. A beautiful machine. With a man like that, you'd have beautiful clothes, you'd never want for anything. Chaveleh would be dressed like a little princess."

"I don't like him," Mama said.

"So. You liked Nathan? Of course, you loved Nathan! And what did that get you? Misery. *Tsuris.* Grief. You run around the city like a madwoman. One child is in an orphanage, and one sits here idly playing with strings and never eats a bite. Is that what you want?"

Mama continued laying her clothes in the suitcase.

"All right, I admit it, he's no beauty. Handsome is not everything. Cultured is important. He likes opera. He has good taste, intelligence."

"He did not shed a tear for his poor wife."

"Tears! How many men do you know who cry?"

"Maybe not cry, but feel."

"What do you know what he feels? Did you ask him? His heart is probably breaking."

"This I doubt," Mama said.

Ava was at the table, kneading the dough for *chalah*. She pressed her knuckles into the flour till they hit the bottom of the bowl, then came up and did it again. She was thinking, as she so often did, of her father, of a time when she could be with him and with Shmuel and her mother again. Why was Aunt Rose talking about that man with the pointed shoes? Ava wanted to forget him, his dark little eyes, his sallow skin. She never wanted to think about that day again, with the woman's belly rising like a great fish under the blanket.

"Take the tickets," Aunt Rose said, opening Rachel's pocketbook and tucking them inside. "Think about it."

Ava covered the bowl with a linen towel and set it on the radiator cover. She was afraid that her mother was leaving. Once Mama was gone, Aunt Rose would turn her attention to Ava, and that meant yelling and criticizing. As if Aunt Rose could read her mind, she whirled around and said sharply, "Look at that mess! Flour on the table, flour on the floor. And the dough is too dry, I could tell it from a mile away. Uncle Hymie will come home from a hard day's work, and the bread will be like lead in his mouth. Is that a way to make bread for your uncle?" she demanded. "A man who would give you the shirt off his back?"

"Look, Rose," Mama said, closing her suitcase and setting it on the floor. "I am going to visit Dr. Goldberg at the hospital to see if he has some jobs for me. I'm saving a little money all the time. Soon I'll take Chaveleh to be with me, and that will ease your burden. This won't be forever, and I know Chaveleh will be as good as she can."

"If it isn't one burden, it's another. If Chaveleh isn't eating my heart out, I worry about you. What can I think? You aren't a widow. You aren't a spinster. You aren't—God forbid—a loose woman. So what are you? When my friends ask, I don't know what to tell them what you are."

"I'm your sister. What else do they have to know? Tell them the truth, that Nathan didn't care for me enough, that he went after young girls."

"I spit on him," Aunt Rose said.

Ava gasped and then ran to bury her face in her mother's breast. She wanted to pummel Aunt Rose with her fists. Her mother stroked her hair briefly, then pushed her away. "Don't make a scene, Chaveleh. Go to the other room if you can't stand to hear grownups talking."

"I want to be with Papa," she sobbed.

Mama's face turned hard. "I don't want to hear about him now. Do you understand? I never want to hear about him again!" She began to cry, too. Aunt Rose came toward Ava and grabbed her arm fiercely. She pulled her down the hall, roughly, meanly, and shoved her into the bedroom. She said something terrible, a curse in Yiddish, and slammed the door. Ava tried to stop crying so she could hear what was being said in the other room.

"I must go," Mama was saying. "I will soon have enough money for the divorce, then it will be as if Nathan never was."

"And Shmuel and Chaveleh came from where? From cabbages?"

"Let me live, Rose. This is all I can do for now. I work and I pray I can get from one day to the next."

"There is a way out of this," Aunt Rose warned her. "If you don't see it, you are a blind fool."

"So I am a fool," Mama answered. "And if I am, I am not the only one in the world."

EIGHT

Aunt Rose and Uncle Hymie were having a card party. Ava had been warned several times about what she must do and not do: she must eat an early dinner, she must help Aunt Rose make the house spotless, she must help set out the baked pastries and the silver tea pot and the nuts and the candies. Then she must take her bath and go right to bed. She must not eat any of the chocolates—if there were any left over, she could have some the next day—and she must not come into the living room once the guests had arrived.

Uncle Hymie had come home early and was sitting in his big armchair under the gaslight, smoking a cigar and reading the paper. He had a raspy cough and a raspy voice like his rough and whiskery cheeks. Ava always felt as if her skin were raw and tender when she stood near to him—and that if he touched her, she would hurt all over. He was like an emery board or a square of sandpaper. "C'mere," he would command her, and if she came near, he would hoist her up onto his hard knee and jiggle her up and down, the piston of his strong leg jarring through her body and rattling her teeth. He would guffaw and laugh while she grabbed for him, in order not to be thrown to the floor, and then he would set her down and say, "You like it? You like it?" Then he would forget her instantly.

She kept as far from him as she could while she helped her aunt lay out the embroidered tablecloth that was used only on special occasions. She felt pleased that company was coming—it would distract her aunt from thinking of all the ways Ava was displeasing her, and tomorrow there might be a dish of chocolates and mints for her.

She had plans for tonight—she would take her bath and then read one of the books she got from school when they had lived on Cherry Street. She had not been going to school since then because her mother didn't want to trouble Aunt Rose with all the details of arranging for it. Soon enough, Rachel said, they'd be settled somewhere, and then Ava could go back to school.

"All right," Aunt Rose said. "I'm making this scrambled egg for you now, and I want you to eat it here, standing at the sink—we don't want crumbs all over the dining-room table—and then you go right down the hall and do as I told you."

The egg wasn't bad if she ate it fast, trying not to see the white strings of mucous, trying not to smell the eggy yellow yolk. Sometimes the egg had a red spot in it—it meant a bird would have grown in the shell if a hen had sat on it—and that was even worse.

"Here, have your milk and go," Aunt Rose said. "Remember, I don't want to see your face again tonight."

Ava wiped her mouth on the dishcloth and nodded and ran down the hall, feeling freed for the night. She got her long white nightgown out of the dresser drawer and took it into the bathroom, where she set it carefully on top of the toilet. Then she closed the bathroom door and began running water into the bathtub. She took Aunt Rose's shower cap out of the cabinet and tucked her long hair into it. She was only allowed to wash her hair in the mornings—so there would be time for it to dry before she had to lay her head down on the pillowcase. When she was all undressed and the water was high and steaming in the tub, she tossed the bath towel that was hanging over the edge of the tub toward the toilet tank.

It landed on her nightgown, trembled there for an instant, and suddenly slid into the toilet, dragging her nightgown with it. Ava gasped. She watched the towel and her nightgown fill with water, spreading out like sponges and sinking as they grew heavier.

She tried to pluck her nightgown from the toilet before it was completely saturated, but then realized she had no place to put it! Water would drip all over the tiles, run out into the hall, and soak the long green hall runner that Aunt Rose prized. If she put the nightgown in the tub, it would dirty the clean bath water. And now that her nightgown was wet, what would she wear to bed? She had no other nightgown! She tiptoed to the door, shivering slightly in her nakedness and pressed her ear to the door. Already guests were here. They were coming in now—Ava could hear her uncle greeting them at the door. There was loud laughter, the sound of the women exclaiming at the food Aunt Rose had baked for the party. Ava heard the hangers scraping in the closet—Aunt Rose was hanging up her guests' coats.

Ava didn't know what to do. If she took her bath, she'd have no towel to dry herself with and no nightgown to dress in. If she dressed herself in her clothes and rushed to her room and went to sleep, some guest would discover the towel and nightgown in the toilet and tell her aunt and uncle. They would be furious and might even wake her up to punish her!

She paced the length of the bathroom over and over, trying to decide what to do. She got a glimpse of herself in the mirror over the medicine cabinet—an apparition with a balloon head and stick-figure arms and legs. Finally, gasping with fear, she opened the door a crack and called softly down the hall, "Aunt Rose, Aunt Rose."

They would never hear her above the noise in the living room. She called a little louder. "Aunt Rose! Aunt Rose!" Still nothing, no response, no person coming to her aid. Finally, then, Ava screamed for help. *"Aunt Rose!"*

"What's going on?" she heard some woman say, and then her Uncle Hymie was coming down the hall in his flat-footed walk, stomping his way in her direction.

"Hey, hey!" he yelled, coming at her. "We told you we didn't want to hear a peep out of you!" He pushed the bathroom door open. "What's going on here!" he bellowed. "What's this?"

Ava pointed at her nightgown in the toilet, tried to explain to him. Suddenly he began to laugh, his cigar jiggling up and down in the corner of his mouth. "God, you look ridiculous!" he said. "They'll never believe this! Hey, come with me," he said, grabbing her arm, and tugging her toward the hall. "I've got to show them this sight." He began dragging her along.

"Don't!" Ava screamed, digging her heels against the floor, skidding along over the tiles as he dragged her. "Please don't!"

"Come on!" he said, jerking her even harder. "This is something they'll write home about."

"Don't, Uncle Hymie! *Don't!*"

And suddenly she was in the bright lights and smoke of the living room, among all the people.

"Look at this plucked chicken!" Uncle Hymie called out. "Look at this, will you?"

Ava kicked and struggled, desperate to pull out of his grip and run away. She was conscious of her white arms and legs flailing about, conscious of the laughter of the men in the room. Her uncle was shaking with laughter, tears of hysterical laughter rolling down his cheeks.

"Let *go!*" she shrieked and ripped out of his grip. She ran to the kitchen, where she wedged herself in the corner between the sink and the wall.

"Hey," he called, coming after her. "Come back here. Not everyone got a good look at you."

Aunt Rose was just taking a *kugel* out of the oven.

"What is this?" she said. "What's going on? What's so funny in there? Ava! What are you doing here naked?"

Uncle Hymie grabbed for her arm again, and Ava clung to the towel rack with all her strength.

"Hymie! Have you lost your mind! What are you doing?" Aunt Rose cried. "Leave the child alone!"

"I want her to come back in the living room!" he said. "This is better than vaudeville."

"Are you crazy?" Aunt Rose cried. She turned to Ava.

"What happened? Couldn't you take your bath? What are you crying for?"

Uncle Hymie continued to pull at her arm. He gave a tremendous tug and suddenly the towel rack ripped out of the wall, flinging them both across the kitchen. Ava fell to the floor with her arm under her. She felt a burning pain shoot through her wrist.

"Get out of here!" Aunt Rose shouted at Uncle Hymie. "You drank too much schnapps, that's what's wrong with you."

When her uncle had gone back to the living room, where laughter was still rippling, Aunt Rose came and lifted Ava off the floor. "Tell me now, what is wrong?" she asked, but Ava was shrieking. She held her arm forward for her aunt to see.

"Oh my God in heaven!" Aunt Rose gasped. "The bone is showing. The child's bone is sticking out of her body! Hurry someone and bring a blanket, we must wrap her in a blanket and run for the doctor."

NINE

They raced through the streets. The cold high black sky was above her. Her aunt had borrowed a stroller from a neighbor and deposited Ava in it, some-how, though she was much too big for it and her knees stuck up almost in front of her eyes. The wheels jostled and thumped over the sidewalk. She called out, "Mama, Mama." She remembered the night her mother had run with her through the streets to look in the window where Papa had been holding the young girl's hand. She thought that when women ran with chil-dren, it was always to some terrible place where terrible things happened. The pain had moved from her wrist, up her arm, and into her shoulder. It was a pain so sharp and so hot, she wondered if she would die.

In the street they passed an open sewer hole, surrounded by burning smudge pots. She could see down into the hole; it was deep and dark. Her aunt was mumbling as they ran: "God in heaven, what did I do to deserve this? Why am I being punished this way?" The rough wool surface of the blanket Ava was wrapped in rubbed against her bare body. She tried to think about the places where it scratched her in order not to think about her arm.

"Thank God, thank God, this is the street," Aunt Rose said to herself, panting and gasping as she turned the corner. Her aunt pulled her out of the stroller and ran with her up a narrow staircase.

"Dr. Schwartz! Dr. Schwartz!" Aunt Rose cried out. With Ava in her arms she could not knock on the door with her fist, so she knocked with her head. "It's an emergency! Please hurry."

A man wearing a bathrobe came to the door. "My sister's child," Aunt Rose gasped, thrusting Ava into his arms. "She was playing, she fell. The bone, the bone . . . "

Ava felt the doctor take her in his arms and put her down on a hard table, felt the cold air on her naked body as he opened the blanket.

"Did she fall in the tub?"

"Yes, yes," Aunt Rose said. "Always playing carelessly . . . "

"Let me see, little one," the doctor said. "Don't be afraid." His voice was kind and soothing. Ava felt her fear diminish; the doctor would take the pain away and keep her here. He would never turn her over to Uncle Hymie. She felt his fingers moving over her arm gently, turning it over, touching it.

"Stand back!" the doctor said to Aunt Rose. Ava felt his grip tighten on her arm. Suddenly he squeezed and twisted her arm. He twisted it with such force that she saw a red explosion before her eyes. The pain was more terrible than anything she had ever known, much worse than the worst Indian burn Shmuel had ever given her. The doctor kept twisting till she thought she heard a crack, but her screaming was louder than the crack, louder than Aunt Rose's cries to God in heaven.

When she opened her eyes again, she felt numb, drugged. Her teeth were chattering. The doctor's wife was spooning some lukewarm sweet tea between her lips.

"*Schoen meydele*," the woman crooned. "Darling child."

"I want Mama . . . " Ava sobbed.

"You will have your mama very soon," Aunt Rose said fiercely. "I am finished with you. This is all I can take, this is the end. You will go back to your mama the minute I can find her!"

TEN

Rachel sat—as if on a mountaintop—in the farthest reaches of the balcony of the Metropolitan Opera House. Beside her sat Isaac Sauerbach, peering through the opera glasses he had rented in the lobby below. He sat stiffly, his back erect, his lips set sternly together. The round starched collar of his white shirt seemed to support his neck at an unnatural angle; with his beaked nose and the small glittering circles of his black eyes, he looked like a scrawny bird.

Rachel felt dizzy from the height. The shimmering curtain under the carved wooden arch had not yet parted; the music had some moments ago begun rising from the orchestra pit. They sat so high up that the ceiling of the immense building was not far from their heads. The last time Rachel had been in a building with so many people was when she had come to Ellis Island from Poland as a girl of sixteen.

But it was so different here! Below were all the grand ladies wearing velvets and jewels, sitting next to well-dressed and wealthy men. Ellis Island had housed only the frightened, the desperate, the yearning. There the women had worn clothes they had traveled the ocean in, had covered their heads with woolen shawls. Here the women wore ostrich and egret feathers in their felt hats.

Rachel was wearing her fanciest clothes; a dark blue silk middy blouse with fine blue wool cuffs on the sleeves that ended just below her elbows. At her throat was a seed pearl brooch that had belonged to her mother. Her long black skirt fastened with four tortoise-shell buttons on the left side. She had taken from their hiding place the diamond earrings Nathan had given her on their wedding day; she wore them not out of sentiment, but because she wanted it to seem clear that she was not poor, not desperate.

Isaac already knew she was a woman of some skill, a woman who could earn money—though sadly her skill had not been enough to save his wife. When she had knocked on his door and offered him the pair of tickets, he had shown almost no emotion.

He had said, "What is the opera?"

"I don't know," she said, "but Caruso is singing."

"Yes," he said, "I will go, then." He had not invited her in or offered even a cup of tea. When she had got back to her sister's door, she had flung her pocketbook on the table in humiliation and anger. Ava, sitting on the couch with her arm in a cast, looked up with fear in her eyes.

"He is like a wooden stick," Rachel had said.

"Sticks can be made to burn," Rose answered. "You'll see."

"He didn't even say he would come here to call for me."

"He'll come. His life is no bed of roses."

"I may decide not to go. What do I care about the opera?"

"You have no choice," Rose had said, with finality in her voice. "It is not opera we are talking about here."

Now the curtain parted slowly, majestically, folding back upon the lighted stage. The audience gasped with pleasure. Isaac leaned forward tensely. Except for his dark curly hair, parted in the center, the rest of him was perfectly tight and straight as a ruler.

Rachel wondered how long this opera would take. She was worried about Ava, who seemed a different child since she had broken her wrist. She ate almost nothing. She had lost weight and spoke only when she was forced to speak. She hid in her bed whenever Rose would let her get away. Because Ava could do no housework now, Rose was angrier than usual. Rachel knew she could not leave Ava there much longer. Something had also happened between the child and Hymie, though Rose denied any such problem. Yet when Hymie was in the room, he didn't glance at the child, never greeted her, never teased her or bothered her as he used to do.

Time was running out. If Rachel's life did not change, Ava would also have to go to the orphanage. And what were the chances for change?

The man beside her sniffled into his handkerchief. Rachel glanced at his face—it was seamed and pitted, as if he had been scarred by some terrible disease. Yet he was so young! Only twenty-five: Rose had found out his age from Sophie's sister, Dolly. Rachel felt as if she were much older than her own age of thirty-five, much older, yet she imagined this sober man to be more in control of life than she was. He had an air of certainty about him, of strength, as if he had the knowledge of how to live and survive.

Though they sat together, he never glanced at her. She could make no sense of what was going on down there on the stage. A short, fat, mustached man was parading around, dressed in a plumed hat, carrying a sword, and singing at the top of his lungs. This was America, so why was he singing in Italian? She had gone to night school to learn English, and her children could already read and write better than she could. Why would Americans come to a theater to listen to people shout and rant in a foreign language?

She would never waste her time on such nonsense again. The Jewish theater was different—it was in Yiddish, so anyone could understand it. And the stories were about people like herself and her family, not about dukes and duchesses! Sometimes the Jewish theater was so funny it brought tears to her eyes—the way the actors strutted around on the stage and carried on. But this! It was all screeching and posturing!

She was getting a headache. She wondered if Isaac might be willing to leave at the intermission. She looked at him again—he was rapt! Beaming with attention and interest. His mouth hung slightly open in wonder as the fat man bellowed out the longest, highest notes Rachel had ever heard in her life. Isaac's face had the faintest smile upon it.

Suddenly she thought of Nathan—of how his smile had been so wicked and delightful, of how his hands looked when he wore his father's rings on his powerful fingers. Why was it that when she least expected it, some vision of him appeared in her memory, unprotected by her hatred, her shame, her anger? He should roast in hell for what he did. Her own mother had warned her when she was a girl: *Marry a homely man and you won't have to worry.* Instead she had married Nathan, who was handsome, extraordinary, with fire in his eyes and magic in his lips. She thought of how sometimes when she was unclean, was bleeding, when it was not time for it, he whispered in her ear—Who would ever know? Why could he not come into her bed and take his marital rights? She flushed to think of it. Such a wicked man!

A hand touched her arm; she jumped in her seat. Isaac was offering her the opera glasses and pointing to the stage. She held them to her eyes—she saw nothing but the blur of boxes full of little heads, and a rush of velvet curtain, and the string of lights of the musicians below. Her hand shook and wavered; Isaac directed the lenses downward and centered them on the stage. Now she saw the fat man up close, bowing and strutting, shouting like the neighbors across the air shaft used to shout when she had lived on Cherry Street. She handed the glasses back to him and sank down in her seat. She would just sit here and rest till it was over. It would be for only another hour or two, not a lifetime. She was just so tired.

She had been with Dr. Goldberg on a difficult case when word came that Chaveleh had broken her wrist, that she must go to Rose's at once. By then she had not slept for two days. She arrived at her sister's full of fear, but when she realized that Chaveleh was all right, that her arm would heal, she thought she could rest. But no! Rose began early in the morning to harass her, to threaten her, to warn her. She could not keep the child any longer.

Even if Ava were not such a difficult child, even if she were not such a bur-den, they had to rent her room to a boarder. Hymie had said times were hard now—his store was doing badly, and the two dollars and fifty cents a week they could get for a boarder was important for them to have. Furthermore, Rachel had to be practical—she was getting old!

"Look," Rose commanded, "look at yourself! Already there are wrinkles around your eyes. And your hair—it's turning white already. In a few years, you will be an old lady!"

Rose went on this way till late at night. A woman who was decent should not work; she should stay home and raise her children. And if she had been stupid enough to marry a pig, a thief, an adulterer like Nathan, she didn't have to suffer for it till her dying day. This was her chance! She must marry again—and who was more convenient than Isaac? He lived only around the corner, he was a fine tailor, he had rooms well furnished and a gas stove; he owned a Victrola, a Singer sewing machine. Rose threw her arms up in exasperation.

Didn't Rachel have a drop of sense? She must obtain the "get"—her di-vorce papers—from the rabbi immediately. Hymie had agreed that they would advance her the additional money she needed. She could pay them back later, when her life was settled. But she must not waste a minute—she would have to wait for the period of ninety-one days after she obtained the papers and before she could marry. It was required so there could be no doubt as to who the father of a baby conceived in the early days of marriage might be. And Isaac was pious, Rose warned her. There would be no margin for sloppiness.

She stared at Rachel as if to indicate she knew how sloppy Nathan may have been about following the laws and rituals. Rachel lowered her eyes.

"What if I can't find Nathan?" Rachel asked.

"We will find a rabbi who will consent to issue the divorce with or with-out him. There is no question he has abandoned you."

"He probably has another wife by now," Rachel said bitterly.

"Good riddance to him and a pity on her," Rose said with contempt.

Rachel was roused from her reverie by the cries of "Bravo! Bravo!" and she realized the opera had ended. Thunderous applause shook the opera house, the singers bowed, the curtain went up and down, up and down. She applauded as well, with relief.

Isaac made his way carefully to the aisle, and she followed him, fearful of getting lost in the crowd. It took forever to get out into the cool air of the street. Carriages were lined at the curb, taking on passengers. Rachel made a little agreement with herself—it would be a test of his suitability: if Isaac hired a carriage for them, she would marry him; if not, she would not. He began to walk down the street in his stooped, round-shouldered way. Clearly they were walking, not riding. She stood indignantly for an instant as her mind circled the alternatives again. Then she hurried after him. She was in no position to give tests. But he surprised her. "I thought," he said kindly, "that we might stop for a little ice cream and then take a carriage home."

Rachel's answer was astonishing, even to herself. She turned to him and said, "Thank you—and if it is convenient for you to marry me, I agree to it."

ELEVEN

Now Ava's mother had no time for her. Ava could tell she was busy thinking about Isaac; all day Mama and Aunt Rose sat at the dining-room table and talked about Isaac this and Isaac that. They wondered how much money he might have saved, and would he use it to buy a house someday, or was he saving up to bring the rest of his family from Poland to America? And when should Rachel tell him about Shmuel in the orphanage—that she had two children, a son as well as a daughter? And what about Nathan? Should they tell Isaac the truth—that he had run off and left Rachel—or pretend that she was a widow who had lost a young husband to tuberculosis?

The women sat arguing and debating these points like the old Jews Ava had seen on the street arguing questions of Talmudic law. They stood there in their high hats and long black coats shouting arguments and challenging one another.

Mama sat holding a skein of yellow wool taut across the bridge of her hands while Aunt Rose rolled it rapidly into a neat ball, and the women talked with that same intensity, arguing each issue with passion and conviction.

"Maybe it's better he should think I'm a widow," Mama said. "It's more respectable."

"But if Nathan ever comes back! What then? I always worry he will come back and kidnap Chaveleh. She was his princess, his precious *kinde*."

"He won't come back," Mama said. "What do you think? He'll come back to give me money for the children? When Chaveleh was a baby, I had to put half-milk, half-water in her cup, we had so little money. To him gambling was like breathing."

"All right," Aunt Rose said. "We'll tell Isaac you're a widow."

"God in heaven!" Mama said, moving her hands so that the wool nearly slipped off them. "I just remembered—your friend Dolly knows about Nathan, doesn't she? She's Isaac's sister-in-law; he must already know about Nathan."

"Dolly is a *dumbkopf*," Aunt Rose said. "What goes in one ear comes out the other. She doesn't remember tomorrow what I told her yesterday. Also, she doesn't talk to Isaac. He insulted her mother once; he said her *kugel* gave him heartburn."

"All right, then, it's settled," Rachel said. "I'm a widow." She turned to Ava, who lay on the couch, her left arm in a cast. "If Isaac ever asks you, your father died long ago. Can you remember that, and can I trust you?"

Ava shrugged, then nodded. She was sick of all this talk. She was sick of her broken arm. Underneath the cast she had wild itches. At night she could not sleep and could not escape. She sometimes imagined that she could slip out of her body, leaving it there like an old rag in the bed, and then she would fly like a hollow bird to wherever her father was. They would walk through green fields and feed ducks in the ponds. He would buy her a grand baby buggy to put her doll Peggy in—he would feed her nothing but *halvah*.

But every morning she was there in her bed, hiding under the covers until she heard Uncle Hymie leave for work, later smelling the foul odor of his cigar heavy in the bathroom when she went in to brush her teeth. She had not looked at his face since that night he'd pulled her naked into the living room.

Rose and Hymie had agreed that since Mama was going to marry Isaac as soon as the ninety-one days had elapsed after the divorce papers were drawn, it would be all right for her and Ava to stay there until the wedding. They would get their boarder afterward. Letting them stay might not be as big a loss as they thought, Rose said, because with Isaac a tailor and Hymie having a dress store, they might be able to profit from one another.

Ava had nothing to do during the days. She couldn't play ball, couldn't crochet potholders, couldn't even dry dishes or help make *chalah*. Once a week she had to go to Dr. Schwartz's office, put her hand in a paper bag, and stick it into a machine that was like a small oven. It was supposed to help her wrist heal faster. She missed Shmuel, but was comforted by the thought that soon they all would be together again.

"Let's make plans for the wedding," Aunt Rose said. "We must think about food, presents. What things would you need in a house that once had a wife? Would he ever let you investigate the kitchen, see what pots, what silver, what linens poor Sophie had?"

"He wants no one at the wedding," Mama said. "Only the rabbi."

"What kind of a man says a thing like that? Your sister? Me? I don't deserve to be there?"

"He is strange and private. I hardly know him. We must not press him to do things he doesn't want to do."

"A pious man doesn't want witnesses?"

"There will be whatever witnesses are necessary."

"And when will it be?"

"Very soon, as soon as it is the right time. He is tired, he said, of eating alone."

"Then when will you tell him about Shmuel?"

"Today. Tonight. He is coming here after work to see me."

Aunt Rose turned to study Ava on the couch. "Chaveleh," she commanded, "when Isaac comes tonight, I want you to go and kiss his cheek. Show what a good sweet girl you are. Climb on his lap. Sit on his knee. Make him grateful he will have a ready-made daughter, affectionate and beautiful."

"I don't think that's a good idea," Mama said.

Ava made a face. She thought of the piston of Uncle Hymie's knee, shaking her up and down till her insides hurt.

Later, when there was a knock on the door, she was instructed to open it. Fresh tea stood in the teapot, and sugar cookies were arranged on a silver tray on the table.

"Remember to smile at him!" Aunt Rose whispered.

Ava opened the door and smiled. Isaac stood stiff as a stone on the threshold.

"Welcome to our home," Aunt Rose said. "Come in, have a seat, make yourself comfortable."

He walked past Ava as if she were invisible and took a seat at the table. Aunt Rose scurried about. "Tea? With sugar cubes? A cookie or some honey cake?"

Rachel sat shyly, her hands folded in her lap, her hair, threaded with white, gently fastened in a bun. Her blue eyes shone with relief. Marrying Isaac would mean no more traveling with Dr. Goldberg, no more delivering of babies. It would mean having Shmuel, her darling boy, at her side. So what if Isaac liked opera? So what if he wanted no one at the wedding? A man who has lost a young wife cannot be expected to act in an ordinary way. She could put up with his strange ways, his odd habits. Rose had convinced her this was the only solution. She had come to believe it.

Ava could see that her mother was resigned; her face had lost some of its tightness, and now her clear white skin lay soft upon her cheeks. There was a faint smile on her face as she passed the plate of cookies to Isaac.

"To return the favor of your taking me to the opera," he said to Rachel, "I have bought tickets to the Barnum and Bailey circus next Saturday. If you will do me the honor."

Rachel bowed her head in agreement. Aunt Rose signaled to Ava: go and kiss him, sit on his lap. Ava felt weighted by her broken arm as if lead were in the cast. She could not move. Aunt Rose's eyes indicated an urgency, a threat. Very slowly Ava moved herself across the floor to where Isaac sat. She was imagining how she could make herself kiss him. How could she plant her lips upon that pockmarked face? How could she jump upon those bony black knees? Aunt Rose was waiting, her secret face—which Ava knew too well—fierce and frightening.

"Oh, how nice that will be!" said Mama. "The circus! How nice that you would like to take Chaveleh and me to the circus."

Just at that moment Ava leaned against his black suit, reached up to hook her good arm around his thin neck to hug him. She was not prepared for the violence with which he pushed her away.

"What are you doing?" he cried hoarsely.

She ran to her mother and hid her head against her breast.

Mama said, "The child has not been well since she broke her arm. Forgive her for being so forward." She took Ava by the shoulders and led her down the hall to her room.

"He did not mean anything by pushing you away," Mama said. "He is like my grandfather in Poland. Orthodox men cannot touch women, and he is not used to children, he has never had any."

"Aunt Rose made me do it," Ava said, tears falling down her cheeks. "I know he hates me; he'll never take me to the circus now."

"That may be," Rachel said. "It doesn't matter. I promise someday you will go to the circus."

"Don't you go with him," Ava begged. "Please, Mama, don't you go."

Rachel pushed her away and straightened her hair, looking in the mirror over the dresser. "I'm going with him, Chaveleh. I am going with him wherever he goes. It's the best thing for all of us."

1907

TWELVE

In the same bed where Isaac's first wife, Sophie, had lain dying in childbirth, now Rachel lay in labor, her pale cheeks flushed with effort, her blue eyes tense with concentration. "Don't be worried, Chaveleh," she reassured Ava, who clung to the bedpost waiting for instructions. "It's not as bad as it looks to you. Don't be afraid. All women have to do this, or the world would not go on. And I think it will be fast. Maybe you could run to Aunt Rose's and tell her to get Dr. Schwartz to come here as soon as he can."

She gasped, and her features twisted into an unrecognizable shape. Ava could see the great mound of her mother's belly rise and heave with the contraction. Her own body tightened and reacted to each wave of pain as her mother moaned and stared helplessly while the spasm rocked her. She knew Mama was not frightened; childbirth was her mother's business, and yet . . . how could Mama know she would not die? Was it bad luck to be giving birth in a bed where another woman's birth had gone wrong?

"I don't want to leave you," Ava said.

"Leave me—what can happen?" her mother answered. "Do you think I'll run away? Go, go, go!"

"All right," she said. "I'll be back as fast as I can."

Ava grabbed her coat and jammed her feet into her galoshes. She raced down the steps and through the streets to Aunt Rose's. The streets were slushy, and her feet slipped and slid in the slick icy places at the edges of the sidewalk. Old Mrs. Mirsky was sitting outside in the winter sun, her feet wrapped in a blanket, shaking the pearls through the holes in her box.

"Oh—how I miss you, *bubbeleh*," she said to Ava. "A whole year now you're living with your new father. Has this good tailor made you a new coat yet?"

"I can't talk," Ava said. "Mama is having her baby! I have to get Aunt Rose and tell her to get the doctor."

"Rose? She went out—maybe a half-hour ago. She likes to bring Hymie a hot lunch at the store. She brings lunch to your brother, Shmuel, also. So how do you like having Shmuel home from the orphanage? He's a good boy, no? He works hard."

"I have to go, I can't talk now, Mrs. Mirsky."

She fled, running toward Orchard Street. She was thinking that she didn't see her brother much more now than she had when he was at the orphanage. He worked for Uncle Hymie during the day, and for an extra twenty-five cents he slept on an old couch in the back of the store at night, acting as a watchman. So it was only on Shabbos that he was home with them for dinner, and then Isaac was very strict about all of them behaving properly—they all would have to stand as Rachel said the blessing over the candles and then sit quietly while Isaac gave the blessing over bread. They had to eat in silence since Isaac believed that there should be no talking during meals. Sometimes Shmuel would reach under the table and grab Ava's leg, and she would smile at him, but they had to be very careful not to ignite Isaac's wrath. After dinner, he would expect them to sit in the living room and listen as he played records on the Victrola, of Caruso singing or of famous cantors dovening and crying out at the top of their lungs.

Rachel always sat patiently, knitting or crocheting. She seemed peaceful and content, happy to be living in a home, not working, not having to leave her children. She was grateful every day to Isaac and told Ava to be grateful, too. If he hadn't rescued them, she would still be scrambling for a living, and the children would still be separated. Sometimes Ava would look at Isaac's cold, distant face and then remember Uncle Hymie, with his sharp whiskers, his foul cigar, and she had to admit to herself that this was better. At least now she was going to school again, she was able to lead a normal life.

But her mother had no time for her—she was always busy with Isaac, and Shmuel was never there to talk to her or play with her. Whenever she could manage it, she would pass Kaplan's store and look inside, hoping to see her father waiting there by the pickle barrel, waiting to take her away. But it never happened. She saw only strangers or neighbors of Aunt Rose's—but never her father with his smile that could light up a city.

She rushed into Uncle Hymie's clothing store and hurried to the back. The stink of his cigar smoke was like a curtain that flapped in her face. He was sitting in the dimness, at a big desk. Shmuel was just pushing a rack of heavy coats from the storeroom and didn't see Ava. She could hear him grunt as he shoved the heavy rack in front of him. He was a big boy now, past thirteen. He was tall, with strong arms and legs, and his voice had changed to a deep baritone. Ava had once asked him if he wasn't afraid to sleep alone in the store all night. He had told her that there were rats that ran across the floor. But it was important for them to have the money—someday they would need it, they would buy a house, they would get their mother a new fur coat. Ava reminded him of their mother's skunk coat—but Shmuel said she had given it away to charity. She had kept nothing that belonged to Nathan once she married Isaac.

"Where is Aunt Rose?" Ava asked. "I must see her."

"What's the big excitement?" Uncle Hymie said to Ava. Only for her mother would she even come this close to him, only in an emergency.

"My mother is having her baby," Ava said. "We need a doctor."

Shmuel came out from behind the coats. "I'll go and get the doctor!" he said. "Aunt Rose went shopping to find bargains on the pushcarts." He grabbed his coat off a hook.

"There's work to do here," Uncle Hymie shouted at him. "Where do you think you're going?"

"Didn't you hear?" Shmuel said. "We need the doctor at home."

"If you leave, you don't get paid for the day," Uncle Hymie said, shaking a cylinder of black ash from his cigar toward Shmuel. "Let Chaveleh get the doctor."

"She can't run as fast as me," Shmuel said, flying out the door. "You go home!" he directed Ava over his shoulder. "You go to Mama!" She stood there confused. Shmuel stopped, came back toward her, and shook her gently.

"Don't be afraid," he whispered. "Just go home and sit with Mama. She knows all about these things, and she's had two babies—you and me—so she won't have trouble. Nothing bad will happen." He bent and kissed Ava's cheek. "Go, I'll be there soon." Then he was gone.

Uncle Hymie got up and walked toward her. "So," he said, "I see the skinny little chicken is filling out. Getting to be quite a beauty." He reached out and felt her shoulder. "And how's the broken arm these days? All healed up, good as new, I bet." Ava jerked her arm away.

"And how's your new daddy treating you? Better than I did?" her uncle said. She wanted to knock the cigar from his mouth and grind it into the floor of his shop. But she knew that Shmuel would only have to clean it up.

"Why all the hard feelings?" Uncle Hymie said. "It was only a little joke that night. Do you have to hold it against me always? Maybe we can be friends, make up, have a little kiss." He moved his face toward her. "I know Isaac doesn't kiss you," he said. "Just think what he's missing." He bent toward Ava as if to kiss her. She flung her body away from him and ran out the door of his store. Her uncle called after her, "Someday you and I will make friends, sweetheart. You'll see."

THIRTEEN

Ava could hear her mother's moans from the street. "Oh please, Shmuel," she prayed. "Hurry!"

"Mama, I'm home!" she called out, pulling off her coat. "Are you all right?" She wanted only to hear her mother's ordinary voice—not those foreign and terrifying grunts, sounds that might come from an animal. She was afraid to go into the bedroom. What would she see?

"Oh—ooh—ooh! God in heaven!" Rachel groaned. As Ava came into the room, Rachel became quiet. Then she raised her head and waved a hand weakly at Ava. At least she looked alive, she looked like Mama. When she finally spoke, gasping, she whispered, "These screams just come out, Chaveleh—everyone having a baby screams like this. I'm not dying, don't be afraid. The cries just come out of my mouth. Come here to me, come to Mama, take my hand."

Ava approached her mother slowly, afraid she would suddenly change into that other wild creature who writhed from side to side in the bed and screamed in terror. She took her mother's hand, which was cold and damp.

"The doctor is coming?"

"Shmuel went to get him."

"There is no time," Rachel said. "I feel the baby coming." Her face froze; she was attuned to something happening inside her. "It's coming, Chaveleh . . . right now!" Her voice rose high and loud on the last word. The grunts were starting to come from her mouth again. She was trying to talk to Ava between them, but they seemed to be pulling her down into some pit, some inward place where Ava could not follow.

"Get a pot of water on the stove," her mother gasped. "Boil the water . . ." But the inner waves had started again, and the body in the bed toiled and shook with the terrible process. Ava clung to the bed, watching her mother's face for some familiar sign that she was still in there, inside her head, inside her body. Her mother screamed and threw off the covers. Ava saw blood in the bed.

" . . . Boil a hair ribbon and scissors," her mother gasped. "We . . . have to . . . do it ourselves. I'll tell you what to do. Not hard . . . but easy, Chaveleh."

Ava sped to the kitchen, relieved to be out of there, happy to be busy, moving her own arms and legs. But it took three matches before the gas stove lit, and then it took a hundred years for the water to boil. She thought she should go back to her mother while it was heating, but she didn't want to be in there, watching that struggle. Twice she went to the doorway and looked downstairs to see if Shmuel were coming. Finally she returned to the bedroom. "It's boiling, Mama—the ribbon and scissors are boiling in the pot."

Her mother was silent. It was not a quiet silence, but a silence of containment like the stillness in a balloon before it bursts. Her mother's cheeks were red with exertion, her lips clamped shut and her eyes squeezed closed as she bore down with all her might. When finally she exhaled, the wind of her hot breath blew Ava backward.

Her mother's head fell weakly against the pillow, and from below, from the tangle of bedclothes, came a tiny whimper. A baby's cry. Rachel's eyes opened. She smiled very slightly. Ava ran to the kitchen, poured the boiling water into the sink till only the hair ribbon and the scissors remained in the bottom of the pot. She carried the pot back into the bedroom.

"Mama, can you tell me what to do now?"

It seemed Rachel was almost asleep. Then she spoke in a low voice. "I feel the baby, Chaveleh. Look. I feel it moving—can you see it?" Between her mother's legs lay a creature so tiny that Ava was afraid of it. Its legs were like little red worms, its face like a dried apple. When it opened its mouth to cry, its purple tongue flailed and rattled in its mouth. There was blood on its limbs, and a white scum like the kind that rose to the surface on a pot of chicken soup.

"It's a girl, Mama."

"Aah," said Rachel. "Isaac was hoping for a girl. He has always wanted a daughter."

I am a girl, Ava thought, I could be his daughter. But she said nothing.

"Wrap the baby in a big towel," Rachel said. "Hold it very carefully and then lay it down right there—you see where it's still attached to me?" She seemed exhausted from having talked so much and closed her eyes. After a long moment she opened them again. "The afterbirth is coming," she said. "As soon as it comes out, I will tell you how to cut the cord."

Ava was holding her breath. She didn't want to touch the tiny creature that had come from the inside of her mother, where Ava herself had grown. How terrible, really, that human beings had to start life in a bath of mucous and blood. Yet, steeling herself, she made her hands touch the little red worms of the baby's arms; she slid her palm under the baby's pulsing back and put a dry towel between the baby and the mess in the bed. At her touch the baby began to scream in loud regular shrieks, letting the cry go on till all its air was gone and then gasping to draw in another thimbleful of breath, enough to cry with for another long moment.

Rachel gave one brief groan, and a lump of tissue came flooding out of her body onto the bed. "All right," Rachel called, when she could talk again. "Now this is what you do. You see the cord coming from the baby's belly button? You see how it's throbbing? In a minute that will stop. As soon as it stops, I want you to take the hair ribbon and cut it in half. Tie one piece around the cord, very tightly, about an inch from the baby's body. Then tie the other piece an inch away from that."

Ava nodded. The pot was now cool. She reached inside it and got out the pink hair ribbon, then took the scissors and did as her mother instructed, very carefully, all the while aware of the heat and life in the baby's screwed-up red face. Her hand was bigger than the baby's whole chest. When she had the two pieces of ribbon tightly tied, she looked up at her mother. "What do I do next, Mama?" she asked. Rachel was perfectly silent, her eyes closed. Had she died? Was she dead? Would Ava have to be the mother to this baby now?

"Mama!" But Rachel was breathing; Ava could see her chest rise and fall. Her nightgown had fallen to the side, and Ava saw with wonder that her mother's breasts were swollen and huge, and seemed ready to burst, just as her belly had been swollen to bursting. Ava drew her mother's nightgown closed. Her mother was sleeping, and something important still had to be done. The baby lay on the bloody bed, between her mother's legs, the towel now getting wet with new fluids coming from her mother's body.

Surely the baby had to be put somewhere else now, somewhere soft and clean. But it was still attached to her mother. She could only guess that the scissors were meant to cut the cord, there, between the two ribbons. But dare she do it? What if it were the wrong thing to do, and she killed the baby? Or her mother? What if they both bled to death under her eyes? The baby was crying and thrusting its arms and legs in the air. It was so tiny, so very help-less. The towel opened and exposed its tiny limbs to the cold air. Ava made the decision to cut the cord. She did it very carefully, pointing the sharp tip of the scissors away from the baby's body. When it was done, a tiny bit of blood pulsed out and then stopped. The baby was free. Ava lifted it in her arms and held it close against her body.

The baby stopped its screaming and closed its eyes. In a moment it was rooting against Ava's chest with its mouth. Her own breasts had only just started to grow a few weeks earlier. On each side, under each of her small flat nipples, was a tiny, hard, marble-size lump. The lumps were tender to the touch. When she rolled her fingertips against them, she gasped at the feel-ing and at the knowledge of what it would be like to have breasts. But could they ever be like her mother's? Taut and tight to bursting? With nipples as big as saucers?

The baby's head was still wet and slick with the foam of its birth. Gently, Ava rubbed the towel over her head, drying her sister's hair. And then sud-denly, to her surprise, she lowered her lips and kissed the baby's forehead.

FOURTEEN

"We will name the baby Musetta," Isaac said, sitting proudly in a straight chair at the foot of the bed. "I will take her to the opera as soon as she is old enough."

"What kind of a name is that for a Jewish child?" Aunt Rose said, lean-ing in the doorway with her arms crossed. "Why not call her Ruth, Leah, Rebecca? Why not Sophie, after your first wife?"

Rachel, propped up in the bed, nursing the day-old baby, seemed oblivi-ous of the discussion. Ava had brushed her mother's hair that morning and tied it back. She had been in charge of the new baby since yesterday, changing its diapers, bringing it to her mother to be fed, taking it back to its cradle, rocking it to sleep. Dr. Schwartz had never arrived at the house. When Shmuel finally returned, he had with him a midwife located by Dr. Schwartz's wife, but they all found the baby safely born, its mother sleeping peacefully, and Ava proudly keeping watch over both of them. The midwife, who knew Rachel from their work with the doctor, expressed wonder at how well Ava had done in helping her mother to deliver the baby and in cutting the cord neatly and hygienically.

"Maybe Ava will grow up to be a midwife," Aunt Rose said. "It's good money."

Ava felt Isaac looking at her. Was he thinking about who she would be when she grew up? She often felt he wished she were grown up and gone from his sight. He never spoke to her directly, but always asked Rachel to give her some command or other. It was her duty, as soon as she came home from school, to wash the kitchen floor. When Mama protested that it did not need to be washed every day, Isaac said that the importance of this routine was that the child be trained. If she did not develop good habits now, when would she?

Ava always felt she was in his way. If she sat at the table playing checkers with her girlfriend Tessie, who lived across the street, Isaac would indicate he needed the table to lay out a length of cloth. He often brought home work to do, and the sound of the sewing machine in the alcove was a frequent buzz in the evenings. When he wasn't sewing, he was playing his Victrola, sitting upright in his hard chair and becoming fiercely angry if anyone disturbed him. Ava learned to keep out of his way, to stay in her room and do her homework, to work on her reading and writing far from his gaze.

"Who is Musetta?" Rachel asked idly, stroking the baby's tiny head.

"Aha," Isaac said in the lively voice he used only when he talked about his music. "She is the great spirited beauty in Puccini's *La Bohème*. She has fire, she has passion!" He looked lovingly at the infant in the bed. "She is like this beautiful daughter of mine, lusty and temperamental!"

"I can't see you putting up with a willful child," Aunt Rose said.

"If she has talent," Isaac said, "willfulness is to be desired." Then, as if something had just occurred to him, he glanced at Ava.

"Rachel," he said, "Have you told the child that she must get ice for the ice box today?"

"I thought today we would buy from the ice man and save her the trouble," Rachel said. "She worked so hard yesterday; I thought she could have a little rest."

"She has responsibilities, like the rest of us. Tell her to go now and get the ice."

"There is plenty on the windowsill," Rachel said.

"But if the sun shines, there will not be," he persisted. "Tell her to go."

Rachel looked apologetically at Ava. "Go," she said. "You heard your father."

Ava threw him a vicious glance and stamped from the room. He was not her father; he would never be her father. Her father was handsome and loving and good, and someday he would come and take her with him, maybe this very moment. Today she felt she could leave her mother without regret in an instant. Mama had totally given up defending Ava and agreed always with Isaac. Now with the new baby—"Musetta"—Mama would not have a minute to spend with Ava, anyway.

"Oh, come for me, Papa," she prayed, as she took money from the sugar bowl, got her coat, and headed toward the East River. On the docks she could get ice for five cents less than the ice man charged. But she had to walk a long way to get it, and it was heavy to carry back. She checked to see that she had gloves in her pocket; without them, her fingers would turn numb and white from holding the ice.

"Chaveleh, wait for me, where are you going?" Shmuel, carrying an armful of trousers, caught up with her on the street.

"He's making me get ice at the docks," she said. "There's ice on the fire escape, there's ice on the windowsill. Look—it's going to snow again, but he has to have ice."

"Isn't he grateful for what you did for Mama yesterday?"

"He doesn't care. He's horrible."

"He's not so bad," Shmuel said. "He's made life much easier for Mama."

"Well, he likes you," Ava said. "You work. You bring him money. As soon as there's enough money, he's going to bring his parents here from the old country. But me—he thinks I just take up space and eat his food. When he brings his mother and father, there won't be room for me."

"Maybe you can work soon. Then he won't be so hard on you."

"I'm not old enough."

"Maybe not now. But soon you can get your working papers."

"I have to be fourteen."

"No, no, you just have to be a little taller. I'm not quite fourteen and I have them. There's a notary Uncle Hymie knows who will give you working papers for fifty cents no matter what your age is."

They came to a corner. "I have to go down this way now, Shmuel—good-bye. I'll see you at home."

"No—let me come with you. I'll carry the ice, you can carry these pants; they won't be as heavy as the ice."

"Uncle Hymie will be angry if you're late."

"We'll hurry, he may not notice how long I'm gone."

"You're such a good brother," Ava said. "You're so good to me."

"You're my little sister. If I don't take care of you, who will?"

1910

FIFTEEN

"Put down the feathers and do what your papa says," Aunt Rose said.

"What did he say?" Ava asked. She was knotting feathers into long plumes. A lady in the building had shown her how to do this and paid her one cent an inch. Then the lady attached the plumes to hats that she made and then sold for high prices.

"She knows what she has to do," Isaac addressed Aunt Rose.

"Let her finish the plume," Aunt Rose said. "Money in her pocket is less out of yours."

"The baby is hungry," Isaac said.

"Babies are always hungry."

There was a *new* baby now. Isaac had named the second daughter "Gilda." This one screamed day and night. She was sickly. She had a pasty complexion. She woke from her naps crying and kicking, her ugly little face red and angry.

Ava didn't mind the first baby, the baby she had helped come into the world. Musetta loved Ava's dolls and toys. She smiled and played. Sometimes she made Isaac laugh; not often, but when he laughed he forgot to criticize Ava, and that gave her some peace. But Gilda, the new baby, was nothing but a problem. She choked when she nursed at Mama's breast and turned blue. She refused to drink and fell asleep after two pulls, and then woke in ten minutes screaming.

Now Mama was in the hospital; she had developed a terrible pain in her ear. The doctor had come and said it was the mastoid sickness and that she had to have an operation. Now that she was recovering, it was Ava's job to carry the new baby three times a day to the hospital, which was twenty blocks away. It seemed to her as if she had just come back and sat down with her feathers—and now here was Isaac saying that it was time to go again.

"You'd better go now," Aunt Rose said. "The baby will starve to death, skinny thing that she is, if she doesn't get all she can."

"All right," Ava said. "I'll go." Musetta was crawling about on the floor, playing with a ball of wool. Aunt Rose was knitting matching red sweaters for the baby and Musetta. Ava asked her if she would knit one for her, too.

"If your papa agrees, I'll make one for you, too."

Isaac shook his head. "She is to wear nothing bright."

"Oh," Aunt Rose said, "Why not? A sweater is not the same as scarves and bangles."

"No," Isaac said, and that was the end of it.

When Ava told her friend Tessie she was not allowed to wear anything bright, Tessie nodded her head knowingly.

"My mother told me all about what can happen," she said.

"What?"

"Don't you know about the bad men?"

Ava shook her head.

"There are bad men," Tessie said, rolling her eyes deliciously, "who grab young girls and then they disappear."

"What happens to them?"

"Why don't you ask your brother Shmuel? I'll bet he knows all about that."

"Shmuel wouldn't know about bad men. He's a good man."

"My mother says all men are bad, under the right circumstances."

Ava wondered if Tessie would be in danger just because of her bright red hair. She could be seen blocks away with that hair, it was so brilliant, so long, so wavy. Tessie had become very beautiful in the last few months. Isaac now turned his back to her whenever she came to the house.

"All right, give me the baby," Ava said, putting on her coat. "I'm ready to take her to Mama."

Aunt Rose bent over the cradle and scooped the baby up. "Come, come," she crooned. "Gildala, my golden Gildala." She wrapped the baby in a heavy wool blanket and placed the bundle in Ava's arms. "Go carefully now."

"Tell her not to talk to men," Isaac instructed Aunt Rose.

"You heard," her aunt said.

"I know," Ava said. "Three times a day he says it."

"Don't refer to him as 'he'—it's disrespectful."

"Sorry," Ava said, taking the baby out the door. "I'd better go now."

At least it wasn't so bad holding the baby out in the street. In the house there was always the smell of the baby's full diaper or her spit-up. Ava couldn't remember that Musetta had smelled so badly. Maybe she felt a special warmth toward Musetta because she had been there when the baby was born. But that wasn't the only difference—Musetta, from the very beginning, had been more bright-eyed, more curious. Small as Gilda was, Ava thought she looked like a little tiny Isaac, with the same closely set eyes and the same tight mouth.

When she got to Hornstein's Bakery where they always bought bread, she went inside for a minute to get warm and to rest. She was out of breath—the baby was heavy in all those blankets, and they still had a long way to go. Balancing Gilda in one arm, she felt in her pocket for her money. Now that she was knotting the feathers, she always had a few pennies for cakes or candy.

"Hello, Chaveleh. How are you today?"

"Fine, Mrs. Hornstein. Could I have three sugar cookies, please?"

"Your mama is doing well since her surgery, I hear. When will she be home?"

"Probably in a week."

"And every day you take the baby to her? What a thoughtful girl."

"I go three times every day."

"A jewel of a child you are," Mrs. Hornstein said, handing Ava the cookies in a sheet of waxed paper. She walked a few steps to the rear of the store and yelled, "Henry! Chaveleh is here again. Come and say hello."

"No, no, don't bother him," Ava said. "I have to go now . . . "

But Henry was already bursting through the door, wiping his floury hands on a white apron. His grin always made her heart jump—it was shy, and his face was always full of pleasure when he saw Ava. He was the same age as Shmuel, sixteen, but not quite as tall. He had blue eyes and curly light brown hair.

"Hello, Chaveleh, I'm making bagels."

"That's nice."

"Would you like a bagel?"

"I just bought some cookies . . . " She held out the cookies toward him. "Do you want one?"

"No, that's okay. I have a lot of cookies here."

Mrs. Hornstein smiled and walked away to wait on a customer. Ava shifted the baby to her other arm. Its face was covered under the blanket. She hoped it could breathe, but wasn't sufficiently worried to turn back the blanket and check.

"What else are you baking?" Ava asked.

"Early this morning I did rye bread without seeds. Then I did rye bread with seeds. Now bagels. Later *chalah*."

"Do you enjoy it?"

"If I have to work, I'd rather be baking than sewing trousers."

"What I do is knot feathers," Ava said. "I get a penny an inch."

Henry made a face. "Not good pay," he said. "I know a shoe store where you can make seventy-five cents a day."

"Where?"

"I could take you over there. Do you want to go?"

"That's a lot of money," she said. "How far is it?"

"Just a block from here." He untied his apron. "Mama, can I have ten minutes? I want to take Chaveleh over to Mr. Carp's shoe store—maybe she can get work there."

"Certainly, certainly. Here—give me the baby for two minutes, Chaveleh. I'll put her down in the back. She's sleeping, she won't be any trouble."

"I don't know if I should leave her . . . "

"Go," Mrs. Hornstein said. "It won't be a problem."

When Ava gave up the baby into Mrs. Hornstein's arms, she felt as if she'd just set down the weight of a mountain.

"Come on," Henry said. "Let's hurry." He raced out of the bakery, and she flew behind him, running down the street. The feel of the wind in her face made her laugh. She pulled off her shawl and let her hair blow behind her.

"Faster," Henry said, pausing to grab her hand and pull her along. "Faster! We don't want someone else to get there first and get the job. Mr. Carp was just in the bakery yesterday, saying he needed someone to work, selling shoes."

"I don't know if . . . " The wind filled Ava's mouth and choked off the words. "I don't think Isaac would let me."

Henry slowed till they both were walking briskly. "Why not? Don't you need the money? Doesn't every family need all the money they can get?"

"He's afraid to let me go out. I don't understand, really. Tessie says he's afraid bad men will get me." Ava laughed. "Maybe bad men like you, Henry."

Henry flushed under her gaze. "No, seriously, Chaveleh. Would he really prevent you from taking a job? You have working papers now, don't you?"

"I've had them for a year already. Shmuel helped me get them, but it didn't matter. Isaac wouldn't hear of my working. I can't see why—he hates to have me there at home. I know he always wishes I were gone."

"It must be hard, not to have your real father there."

"It's terrible."

"Maybe someday you'll see your father again. My mother told me he was very handsome."

"He was as handsome as Isaac is ugly. Isaac never talks to me. He has never called me by name. All he wants is for me to scrub the floors, get ice, carry the baby, play with Musetta and keep her quiet so he can hear his records. And Mama lets him be mean to me day and night. She says he saved us—he took Shmuel out of the orphanage, he gave us a home. Sometimes I'd rather be in an orphanage."

"There's Mr. Carp's store—do you still want to try for the job?"

"Yes!" Ava said. "Even if I have to fight with Isaac."

"Still, he isn't entirely wrong when he says there are bad men," Henry said. "I've heard of such things."

"Well—what would bad men want with me? I don't talk to strangers. I go to school and come home. But Isaac won't even let my Aunt Rose knit me a red sweater. No bright colors, he says."

"There are men that kidnap girls and send them to other states," Henry said. "It's called White Slavery."

"What do they do with the girls?"

"I'm not sure, but you wouldn't want to find out."

"But Isaac won't even let me wear a red ribbon!"

"I know how you could wear a red ribbon," Henry said. "My mother pins one on her slip every day. She says it keeps away the evil eye. It keeps her safe. So you could wear one and tell Isaac it's for protection."

"It wouldn't be much fun to wear a red ribbon under my clothes. And I don't even know if I believe in the evil eye. Maybe I just believe in good luck and bad luck."

"Here's the shoe store now," Henry said. "Shall we go in? It could be the start of a whole new life for you."

"Yes," Ava said. "I'm as ready as I'll ever be."

SIXTEEN

"Well?" said Mrs. Hornstein when Henry and Ava got back to the bakery. "Well? What happened?"

"Good news!" Henry said. "Chaveleh starts to work there tomorrow."

"Mazel tov!" said Mrs. Hornstein. "Now come in the back, Chaveleh, and see the surprise I have for you. Henry, you stay here in the front in case customers arrive."

Ava, thinking Mrs. Hornstein had made some delicacy that she wanted Ava to taste, was astonished to see a fat woman sitting in a chair, her blouse open, and the baby, Gilda, held against her bare breast. Ava stared at the woman in confusion.

"This is Mrs. Ianello," Mrs. Hornstein said. "She came in to buy some coffee cake and heard the little one screaming in the back. The minute you walked out, Chaveleh, the devil came in and woke her. I never heard such yells. I didn't know what to do with her; I was afraid the customers would think I was murdering her."

"She always yells like that," Ava said.

"So then Mrs. Ianello came in." The fat woman smiled at Ava, showing a space where two of her teeth were missing.

"It's no trouble," she said. "My Anthony—he's six months old—he's fast asleep at home with his big sister, Angelina, and I thought I'd take ten minutes to run out and get some shopping done. So then I heard your poor little baby screaming, and I thought, 'Well, my Tony's just been fed, he's had plenty, I got lots to spare.'" She patted her huge breast, the one at which Gilda was now sucking vigorously. "When I can do a good deed, I'm glad to."

"You'll go to heaven," Mrs. Hornstein said, smiling.

"Oh yes," Mrs. Ianello said, completely serious. "I pray every night that I will."

"Don't look so worried, Chaveleh," Mrs. Hornstein said. "It will save your mama the trouble. Later, tonight, the baby can have her mama's milk again."

"I have good milk, don't worry," Mrs. Ianello said. Her breasts were three times the size of Mama's; Ava had never seen such breasts in her life. They were swollen and white, lined with veins and wormy with blood vessels.

"Well, that's settled," Mrs. Hornstein said. "Now when the baby is full, we can put her down again, she will sleep, and you can stay in the back and keep Henry company while he makes strudel dough."

Mrs. Ianello nodded her agreement. "A sweet boy, Henry is," she said. "Look how he helps his mama. A boy so helpful would make a fine husband for you."

Ava looked down at her shoes.

"Don't tease the girl," Mrs. Hornstein said, smiling. "Take off your coat, Chaveleh. Relax. When Henry comes back here, you can have milk with your cookies. Mrs. Ianello has solved our problems for the time being . . . "

When Mrs. Ianello had finished feeding the baby, she held her over her shoulder and did not even flinch when Gilda made a funny noise and a flood of milk came spilling out of her mouth. She pulled a handkerchief from her pocket and wiped up the mess.

"Good, good, let all the air out," she said. "You had a good meal, yes?"

Then Mrs. Hornstein lifted Gilda from the woman and lay her down on a small cot in the corner. In an instant, the baby was asleep.

"I'll call Henry in now," Mrs. Hornstein said. "He can get back to work."

With Gilda fast asleep, Ava spent some time helping Henry roll out the strudel dough and filling it with chopped prune filling. Together they rolled the long lines of dough till they looked like sleeping white snakes. Then Ava brushed them with melted butter while Henry began preparing the flour mixture for the next batch. When everything had been put in the oven to bake, Henry took a bottle of milk from the ice box and served a glass to Ava along with a square of rich marble cake.

"I'll never be able to eat dinner," she laughed. "Aunt Rose is probably making chicken and soup; I think it's the only thing she knows how to cook. When I used to live with her, I think we ate nothing else."

"Chicken soup isn't bad," Henry said. "After all—what else is there, really?"

"Cake!" Ava said, stuffing her mouth. "Pies!"

"I have no more baking to do today," Henry said. "Shall we take a walk down to the river? The baby is still fast asleep."

"Well—" Ava hesitated. "Maybe a short walk, but then I definitely have to go home, and then tonight Shmuel will walk to the hospital with me, so Mama can feed Gilda then."

SEVENTEEN

When Ava came in the door, Isaac lunged at her. "Monster! Thief!" he shouted. "Where have you been?" He stood trembling before her in rage. "I thought you ran off with my little Gilda," he shouted, pulling the baby from Ava's arms. "I thought the two of you had been sold down the river."

Astonished, Ava looked toward Aunt Rose, who was backed against the curtains, wringing her hands together. Isaac continued ranting, "You evil, miserable child!"

It occurred to Ava, in the clarity of the moment, that this was the first time Isaac had ever addressed her directly.

"Nothing is wrong," she said calmly. "Why are you so upset? The baby is fine."

Isaac was so angry he could not speak. He pulled at the hairs on his head, dancing from one foot to the other in his fury. Aunt Rose stepped out of the shadows and took the baby from him.

"Shmuel went to see your mama in the hospital at his lunchtime, and she asked why you hadn't come with Gilda. Your mama was worried. Her breasts were sore, she wanted to nurse the baby. Shmuel thought maybe you were still here—so he ran all the way home to tell you to go to Mama right away. And then we told him you'd left hours ago! So now he's out on the streets looking for you, Chaveleh. He's frightened. He's probably looking in the river by now!"

"I didn't mean to cause any trouble," Ava said. "And I didn't think about Mama being uncomfortable. I should have. I'm sorry. But don't worry about the baby. She's been fed and she's fine!"

"How could she have been fed?" roared Isaac.

"Should I explain?" Ava asked her aunt. "Does he want me to explain?" It occurred to her that from now on she would address him through a third party.

"Do you want her to explain?" Aunt Rose asked Isaac.

"What is there to explain?" he cried. "She is no good. She is disobedient! She is untrustworthy."

"Aunt Rose," Ava said. "Tell him that I did nothing wrong. Tell him that I was in the bakery, and the baby started crying, and a very kind woman offered to nurse her."

Already Ava realized this would not appease them; Rose and Isaac were staring at one another, both looking horrified. "What do you mean, a 'kind woman'?"

"Mrs. Hornstein's friend Mrs. Ianello. She has a new baby at home. Gilda was screaming. She gave her milk."

"From her breast?" Aunt Rose asked.

"Yes."

"God in heaven!" Isaac moaned, striking his chest. "My baby has drunk the milk of a Christ lover! My God! My God!"

"We can ask the rabbi," Aunt Rose said. "It could not be helped."

"My Gilda is ruined!" Isaac cried to the heavens. "This woman drinks milk with her meat. She eats pork, shellfish. On this she fed my baby!"

"I'm sure she has a very clean home," Ava volunteered.

"*Gay in d'rerd arayn!*" Isaac bellowed at Ava. "Go to hell!" He suddenly swung his arm, opened his hand, and slapped her face. When he pulled back to strike her again, she ducked, and he struck his fist against the wall. "*Mamser!* Bastard!" he cried. "I have broken my fingers!"

"Let me see," Aunt Rose said. "Quick, come in the kitchen, we'll get ice."

"I won't be able to work!" he moaned. "I won't be able to sew."

Ava stood serenely while Aunt Rose lay the baby down, hurried with Isaac to the kitchen, began to chip ice from the block with a pick. She slowly pulled off her shawl and coat and hung them in the closet. All the while Isaac moaned and cursed, mumbled and threatened. The truth was that he had no real power over her. She would eventually leave here. Now she had a job. Soon she would grow up and go away. It didn't matter if it wasn't tomorrow. Someday it would happen, and she could live for that day. She didn't have to be afraid anymore. And she didn't have to try to love Isaac or his children—ever.

1915

EIGHTEEN

"On the mountain stands a maiden,
Who she is I do not know,
All she wants is gold and silver, All she wants
Is a nice young man. Jump out,
Sadie dearie,
Jump in, Susie."

Musetta held tightly to the red wooden handles of her jump rope and began to jump and count: "One, two, three, four, five . . . "

"Don't get too tired!" Isaac called down from the window. "Don't go over ten."

"Papa!" Musetta said breathlessly, losing count and at the same time tripping on the rope. "I didn't know you were listening."

"Come upstairs. Papa will play with you."

"Mama wants me to have some fresh air."

"You'll get plenty—in the summer, in the country. But now come up—we'll sing songs together."

"I don't want to catch Gilda's cold."

"You won't. Come up. It's lonely here, with Mama gone shopping."

"Well—all right. I will. There's no one to play with anyway."

Musetta ran up the steps of the tenement building. Isaac was waiting at their door for her. "Such a cold nose you have," he said, bending to kiss her. "You should wear a scarf on a windy day and cover your face with it."

"You shouldn't worry so much, Papa," Musetta said. "Mama says you will die early if you worry so much. Children are strong, she says."

"Look at your sister," he said. "Gilda is not strong. Again she is sick."

Gilda, already five years old, looked only about three. She was thin and pale. During the night she had had an attack of the croup, and Papa had been up walking with her, giving her tonic, then hot tea with honey. It annoyed Musetta, who slept in the same bed with Gilda, that her sister was sick so often. It meant the light had to be turned on, that there was noise and commotion, and in the morning, when Musetta had to go to school, she was tired and found it hard to concentrate. Since school was her favorite place, she wanted always to be alert there and not miss a single fact, a single spelling word. Her teachers were astonished by her spelling and her reading.

Miss McGinley had given her special books to take home, not the ordinary readers, but books that were meant for children in advanced grades. She could hardly wait to get to school in the mornings—it was exciting there, and Miss McGinley was beautiful and mysterious. Very tall and thin, she often wore a red suit to school and a red wide hat with long white egret feathers on it. Ava had told Musetta that egret feathers were the fanciest kind and cost the most. Also, Miss McGinley smelled of a marvelous lily of the valley perfume that Musetta could inhale from her own clothes when she got home from school. When the rooms at home smelled of *kugel*, of onions and chicken fat or barley soup or stuffed cabbage, Musetta would sometimes go to the closet and sniff her school dresses, hoping to get a scent of school and Miss McGinley.

Musetta knew her teacher must lead a completely different life from hers because Miss McGinley brought to school fresh flowers, which she told the class she had picked in her garden. If she had a garden, then she certainly did not live in a tenement building with only two windows and a dark air shaft for light and air. Musetta had come once to the teachers' lunchroom with a message for Miss McGinley from the office and had seen her teacher eating slices of pink meat from a wax paper sheet. When she stared at them too long, her teacher had offered a slice to her. "Would you like some ham?" Musetta shook her head. Her teacher said, "Oh, you probably can't eat ham, isn't that so?" The meat looked delicious, and Musetta wondered why foolish rules that had nothing to do with her prevented her from tasting the meat. All that nonsense—that she could not eat ham or eat meat with milk or eat ice cream even an hour after a chicken supper. Once she had forgotten the rules and poured herself a glass of milk after a salty pot roast dinner, and

Mama had yelled at her as if she had seen Musetta drinking iodine. "Never do that again! What if your father had seen! A calf must not be eaten in its mother's milk, it is forbidden, Musetta!" How much nicer it would be to have the freedom that Miss McGinley had, the freedom that everyone who wasn't Jewish had.

Now Papa held out his arms and said, "Come, stand here by me, we'll sing a song together."

"I want to sing, too," Gilda called from the couch where she sat wrapped in an afghan. Her voice was whispery and hoarse.

"No, you can't sing today, little one," Papa said. "You're sick. You just sit and listen. Listen to Musetta's beautiful voice. Someday she will be an opera star."

"I'd rather be a pianist," Musetta said. "I wish I had a piano, Papa."

"Do you?" he said. "Well, we'll have to think about that."

"I would play on it every day!" said Musetta.

"Yes, I think you would," Papa said. "Come now, and sing. At least until we have a piano we can make music with our voices. And if you're a good girl, I will take you to see Caruso one day soon."

"Mama told Aunt Rose that Caruso is fat and screeches at the top of his lungs."

"Mama does not have musical understanding," Papa said. "For that she has to be forgiven. She is a good wife and mother in every other way. Now— we'll sing 'Unter a Kleyn Beymele.' That's one you like, am I right?"

"Yes, I like that one," Musetta said. "If Gilda keeps quiet."

Gilda coughed loudly. "If I make noise," she said, "it's because I can't help it."

"All right now," Papa said. "Here we go. *Unter a kleyn beymele zitsen yina-elech tsvay. . . .*" The song was about two young boys who are sitting under a tree, talking about a girl. Musetta loved the song, it was so pretty; it made her hope that someday boys would sit under a tree and talk about her. She knew she was pretty—she had long golden hair that Rachel sometimes dipped in sugar water in order to make long thin curls that swirled down Musetta's back. She had almond-shaped brown eyes and a dimple in her cheek when she smiled. She would stare in the mirror for a half-hour, practicing smiles, practicing how to look glamorous. Sometimes her sister Ava, who was almost twenty and worked now as a buyer of coat trimmings, let Musetta use her lipstick and powder. The powder made her cheeks look smooth and pale; her dimple was like a little pocket of mischief, appearing and disappearing. Shmuel loved to stick the tip of his nose in her dimple and pretend the dimple was going to gobble up his nose. She loved Shmuel—he was so good-natured and kind to her. Sometimes he seemed more like her father than Isaac—it didn't seem possible that Mama could be her mother and also the mother of the grown-up Shmuel.

"Now let's sing another," Papa said. "What about 'Ofen Pripichek'?"

"I want to sing that one!" Gilda insisted. "That's my favorite."

"You are too sick," Papa said.

"No I'm not!" Gilda screamed and suddenly burst into a fit of coughing.

"Musetta, get your sister her tonic—Do you know where it is? Mama said that if she was still out, we should give it to Gilda."

"Yes, I know where it is," said Musetta, going to the cabinet and getting down the brown glass bottle and a spoon. She came back with a cup of water and the medicine in a teaspoon. "Open your mouth," she said to Gilda. "Hurry, before I spill it."

Gilda, who was very fussy about everything, said, "First I have to smell it." She sniffed at the medicine and started to scream, "Musetta is trying to poison me! That's not my medicine!"

"Yes it is!" Musetta yelled back, "It was right there in the cabinet where Mama said it would be."

"It's horrible, it's poison!"

"Take it!"

"I won't!"

Musetta lunged with the spoon at her sister's stubborn, sealed lips, and Papa interrupted her. "Let me have that, Musetta. Let me smell it." He sniffed. "This smells like alcohol. That's what it is."

"See? See?" Gilda cried.

"Come here, Musetta, and smell it," Papa said. "You will see what a terrible mistake you made! Alcohol could kill a person!"

"I wasn't going to kill anyone!"

"Yes—but you could have, by mistake. You must be careful! Gilda is your little sister, you are responsible for her; it's your duty in life to see that she is safe and well."

"She wanted to kill me!" Gilda cried. "She hates me."

"Shut up," Musetta said, thinking that she did hate her scrawny dumb little sister who went around smelling everything—smelling coats and smelling food and smelling people. Gilda often said that Uncle Hymie smelled like the doctor and that Mama smelled like wet fur. Musetta didn't go around sticking her nose where it didn't belong.

"Why don't you hit Musetta, Papa? She told me to shut up!"

"Hitting isn't the way to solve things," Isaac said.

"Well—you hit Ava," Gilda said, " . . . but that's because she isn't really your child."

"Who said that?" asked Isaac, his face getting red.

"Shmuel told me that's the reason you're so mean to Ava."

"Never mind. Be quiet. No more of this talk." He went into the kitchen, where Musetta heard him fill the kettle with water and put it on the stove. Then she heard the whisk of the match and the pop of the burner being lit. Soon there was a sound in the hall, of footsteps coming quickly toward the door.

"Chaveleh's coming home from work," Gilda said. "I hope she brought me a present."

"Ooh, she has a new coat!" Musetta said, as her sister came into the room, bringing with her a breeze of cool air and a scent of perfume.

"Well, how are you feeling today, Gilda? Any better? Guess what? I brought you a present."

"I knew it!" Gilda said. "What is it?"

Ava turned her pocket inside out and came forward with a handful of buttons. "More broken buttons for your collection. I have everyone on the lookout for you—the cutters, the pressers, the seamstresses. They're all saving broken buttons for you. See? Here's a leather button, and here's one that's shaped like a star."

"I like the ones that look like rubies," Gilda said. "Have you any of those?"

"Not today," Ava said. "Maybe next time."

"Where did you get that new coat?" Musetta asked. She stroked it—the coat was made of soft beige wool and had a thick fur collar.

"Do you like it?" Ava said, spinning around to show it off to the girls. "I modeled it for Mr. Berk's salesmen this afternoon, and then Mr. Berk said I could have it instead of a week's pay. It's worth at least a month's pay! Isn't it pretty? I selected all the trimmings for this model— the buttons and the fur."

"You're lucky to get a new coat," Musetta said. "Now maybe you won't be so angry about the time Papa made coats for Gilda and me but not one for you."

"I don't care about that anymore," Ava said. "I cared about it then." She glanced toward the bedroom. "Isn't Mama home?"

"She's shopping."

"I guess I'll have to start making dinner for you, then. But I'll have to hurry because I'm going out in a little while."

"Are you going with Henry from the bakery?"

"No, not tonight. Tonight I'm going to Coney Island."

Just then Isaac walked into the living room. "That coat," he said to Musetta. "Where did she get it?"

"Chaveleh's boss gave it to her."

"She will have to give it back," Isaac said.

"She earned it instead of pay," Musetta explained. She was used to carrying messages between her father and her sister, who did not speak to each other directly.

"Tell her we expect half her pay. She cannot cut her coat in half, can she?"

"Can you?" Musetta said to Ava, feeling a thrill of power, to be involved in this battle of wills.

"Tell him I do my work well, and this is how Mr. Berk wants to thank me for it. I will give Mama half my pay as usual, this month. But I will keep the coat."

"Tell her," Isaac said, staring out the window, "that this family does not accept such presents. And that kind of thanks is no pay for work unless it's some *other* kind of work."

"What do you mean?" Ava cried to Isaac, then spun toward Musetta. "Ask him what he means by that!"

Ava deliberately went to the closet and hung her new coat on a hanger.

"What do you mean by that?" Musetta said.

"She knows what I mean." Isaac walked to the closet, pulled the coat off the hanger, and tossed it to the floor. "It will have to go back to the factory."

Ava swept up the coat and held it against her. "Don't tell me what to do," she said directly to Isaac. "Don't ever tell me what to do again."

"You'll do what I say," he said. "For one thing, you will give back that coat. For another, you will not go out tonight; you will stay here and wash the walls."

"I am going out in twenty minutes."

"You will give the coat back," Isaac hissed. "I won't have you living here with people talking of how you got that coat."

"How did I get it? I worked hard!" Ava cried.

"People will talk and say what you are," Isaac said. "What you truly are."

"And what is that?"

"You are a whore," Isaac said softly. "That's what you are."

"You're crazy!" Ava cried. "A crazy man."

Isaac lunged toward her and smacked her face. "I have always known what you were. Now I have proof."

NINETEEN

The train rocked along its tracks, and Ava leaned her chin into the furry collar of her coat, savoring the soft reassuring touch of it against her skin. She tried to breathe slowly and calm the panicked beating of her heart.

She was on her way to Coney Island, to meet her friend, Johnny Quinn, a tall blond fellow she'd been going out with for a few weeks. He was a dancer in an open café on the boardwalk; he and his partner, Tony Angeloni, did five buck-and-wing dance acts every evening, the last one at midnight. Johnny had apologized to Ava that he couldn't pick her up, but he promised he would certainly take her home if she didn't mind taking the train out to Brooklyn by herself.

She liked the idea of having a reason to leave home after dinner, to take a long train ride, to sit in the café with Toni Angeloni's girl, Maria, and watch the boys do their dance. Anything was better than sitting home with Isaac and Mama, listening to his Caruso records or watching him coddle Musetta and Gilda as if they were made of glass and would break if asked to do anything. Ava would come home, do her chores as quickly as possible (she still washed the kitchen floor every night), and then leave to take the elevated train to Coney Island.

There was hardly anyone on the train at this hour; she could see only an old woman sitting at the other end of the car, her head resting against the window glass, her hair covered with a black shawl. She hated to worry her mother by going out every evening and coming home at 2:00 A.M., while Rachel was concerned that Ava would get sick because of not sleeping enough and going to work every day tired and exhausted. She didn't like Ava's going out with Johnny Quinn, whom Ava had met at work, but she agreed to pretend he was Jewish so Isaac didn't interfere. Rachel had told Isaac that "Quinn" was from the name "Cohen"—that the boy called himself that for convenience in business. The truth was that Johnny was Irish and that he went to mass every Sunday.

Once, when he wanted to change into a clean shirt, Ava had gone to his house with him. A painting of Jesus hung over the kitchen sink. There was Jesus, whose name could not be spoken in her house, with his sweet girlish face, wearing a pink robe, staring at her with his deep, soulful eyes. This was the kind of father who could love and protect you, a father to come home to. Maybe because of him Johnny had that kind of confidence in life that made him fun to be with—he joked and kidded and danced like a dream. Sometimes, after his show was over, the four of them, Tony and Maria, Johnny and Ava, would go to a nightclub and dance. Johnny was so different from serious Jewish boys. He had a light sunny touch about him.

Ava had been going out with Henry Hornstein almost every week since she'd met him in his mother's bakery years ago, but Henry was so earnest, so sincere, so predictable. Ava was tired of Jewish boys. Those she knew were tied to their mothers, always trying to please them, always trying to please Ava as well. There were no surprises in being with them.

The lights in the subway car blinked and dimmed; Ava read the ads plastered on the walls of the train—for hair tonic, for cod liver oil, for cigarettes. She was so relieved to be away from Isaac. How dare he smack her, as he felt was his right? He never hit Shmuel. For one thing, Shmuel was taller than Isaac now and much stronger. For another, Shmuel didn't seem to excite in him the kind of rage Ava caused. If Ava looked especially pretty, Isaac was infuriated. If her hair was curled, or if she wore it some new way, he would say to Rachel, "Tell her to change it back, I don't like it that way." And her mother was always torn between her daughter and her husband. Mama needed Isaac; he was good to her and saw that she and her children had food and clothing, nice furniture, good shoes to wear.

Isaac worked hard—he worked in the factories in the season, and in the off-season he helped Rose's husband, Hymie, in his store or did private dressmaking for rich ladies who wanted well-made clothes. He saw to it that Musetta and Gilda had beautiful new coats, and once, buying scraps of leopard fur from a furrier, he had sewn each of his little girls matching hats and muffs. His talents in copying design had been noted by his boss, who sent him to study the new styles in the windows of department stores, which Isaac then would copy and make patterns of.

Ava could see how difficult it was for her mother to criticize Isaac. He had saved them all from a terrible life, and they were forever in his debt. Yet Ava had to get away from there; she could not bear his disapproval day and night. Always in her heart was the image of her beautiful papa who adored her, who had promised someday to come and get her. Would she ever see him again?

She rested her head against the window and dozed a little until she was aware of street names in the stations that meant she was approaching Coney Island. When her stop arrived, she got up and entered the station. She was the only one on the platform. Her shoes made a clanking sound on the wooden boards below her. There was a strong smell of salt sea in the breeze that fanned her face as she opened the doors to the stairs and stepped outside. She shivered in the chill wind and hurried down the stairs.

Since it was a weeknight, most of the rides were shut down, the souvenir shops closed, the food shops locked up. From somewhere came the music of an organ grinder. Ava hurried along and turned into the Starlight Café, nodding at the proprietor, a small, mustached man who sat on a wooden chair near the door. He in turn nodded toward the stage, where Johnny Quinn was doing his duet with Tony Angeloni. Ava took off her coat and made her way to a table on the side, where Maria was watching the boys. She was a sweet Italian girl, a little fat already, a little like those wide, kind-faced women who went to St. Joseph's Church near the factory where Ava worked. She held out her hand to Ava, and they clasped their fingers together in greeting. Tony and Johnny were made up in blackface, their mouths wide white circles. Both of them wore hats and carried canes. They were dancing a fast jig, exchanging their canes and hats with one another at lightning speed.

Ava ordered fruit juice from the waitress. She was so tense—she wished she could unwind, relax. But in her mind was the anticipation of the ride home, hours from now, and the worry of coming back to Isaac's house. She had the feeling she could never lay her head down under his roof again after what he had called her tonight. But what alternatives did she have?

During the break between shows, she sat with Johnny on a bench on the boardwalk and told him about the fight with Isaac. Before them the ocean rolled and shimmered under the moon. She listened for the sound of the waves crashing on the sand. She could almost sense the foam creeping toward them, then sinking slowly back into the sea.

"The rotten bum," Johnny Quinn said. "You want to come home with me tonight?" He leaned over and hugged her. "I mean it, sweet girl, and you know I do."

"I know you do," Ava said. She sighed. "Thanks, Johnny. I don't think that will solve my problems."

"You mean I have to marry you to get you out of there?"

"Not exactly, Johnny, but you're sweet to be thinking of it."

"I could marry you, you know!" Johnny said. "I think you're ultra. We could run off, elope."

"Thanks, Johnny. Isaac would murder me. But you're a fun kid. Why don't we just try to have some fun?"

"Great idea," he said. "Only two more shows, and then we'll go dancing." He checked his pocket watch. "Time to go in now, are you ready?"

"I'll just sit here a while and look at the ocean," Ava said. "It's a bit smoky in the café, you know."

"Righto," Johnny Quinn said. "Come in when you're ready."

He bent and gave her a quick kiss. "Till later, sweetheart."

TWENTY

It was 3:00 A.M. Johnny was a little drunk and very unsteady. He was humming "When Irish Eyes Are Smiling" as he walked Ava from the elevated to her tenement building.

"Don't come up," she said. "There's no point. It's so late, and you still have to go all the way back to Kings Highway."

"All right, luv," he said. "Just point me in the right direction."

"Thanks, Johnny—you're a dear boy. You cheered me up, no end."

"See you tomorrow? Will you be at the café?"

"I'll try, I'll do my best to come."

"Think about my offer," he said. "I'll marry you in a wink."

"I don't think I'm ready for that yet, Johnny."

"If I was one of those Jews with a long beard, would you then?"

Ava laughed. "Oh—I don't think my heart is set on one of those!"

"But you want a Jewish husband," he said. "Tell the truth."

"Who knows? Maybe." Ava said. "I just want someone nice."

"But one who doesn't go after the bottle like I do, right?"

"I never said that, Johnny. Maybe the bottle bothers you more than it does me."

"I do have a yen for it, quite a bit," he admitted.

"Go home and go to bed now," Ava said. "Go right to sleep when you get there."

"Farewell, my lovely," Johnny Quinn called, weaving his way down the street and calling over his shoulder. "Farewell, my princess, my sweet face, my red rose . . . "

Smiling, Ava ran up the stairs and then gasped when Rachel opened the door suddenly to let her in. Her mother was wearing her blue housecoat; her hair, nearly all white now, stood out in shadowy swirls around her pale face.

"Your papa wants an apology, Chaveleh. He made me wait up for you."

"My papa? You mean Isaac? Please, I've asked you not to call Isaac my papa."

"He wants you to promise to give the coat back to Mr. Berk."

"That's ridiculous, Mama. You know it is. I love this coat. It's the warmest I've ever had, and the prettiest."

"I know, I know, darling," Rachel said. "Myself—I think you should keep it, what's the harm? You earned it. But your papa, I mean Isaac, he sees different, he doesn't want you to have it."

"I'm keeping it, Mama." She gently nudged her mother through the doorway, so she could get inside herself. "Let me come in and go to bed, Mama. I'm exhausted."

"Chaveleh. Isaac doesn't want you to come in unless you apologize to him and agree to give back the coat."

"Now? You want me to apologize to him now?"

"No, no, in the morning," Rachel said. "But only now I can't let you in unless you agree."

"Mama! You wont let me into my own home?"

"It's his home, Chaveleh. That's what he says. Of course I don't agree—your home is wherever I am and wherever Shmuel is. And Gilda and Musetta, also. But he has a strong mind, Isaac."

"Strong? I think he's crazy, Mama."

"Don't say that! Bite your tongue! Who gave us a home, took us off the streets? Your poor brother would still be in an orphanage if not for Isaac and his charity."

"Charity! Is that what this is? So our home is like an orphanage if it's charity we're getting! Don't you see? We give, too! You made a home for him. You cook and bake and keep him content. You gave him the precious children that he adores so much, his little opera singer, Musetta, and his little delicate flower, Gilda. We aren't only taking from him. We're giving. And don't I work and give him half my pay?"

Tears began to slide down Rachel's cheeks. "Only I can't fight him, he has a will like iron," she said. "Don't hate me, Chaveleh—to me, he's good as gold. I can have anything I want, pearls, diamonds, if I asked; he would work all day and night so I could have them."

"But you won't let me in to go to bed?"

"What can I do, Chaveleh? Tonight he was like a tyrant."

"Only tonight?"

"Don't make it hard, darling. Just say you'll give back the coat. And in the morning you'll say, 'I'm sorry, Isaac.'"

"No, I'm sorry, Mama. I'm sorry to put you through this, but I won't apologize to him." She turned in the doorway and said, "Johnny Quinn said I could come to his house for the night. Maybe that's what I'll do. I'll take the train back to Brooklyn."

"No, no, no! Don't do that!" Rachel begged. "He's not for you, the Irish boy, the blond-headed goy."

"Well, then—if I have to, I'll go to Aunt Rose's for the night. I'd rather do that than give away my new coat."

"It's too late to walk to Rose's now. Come in, please, darling."

Ava leaned forward and kissed her mother's forehead. "You go to bed now, Mama. I can't agree to this thing. We'll talk about it tomorrow, but now I'll go to Aunt Rose's."

"At least let me wake Shmuel, he can walk with you."

"Well, all right, if you think it's important. But don't be so afraid, Mama. Isaac isn't going to kill me. Or you."

"But this aggravation might kill him," Rachel said, drying her tears. "And then where would we be?"

TWENTY-ONE

Ava turned back the white chenille bedspread and kicked off her shoes before she lay down on her old bed. The room smelled familiar—the polished wood odor of the oak dresser, the slightly musty scent of the curtains, and just a tinge of carbolic, the result of Aunt Rose's scrubbing the woodwork and walls weekly.

She sighed and let her head sink into the pillow. She was almost too tired to sleep. In a few hours it would be morning and time for her to go back to Mr. Berk's factory again. Sometimes it seemed there was nothing to do in life but work: work at home, work at work. Even sleeping was work—it had to be done at a certain time in a certain place, and there was an urgency about getting it done. If, like tonight, she didn't get her sleep, she would be exhausted, she would not be able to do her work well, and she would feel guilty. She didn't mind work; what she minded was the feeling that there was no end to it. Would her life ever change? Would she always be working and going back to Isaac's house at the end of the long day?

She reached down to the foot of the bed and pulled her coat up to cover herself. The fur collar was soft and warm; she stroked it and felt her breathing become calm and even. The fur had a special smell, slightly sour, acrid. Musetta's and Gilda's leopard hats and muffs smelled this way, too. Long ago, Rachel had had a coat, a skunk coat that had this strong odor. Ava remembered it so clearly—the little black hooks that lay buried in the fur, the way the long black hairs of the fur had tickled her nose. She wondered where that coat was now? Shmuel said Mama had given it to charity. She hadn't seen it since the night they had discovered her father with the red-haired girl.

Ava felt her eyes flood with tears. How long ago that seemed, but how vividly she recalled the scene—that brightly lit window, like a stage, on which her father played the villain. How cold it had been that night! The panic and fear on her mother's face, the terror in her own heart! She must try to sleep now. There was no point in remembering such painful feelings. Things had moved on—her mother had a new life, Shmuel had been rescued from the orphanage. Surely things were better now.

But were they? Ava wiped her eyes and tried once again to quiet her mind. On the dresser she could see the flower vase that had always been in this room in Aunt Rose's house; she followed the lines of it with her eyes, its comforting curve. Finally she felt her heart slow down, her limbs relax. She rubbed her chin against the soft fur collar and gave herself up to sleep.

"Shh! Don't say one word!" a voice whispered in Ava's ear, and she struggled to sit up, but felt a heavy weight across her chest.

"Don't worry, it's only your uncle Hymie."

Ava tried to move, but his weight held her down "What? What are you doing in here?"

"Don't talk. We can't wake your aunt. And if we do, I'll tell her you invited me in here. It wouldn't surprise her, from what we hear about you. The way Isaac talks about you, it wouldn't surprise anyone, I can tell you that."

"Are you crazy?"

"I'm not crazy, Chaveleh. Ever since you were a little girl, you've had that look about you. A little tart! The way you toss your hair back!"

Ava could smell the foul cigar odor on his breath. His head was like a black rock above her, about to tumble down and crush her. He moved his hand toward her breast.

"Don't you remember how you used to run around naked when you lived here with us?"

"I never . . . "

"Don't give me that!" he hissed in her ear. "One night we had a party, and we told you to keep out of the way, to go to bed, and you came parading without your clothes in front of all our guests. You humiliated your aunt Rose and me."

"You are crazy," Ava said, pushing his hand away. "You pulled me out of the bathroom . . . "

"I don't want to hear your lies," he said. "I just want you to make up for all the trouble you caused us, all the money you cost us! All we do is give to your family. I pay Shmuel good money to work for me, and half the time he's dreaming up some scheme or thinking about joining the army. I don't get any work out of him, and I pay and I pay. Handouts! That's what your family likes—your mother, always pitiful, always in tears about something. Why didn't she think about reality when she met your handsome father, a man who ran around with women and gambled and didn't have the responsibility of a worm? Did she realize who would have to pay the bills after he left? Did she realize that every meal you ate here cost us, not her?"

"Get away from me, Uncle Hymie, or I'll scream."

"Don't threaten me, Chaveleh. If you do, I'll arrange to talk to Isaac about how you came into my bedroom tonight and invited me to your room."

"Even Isaac would never believe that," Ava said.

"Yes, he would—because he's only human. How do you think he feels, having you around all the time—a young beautiful girl? With a figure like you have?"

Ava brought her knees up as hard as she could, ramming her uncle off balance so that he nearly fell from the bed. Ava pulled herself to a sitting position.

"Get out of here!"

His hand was gripping her arm. "Now don't get all excited," he said. "I'm not going to hurt you. All I want is a little thank you for all I've done for you and your family. A little kiss, a friendly hug, nothing more."

"You stink of tobacco," she said. "You're mean and ugly and cruel. My brother works for you till he can hardly stand, and you pay him almost nothing. God only knows how Aunt Rose can bear to live with you, you're disgusting!"

"Ungrateful brat," he said, shaking her so hard that her teeth rattled.

"Aunt Rose!" she screamed.

He slapped her face.

"Aunt Rose!"

Her aunt came running in, wrapping her robe about her. She turned on the lamp. Hymie, his face hairy as a bear's, lumbered to an upright position from the bed and looked down at his rumpled pajamas. "She was having a nightmare," he mumbled. "Bad dreams."

Ava was crying, clutching her coat to her face, feeling her tears dampen the fur. In the distance she heard a fierce knocking.

"Now what?" Aunt Rose said. "The noise will wake the neighbors. Who could be at the door at this hour?"

Aunt Rose hurried out of the room; Hymie stood there, his unshaven face red under the stubble of his whiskers, his jaw set angrily.

"You'll pay for this," he said. "All I want is a little cooperation. Nothing serious. Just a little cooperation."

"Filthy dog," Ava sobbed. "Get out of here."

And then—like a miracle—she heard Shmuel's voice in the living room. She flew from the bedroom and into his arms.

"Oh—what are you doing here?" she gasped, hugging him and wetting his face with her tears.

Aunt Rose stumbled into a chair, crying, "My God, my God, what's going on here?"

"I don't know what's going on here," Shmuel said, "but I can tell you what happened to me." He moved with Ava to the couch and sat down with her, holding her close. "I got home, and Mama was still up, and she said to me, 'So did you walk Chaveleh to Rose's? Did she get there safely?' And I realized that I was so sleepy I couldn't remember if I had taken you there or not. So I told Mama I wanted to go back and make sure you were okay; she didn't ask any questions. I just ran back down the stairs and ran all the way here, and when I got to the door, it was so quiet I realized everyone must be asleep inside. So I just sat down in the hall there by the front door and dozed off. Until a minute ago, when I heard you cry out. You sounded so frightened! So I knocked at the door."

"I'm so glad you're here," Ava sobbed.

"Tell me what happened to make you afraid," Shmuel said, stroking her forehead. "Tell me."

"Tell us, this is making me crazy, all this trouble and I don't know what it is," Aunt Rose said.

"It's nothing," Ava said. "I just had a terrible nightmare and I was frightened. But don't worry, I'll be all right now."

"All right!" Aunt Rose said, clapping her hands together. "Let's stop this nonsense now. You go home and back to bed, Shmuel, so your mother also doesn't run over here in ten minutes."

Ava stood up, "I don't think I could go back to sleep here now," she said. "Maybe it has something to do with my being in my old room. If you don't mind, Aunt Rose, I'm going to have Shmuel walk me over to my friend Tessie's, and I'll spend the rest of the night there, if they let me."

"I won't argue with you," Aunt Rose said. "Whatever you do, do it. We need our sleep. Hymie works hard, and we can't have any more commotion tonight."

Ava turned to Shmuel. "I'll get my coat," she said. "Then you can walk with me to Tessie's house."

TWENTY-TWO

Musetta was in a hurry to leave the house for school. It had been a terrible night—there had been noises and whispers in the living room; Gilda had pulled off the blankets and then sniffled and snorted for the rest of the night. Mama was in an angry mood at breakfast time, banging pots and slamming cabinet doors. Papa had read the Jewish newspaper sullenly without once reading out loud any of the items in the Bintel Brief section about love problems or about Jewish girls in love with gentile boys.

"Where is Chaveleh?" Gilda asked, eating only the white of her egg. "I want to give her the yolk."

"Never mind," Mama said.

"She'll be late for work," Gilda insisted. "I'll go wake her up."

"She's not home," Musetta said. "Don't bother."

"Where is she?"

"Out all night," Musetta said.

"Never say that about your sister!" Mama insisted.

"Well—she's not in her bed," Musetta said logically. She noticed that Papa was frowning.

"Eat your breakfast and get ready for school." Mama began measuring flour into a bowl, getting ready to make *chalah* for Shabbos dinner. Musetta pushed back her chair and gathered up her books.

"Look at the knots in your hair!" Mama said. "You didn't brush it."

"Yes, I did," Musetta said. "You didn't braid it for me last night."

"Can I do everything?" Mama asked. "Do I have ten hands?"

"Bye-bye," Musetta said. "I'll see you after school." She touched Papa's arm. "Good-bye, Papa." He jerked his elbow as if she were a fly that had landed on it.

In the street she felt better. Her heels clicked on the pavement—she felt she had taken charge of herself as soon as she walked out the door. The air was cool in her lungs. She liked the feel of the books in her arms, the breeze in her long hair. She hated the feeling of the house, the heavy smells of cooking and baking, the acrid smells of ammonia and carbolic, the medicinal smells of Gilda's various tonics and syrups. Papa was so unpredictable. Sometimes he would be so cheerful, humming and singing, playing his records, having Musetta and Gilda sing with him, and sometimes he would turn into a block of sooty ice, dark and cold, ugly to look at, chilling to be next to.

It was only out here in the world that Musetta felt she had some control. No one would suddenly get angry with her for something she did not do. No one would suddenly assign her a chore she was not responsible for and had no interest in doing. At school she was appreciated. She was asked, not told, to do things, and she was happy to do them.

Miss McGinley trusted her—she often sent Musetta to the office with important messages. She regularly sent her out into the hall to check the time on the big hanging clock since Musetta was the only one in the class who could tell time accurately.

And wasn't that Miss McGinley up ahead of her in the street right now? Musetta's heart began to pound. If anyone really knew her, it was Miss Mc-Ginley: not Papa, who liked her only when she was interested in his interests; not Mama, who liked her only when her hair was smoothly brushed and her bed neatly made; not Chaveleh or Shmuel, who thought she was a cute and bright little sister; not Gilda, who saw her as a bossy older sister.

Miss McGinley knew her as she really was—a student who loved to read, who learned ideas the minute she was taught them, a girl who was going to travel in the big world when she grew up and wear nice suits and leather shoes and maybe, someday, big hats with feathers in them, hats like Miss McGinley wore. Musetta quickened her steps. She would catch up with her teacher and walk the rest of the way to school with her.

Miss McGinley stopped to talk with a woman who came out of a dress shop. Good—now she would pause there, and Musetta wouldn't have to run so fast and lose her breath. The last thing she wanted to do was appear childish.

When she got close, she could almost feel the aura that surrounded Miss McGinley—the cloud of fragrant perfume, her tall, elegant being, her soft-spoken voice, her caring manner. Why was she so different from all the people at home, from all Musetta's relatives, from all her mother's acquaintances?

Was it simply that Jewish people were loud and angry most of the time, but gentile people were calm and controlled and dignified?

She tapped softly on Miss McGinley's arm. Her teacher, still talking to the woman in front of the dress shop, glanced down at Musetta but gave no sign of acknowledging her—she simply looked back at the woman and continued to talk. Musetta stood patiently beside her, feeling proud that she had the courage to stand and wait, like an adult. But soon she began to feel impatient. Her books were heavy, and she didn't want to be late to school. Her teacher could be late, but Musetta couldn't be—children had fewer rights than adults. When she heard the school bell ring in the distance, she could no longer control herself. She tugged at Miss McGinley's arm once again.

Her teacher looked down.

"Miss McGinley don't recognize me," Musetta said, as a kind of light-hearted challenge. And then she heard what she had said! Bad English! Bad grammar! Dumb! Stupid! Wrong! Miss McGinley would think the worst of her, would never forgive her for being ignorant! Even more terrible, Musetta felt she would never be able to forgive herself. She had just ruined her life, ruined her future. Now she was just like all the other restless, stupid students Miss McGinley had to put up with.

She felt herself ready to cry. It was as if she had done something irretrievable, permanently ruinous. "Why—Musetta!" Miss McGinley sang out. "How nice to see you here! I didn't realize it was you." She put her arm around Musetta's shoulder and said to the woman in front of the dress shop, "This is one of my very best students. Her name is Musetta. She's my most reliable messenger and the best reader I've had in my class for years. I'm so proud of her."

The woman smiled at her.

"I think she's going to go very far in life," Miss McGinley said. "Aren't you, Musetta?" She looked down, and Musetta gazed up into her beautiful face, into her clear blue eyes.

"I hope so," she answered.

"I know you will," Miss McGinley said. "I am absolutely certain."

"Then I will!" Musetta promised, wanting to laugh and cry all at once. "I'll do whatever you think I should do."

"No—you'll do what you want to do, my dear," her teacher said, hugging her. "What's important is that you know you can do anything you set your mind to. Armed with the knowledge of your abilities, you can fly if you want to."

"I can almost fly now," Musetta assured her.

Miss McGinley laughed. "Then fly on to school, little one. And when you get to class, do me a favor—call the roll for me . . . all right?"

"I'll do anything in the world for you!" Musetta promised. "Anything you ask!"

TWENTY-THREE

The salesman had a line of belts and buttons he hadn't shown Ava yet. Mr. Berk was closing up the factory for the night; most of the lights were off already.

"I can't see them tonight," Ava said. "But I'll tell you what, Mr. Dubinsky— if you come back in the morning, I'll look at them before I do anything else."

"In the morning!" he said. "Do you think I have no place else to be but at Berk's? Today was my day for Berk's; tomorrow I go to . . . let me see . . . " he pulled out a pad from his pocket and consulted his list. "Tomorrow is Goldstein and Press in the morning, Katz and Gerber in the afternoon."

"Well, then," Ava said. "Perhaps the line of belts and buttons can wait till next month. I think Mr. Berk has quite a good supply now, anyway."

"Well," said Mr. Dubinsky, "if you want to be a month behind the times . . . if you want Berk's coats to be out of style, that's your business, but it would seem to me, for your own good, that you'd want to have the latest fashions so the others don't get way ahead of you."

Just then Mr. Berk came striding by. "Good night, Ava; good night, Dubinsky."

"Your girl here won't give me ten more minutes," Mr. Dubinsky said. "To show her a line that's out of this world."

Mr. Berk smiled. "Out of this world? Don't get so dramatic, Dubinsky. When we're finally all out of this world, we won't worry about coat trims."

"A point well taken. But while we're in this world, we have to do what we can, wouldn't you agree? If Goldstein and Press get a foot in the door first, you'll be out of luck. Even with your reputation, Berk, with your quality, if you have out-of-style buttons, who wants to wear your stuff?"

"Ava," Mr. Berk said. "Do you have time to look at his line?"

"It's really late," Ava said. "It's been a long day, Mr. Berk."

"The girl is hungry, Dubinsky. Her dinner is waiting at home."

"So I'll be glad to buy her supper. And don't think it's because I'm such a generous person; the fact is, it's cheaper to buy her supper than to come back another day."

"Well, Ava—what do you think? We should probably see the new line, but I'll leave it up to you. If you think we have enough trim in stock, then don't worry about it."

Ava took her coat off the rack and put it on. She was planning to stay the night at Tessie's—but she knew that if she didn't arrive there, Tessie would think she had relented and gone home. But Mama would think she had gone to Tessie's if she didn't come home for supper.

She had stopped to see Mama on the way to work this morning when she was sure Isaac had left for the day. She told Mama that it was best that she stay with Tessie for a few days.

"Why not stay at Rose's?" Mama had asked.

"It's . . . well, it's not very satisfactory there. She treats me as if I were still ten years old."

"But what if it's too much work for Tessie's mother? Then, God forbid, you might go to stay with Johnny Quinn and that would be the death of me."

"Why would I want to stay with Johnny Quinn?" Ava assured her mother. "Don't I have enough troubles as it is?"

"It could happen," Mama said ominously.

"Mama, you know Tessie. You know Mrs. Rabinowitz. It's just like home over there."

"What about her boxer son? Her little Lenny, who calls himself Big Len, he's a gangster now."

"You're worried about Big Len? He's never there, Mama. And he's not interested in girls like me. Tessie says he likes big blondes."

"Go already," Mama had said. "You'll be late for work."

Now Ava said to Mr. Dubinsky, "All right—you can show me the trim." She began to slide her coat off her shoulders.

"I'm serious about supper, young lady," Mr. Dubinsky said. "We'll go two blocks, over to the Victoria Hotel. We'll have a nice lamb chop, so you won't feel I made you miss your meal at home."

Ava felt she would rather stay here in the factory where she was on familiar ground, but Mr. Berk had his key ring in his hand; she could see he was anxious to lock up for the night and go home.

"All right," she said, "Let's go."

Ava had heard about dining rooms at hotels like the Victoria: low lights, pure linen tablecloths, fine silver, candles on each table. In the dim light she looked at Mr. Dubinsky's thin, spectacled face, and sighed. Another man she had not much respect for. He had taken his sample case into the hotel and now was opening a black leather satchel right on the linen tablecloth. He began to point out certain elegant buttons to her—tortoise shell, ebony, mother-of-pearl. She thought about the men she knew; sweet Henry Hornstein, who still worked in the bakery and still came around to see her now and then; Johnny Quinn, the charmer, but dangerously unstable and likely to be a drunkard; Shmuel, her brother, handsome and wonderful; her papa, handsome and unfaithful; Isaac, small-minded and mean in spirit. Would there ever be a man who was all the right things for her?

Mr. Dubinsky had a sly smile on his face. He was holding out a tortoise shell belt buckle toward Ava. His fingers were long and skinny, with yellowish, clawlike nails.

"This . . . " he whispered, "is for you. Off the record. I won't charge Berk for it. It would go on that coat of yours like a marriage made in heaven. Berk gave you that coat, right? I recognized it from his line, and I know a girl who earns what you earn could never afford it, so I put two and two together, you know?" He leaned toward Ava across the table and touched her hand. She pulled it back as if a snake had struck at it.

Just then a waitress came by. "Would you like a drink?" she asked. Ava glanced around to see where she could find the bathroom.

"Excuse me a minute," she said to Mr. Dubinsky.

"I'll order you a drink, darling," he said. "Don't worry, I'll take care of it—you just come right back."

Ava hurried through the roomful of tables and wished she had taken her coat with her! Then she could leave, just run out the door. She glanced back at the table. Mr. Dubinsky was touching the buttons in his sample case, rubbing his fingers over them as if he were conjuring a magical spell. In a moment the waitress came back with two glasses of wine. When she had walked away from the table, Ava saw Mr. Dubinsky reach into his pocket and take out a medicine vial. She moved back behind a potted plant and watched him. He emptied the powder into one of the glasses! She had heard about such things! She would be drugged, and then he would carry her upstairs to one of the rooms, where he would dishonor her! He was a traveling salesman. He had probably done this to other women before.

A weakness, a kind of despair, came over her. Did a woman always have to be on guard against men? Would she always have to be suspicious of them, distrust them? Last night Uncle Hymie, tonight Mr. Dubinsky! And had not Papa betrayed her, promising to come back for her one day? And was not Isaac proof of the kind of tyranny a man could be guilty of?

Only Shmuel gave her hope—but he was her brother, flesh of her flesh, almost the same being as she was. Would there ever be a man out there in the world for her who would care about her, care for her, allow her to let down her guard, be herself?

How smug and evil Mr. Dubinsky looked, sitting there, as if he already had her asleep and in his power.

"Go to the devil!" she thought, swooping fiercely through the room to her table where she wrenched her coat away from the back of her chair to the astonishment of Mr. Dubinsky and the waitress who had come back to take their dinner order.

"Go to hell," she hissed at Mr. Dubinsky. "You will never take advantage of me, you sour old piece of cheese!"

TWENTY-FOUR

"Guess what?" Tessie said as she threw open the door for Ava. "My brother is here for dinner!"

"I can smell his cigar!" Ava said. "Maybe I'd better leave."

"You're not afraid of Lenny, are you?" Tessie said, pulling Ava inside and helping her off with her coat. "You remember little Lenny and his collection of doorknobs? When we were kids, he used to let you line them up according to size."

"I haven't seen him for years. Does he still collect them?"

"He's into bigger and better things. Come on in and say hello."

Ava followed Tessie into the dining room. Tessie was still wearing her work clothes—a green silk dress and alligator-skin high heels. She worked as a bookkeeper in a fancy dress shop and was allowed to buy sample dresses at half price. Her boss liked her to look elegant. Ava considered her friend a great beauty, with her dark red hair piled high on her head, her wide swinging hips, her shapely legs. She had had offers of marriage from four men in the past year—but as she had told Ava, until the king of England came around, she could afford to be fussy.

In fact, this summer she was going to England on the *Lusitania*, a great ship. Her boss was paying her way—she was going to bring back English patterns and drawings of English dresses. The wives of well-to-do businessmen in New York had a great interest in elegant foreign clothes. She might even go to France as well!

Ava felt that Mr. Berk was a good employer, but heaven knew he would never send her to England and France.

"Hello, Mr. Rabinowitz," she said to Tessie's father. He reached a hand out for her and pulled her to him.

"Chaveleh! I am always so happy to see you! Why don't you come here more often?"

Ava smiled. "I was just here last night, don't you remember?"

"That didn't count. Coming at dawn doesn't count!"

Ava let him hold her hand, but was aware of Big Len's eyes on her. He sat like a squat wide monkey at the far end of the table, wearing a pin-striped suit with a vest buttoned tightly over his barrel-shaped chest. He had Brillo-like dark hair, tightly curled against his large head, and wore thick eyeglasses. He had looked monkeylike when he was a young boy, and Ava had always been a little afraid of him. Now he studied her intensely as she pulled out a chair and sat down.

"Ava!" he said. "I think you still have my glass doorknob!"

"What?"

"I once let you take my glass doorknob home, just for overnight, and you never brought it back."

"I never did any such thing!"

"I never forget. I'm like an elephant!" Lenny said. "It was my prize. I stole it from the public library—it was like crystal; no, like a diamond. You liked to look at the light through it, it reflected light like a prism. So one night I let you take it home, and you never returned it. You owe it to me. Or you owe me a replacement!"

"Don't pester the girl," Mr. Rabinowitz said. "Selma, give her some of your vegetable soup, she looks pale and undernourished."

Blushing, Ava began to pull a roll apart. When she tried to chew it, she found her mouth dry and her throat unwilling to swallow. She wondered if she would ever have a peaceful moment again, a quiet evening, a time that did not feel like a crisis, an emergency. She didn't even have a corner of the world to call her own, her own bed, her own home. How long could she stay at Tessie's? What were her choices?

Suddenly Lenny flung something across the table at Ava. It was a gold pocket watch on a heavy gold chain.

"I'll trade you," he said. "This for my precious doorknob."

"Oh, go on," Ava said. "You know I don't have it after so many years. I probably never did."

"Aha—now you say 'probably'!"

"I know I didn't," she said. "You know I didn't."

"We'll have to talk about it after supper . . . in detail."

Tessie leaned over to poke her brother's arm. "Oh, leave her alone, Lenny. You were always such a big bully."

"Little guys need to be big bullies," Lenny said, putting his napkin in his lap and beginning to slurp his soup noisily. "Otherwise they get run over."

Ava and Len sat in the parlor long after Tessie and her parents had gone to bed. It was just as well; after her recent experiences, Ava was not anxious to be left alone in the dark with her thoughts. She was very tired, it was true—but she was uneasy about relinquishing her vigilance; she wanted to remain on guard. She used to think that when she was in her papa's arms again, she would be able to relax and surrender herself in trust. But of course she no longer believed that.

Big Len sat in the overstuffed flowered chair, and Ava sat on the couch. He was so short that his feet did not quite touch the floor. His black shoes, shined to a high gloss, occasionally scraped against the dark red rug. On the table between them was a bowl of raisins and nuts. Len scooped up a handful of them in his palm and then threw them forcefully into his mouth.

"Watch out you don't choke to death," Ava said.

He stared at her through his thick glasses. "Do you care if I choke?"

"I'd rather you didn't," Ava said.

"You care about me? You want me to live?"

"I wouldn't want to see anyone choke to death," Ava assured him.

"But me especially. Would you especially not want me to choke to death?"

"Yes. What do you want me to say? That I don't care?"

"No, no! I want you to say you do care."

"Well, of course I care. If you died, your sweet mother would be devastated. And even Tessie probably would want you to live, though I remember what a terrible brother you were—bossy and braggy and mean as a bulldog."

"I'm still mean as a bulldog," Len said.

"I believe it," Ava said. She realized that her feet ached and she kicked off her shoes.

" . . . I hold on forever," Len added.

"What do you mean by that?"

"I'm tenacious, like a bulldog. In the ring I get a fix on one rib, and I go for it, my attention never wavers."

"In the ring?"

"I'm a boxer, a lightweight—you wouldn't think so by looking at me, would you?"

"You don't look like a lightweight to me. Not in any sense."

"That's the advantage I have over the taller guys. I've got all my strength concentrated, like lead, right in my center." He stood up and pounded on his stomach. "Come feel this," he instructed Ava.

"I don't need to, I believe you," she said.

"Come feel my gut," he said. "It's an experience you won't forget."

Ava slid her hands under her thighs, as if to hide them. But Len came toward her, leaned over her and extracted her hands as if they were matzos she had hidden under the cushions.

"Feel," he said, guiding one of her hands to his gut, where she felt the muscles like steel girders under her fingertips. "I bet you've never felt anything like that before."

"I haven't," Ava said, pulling her hand away as if she had touched a hot stove. "But I think it's stupid to be a prize-fighter."

"Why? Because I might disfigure my pretty nose?" He turned his profile to her, and she saw his blunt wide nose, off center, not graceful.

"Not only that," she said, "you might get killed. You might go blind. You might become retarded if someone hits you hard enough in the head."

"Some think I'm already retarded."

"I don't," Ava said. "If anything, you're much too smart to do stupid things like fight in the ring."

"There's more money in that than in selling sweet potatoes, my girl."

"I'm not your girl, Len."

"I'd like you to be."

"Be the girl of a prize-fighter? Are you crazy?"

"I'm a nice Jewish boy," Len said.

"Mama would have a heart attack if you came to call on me."

"What about Papa?"

"I have no papa, you should know that by now."

"I meant that son of a bitch, Isaac."

"What has Tessie told you?"

"Enough, enough."

"He takes care of Mama."

"So because of that he should be able to tear your heart out?"

"He wouldn't let you set a foot in his house, Len—a man who makes his living the way you do."

"So I don't have to come calling there. Why should I? You're living here. All I have to do is let myself in with my key."

"I can't stay here for long. Just until I figure out what to do. I'm having trouble at home, and I can't stay at my aunt Rose's—but I'm here only temporarily."

"You could come to my rooms."

"Oh—sure. Just like that."

"You could marry me."

"My God, Len, you haven't talked to me for years. All you know is that maybe I took your glass doorknob."

"One look reminds me of what a special high-class girl you are. And a beauty."

"Thank you, Len. But I don't want a gangster for a husband."

"Who said gangster?"

"I've heard things."

"But not from me."

"No, not from you."

Len bent down and picked up one of Ava's shoes. "Give me a chance," he said. "Just a chance. I looked at you all through dinner, and I loved what I saw. I want you. I'll kiss your feet." He knelt and before Ava could snap her foot back, he had it in his warm hand and was kissing it.

"I will drink from your shoe."

"Don't, don't," Ava said, half afraid of his intensity, but somehow amused and pleased by it. "My shoe isn't that clean."

"For you I would risk anything," Len said. He was still holding her foot as she tried to pull it back, tried to stand up. Losing her balance, her hand came to rest on his springy hair. Her hand felt shocked by the heat and resiliency of his curls. They were not stiff and wiry as she thought, but soft and warm.

She sat down, confused. "I'm so tired, Len," she said. "I think maybe I'll go into Tessie's room and go to sleep now."

"I'll let you go for now," he said. "I'll go home to my place now, but I'll see you back here tomorrow at dinnertime. We'll make plans. We'll go out together."

"Isaac would kill me," Ava said.

"Don't worry, I can take care of him," Len said. "He's a featherweight."

TWENTY-FIVE

"He wants you for immoral purposes," Mama said. "You mustn't see him any-more. Sadie Rabinowitz tells me what's going on. How after Tessie goes to sleep, you sneak into the living room and stay there alone with her son, the gangster."

"Oh Mama, what are you talking about? He isn't a gangster. He's a busi-nessman. He owns a pool hall."

"That's a business for a decent man?" Even though Mama was indignant, she pushed a plate of *mandelbrot* toward Ava. " . . . Have another one," she said. "You look skinny to me, you're not eating enough over there."

"He's not going to stay in that business forever," Ava said. "It happens to be profitable right now. He just fell into it."

"But he also fell into the wrong crowd. Bums and prize-fighters. He's break-ing Sadie's heart. Although I must admit he bought her a very beautiful hat."

"He's a very good son, Mama. He's a good person."

Ava sipped the strong tea Rachel had prepared for her. It was Saturday morning; Isaac was safely at shul, and Ava had come over to visit with her mother. Musetta and Gilda were playing jacks on the living-room floor.

"How long do you think you can stay with Sadie?" Rachel asked. "It isn't right, you know—to take food from their mouths when you belong here with us."

"Isaac doesn't seem to think so," Ava said.

"He's sorry, he's sorry," Rachel said. "He sees I'm so sad all the time, and he's sorry."

"So why doesn't he apologize to me?" Ava asked.

"He's a proud man, he can't. All you would have to do is not wear that coat anymore. You could say you gave it back to Mr. Berk—but you wouldn't even have to do that. We could hide it . . . at Aunt Rose's maybe."

"I don't want to do that, Mama," Ava said. "I wasn't wrong, taking that coat; Isaac was wrong, accusing me of what he did."

"He knows what men are like—he was afraid Mr. Berk was taking advantage of you."

"Maybe he knows what he's like, maybe he knows his own conscience, and he imagines all men are like him, but it just isn't true. Mr. Berk is a sweet, good man. He's like an uncle to me." Suddenly Ava thought of her uncle Hymie and added, " . . . or like a brother."

"Aah, your brother," Mama said, finding a new subject. "Do you know what? My heart is breaking. Shmuel is going to join the army."

"He is? Why? When?"

"Soon, soon," Mama said. "He tells me Uncle Hymie won't pay him for all the time he works—he takes off money for this, money for that. If Shmuel stops to blow his nose, Hymie says he isn't working and takes a dollar off his pay, sometimes two dollars—for nothing! For nothing at all!"

"The army," Ava said. "It's dangerous."

From the living room, Musetta called, "He might even get killed!"

"God forbid! The evil eye mustn't look on us," Mama said, knocking twice on the wooden tabletop. "We've had enough misery."

"For heaven's sake, Mama!" Musetta called loudly. "Why are you so superstitious! Do you think hitting the table or wearing a red ribbon pinned to your slip can stop bad things from happening to us?"

"God willing, nothing bad will happen."

"How come you're always talking about God?" Musetta said. "Has anyone ever seen God?"

"Don't be so fresh," Ava cautioned her little sister.

"There is no God," Musetta said.

"I'll tell Papa what you said," Gilda piped up. "He'll smack your face."

"Who told you such nonsense?" Mama demanded, getting up and walking to stand closer where the girls were playing jacks.

"I just know," Musetta said. "I think about these things and I just know."

"It would kill your papa if he heard you say such a thing."

"I don't believe in God or heaven or all those other superstitious things you warn me about all the time. Like I should cross the street if I ever see a gypsy coming toward me."

"Oh—but you must," Mama said. "You must never let a gypsy close to you. If she breathes on you, you could break out in boils all over your body."

"That's the silliest thing I ever heard," Musetta said.

"In the old country . . . " Mama said.

"I don't want to hear about the old country!"

"Listen!" Mama said. "I never told you this before, but once, in the old country, I was crossing a big field, and I saw a gypsy coming toward me. I was about twelve years old; my mama had warned me just like I'm warning you, never to talk to a gypsy, but this gypsy woman came right toward me, her colored scarves blowing in the wind. I could hear her jewelry jangling, her bracelets ringing together. I tried not to look at her, but she was so beautiful . . . "

"What did she say, Mama?" Ava asked. "You never told me about it."

"She came up to me in the field and she said, 'How much money do you have?' I said 'I have no money,' and she said, 'Give me your earrings then, and I will tell your fortune.'"

"What did she tell you, Mama?" Gilda begged.

Rachel crossed her arms over her chest and whispered, "She told me the truth! She told me that I would cross a wide water and meet a handsome man, but he would be bad, and the marriage would come to a bad end. But that later I would meet a dark-haired man, and it would be good."

"Is that Papa?" Gilda demanded.

"Of course it's Papa," Musetta said impatiently. "But the gypsy was wrong because Mama never had a bad marriage; her first husband died, no one could help that, right, Mama?"

Musetta looked to Rachel for confirmation; Rachel was looking at Ava.

"Come into the kitchen with me, Chaveleh," she said. "I want to show you something there."

Ava followed her mother into the kitchen. Rachel turned to her and put her hand on Ava's cheek. "They don't know about Nathan, Chaveleh. Even Isaac doesn't know. All these years I've kept it a secret, I've told them my first husband died of consumption."

"I know that, Mama," Ava said. "You always used to warn me, never mention Papa and what happened. Why are you so nervous suddenly?"

"Because I almost told them myself just now. What the gypsy said—I was going to tell them it was all true."

"They're just children, Mama. They can't understand these things. And you didn't tell them it was all true."

"But I almost did . . . "

"It's all right, Mama. It isn't such a shame—even if they found out someday—even if Isaac found out—it isn't your shame. You didn't do anything bad."

"But I think about your father every day, Chaveleh. I think about Nathan, and I cry myself to sleep."

Ava put her arms around her mother. "Oh, Mama! I think about him too! I pray he is alive and well somewhere. I dream that he will someday come back and take me to live with him."

"I miss him," Mama said, crying quietly. "He was so gentle . . . when he still loved me. He was so sweet, he always smelled like . . . springtime." Ava and her mother rocked together in the little kitchen. Finally Mama said, "The gypsy knew, Chaveleh—she knew what my whole life would be."

TWENTY-SIX

A dark snake was wrapped around Gilda's chest, coiling itself around and around like a spring, tightening till she could not draw a breath.

"Take him off!" Gilda cried, thrashing under the covers, throwing off the blankets. "Mama! Pull him away!"

"Sha, sha, *bubbeleh*, don't yell, you will get all tired." Mama's voice seemed to be coming from a pinkish cloud that floated just above the body of the snake.

"Drink this, try to take a sip, Gildala. For Mama—please, do it for Mama." But Gilda's throat felt like a tube of fire, a glowing red tube.

"Call Shmuel," Gilda cried. "I know he can make the pain go away."

"Someone get Shmuel," the tall man said. He was the doctor.

"Shmuel is at work," Chaveleh said.

"Can't he be called? The child might cooperate with him."

"He's delivering trousers for my brother-in-law in Brooklyn!" Mama cried, as if Brooklyn were a place farther away than heaven. "How can we find him in Brooklyn?"

"I can't breathe!" Gilda screamed. "I want Shmuel!"

"Take the rugs out of here!" the doctor commanded. "Someone move out that big chair. Open the windows wider. Take down those curtains. There's not enough oxygen in this room!" Gilda heard a big commotion, a horrible scraping, like the needle of Papa's Victrola tearing across the record. The snake looked at her with its red eye, holding its head curved like an umbrella handle just above her throat. She could see its tongue flickering, a fiery dart that would not keep still.

"Drink, drink, you must, you're burning up," Mama said, and something wet poured over her chin, down her neck, then puddled in the curve of her throat. The snake, thirsty because of its burning tongue, lowered its head to drink from the watery hole, and she felt its fangs pierce her.

"She's turning blue, God in heaven!" Mama screamed.

But Gilda was breathing; she knew that she was from the sizzling thread that burned through her lungs as she inhaled. Now she opened her eyes and was still. The doctor was taking something from his bag, a set of teacups, or was it a bag of seashells? They tinkled upon one another as he set them on the table beside her bed. They looked like clear glass bells. Now he tore a bit of fluff from the cotton cloud over her bed and painted the inside of the bells with tonic . . . no, with alcohol, the alcohol with which Musetta had once tried to poison her. The snake had rotated his red eye and was watching the doctor just as Gilda was watching him. Like a magician, the doctor snapped his fingers and the little glass bells burst into fire. He pointed his burning forefinger into the center of one little bell and a flame came up to the rim. Then with a swish of his arm he pulled the bedclothes from Gilda, flipped up her nightgown and fastened the burning cup to the skin of her chest. She screamed; the snake slithered off and the bell sucked at her nipple like a tornado, pulling her breast into a cone shape, swallowing her.

"Hold her hands!" the doctor said, "Don't let her pull them off." One after the other, he made the bells blaze with fire and welded them to her chest till she was sucked into the whirlwind. When she opened her mouth to cry out, they poured liquids down her throat till they nearly drowned her. She was turned on her side, and the burning brands were applied to her back. She saw her sister's face loom near. *Now I will have the bed to myself,* she seemed to be saying to Gilda. And Papa's small dark eyes were sitting on her shoulder. His skullcap and his tallis swam empty in the air.

"*Boncas,* we are giving her *boncas!*" Mama said to Papa. "It is the only hope."

Like a thousand sucking lips, the cups pulled at Gilda's flesh, and then Papa pushed the doctor out of the way.

"Gilda, my precious child," he said. "Get better and we will go on a vacation to the country. I promise to take you where there are cows and horses and corn growing in the fields. You know how you always talk about seeing ducks and chickens? Well, we will go there, and you will feed them yourself. Be still and don't fight. Drink, drink the water and then sleep, and when you are all better, we will go to the country."

Gilda saw the snake slither into the heart of the pink cloud and leave his black skin behind. A mucous trail shone behind him as he poured away between the floorboards.

The place called "the country" glistened clear and green in the distance. "Will there be a haystack?" Gilda asked, and suddenly Papa began to cry.

"I didn't know a grownup could cry," Gilda said. But now Papa was laughing, laughing and crying at the same time.

"Go away, everyone," Gilda said. "It's too noisy for me to sleep."

TWENTY-SEVEN

They had been in the country only an hour and already Mama was making matzo balls. Musetta tugged on her apron impatiently. "At least come down and see the lake! Gilda wants you to watch her feed the chickens."

"I'm already looking at a chicken," Mama said, patting the pale salted skin of the bird on the counter. "What do I need to climb down a hill to look at chickens for?"

"Because this is the country!" Musetta said. "Because we're finally here!" She could not understand why Mama had brought the contents of her whole kitchen on this vacation—bags of dishes and pots and silverware—when she could have borrowed anything from the hotel.

But Mama said that would be too dangerous—you could never trust that things were kosher unless you brought them yourself. Especially in a *kochalayn*, where not all the women who shared the kitchen with you were dependable. How could she be sure that she wasn't using a pot for meat that had boiled a cup of milk an hour ago? What if when Isaac came up for the weekend tonight he had a suspicion that a calf had been cooked in its mother's milk?

Musetta wanted to say that she didn't think the world would come to an end if that happened, but she had been warned to watch her "smart mouth," and she didn't want to get Mama edgy now that they were finally in the beautiful Catskill Mountains and out of the crowded smells and noises of the tenement building.

Just then the door burst open, and a very large, heavy woman came tramping in carrying a big satchel. "How do you do? I'm Mrs. Carp from the Bronx. Ida Carp."

"Rachel Sauerbach from the East Side," Mama said. "And this is my daughter, Musetta."

"What kind of a name is Musetta?" Mrs. Carp asked. "It's not a Jewish name, that I know."

"My husband named her for someone in an opera," Mama said apologetically. "He adores Caruso."

"Oh—the Italian," Mrs. Carp said. "So you named your daughter an Italian name?" She began to unpack her satchel, dumping piles of utensils into the cupboard she was claiming as her own.

Musetta made a face. "I'm going, Mama," she called. "We'll see you later."

"Could you take my Bryna with you?" Mrs. Carp asked. "She's right outside."

"I'm sure my daughters would be delighted to make a friend," Mama said, throwing Musetta a significant look.

"Come on, Gilda," Musetta said to her sister, who sat on the porch railing in her long city dress, her white shoes buttoned up to her calves, her long fair hair braided neatly down her back. And to the fat freckled girl who sat on a wicker rocking chair, Musetta added, "You can come along with us—your mother said you should."

"We come here every summer," the fat girl said. "My father likes to have peace and quiet in the city. He never comes up here to be with us if he can help it."

"My father is coming tonight," Gilda said.

"How come he didn't come with you?" Bryna said.

"Because he had to work today," Gilda answered. "He works very hard."

"My father sells gold and diamonds," Bryna said.

"Our papa is a lawyer," Musetta said suddenly.

Gilda threw her a dirty look, and Musetta took her arm and pulled her along down the hill.

"Come on," Musetta said, "Just breathe the fresh air, Gilda. Your lungs need it." Gilda pulled her arm away. She explained to Bryna, "I was very sick this winter, I almost died. They had to use *boncas* on me."

"My God," Bryna said. "You should be very happy to be here then."

"Oh—I am," Gilda said. "I am."

Musetta stopped suddenly and pulled at the buttons on her shoes. "I have to take these off," she said. "Go ahead without me, I'll catch up."

Gilda looked worried. "Just don't fall in the lake," Musetta warned. "Mama will kill me if you do."

She lowered herself to the sun-warmed grass and watched her little sister walk off with the fat girl. Flinging herself back on the fragrant softness, she let the sun make brilliant rainbows under her eyelids. Oh—how wonderful this was, how perfect. Why did people have to live cramped together in the city when there was all this space and all this perfumed air? How could Mama lock herself up in that kitchen, worried only about getting dinner ready for Papa, when she could be out here exploring the new sights and feelings of the country? Musetta loved Mama, but was puzzled by her fear of Papa, by her unwillingness to do things she might want to do but was afraid to do. It seemed as if Mama never asked herself what she wanted for herself, but rather only what she thought others wanted her to do for them.

It irritated Musetta that they were in the country simply because Gilda had almost died; it didn't seem sensible to reward someone for something accidental like catching pneumonia. If Papa thought it was a good idea for them to go to the country, and if they had enough money to do it, they should have done it just because it would be fun and wonderful. Now Gilda would always be throwing it up to her that they were here because of her, that if she hadn't gotten sick (or if she had died), they wouldn't be here at all. So Musetta had better be nice to her. There was something sneaky and false about Gilda—she wasn't always as delicate and dumb as she seemed. She fooled Mama and Papa by her sly ways—she got things without asking outright for them, like Musetta did, but instead pretended to be weak or sick or even too stupid to figure something out.

It was ungenerous of Musetta to be thinking this way. Gilda had been very sick—that night, when the doctor had applied the burning cups, Musetta had feared that Gilda would indeed die. And in all the weeks afterward, when Mama had to spoon-feed Gilda hour by hour to keep up her strength, Musetta had almost wanted to pray that her sister would not die. But she knew she could never pray! To everyone she knew, praying was almost a reflex. Papa wandered the house all the time, dovening to himself, his nose in a prayer book. But praying to whom? For what? There was no God. Musetta was certain of it. What kind of God would be listening to everyone's petty problems? It was ridiculous to imagine that God would care about whether people got their wishes—their new muffs or puppies or trips to the country or diamond rings.

She arched her back and sighed. She didn't want anything but the chance to be left alone and think her own thoughts. She wanted to have privacy and be able to read and think about the future when she would be grown up and free of all restrictions.

She heard a cry. Sitting up, she shaded her eyes and saw her sister with the fat girl down by the lake. They both were kneeling down, huddled over something on the ground. Musetta took her shoes in her hand and began to run down the hill over the grass. As she got closer, she could hear Gilda sobbing. What had she done now? At least she hadn't drowned in the lake. But when she got near, she saw that something serious had happened; there was a dead creature on the ground, a little duckling.

"She didn't mean it!" the fat girl cried to Musetta. "She just wanted it to stop, so she threw a stick at it."

"What are you talking about?" Musetta demanded. She knelt and examined the limp fuzzy chick.

"Your sister—" Bryna explained, "she saw a mama duck walking along and all her little ducks behind her, and she wanted to hold one, but they were going too fast, so she picked up a stick and threw it at them, and it hit the last one, and then it just died. Just like that. She killed it."

Gilda held up her tear-stained face to Musetta. Her mouth was trembling, and her whole body was shaking. My God, Musetta thought, now she'll collapse, and we'll all have to go home so she can recover.

"Oh—don't carry on so much," Musetta said. "It's just an accident, Gilda. You didn't mean it, and maybe the duckling was sickly or something; it was probably a weakling and wouldn't have lived very long anyway."

"Papa will yell at me," Gilda sobbed. "He says girls have to be gentle."

"We won't tell Papa, for heaven's sake. So you don't have to worry about that. No one will ever know."

"God knows everything," Gilda said, wiping her eyes with her fingers. "He'll punish me."

"That's plain nonsense," Musetta said. "Forget about Papa and God for now, forget about this dead bird. Here, I'll throw it in the lake, and it will be gone. Even the mother duck won't remember it. And let's try to have some fun. Let's go over there to the barn and look at the horses inside. Let's just try to enjoy ourselves."

The three girls walked along and breathed the country air. They climbed a big apple tree and sat in its high branches. Gilda whimpered and complained that her dress would tear or get dirty, that Papa would be angry when he came tonight for the Sabbath and saw that she had a rip in the dress he'd sewn for her.

"Stop complaining," Musetta commanded. "Don't you realize you can't have a happy vacation if you keep complaining?"

"Maybe she has a lot to complain about," Bryna said. Musetta sighed. She wished she could find some friends who weren't her relatives or people she just bumped into in a public resort. She wished she could find a girl like herself, who thought the way she did. She had a feeling it wasn't going to be easy. Most of the girls she knew in the city were just like each other and just like their mothers. They talked about clothes and giggled about boys and thought about food. Only Miss McGinley seemed the right kind of person—elegant, wise, beautiful, graceful. Musetta wondered what kind of woman she'd be when she grew up. She knew she wasn't going to be like Mama or Aunt Rose. Not even like her sister Ava, whom she loved. But Ava worked at a boring job and was going to marry Big Len, an ugly, short, pushy little man who Mama said was a gangster. She guessed that Ava liked him well enough; she always smiled and laughed when she was with him, but she'd never seen Ava touch him lovingly or pat his shoulder when she passed him. He grabbed her enough—smacking her behind or cupping her chin in his squat little hand when he walked past her. But there was something wrong there, something missing.

Papa had not even met Big Len; he and Ava had a war going between them, something Musetta did not understand. Ava had not been in the house at the same time as Papa since the day Gilda had been so sick. But sometimes Ava came to the house with Big Len on Saturday mornings when Papa was at shul and visited with Mama then.

Len was nice to Musetta. He bought her chewing gum and sometimes *halvah*. Once he had given her a bottle of expensive perfume, and Mama had been horrified. But he had only laughed and promised to get Mama a bottle, too—and that had pleased her.

The fat girl handed Musetta an apple she had just picked, and it reminded Musetta that there was no sense thinking about home when she was here. That would just defeat the purpose of being in a vacation place. She rubbed the red skin of the fruit on her dress till it shone and then bit into it fiercely, feeling the juice burst onto her lips and the fresh tart taste pour into her mouth.

"Where are the horses?" Gilda demanded.

"They're in the barn," Bryna said.

"Can't we go in and see them?"

"As soon as those boys leave," Musetta said. She had noticed two farm boys going in the barn door as they came up the hill from the lake. She hadn't liked the looks of them and wanted to wait till they were gone.

A soft breeze blew over the meadow and lifted the hair on Musetta's neck. She breathed deeply and then looked around warily.

"Do you smell smoke?" she said to Gilda.

"No."

"Do you?" she asked Bryna.

"Maybe, I'm not sure," she said.

Musetta felt her eyes narrow—she was sure she smelled smoke. She stared at the closed barn door and saw that a grayish line of smoke was sifting out the crack in the door.

"Look! Don't you see that?" she cried. "Isn't that smoke?"

Suddenly the barn door flew open, and the two boys, wearing overalls and straw hats, dashed out. An instant later the roof of the barn burst into flames with a roaring, blowing sound. From their place high in the apple tree, the girls could see the roof burning.

"Oh God!" Gilda cried. "I'm scared."

"Shut up," Musetta said. "Just let me think." She was trying to figure out if they should stay in the tree or try to run back down the hill to the lake. She wasn't sure which way the wind was blowing, or if they would be in the path of the flames.

Now the walls of the barn were going up in a wild blaze. Over the whoosh of the fire, Musetta heard a cry. It was Mama—coming from the hotel, rushing toward the barn, her apron whipping around her waist as she cried, "Musetta, my Musetta, her hair, her long hair!"

"Mama! Mama!" she called and waved from the tree, but her mother had eyes only for the barn, where she must have believed her daughters were playing. Then a strange dreamlike sight appeared at the barn door—a line of horses came spilling out, their manes and tails aflame. They ran out into the green fields, bumping and smashing into each other, their eyes blank, blinded, as they burned and burned.

Musetta heard Mama screaming her children's names and then falling in a faint on the grass. The horses ran in every direction, their bodies burning. Musetta and Gilda reached for one another as the horses fled into the woods, some falling to the ground, still on fire. Then, dazed and shaken, the sisters climbed from the apple tree with Bryna, and together they went to Mama and shook her gently till she awoke and told her they were not dead.

TWENTY-EIGHT

"Go and gather blackberries," Mama said the next morning. "You can't just stay on the front porch and rock in the rocking chair."

"I don't want to go anywhere," Musetta said. "Everything smells of burning . . . of smoke and burning flesh."

"The barn is still smoking," Gilda said.

"And the horses are still dead everywhere," Musetta added. "At least don't make me go anywhere till they take away the horses."

"I thank God every minute you weren't in that barn," Mama said.

Thank me, Musetta thought, not God. Then she wondered if she ought to tell Mama about the boys in overalls. She considered it only for a second; she was not anxious to "tell" anything to anyone. Whenever she did, someone blamed her for it long after she had forgotten it and managed to bring it up at just the wrong time for the wrong reason.

She had once confessed to Mama that she thought she was too skinny, that her clothes hung on her. Mama had hugged her and reassured her that she was pretty enough, that with her face and hair boys would look at her wherever she went. Even at that moment Mama had the wrong idea; Musetta wasn't worried about boys looking at her; she was thinking about her own feelings about herself. But a day later, when Musetta didn't want to eat the *kugel* Mama had made with too many onions, Mama had attacked her by saying, "No wonder you're so skinny, no wonder your clothes hang on you—you don't eat what you're supposed to eat." It was too dangerous to confide any secrets to anyone—in a minute the person you'd trusted could spin around and attack you with the information.

If Musetta told her mother that she had seen two boys go into the barn, Mama might blame her for not telling the hotel owner right away—as if she could have known they were going to set the barn on fire! Blame was something else Musetta didn't see much sense in attributing to people—things just happened. Maybe the fire had started by accident, maybe not. The results were just as terrible, the horses dead.

The screen door on the porch squeaked, and Papa came out carrying the Jewish newspaper. "Where's Gilda?" he said before he had even looked around. "Come here," he said when he saw her sitting on the porch chair. "Come here and stand in front of me." He sat down, and his expression became stern. Gilda came to stand in front of him, looking fearful. Her white dress and white stockings made her look like a little blonde angel. "What is this I hear about the duck?" he said.

Gilda bowed her head. "I didn't mean it," she whispered.

"That girl Bryna just told me about it in the kitchen. Her mother is in there making jam. Why didn't you tell me about it?"

He looked up at Musetta, and his voice became even harsher. "Why did you not tell me about it, Musetta?"

"Because it was an accident," Musetta said. "It just happened, and there didn't seem any point in making a big fuss about it."

"Your sister killed a living creature," Papa said. "Is that of no concern to you?"

"She didn't kill it, Papa. That is, she didn't mean to, even if it died."

"A girl doesn't throw sticks at any living creature," Papa said, hitting the arm of the chair with his newspaper. "Not one of my girls."

Gilda began to cry. Even though Musetta thought Gilda was an annoyance much of the time, she felt sorry for her sister now. When Papa got angry, he could go on and on.

"Do you know what, Gilda?" he said fiercely. "Do you know that one of God's commandments is 'Thou Shalt Not Kill'? And do you know that God punishes those who disobey his commandments? And do you know the way God is punishing you? He is punishing you by having made you witness those horses burn to death. Those horses caught on fire to show you that you must not kill."

Musetta felt herself get hot and itchy all over. She wanted to tell Papa to shut up, to stop this nonsense. She couldn't believe this was the same Papa who sang the wonderful music and took her to stand in the back of the Metropolitan Opera House so she could listen to Caruso sing. This was a different Papa, a crazy Papa, a man whose eyes were narrow and yellow, whose nose was like a vulture's beak. To tell Gilda she had been the cause of all those horses burning to death—that was crazy!

"Where are you going, Musetta?" Mama called as Musetta began to back away down the porch steps. On the bottom step was a large white bowl, drying in the sun. Musetta scooped the bowl up into her arms. "I'm going to gather blackberries," she said. "I'm going right now." She began to run down the path toward the lake, and beyond it, toward the woods.

"Wait!" Papa yelled after her. "I want to talk to you, young lady. I want to know why you didn't tell me immediately that Gilda had killed a living creature."

Oh shut up, Musetta thought, running as fast as she could go. Just be quiet. Grown-ups knew nothing; they were not so smart or so wise. They were just like children, losing their tempers, wanting to strike out and hurt others. But they had so much power! Someday Musetta would not be under their power. She kept thinking of Miss McGinley and her quiet, gentle, orderly life. She would do something important like Miss McGinley. She would be a musician or a writer or a teacher—she would not grow up just to be a boss to others, to push around people less powerful than she was.

She ran and stumbled into the woods where the blackberries grew heavy on the vines. It was dark and cool in the shadows under the trees, and it felt good to pull the bursting berries from their stems and watch them drop and roll into the white bowl. She tried not to think of Gilda still on the porch, still being yelled at by Papa. If Papa was so happy Gilda had not died of pneumonia, why didn't he cherish her every day of his life? How could he forget so easily that she could be dead now like those horses lying in the fields and woods, flies already clustering on their flanks? People like Papa got humble only for a few minutes, when they were frightened, when they bowed their heads and prayed to God. But as soon as the danger was past, they raised their voices and started telling everyone what to do, how to live. Didn't Mama see how wrong that was? Couldn't she think clearly? As Musetta thought about it, she realized that Mama didn't seem to think much at all, but rather acted quite automatically, doing the things she was used to doing, never questioning anything.

She sometimes wished that she could quiet her mind, that she herself could be more accepting and unquestioning. Why not just stop thinking? Pluck the blackberries, let them roll in the bowl, eat them later buried in sour cream, with sugar sprinkled on top.

Musetta began to pick furiously, using both hands, stripping the berries from their branches. At least she could guarantee herself this pleasure—at least she could count on doing this. Her mouth began to water as she imagined the sugar crystals melting on the sour cream, the tart taste of the berries bursting in her mouth. She heard a crashing in the brush; someone was coming along the path very fast, crunching on leaves and pine needles.

"Musetta, Musetta!" It was Mama, coming after her. For what? Had she not peeled enough potatoes this morning for tonight's pot roast dinner? Why couldn't they leave her alone for ten minutes?

"I'm here, Mama," she called. "Picking berries!"

Mama came into view on the path, her white hair awry, her hands clasped to her breast.

"Oh my God," Mama said, "I knew it, I knew it. Can't you do anything right?"

"I'm only picking berries," Musetta said, holding the bowl forward for Mama to see. "The bowl is nearly full, what is wrong with that?"

"You took that bowl from the porch? That's Mrs. Carp's bowl."

"Maybe it is," Musetta said, " . . . but I didn't know that. Don't worry. As soon as we get back, I'll give her back her bowl."

"You *dumbkopf!*" Mama cried, tearing at her hair. "Do you know what that bowl is? A *cockteppel!* What Mrs. Carp keeps under her bed to pish in! So it was drying on the porch, and you took it to put berries in!"

Musetta stared into the bowl. She yearned to take out just one berry and eat it, there, in front of her mother. But she knew she was still a child and had long years to live at home.

"All right, Mama," she said. "I'm sorry . . . " And she tipped the bowl upside down and watched the berries stream in a black torrent down into the dirt. "I'll try to be good from now on."

TWENTY-NINE

Mama decided she wanted to leave for home the next morning. Mrs. Carp had stolen Mama's matzo meal from her cabinet, and there was nothing in which to dip the flounder. Mosquitoes had buzzed around Mama's head all night, and the scorched smell from the burned barn gave her a headache. What's more, Gilda was catching the sniffles, and Mama said Musetta's angry face was something she didn't want to look at anymore. She didn't need all this aggravation, not when it was costing them money every day.

Papa was anxious to get back to the city. He had planned to return alone, but now that they all were coming with him, he said he had to make some special plans.

"You will have to take the children to your sister's," he said to Mama on the train on their way home. "You cannot come directly to the house."

"What is this big secret?" Mama asked.

"You are full of questions when you shouldn't be," Papa said. "You will see when it's time to see. I thought you would stay in the country another week and give me time to get some matters settled."

"A surprise?" Mama asked. "You bought a house in Brooklyn?"

"Not yet," Papa said. "We will have to wait a little longer for that surprise. This is different."

"For the children?"

"For the children and for everyone." Papa smiled. He smiled at Gilda; he smiled at Musetta.

Musetta sat with her chin drilling itself into her chest. How could he be so fierce one minute and so cheerful the next? It was as if he had no memory and thought his children had no memory. He could shout at them and accuse them of every evil deed, humiliate them and fill them with guilt, but the next day be full of surprises.

"Come here, little one," he said to Gilda, and like a grateful bunny she hopped across the aisle of the train and gave Papa her hand. "And you, too— my big girl," he said to Musetta. "Come to your papa."

"Not now," Musetta said. "I'm too tired."

"You will be happy to get back to the city," he promised Musetta. "You will see."

"I hate the city," she mumbled.

"Wait, wait," Papa said. "It will be a different city this time."

When the train got to the city, Mama, Musetta, and Gilda went to Aunt Rose's house, where she served them pickled herring and boiled potatoes. Papa had said they could come home after supper. Uncle Hymie was slouched at the table puffing a cigar. Musetta could see why Ava didn't ever come here anymore; the whole apartment stank of cigar smoke.

"So how was your vacation?" Uncle Hymie asked. He turned to Aunt Rose. "How do you like it—these aristocrats go on vacations, while we poor Jews stay in the city and slave!"

"Oh shut up," she said. "You have more money than God himself, Hymie. You'll die with a tape measure in your hand."

"What's the matter with you?" he snapped. "You don't like money?"

"I want to enjoy some of it before I die," Aunt Rose said.

"Big mouth," he said. "Bring the strudel and tea, and be quiet."

"Oh drop dead," Aunt Rose said.

Gilda clapped her hands over her ears.

"Please . . . " Mama said. "Don't fight for nothing."

"It's nothing, nothing, Rachel," Uncle Hymie said. "We always talk like this. It's nothing."

"The girls don't know it's nothing."

"So let them grow up," Uncle Hymie said. "Right, girls? You have to grow up sometime!" He reached over and pinched Musetta's cheek.

"Please, Mama," Musetta said. "Supper is over now. Papa said we could come home as soon as supper was over."

"Yes," Mama said, standing up. "I think we'll go now. Thank you for feeding us on such short notice, Rose. Good-bye, Hymie."

He blew a black cloud of smoke at them. "Don't mention it."

● ⸙ ●

At their own front door Mama warned Gilda, "Knock first, I think we better knock."

"At our own house?"

"Papa has a surprise—we have to make sure he's ready."

Musetta saw her mother smile a kind of secret smile. What did she expect Papa would have waiting for them? Whatever it was, Mama seemed to feel it would be wonderful.

"Knock," Musetta said, nudging Gilda, who stood in front of her at the threshold. She wanted to get inside and be alone; she wanted to read her special book that Miss McGinley had given her as a prize for winning the spelling bee. The last word in the contest had been "philanthropic," and Dan Flaherty, the bad boy of the class, kept trying to distract her so she'd miss it. But she finally got it all right, and Miss McGinley had applauded delightedly. "You're the winner, Musetta!" she had said. " . . . And do you know what that word means?"

"It means 'ch . . . ch . . . ch . . . charitable!" Musetta finally was able to say, her face flushing with embarrassment. But when the class was dismissed, Miss McGinley detained Musetta to give her a special present, a book titled *Deborah, the Story of a Young Girl*.

"I want you to have this," Miss McGinley told her. "It's a little advanced, but I think you'll enjoy it." The book was lavender in color with a gold binding; Musetta had wanted to take it on their trip to the country, but Mama had not let her pack it. "You read too much! I don't want you spoiling your vacation by reading," she had said. "Soon you'll need eyeglasses from so much eye strain."

Now Musetta longed to get into the house and into her bed, where she would do nothing but read and read to wipe away the memories of the past few days.

"Knock again," Mama said, in agreement that they had stood waiting long enough.

"Who is it?" Papa sang in an unnatural voice. He abruptly threw open the door, and there in the living room were two strangers behind him, an old man and an old woman, shuffling forward, bent, their sad eyes a thousand years old.

Papa herded them toward the door so that they stumbled on their feet, knocking their heavy black shoes together. As they came closer, Musetta inhaled a musty smell compounded of wool and worn leather and the breath coming from their toothless mouths. She could hardly stand to breathe. She backed away and stepped on her mother's toes. Mama was staring at the old people; her mouth hung open.

"Meet your *bubbeh* and your *zayde!*" Papa cried in triumph. "They're going to live with us now!"

"But Isaac . . . " Mama said. "I thought not for a few years . . . at least not till Chaveleh gets married, moves away."

"She no longer lives here," Papa said, his eyes narrowing. "She lives with Sadie Rabinowitz."

"But not forever," Mama said. "That's still her room in our place . . . "

"Now Bubbeh and Zayde have that room!" Papa said emphatically. "So that is that." He bent and said loudly, in Yiddish, in his mother's ear, "Mamaleh, this is my wife, Rachel. You can tell from the pictures I sent to Poland, no? And my girls, Musetta and Gilda."

The old woman nodded her head and smiled. The inside of her mouth was dark and red; Musetta could almost hear the dark gums slap together as the old woman closed her mouth.

"And Papa . . . " Papa said to the old man. "Here is my family. Now they are your family."

The old man blinked his watery pale eyes and reached down to Gilda. To Musetta's astonishment, Gilda threw her arms around the old man and flung her face against his hollow chest; the scraggly hairs of his long white beard swung above her golden hair.

"Oh—I'm so happy you're here!" Gilda said.

Papa looked at Musetta, his eyes saying, "Well, what are you waiting for?" Musetta stepped forward and took her grandmother's hand. It was dry and light as a leaf. "I'm glad to meet you," she said in English.

"All right, all right," Papa said. "Come in and have tea, and then there will be another surprise!"

"What, you brought your aunts and uncles from the old country, too?" Mama whispered in Papa's direction. The old people shuffled slowly to the dining room, where Papa had shined the silver samovar that had once belonged to his great-uncle.

"Tea is cooking," Papa said. "And special cakes from Hornstein's Bakery."

"Such a party," Mama said to Musetta. "Chaveleh should be here. And Shmuel."

"Ava isn't allowed here when Papa is here," Gilda explained to her grandparents, but they seemed not to understand.

Papa was in high spirits. His face had more color in it than Musetta had ever seen. He didn't seem to notice how crowded the table was with six people at it; she was sure he would never consider that now Musetta would have to peel more potatoes every night, that there would be more cups to wash, more towels to hang on the lines across the courtyard.

The old people were now speaking to each other, leaning close and talking in Yiddish, but Musetta hated Yiddish; it was a foreign language in America. She was certain that Miss McGinley's mother and father, grandmothers and grandfathers, didn't huddle about speaking a foreign language to one another. She shuddered, thinking that now she would have to hear it spoken all the time, every day. At least Mama and Papa spoke Yiddish only half the time. Now they would have to use it to make themselves understood to the old people, and it would ring in Musetta's ears day and night. She felt the world was closing in on her, everything going wrong. She no longer had Chaveleh here to discuss things with; Gilda was brattier than ever; Mama was just an echo of whatever Papa wanted; and now these frail, noisy, smelly old people who couldn't speak English were now permanently part of Musetta's household!

"Excuse me," she said, pushing back her chair. "I have to get something in my room." She was thinking of the book *Deborah*, thinking of how it would feel in her hand.

"Don't open the door to Chaveleh's old room!" Papa said suddenly, standing up and holding his hand out like a policeman. "Not till I say!"

Musetta shrugged. Why would she want to go in there? To see the old people's belongings, old sacks filled with even older clothes?

"On second thought," Papa said, "Let's all go into Chaveleh's old room right now. Come, Mama, come, Papa—" he said to the old people, acting most strangely. "Get up now, we all have to go into the room together. Musetta, you come here, in front."

Musetta glanced at her mother; Rachel shrugged, raising her eyebrows. Isaac was acting crazy, she seemed to be saying. Musetta led the parade down the hall to Chaveleh's old bedroom.

"All right now," Papa said. "Open the door!"

At first Musetta saw only the big old bed and the usual other things—the dresser, a wooden chair. But suddenly something seemed to grow out of the shadows, something seemed to smile at her with a row of white gleaming teeth.

"A piano!" she cried, running forward to touch it. "Papa! A piano!" She touched an ivory key, and a bell-like tone rang through the room. "Oh—how beautiful, how beautiful."

"So," Papa said, clasping his hands. "Which is better? The country or the city?"

"Oh Papa," Musetta said. "May I learn to play it?"

"On Monday morning Mrs. Goldfarb's niece will be here to give you a lesson. A nice young girl, very talented."

"Oh—I can't believe it," Musetta said, pulling out the bench and sitting down to rest her fingers on the keys. "This is what I've wanted more than anything."

"Your Papa is not so bad, is he?"

"I never said . . . "

"No, no, you didn't. But sometimes I see it in your eyes."

"Can I get a violin then?" said Gilda, from where she stood in the doorway holding her grandfather's hand.

"Girls don't play violins," Papa said. "Only boys play violins."

"What do girls play?" Gilda asked.

"The piano, the piano!" Isaac said. "Musetta will be our virtuoso!"

Musetta examined the burnished wood, the gleaming bench on which she sat.

"Only one thing to remember," Papa said. "When Zayde and Bubbeh are napping, there is to be no playing."

"And the rest of the time?" Mama asked, holding her hand to her head in anticipation of his answer.

"Practice! Practice! Practice!" roared Papa.

THIRTY

There was a smell of wet wool hanging in the air of Mr. Berk's factory. The sponger had overturned a jar of water on the table, soaking through the cut-out backs and sleeves of a dozen suit jackets. The presser, trying to dry things out, only made things worse, ironing the wet bits of fabric, sending up hissing clouds of acrid-smelling steam. Ava held her handkerchief over her nose and glanced at the clock. She was so tired—and the sharp smell had given her a headache. She had to work for another hour till she could go home. She had a funny ache all down the side of her face and a pulling sensation at the edge of her eye, as if her eyebrow were weighted with lead and dragging her whole head downward.

She intended to stop at Mama's on the way to Tessie's to ask what might be causing the pain. Mama had worked so often with doctors that she seemed to know something about every ailment and its treatment. Maybe after Len came to pick her up at work they could go over to Mama's. If they hurried, they might be able to get there before Isaac got home. She dreaded seeing him and avoided going home when she knew he would be there. He had never met Len, and if Mama had told Isaac what Len did for a living, he would refuse to meet him.

But Ava had a reason for wanting to bring Len home. If she decided to marry him, it would be necessary to approach Isaac about making a wedding. He would probably refuse to give her one, but if the alternative were having her move back to live with them, he might consider it.

This could be a strategic time to bring up the matter; Musetta had told Ava that Isaac was less cranky these days. Now that he had brought his parents over from the old country, he was glad to appear the dutiful son. The old people thanked him every day for his kindness in taking them in—although clearly it was Mama who had the burden of all the work upon her.

It was obvious to Ava that she could not stay with Tessie Rabinowitz and her family indefinitely, although Mrs. Rabinowitz had said to her just the other day, "If it were not for you being here, I would never see my Lennie; he used to come maybe twice a year, for a seder and for Rosh Hashonah. Now, it's magic, he comes to dinner every night to see you. You should only be my daughter-in-law, nothing would make me happier."

Ava was considering it. She knew she did not love Len. There was a part of her that felt cold and cut off from love, something in her soul made her withdraw from the element in men that made them hoarse and rough breathing and wild, the part that made Papa—so long ago—deceive both that young girl and Mama, the part that made Uncle Hymie come to her bed and lean over her, pressing her breast with animal hunger.

Yet Len himself did not frighten her; he seemed quite familiar with that part of himself, his needs and all his appetites. He did not force them on Ava, but seemed perhaps to satisfy them elsewhere, somewhere in that wild part of his life that had to do with the pool hall and his prize-fighting and his gangster friends. His fierceness was never directed against her, but rather wrapped itself around her protectively.

One night last week he had taken her to dinner, and afterward, on their way home, he had leaned close and said, "Swear to God you'll marry me, Ava."

"And if I don't?" she asked.

"Well, then—I might have to kidnap you and take you to a desert island," he answered. He reached for her hand and squeezed it in his huge paw. She had a sense of wanting to burrow into his thick fur, to hide her face against his barrel chest and be protected for the rest of her life.

"That doesn't worry me, I'd like living on a desert island," she said. "But if I marry you, it will be because I would marry even a Chinaman to get out of Isaac's house."

"I'm too hairy to be a Chinaman," Len said. "Wait till you see my bare chest." Then he added, "You don't ever have to look at my bare chest if you don't want to Ava. Not ever."

Before going home today, she had to arrange the fox-fur trims in the cold storage room. As she worked there, Ruthie, one of the models, came in and asked her if she would do a favor for Mr. Berk. Esther, their other model, was out sick, and four salesmen were waiting to see the new line. Would Ava mind just putting on the plaid spring coat, the "Passover" model, to show it to the salesmen?

"Oh—I don't know, Ruthie. Something's wrong with my face, I have an awful headache, and I know I don't look too good. I guess I could . . . if I have to."

"You have to," Ruthie said. "When a boss asks a favor, you have to."

Ava followed Ruthie to the dressing room and stood listlessly while Ruthie draped the coat over her shoulders. "Put your arms in the sleeves, sweetie, it looks better that way. And dredge up a smile. There's a millionaire department store owner from Texas out there."

In the showroom she could tell who the millionaire was immediately—a man six and a half feet tall wearing boots and smoking a cigar. As soon as he looked at her, she knew she'd better keep her eyes down; he was interested. Her heart began to pound. He came up next to her and fingered the velvet collar of the coat, then let his fingertips brush her cheek. "Smooth as silk," he murmured. Ava tried to smile. Mr. Berk was there, nodding approval.

"You like the style?" he said to the Texan.

"Love it," the man said. He put his hand on Ava's shoulder. "Nice-quality wool. Maybe I could use ten dozen. More if your girl comes with them!" He laughed.

Ava had a flash of her life to come: men handling her, making jokes at her expense. Leering, blowing cigar smoke into her face. What was there to wait for? True love? What was that? Had Papa given it to Mama? Had Aunt Rose gotten it from Uncle Hymie? There was nothing to wait for. Love didn't exist.

As the Texan managed to slide his hand down her back, she saw the top of Len's fuzzy head emerging from the stairwell. She realized he had come to pick her up, to make sure that salesmen like Mr. Dubinsky were not taking advantage of her. His wide monkey face appearing in the cold factory warmed her, reassured her. At times, he seemed to her like a tank: square, armored, impenetrable. Inside him she could hide. There was no grace, no beauty, no style to the tank, but it was at least perfectly secure.

"Excuse me," she said to the Texan, "my boyfriend, the prize-fighter, has come to pick me up." She slid her arms out of the coat, letting it slip to the floor in front of Mr. Berk's astonished eyes. "I'll be right with you," she said to Len.

THIRTY-ONE

"What's wrong with your face?" Mama cried. "Your mouth is drooping like you had a stroke!"

"I don't know," Ava said. "I told Len I wanted to come over here on my way to his mother's house to ask you about it."

"What about your eye, can you close it?" Mama asked.

"I—I don't know," Ava said, going to the living room and looking in the big mirror on the wall. "I can't feel anything there. No, I can't close it." By now the side of her face seemed frozen, a corner of her mouth drooping. She could see a drop of saliva sliding down her chin, although she could feel nothing.

"Oy vey," Mama said. "*Tsurus* like this we don't need."

"Don't get so dramatic, Mama," Ava said, although she felt frightened. "I'm not dying." She turned to Len. "Come in and sit down," she said. "You don't have to stand there in the doorway."

"Of course, of course," Mama said. "I don't mean to ignore you. How are you? How is your mother?"

"Fine, fine," Len said. "Do you know what's wrong with Ava?"

"It could be anything," Mama said. "Did you sit in a draft? Were you by a fan, maybe, in the factory? Did it blow on you?"

"I don't remember," Ava said. "Maybe . . . "

"We'll have to go to the doctor," Mama said. "We can't take chances."

"I'll take her right now," Len said.

"I want to come, too," Mama said. "Where is my pocketbook? Where is my hat?" She spun around. "I'm like a chicken without a head."

They heard a shuffling sound in the hall. Bubbeh and Zayde were creeping along, feeling their way, holding onto the walls. They were like two little blackbirds, with their thin long noses, their hunched backs. As they came into the living room, Ava heard the sounds of a piano.

"Listen to that!" Mama said, clapping her hands to her ears. "Musetta runs in that room the minute Bubbeh and Zayde come out; she's like a cat waiting for a mouse. The minute she can get to the piano, she starts. Scales, chords, God knows what! A permanent headache I have from that."

"It's good for her, Mama," Ava said. "Good for her to be so interested in something."

"But for what? A great concert pianist she'll never be."

"How do you know?"

"That's what Isaac says. You never know."

Bubbeh clapped her gums together as she always did before she tried to speak. In Yiddish she said, "My head hurts. I'm weak."

"So sit down," Mama said. "I can't worry about you this minute." She continued to look for her pocketbook, her hat.

"You could make my wife some *mamalega?*" Zayde asked.

"Now?" Mama asked. "Now when I'm on my way out?"

"It wouldn't take long," Zayde persisted.

"The corn meal is in a jar," Mama said. "You make it, Zayde. Or let Bubbeh make it."

The old man's mouth fell open. "Bubbeh wouldn't cook in that kitchen. And you think I should cook in there?"

"That's the place we cook in," Mama said. "Unless you want to go back to the old country. Chaveleh, come right now—we don't want to miss the doctor."

With Len on one side of her and Mama on the other, Ava sat in the examining room where nine years ago she had come with her broken arm. Dr. Schwartz looked no older; his narrow pinched face, his round eyeglasses were exactly the same.

"Always something with the children, Mrs. Sauerbach, isn't it?" he said, peering into Ava's face, his long nose a hair's width from her forehead. Ava felt a sense of hopelessness shudder through her. In a silver instrument bowl in the glass-door cabinet she could see a reflection of her face; it had become something separate from her, a monster with a will of its own, something ugly and demanding—twisted and hideous, without sensation. Behind her, flared out and distorted in the reflection, was Len's wide, solid body, his heavy hand resting reassuringly on her shoulder.

"It couldn't be a stroke?" Mama asked the doctor. "Not in such a young person!"

"Not likely—" the doctor said. "But you never know. Anything is possible."

Just as Ava began to imagine herself crippled for life, the paralysis spreading down to her limbs, just as she pictured herself sitting in a wheelchair, like the ninety-year-old ladies who sat, shaking with palsy, in the wan sunshine of the tenement entryways, Len boomed out a denial.

"Of course it isn't a stroke! A gorgeous healthy young girl doesn't have a stroke. Maybe it's a toothache; maybe it's a cold in the muscle of her cheek. But not a stroke. Don't scare the life out of her."

"All right, all right," the doctor said. "Lie down, my dear, we'll test a few things, and then we'll see . . . "

Finally he made a diagnosis.

When they left his office, Mama said, "Bell's palsy, I never heard of it."

"It's just a cold in the muscle of her cheek," Len said, his arm warm under Ava's elbow. "In a few days it will be gone."

"The doctor said it could last as long as six months, even a year in some cases."

"And if it does, she'll still be fine," Len said.

"She won't be able to work. She can't talk properly," Mama said.

"She doesn't have to work," Len said. "When we're married, she won't have to work, so there's no need now."

"She won't even be able to feed herself," Mama said. "Food will dribble down her chin."

"I'll feed her," Len said.

"Someone has to take her for her heat treatments," Mama said. "With Bubbeh and Zayde in the house, I have no time for anything."

"I'll take her for heat treatments," Len said. Ava could say nothing while her mother and Len arranged her future life. She had no strength to fight; it was easiest to let them carry her between them, figure out her future. She felt certain now that she would marry Len. She was in no position to look further—she might be an invalid the rest of her life, she might have this twisted face forever. She could not be a chooser, but had to accept her fate. It was not so bad. Len was kind, he would work hard. She would forever be out of Isaac's way. It wouldn't be too bad a life.

Mama seemed to be thinking along the same lines. She said to Len, "I will talk to Isaac soon about making a wedding."

Ava tried to say something—she felt her tongue rise, her breath poise itself inside her mouth—but when the thought formed on her lips, she could not speak it. *This is all I will ever have.*

THIRTY-TWO

What Musetta needed was earmuffs! There was more commotion at home than out on the playground at school. Bubbeh grumbled and complained constantly in Yiddish. "Rachel, you are out of kosher salt." "Rachel, why is it there is not a *mazzuzah* on every doorway, only on the front door?" "Rachel, this chicken looks like it died before it came out of the egg. Can't you tell the butcher to give you a chicken that has some meat on it?"

And Zayde mumbled also—he shuffled from room to room dovening aloud, wrapping tefillin with their black leather straps around his arms and head every morning, praying and nodding his head as if he were half-asleep.

When Papa was home, they mumbled complaints to him. How come he didn't pray as much as he should? How come he didn't see to it that Rachel kept the kitchen cleaner? Why didn't the girls do more work in the house? What was all this piano playing that Musetta did instead of helping her mother keep the floors scrubbed? Why did he let Gilda spend so much time cutting hearts and flowers from colored paper and arranging them in a scrapbook? Weren't there more important things for girls to learn?

Papa was polite to them, but Musetta often heard angry whispers coming from her parents' bedroom. Sometimes Mama cried; Musetta heard her blowing her nose. One day there were new *mazzuzahs* in all the doorways.

Musetta wished for sunny days; on sunny days the old people liked to take a walk up and down the street, and then the house would become quiet and peaceful. Mama sometimes came to tell her they had gone for a walk. She and Mama would smile at each other when the old folks had gone downstairs. Even Papa seemed to sigh with relief; when they were out of sight, he would put on a Caruso record.

Bubbeh and Zayde hated Isaac to play opera records. One night they accused him of terrible things—of wasting his time on that ridiculous music, of taking his daughters to the opera, where wild women wore low-cut gowns and sang out their private business to the world.

"Oy vey, oy vey!" Musetta heard Papa cry to Mama when the old people had gone to bed. "What did I burden myself with by bringing them here? They hate it—it's too hot, too cold, the food isn't kosher enough, the children aren't quiet enough, the beds aren't soft enough."

Musetta envied Chaveleh. Soon she would be getting married. It was all settled—she wore an engagement ring already, a diamond that Len had given her to seal their agreement. She lived now with Len's family. She had had to quit her job because of her paralyzed face, but Len was going to marry her anyway. Papa had refused to make a wedding; that was another cause of fighting between Mama and Papa, but he said he had enough expenses as it was with Bubbeh and Zayde to support.

"Just this one last thing," Mama had begged Papa on a day when the old folks had gone out to take a walk. "After that Chaveleh will never cost you another penny."

"She spits on me," Papa said. "What do I owe to her?"

"It's you who spits on her," Mama said. "And it isn't to her that you owe the wedding. It's to me."

"To you?"

"I am your wife."

"Yes, yes, I know," Isaac said. "How can I ever forget it?"

"You grow meaner every day," Mama said. "What is the matter with you?"

"God help me," Isaac said. "Forgive me, Rachel. My heart is like a stone."

Musetta didn't want to hear any more. She went to Bubbeh and Zayde's bedroom, her refuge when they were out on their walks, and she played the piano. When the notes sounded in her ears, she could forget the racket, the arguments, the smells of the tenement, her grandparents' ugly lined faces. She could forget how sad Mama looked, how tired Papa looked. She could stop thinking about how Shmuel might fight in the war and die or how Chaveleh might never have her pretty face straight and regular again.

The music made her feel she was flying outside over the treetops, over the river, away past Brooklyn, past the cemeteries and the houses and the endless stores full of dead chickens and glassy-eyed fish. It took her away from Gilda's whining—Gilda, with her pasty complexion and her intense, critical stares. Most of all it gave her something to hope for—a life like Miss McGinley's, measured and soft-spoken and organized and thoughtful. A life without shouts and threats and without that kind of inner, burning anger that those around her seemed to hold in their hearts.

The scales she played were a ladder to a happier life. The chords were the sound of the harmony she wished she had in her own life.

THIRTY-THREE

"Do it for an old woman who is dying," Sadie Rabinowitz said to Ava. "Just so she can die in peace. To me, well, it's not that important, though of course I did it before my wedding, it was not a choice I had. But for Len's *bubbeh*, do it for her."

Sadie took Ava's hands in hers. She was such a warm, generous woman, and she had been so good to Ava. But the idea of going to the *mikvah* made Ava shudder. She had once gone with Mama to the *mikvah* and waited in the dressing room, holding Mama's clothes while the attendant took her to the bathing room and then to the immersion pool. It had stunk of mold and other forbidden smells—women's smells, secret body smells.

"But I have so much to do tonight!" Ava said. "I'm getting *married* tomorrow!"

"Don't I know, don't I know?" Sadie exclaimed. "The happiest day of my life, that my son should get a girl like you." She leaned forward and kissed Ava's cheek. "Such a precious daughter-in-law you will be."

Ava laughed. "Don't mess my fancy hairdo, Sadie," she said affectionately. "I don't want all my curls to be undone before tomorrow!"

"Gorgeous, you look gorgeous," Sadie said. "God willing, all your children will look like you, not like Len. Don't tell him I said it—maybe they could have his brains; he has a good mind, it wouldn't be bad if the children had his brains. But they should have your looks."

Ava laughed again. She held up her hands to examine them—her nails had been done at the same time as her hair this afternoon, they were painted a brilliant red color. She was having trouble getting used to seeing herself so glamorous. . . .

"Thank God your face is normal," Sadie said. "I prayed that by the wedding your face would be normal."

"Len took me for all my treatments," Ava said. "Do you how many hours he waited for me in the doctor's office?"

"He's such a good boy, no?" Sadie asked.

"A good boy," Ava agreed. The two women hugged.

"So will you go to the *mikvah* for Ida?" Sadie asked. "She's coming over tonight with my sister; they want to take you."

"Will you come with us?" Ava asked.

"How can I come?" Sadie said. "My son's wedding is tomorrow. I have to stay up and bake strudel all night!"

Ida, Len's grandmother, was ninety years old. Like an old black crow, she hunched along the street, leaning on her cane, holding on to the arm of Sadie's sister, Len's aunt Bella.

"Could we hurry?" Ava asked. "I would like to do this very fast. I have so much to do tonight. I want to iron all the nightgowns in my trousseau, and I need to sew the pearls on my veil."

"Sha, sha," the old woman said sharply, waving Ava away as if her words were as annoying as mosquitoes in her ears. "This we cannot rush."

People passing them in the street gave them no notice. It seemed remarkable to Ava that on this night, the eve of her wedding, the world went on in its usual way, while tomorrow and forever after that her life would be different. She would no longer be alone in the world; she would have Len at her side, in all his reassuring strength and certainty. Isaac could no longer rule her; Mama would treat her as an equal, a grown woman, not a maiden but a wife; and she would wear a fine gold wedding ring, a symbol of her respected place in the community.

Len had promised that he would eventually find new and safer ways to earn his living—he just needed a little time to figure out the best plan. Ava must trust him and not rush him. He would do whatever was best for the two of them and eventually for the family they would have. Life was going to be easier from now on. She had come to the turning point in her life. Len promised he would always adore her; he expressed wonder that a woman as beautiful as he thought she was would agree to marry him, a "short tough, little brute."

"I like the way you look," Ava had said, smiling into his wide face. "Don't worry, Len. I think you look very handsome."

There was only one heaviness in Ava's heart that she could not share with anyone. Her own papa would not be at her wedding.

Hurrying along the dark street, Ava looked up at the black sky dotted with stars and thought, Where are you, Papa? Why did you not come back to me? I waited and I waited, I dreamed of your coming back and throwing your arms around me, I dreamed of the doll carriage you would buy for me, I dreamed of how much you loved me when Isaac was shouting and giving orders to me.

"Here we are," Bella said. "Don't walk so fast—we're here, Ava!"

"I see, I see," Ava said, turning into the dark doorway and pushing open the heavy door. A strong odor assailed her nostrils; she remembered it from the time she had been to the *mikvah* with Mama. She shivered a little. It reminded her of women's thighs, of Mama's girdle, of elastic, of perspiration, of bloomers and slips and damp bathing suits. Len's grandmother gave her a little shove with the hard claw of her bony hand. "Go with the woman. She will take care of you."

The attendant, a tall, fierce-looking woman wearing the traditional wig, hooked her arm through Ava's elbow and tugged her along. The gray cement scraped under Ava's shoes. She reached up and delicately patted her newly set curls. She hoped that the dampness here would not loosen them.

"You will take off your clothes," the attendant said. "You may wear this robe." Shivering, feeling goose pimples rise up all over her skin, Ava lay her clothes over a chair in the dressing room and put on the rough-textured robe.

"Ready?" the attendant said, standing impatiently in the doorway.

"I suppose so." Barefooted, Ava stepped tentatively on the cold cement toward the woman.

"Give me your hand," the woman said, and obediently Ava held out her hand. From out of nowhere the attendant brandished a pair of small scissors and, holding Ava's hand in an iron grip, began slicing off Ava's newly polished red nails.

"What are you doing?" Ava cried, pulling her hand back.

"Give me the other hand," the woman commanded.

"Are you crazy?" Ava ran through a doorway and found herself in a long cold room where a murky-looking pool sent fumes of disinfectant sloshing toward her. The old woman, Ida, was waiting for her there and said, "Into the water, into the water, right now!"

Ava hesitated on the brink of the pool and thought, I must get this over with, I must do it and get out of here. She ventured forward with her toe, touching the gray foamy water. The attendant came behind her and pulled the robe from her shoulders so that she was bare, totally naked, helpless. She was shoved forward, down the rough-textured steps, into the slimy broth. The slope of the pool's floor veered sharply downward, so that in two steps, Ava was up to her waist in the water.

"Farther! Farther!" the old woman cackled from the bank. "Go in deeper."

"No," Ava cried. Her breasts had shriveled, her flesh was turning gray. And then she felt the tall attendant behind her, right in the water with her, her steely hands bending Ava forward from the shoulders, trying to shove her totally into the water, trying to press her head under, to drown her! Ava thought of her beautiful curls unwinding, filling up like sponges with the foul water, hanging wet and limp like seaweed around her hollow face.

"No, no!" she cried, wrenching herself away from the woman. "I just had my hair done, don't you understand? Tomorrow is my wedding!"

"Go under!" the old woman called, "or you will not be a Jewish bride."

"The hell with all of you!" Ava cried, scrambling up the steps and beginning to cry. "Where are my clothes, you old witches? The hell with Jewish brides!"

THIRTY-FOUR

In her dream Ava married Nathan, not Len, and after the ceremony Len slumped behind a potted plant, his pawlike hands holding onto its branches, while Nathan waltzed with Ava across the polished floor, spinning and whirling with her, making her laugh with delight. When Ava opened her eyes, she was aware of Len curved away from her in the bed, heavy as a rock, tilting the mattress toward his side and giving her a sense that the bed was going down in heavy seas. She turned her head slowly toward him and felt her heart give a double thump.

Was this really the man she had chosen to live with for the rest of her life? Already the stuff of his body had entered hers and was now flowing—she imagined—through her womb. What did he know of her? He knew the shape of her face, her body, the sound of her voice. Her knew the way her hair frizzed on humid days and that she despised the taste of cooked cabbage. And—now—he also knew how her secret places looked, how her left breast was rounder and heavier than her right breast, how her nipples shriveled at any cool breath of air, even how (her secret shame) two tufts of dark hair grew down the inner sides of her thighs.

The wedding itself was already receding in her mind; she had not been clear-headed yesterday or any time since the previous night when she had arrived back at the Rabinowitz's from the *mikvah*, hysterical and furious, babbling her story of how they had nearly tried to drown her, showing them her hand with the nails cut off nearly to the quick.

Tessie had hugged Ava, while Sadie had greeted her outraged sister and mother at the door with the story that Ava had not meant to flee, that she was having last-minute terrors about the wedding, as any good girl might have, especially when about to marry a powerful man like Len.

In the morning Sadie told Ava that the story had satisfied Bella and Bubbeh; they understood how a chaste girl might fear Len, how—realizing that the *mikvah* was the last step in her preparation to become his wife—she might have wanted to run away.

Then, shimmering in her mind, was the blur of the next hours: dressing for the wedding in Sadie's bedroom without Mama there, the sense of being a wooden doll, while people fluttered around her, arranging her veil, her skirts, her stocking seams. It was Sadie's wedding dress she was wearing, its lace still smelling of the old country and its customs.

In the shul Ava was moved like a puppet, placed here, told to stand there, instructed to walk seven times in a circle around Len, gently shoved and tugged, nudged when to hold out her hand, when to sip the wine as her veil was raised, when to stand back after the babble of Hebrew words was heaped upon her ears and Len smashed the wine glass wrapped in a linen cloth under his mighty foot.

On the way out of the shul, Ava looked up and saw Mama in the back row, with Gilda and Musetta holding tightly to her hands. She had come at the last minute, after all, without Isaac. She was crying.

All along Isaac had refused to participate in the preparation of the wedding, claiming it was not his responsibility, she was not his child. It was not his duty.

So Sadie and her husband, in their generosity, had done it all, arranged for the shul, the rabbi, the small dinner afterward in a restaurant owned by a friend of Len's, just across the street from Len's pool hall.

While Ava had stood under the chuppah, stiff as a marionette in her white lace garments, she had thought, Here I am at my wedding without my mama or papa here to see me. When she discovered Mama in tears, sitting with the women in the back of the shul, she had broken down herself, sobbing in a torrent of grief, stumbling and nearly falling, so that Len had to carry her a few steps until she could find her balance.

Afterward, her mama and sisters had disappeared—had not even kissed her. Ava could not remember the wedding meal; she knew she ate nothing and heard nothing, while all around her was the babble of the Rabinowitz family's relatives. At the end of the table was the *bubbeh*, the black crow with the beaked nose, staring with her black eyes at Ava, daring her to be the good Jewish wife she could never really be.

Then, much later, they found themselves in the rooms Len had rented for them. They were only a few blocks from where Mama and Isaac lived with the girls and Shmuel. (Shmuel! Her eyes filled as she thought that he was gone also—gone off to be a soldier in a faraway war she could understand nothing about. He was in some town far in the south, Georgia, learning how to ride horses. He had sent home a picture of himself wearing a uniform, a large hat, sitting on a princely horse. Sweet Shmuel. How she loved him!)

Then Len had taken her to bed. The experience was not so bad. It was not too painful. Len was rough on the outside, with all his springy hair, his fierce beard stubble, his heaviness and density; but inside he was a gentle man, and he did his business with her carefully, not roughly, not meanly.

"Am I hurting you?" he kept whispering, and, quite truthfully, with relief and gratitude, she answered, "No, it's all right, it's all right." She was lucky she knew about the parts of her body; having gone with Mama to see babies born had helped her immensely. She did not know much about Len's body, about a man's private parts, but as for herself, she knew which of her parts would receive his. She did not know his parts would change from small to huge, from soft to hard, like a rubber hose jerking upright when filled with water. She did not know the exact length of time the act would take, did not know he would breathe and huff like a steam engine, did not know his torso would arch and fall, again and again, upon her quiet limp body. But she was not frightened because he did not lose his awareness as he did these things; he remained the Len she trusted. He whispered to her between his hoarse gasps for breath.

"Am I hurting you? Am I hurting you?" It was like a song he was singing to himself, first a slow song, then a faster and faster song, till it was almost a moan, coming desperately between the breaths he first held and then expelled.

Even during these moments she felt she was still beneath her wedding veil, in a cloudy white place, not really herself, but a being who had stepped into a required role, an actress playing a part.

At one point she had felt one sudden sharp pain, a stretching, pulling shock, and afterward a dull burning ache as Len worked along, bringing his song to its end. Then, when he had unrooted himself from her, he had become unconscious—falling into a trancelike sleep that was as solid as death. He didn't stir again all night as she lay sleepless beside him. Then at dawn, she had fallen into the dream of herself and Nathan, of dancing with him.

When would Len wake up? What was she to do now, this first married morning of her life? She supposed she should make him breakfast. She stepped quietly onto the cold wooden floor and realized that her nightgown had been left behind in bed. When had she taken it off? Or had Len taken it off? It was hardly a nightgown anyway, more a piece of lacy fluff that the girls who had worked with her at Mr. Berk's factory had given her. And she could see that Len lay upon it now; it was tangled between his legs, like some unnatural wrapping. White wedding lace over those dark and fibrous hairy legs. Ava stared. There was a slash of red under the lace, right there where Len's knee was angled.

Well, so there it is, Ava thought. My own blood. Now I am a wife.

She found her robe in the closet and went into the unfamiliar kitchen. Len had stocked the shelves with food, all kinds of fine foods that his restaurant friend had helped him buy wholesale. Ava decided to make Len matzo-brie; then she would wake him to come in and eat.

She opened a box of matzo and took out three of the square dry crackers rippled with brown-baked bubbles, smelling fresh, like Passover matzos. She ran them briefly under warm water, turning them on each side, till they had lost their crispness, then crumbled them in pieces into a large bowl.

In another bowl she beat two eggs with a pinch of salt and a few drops of milk; then she poured the mixture over the broken matzos, mixed them through the liquid till they were saturated, and fried it all carefully in butter. She was a good cook. She had watched Mama and Aunt Rose for years; she would be a good housekeeper, a good wife. That's what she would be. Was that all she would be? It seemed there were no choices. It wasn't so bad, having her own kitchen like this, her own rooms, her own man. "Len," she called, as she walked down the hall to wake him. "Come and have breakfast."

When she sat opposite her husband and watched him shovel great mouthfuls of the delicious matzo-brie into his mouth, while he hungrily chewed the food she had prepared, she felt a warm satisfaction flow through her.

She had filled Len's needs last night and again this morning. As he ate, he looked at her and gave her a wonderful smile. It was almost as warm as Papa's had been, almost as adoring. She sighed with pleasure.

There was a knock at the door. Len raised his eyebrows at Ava. She said, "I don't know . . . " and called out, "Who is it?"

"Mama and Aunt Rose," came Mama's voice.

Len, standing up quickly so that his robe came open and exposed his naked body to Ava's eyes, said, "I'll go in and shave fast, and I'll get some clothes to put on." Her eyes followed his swinging penis as he side-stepped around the table. It was a sight she would have to get used to, to accept, so that her heart wouldn't always pound as it was doing now. But it was such a remarkable thing, so mysterious and powerful. She shivered, remembering how she had felt as it worked in her last night, as Len sang his desperate song.

Her face was flushed as she opened the door to Mama and Aunt Rose. It grew even hotter as they examined her face, stared into her eyes.

"Well," Aunt Rose said. "So good morning in your new home."

"Thank you," Ava said, looking downward.

She could hear the sound of running water in the bathroom. She imagined Len, naked, shaving, and was astonished and embarrassed that her mother and aunt had dared to come here, this morning, the morning after her first night with her husband. If she and Len had gone on a honeymoon, this could not have happened, but Len had spent so much money on the wedding dinner and on furnishing the apartment that he thought it would be just as good to hide away here.

He did not know that no one could hide from Mama and Aunt Rose.

"Why are you here?" Ava asked finally, after a long, awkward silence.

"To bring you a present," Aunt Rose said, producing from her handbag a long, slim box. "Since you didn't invite us to the wedding . . . "

"You were invited!" Ava said. "You all *were* invited!"

"Well, since Rachel and Isaac were not going, I didn't feel it was my place . . . "

"Mama came," Ava said shortly. "I mean, Mama was there at my wedding."

"Only for a few minutes," Mama said softly. "Just because I couldn't let my Chaveleh be married without me there. Even though Isaac did not want me to go, I went. I took the children; they should not miss the wedding of their sister altogether. But then I went home right after."

"I wish you had come to the dinner, Mama," Ava said. "Isaac could have waited another hour for you. What difference would it have made?"

"As it was, he and the old folks argued with me the minute I got home. Bubbeh said my place was with my husband, Zayde said a wife like me should be punished, how I didn't listen, didn't pay attention to what Isaac wanted. I think they're all crazy," Mama said.

"So why don't you leave Isaac?" Ava said. "I would have run away years ago."

"What is wrong with you?" Mama said. "I have two little girls to think about."

"So? You left my papa, and you had two children," Ava said. "You weren't worried about us then!"

"How could you compare your papa with Isaac? Did your papa take care of us? Did he support us? Does Isaac run around with women?"

"Sha, sha!" Aunt Rose said. "What are you saying? You'll forget your story . . . "

"Chaveleh knows everything!" Mama said to her sister. "What do you think? She has a memory! The child was there the night we found Nathan with the girl. You remember, don't you, Chaveleh?"

"Yes. I remember all of it."

"But—" Mama added. "Nathan was one kind of man, Isaac is another."

"Sometimes you need to leave both those kinds of men to be free," Ava said. "Isaac is a tyrant."

"Not always," Mama said. "You should see how he loves Musetta and Gilda."

"I've seen . . . " Ava answered.

There was the sound of Len singing in the bathroom. Ava pulled the ties of her robe tighter. What was she doing arguing this way? They had no business being here. "It was nice of you to bring me a present," Ava said, holding out her hand for the gift Aunt Rose was still clutching tightly.

"Don't open it here!" Aunt Rose commanded, pulling the box away from Ava. "Open it in the bedroom. It's something I want you to try on . . . in front of the mirror."

Aunt Rose marched boldly into the bedroom. Ava followed her nervously, with Mama right behind. She felt a throbbing in her head when she saw that the bedcovers were still thrown back, her lace nightgown tangled among the sheets. Pretending to straighten the bed, Ava quickly bent and pulled the covers up over her nightgown.

But Aunt Rose with her eagle eyes cried, "Oh—there's a nightgown under there, it will get lost!"—and she flung the covers back to retrieve the nightgown. They all stared at the blood on the sheet.

Ava turned her head away, but not before she caught the triumphant look Mama and Aunt Rose exchanged with each other. At least Mama had the grace to look out the window while Aunt Rose pulled the tangled nightgown from the bedclothes and folded it carefully into a neat square.

"So!" Aunt Rose said significantly. "Good! Your mother and I are very relieved. We were worried that Len was a no-good."

Ava felt her headache grow to fill her head. She could not speak. What they meant was that they were worried *she* was the no-good, a wild girl, bad. How could they, how could Mama, think that? How could they have dared to come here to search for proof of whether or not she was a virgin?

"Now you could open your present," Aunt Rose suggested. They all looked up at Len's footsteps coming down the hall. He smiled with embarrassment. He was newly shaved and neatly dressed. Ava wanted to run to him and hide her head against his rock-hard shoulder.

"We brought your bride a wedding present for being a good girl," Aunt Rose said. "Open it, darling," she said to Ava.

Holding the box far from her body, as if a snake might leap out of it, Ava opened the lid and saw a string of white pearls.

"Put it on and enjoy," Aunt Rose said. "It's from the old country, your grandmother used to wear it. Come, Rachel, let's leave the young people alone now. It's after all their honeymoon."

1918

THIRTY-FIVE

March 30, 1918

Secret Heart

Papa has given you to me—a leather-bound diary embossed with gold vines— to while away the hours now that I am sick again. Dr. Schwartz says it is my weak lungs and that someday when we can afford to move out of the city, the country air will be good for me. My only worry about this diary is that Musetta will read it. She is not to be trusted. I know she will fly into a jealous rage when she finds that Papa has given me this beautiful book.

She will probably try to make herself sick to prove that she needs one, too. It's funny how well I know her. Just one glance will say everything to me—What makes me think I know how to write when she is, after all, the star student?! Well, I am not like Musetta, but I am no dummy, either. Why should I waste this paper on her? Never mind Musetta.

Life is far from dull here. Since Shmuel has been in the army, he has sent us two pictures from Georgia, one showing him wearing a long coat and a strange hat, and one of him sitting on a beautiful horse. The horse is standing on a country road, and there are tall trees all around. The horse's tail is moving in the breeze, and the road goes into the woods for a long distance. It doesn't look like war. He wrote in his letter that he met a sweet "Georgia Peach." I asked Mama what that means, and she said, with a tinge of anger in her voice, "It means she is a *shiksa*." Everyone knows that a *shiksa* is a bad sweetheart for a Jewish man to have, and a *shaygets* is a bad sweetheart for a Jewish woman to have. I would never have a *shaygets* for a sweetheart because it would break

Mama's heart. Probably Musetta will purposely look for one because she thinks Jewish men are all bossy like Papa. She doesn't like Bubbeh or Zayde either, even though they have no power, they're so little and bent over. She says she can't stand their smell. I don't think that's polite, even to think it. They can't help it if they're too weak to take a bath every day. And it isn't a bad smell. It's just sort of musty. No one can expect them to smell like babies.

How I love babies! I especially love Ava's new baby, born just two weeks ago on March 15. They named him Richard, and he looks like a red prune. Ava let me hold him, but only after she sat me down on the couch with pillows on either side of me and even one on the floor. When Richard opens his mouth to scream, you can see his pink gums and smell his hot sweet breath. He is so strong for such a tiny thing. Ava adores him, her face is so happy when she looks at him!

She and Len have moved into a new four-room apartment on 109th Street and Fifth Avenue. It has steam heat and faces Central Park, and it costs twenty-one dollars a month. Although Len promised Ava he would give up his pool hall, he says he was lucky to get his license renewed and can't take chances making a living some other way, especially now with the new baby. But he knows Ava doesn't like his friends, the gangsters who hang out there, and he promises he will soon go into another business. They want to move to Brooklyn, just as we want to, but we'll all have to save up for it. I hope someday when I have a baby I will be more womanly. I'm so skinny now, I'm like a plucked chicken. That's what Aunt Rose calls me. But Ava is so wide and soft now; she can hardly get her corset on. But she doesn't seem to mind. She nurses Richard and looks like she has a special secret all the time. She's so lucky! Someday I hope to be lucky, too!

THIRTY-SIX

In the next room the baby gave one small whimper, and Ava felt a sweet, stabbing pressure in the points of her nipples. She smiled and waited for the tingling rush, the electric burning fill and the involuntary oozing of the first hot drops from her breasts.

"Aah," she said, coming to the cradle and scooping up the thrashing baby. "Here's your mama, Richard. Come here and I will fill up all your empty spaces." She padded barefoot across the polished wood floor, pressing the baby against her breasts. She could feel them swirling with milk as if they were alive with swimming fish. "Quickly now," she said, unbuttoning her blouse and sitting carefully in the rocking chair. "I am bursting."

He tried to suck her finger as she placed it under the swollen nipple to make it more narrow and pointy. "No, no," she said, "Here, here—take it." With a sob of relief the baby seemed to inhale the nipple deep into his mouth, and at the first long draw he relaxed his flailing arms and legs and centered all his energy in sucking. Ava rested her head against the high back of the wooden chair. She could see herself in the mirror above her dresser, could see her two dark eyes watching the mother and child, feel the electric points of her nipples below.

She sighed in contentment. The baby's delicate blue-veined skull rested softly against her. With every tug on the nipple his temples pulled inward; the effort touched her, extreme as it was, focused as it was. She wanted to assure him she would not pull away, deny him, that she would sit, still as a mountain, till he had his fill. She rocked and dozed, aware of the pleasure in the softening, emptying breast. After a long time she moved the baby away, rubbed two fingers on his back in tiny circles till he released a bubble of air that smelled like sweet cheese, and then placed him firmly upon her other breast.

She sometimes nursed him for an hour; he would suck and then doze, wake with a start and begin again, only to sigh an instant later and fall away. She would watch his eyelids flutter closed and see his tiny lips come together in satisfaction. She could go on forever, just like this, alone with the baby in the apartment, with no thought but for the moment, the sensation of joy almost overwhelming. Sometimes she would feel the tug on her nipple relay itself to low in her abdomen, a quickening in the birth canal, a thrilling shock between her legs. It was happening now. It spread in waves through her limbs, to the edges of her fingers and toes. She breathed shallowly, all her concentration aroused. She stared at the baby's delicate skin, at its miniature features, as it pumped pleasure through her. She had never loved anyone as she loved this child. She knew she would die for him. The nipple flipped from his mouth with sudden force, sending a spray of milk over Ava's breast.

"Oh, don't stop, don't stop," she moaned, hastening to put her reddened nipple back into her son's mouth. He gave one powerful draw and again let go of the soft point of flesh, which flew out and dripped another droplet onto her skin. "Oh please," she cried out. But the baby was asleep. The sensation building within her stayed tense, taut. She began to rock in the chair, feeling the weight of the child heavy on her thighs, pressing in upon her as she rocked far back and sliding forward as she let the chair come forward.

"Oh my God," she said, "Oh my God." She rocked on, crying out finally in her pleasure. For a long time she sat in the chair, still now, tears on her cheeks. It grew dark in the room. She saw herself fade in the mirror, grow gray and indistinct in the twilight. Only when she heard Len's footsteps, heavy on the stairs, did she stir and compose herself.

THIRTY-SEVEN

"Dinner is late, I'm sorry," she said as he came into the dim room. "I'll make dairy, herring and sour cream and bananas. I'm sorry," she said again, getting up from the chair and carrying Richard to his cradle.

"So is my bruiser wearing you out?" Len asked, coming toward the cradle and leaning down to poke the baby's chin with his huge fist.

"Oh don't, he just fell asleep."

"Come over here and I'll give you a few pokes. And how about we go out to dinner tonight? I'm flush."

"And what would we do with the baby?"

"We can take him over to your mama's. Musetta can watch him, she's big enough."

"Gilda has more patience," Ava said. "Musetta doesn't like mess or noise. But I don't want to go over there, you know why."

"Isaac has been nicer since the baby came," Len said.

"Only because Mama has put her foot down, finally. She wants us over there now that there is a grandchild. But I hate to go, you know how I feel."

"So we'll eat here. Whatever you like. Just come over here so I can bite your arm." He came toward her, mouth open as if to tear a chunk out of her arm. His face was oddly flushed and his eyes looked peculiar to Ava.

"Your skin feels hot," Ava said, touching his face.

"Got to get a drink," he said. At the sink he filled a tall glass and gulped it quickly, letting water run down his chin and drip onto his shirt. He did everything wildly. Lately Ava dreaded Len's horseplay. Before the baby came she was resigned to it, was always cheerful, agreed to whatever Len wanted to do to her. He never hurt her in bed, was always considerate, and didn't take too long. It was no worse than having to sit through a newsreel at the movies.

But now when he wanted to nuzzle her breasts, she told him they were sore, too full of milk, too tender. She could not bear the thought of his cigar breath on her breasts or of his lips that had chicken grease on them touching the place where the baby's tiny lips would later nurse.

She was sorry for this turn in her emotions. She didn't like to hold Len off; it was not fair to him, and he deserved her cooperation. But her feelings toward the baby were like nothing else. He was hers and she was his. It seemed Len was extra, an intruder.

"Sit down and eat," she said. But Len was not there; he'd gone to the bathroom.

"Come to eat, the tea is getting cold, the herring getting warm."

"Ava—come in here." His voice sounded strange. She went quickly to the bathroom and found Len sitting on the closed toilet seat. He held the glass thermometer out to her.

"I think something's wrong," he said. "I kept drinking water all day. You know I never drink water." She pulled the thermometer from him and tried to read it. She could see that the mercury was way up, into the red danger area.

"What's my temperature? I can never read those things."

"It's nothing," she said.

"Then why am I sweating like a pig?"

"It's probably just a cold, we'll call Dr. Schwartz."

"He won't come this far."

"So we'll get someone else."

"Ava, you know Charlie who works for me. His mother had the Spanish flu. She died."

"You don't have that," she said. "You're strong as an elephant. Don't worry." She looked away from his frightened eyes. "Come with me, I'll put you to bed."

THIRTY-EIGHT

May 22, 1918

Secret Heart

Trouble again! Ava was nursing the baby, waiting for the doctor to come and see Len, and the baby suddenly went into convulsions. Luckily, Dr. Schwartz was coming up the stairs and went right to the baby. He said he had a knot in his intestines and must go immediately to the hospital. In the meantime Len started throwing up blood, and he also had to go to the hospital. Ava was almost hysterical. The baby had to have surgery, and Len had to have needles in his arms to feed him. Mama went to the hospital with Ava and sat with baby Richard while Ava visited Len in his room. Ava is afraid she will catch the Spanish flu and give it to Richard, but she can't leave Len alone all the time.

Then, yesterday afternoon she got into a hospital bed to nurse Richard, and they both fell asleep, and the next thing she heard was a baby screaming—Richard had rolled out of her arms and fallen out of the bed onto the floor, flat on his stomach, right on the scar where he had his operation. The nurse who was supposed to be watching them thought it was her fault, and Mama said she ran to a church to pray that Richard wouldn't die.

I think Ava is afraid that both Len and Richard will die and she will be alone. Mama is afraid Ava won't eat, and then she'll get weak and get the flu, too. They all could die. I suppose I could die. Everyone could die. All we do in life is try not to die. Keeping warm, and eating, and getting enough sleep—it all has to do with not dying. I sometimes think that's the only thing people think about, and they never have time to enjoy anything.

Bubbeh and Zayde are so old and sick; Bubbeh keeps saying in Yiddish, "I should only live till the New Year, God should only be good to me." And Zayde keeps saying to Papa, "You'll say Kaddish for me when I die?" Sometimes I want to take Bubbeh and Zayde on the train and go to the beach with them, and let them look at the waves and the water. If only I were old enough! Mama says they would trip and fall on the steps of the subway or that Bubbeh would have a heart attack. Papa says, "What do they need to see the ocean for? They had a boat ride on the ocean long enough to last them all their lives!"

I will pray to God that Richard and Len get better and be well, and that Ava doesn't catch the Spanish flu. Or, if she catches it, that they all die together, and not some of them live and some of them die. Musetta can't stand it when people talk about death or buckets of blood or their "moogens." Bubbeh and Zayde always talk about how they can't go to the bathroom or that they need prunes or that they're constipated. They like to tell everyone if they went to the bathroom and how much they "made"—they don't mean to disgust anyone, it's just really important to them.

I don't really like to hear them talk about it when I'm eating my egg for breakfast. Musetta eats the yolk and I eat the white of our eggs. That's the only time we cooperate about anything.

Lately she makes a big deal about my dolls; she says their glass eyes stare at her from the shelf at night in the moonlight and give her the creeps. She wants me to put them in a box so they don't watch her getting undressed. She can always find something to complain about.

She goes to the library on Willis Street nearly every day. I don't complain that her books are all over the bedroom, or that they smell musty, or that when she piles them on the windowsill they block out the breeze. She keeps a little notebook with her all the time, and if she reads a word in a book that she doesn't know, she looks it up in the dictionary and writes the meaning in her notebook. I think the notebook makes her feel important. If I don't know a word, I either skip it or figure out what it means, more or less, from the rest of the sentence. Mama says, "Don't fight." She doesn't care what the fight is about, she doesn't want to hear fighting. Zayde always wants to hear why we fight—he makes us each a cup of tea, and we drink it with sugar cubes between our lips. Now that he knows a little English, he says, "Tell me why Musettala is fighting with you." If she hears him say that name, she makes a face as if she is going to vomit. There are times I wish she'd play with me and my dolls, but I would never ask. A person can't play with dolls unless she wants to have fun, and Musetta never wants to have fun. How can sisters be this different? I'll never know.

1921

THIRTY-NINE

"I don't like how you're dressed," Bubbeh said in Yiddish to Musetta. She appealed to Mama. "You're not going to let her go out that way, are you?"

Mama turned from the sink, where she was cleaning a chicken, and considered Musetta's appearance. Musetta was wearing a Spanish lace shawl with silken fringe that Shmuel had sent her as a present, given to him by a girl he had met when he was in the army. Musetta spun for her mother's approval. She was going to a party at her friend Rozzie's house; there would be boys there. The lace shawl made her feel glamorous. With her pointy black shoes and the long red dress Papa had made for her, she felt like a movie star.

"Disgraceful," Bubbeh said. "Like a *kurve*, a prostitute."

"Go, sit down, Bubbeh," Mama said. "I'll make you some tea."

"Where is Isaac?" Bubbeh said. "Call him, he shouldn't let her go out looking like that."

"He is lying down," Mama said. "Caruso died today. He feels very bad."

"An Italian," Bubbeh sneered. "What does he have to worry about him for?"

"Who should Papa worry about then?" Musetta challenged the old woman.

"If he were a Jew, I could understand it," Bubbeh said.

"Do you think only Jews are human beings?" Musetta asked. Then she said, "Good-bye, Mama, I won't be back too late. Rozzie's brother will walk me across the street."

"Don't let her go!" Bubbeh warned. She walked toward Musetta, her arm raised, and staggered slightly against the wall.

"Don't aggravate yourself," Mama said. "You'll raise your blood pressure."

133

"A pity to have such a wild child," Bubbeh said. "A curse on my son."

"Oh, shut up," Musetta said before she could stop herself. "You talk crazy!"

"Go to the party," Mama cautioned her, "and don't say anything else you'll be sorry for . . . go, go."

Musetta ran down the stairs and wobbled in the unfamiliar shoes across the street to Rozzie's. She glanced back once and saw Gilda looking out at her from the window upstairs. She didn't wave. Gilda was always looking at her—staring at her, studying her. She was like a bat—the kind they used to see in the country—always tangling itself in her hair. Gilda's habits infuriated Musetta, her way of doing things so slowly and carefully, her way of tying little bows on the dresses of her dolls. She was always pointing things out to Musetta—how nice the cake Mama had made smelled and how the rain came down the windows in little ribbony waves. Did Gilda think she was blind? She could see the rain! But rain was rain, flowers were flowers. Mama's cakes did smell nice, but didn't all cakes? One didn't have to comment on every obvious thing every second!

Gilda was always gushing about something. What a fuss she made about little Richard. Whenever they went to visit Ava, Gilda would ooh and aah and clutch at her heart, sighing, "Look at his adorable toes, the dimples in his elbows, his fat little fingers!" When the baby took a step or spit up his applesauce, Gilda would thank God he was well. "He could have died when he was a baby and was so dreadfully sick! We must thank God for being so good to us and letting him live." Musetta would just as soon blame God for giving the baby convulsions and letting him slip out of the hospital bed and onto the floor! Of course she wouldn't have wanted Richard to die, or Len either, but neither one had died, had they? So why worry so much and give thanks to God so often? Why did God have to do with it?

As Musetta reached the entrance to Rozzie's apartment, she heard Rozzie call down the staircase. "Come on up! We have a tango on the Victrola!" But as she stepped inside, someone called her name from across the street in front of her house. It was Shmuel, in his shirt sleeves, running away from their house as fast as he could.

"Shmuel!" she called. "What is it? Where are you going?" He shouted over his shoulder. "It's Bubbeh. She collapsed. I'm going to get Dr. Schwartz."

"Are you coming up?" Rozzie yelled. "What are you waiting for? Don't hold the door open so long." Musetta hung on the doorknob, teetering on her shoes. She could see Shmuel disappearing down the street. Rozzie would never know, or anyone else, that her grandmother had fallen down.

She could just go up the stairs, go to the party, dance and have fun and enjoy herself. Even Shmuel would probably not remember that he had told her what happened. Her parents would not know, certainly Bubbeh would never know. What was she waiting for? Why didn't she just run up the stairs and forget sickness and old age and the smell of death that hung on the old people?

But what if she were the cause of it? She had just fought with Bubbeh. What if she had given her the heart attack or stroke or whatever Bubbeh was having? Could she, by her very existence, cause someone to die any more than God could save someone from dying?

"Come up, come up already!" Rozzie was shouting. Musetta swung back and forth on the door. Let the old woman die, she doesn't enjoy life anyway, Musetta thought. And then I'll have more time at the piano! She stepped inside and began to climb the stairs. "I'm coming," Musetta called. "Here I am."

FORTY

August 3, 1921

Secret Heart

Everything happened yesterday. Papa's idol, Caruso, died in Italy, and Bubbeh had a stroke. Papa is having stomach pains from his ulcer, and he can't get out of bed. Bubbeh is in her bed with her face all twisted to one side, and her arm hanging without feeling, paralyzed. She can't talk, and her eyes are like blue bubbles. I get the feeling she is drowning. Dr. Schwartz says she may get a little better, he can't tell yet. Mama is exhausted because she is like a nurse and knows how to take care of Bubbeh, so she has to do all the work. If she weren't a nurse, we would probably pay to hire one or Bubbeh would go to the hospital. Bubbeh has a little bell beside her bed, and whenever she wants anything, she rings it. She rings it all the time! Ring! Ring! The noise is making us crazy! And when Mama runs in there and says "What do you want?" Bubbeh, of course, can't tell her—she just waves her good arm in the air and grunts.

Musetta took one look at Bubbeh and ran away to gag. She is pacing the house like a lion. She can't get near her piano, and now that Bubbeh is so sick, she may never get to practice at all. Zayde hobbles up and down the hall, mumbling to himself. His hands are cold, even though it is such a hot summer. His lips always seem to be trembling, he can't eat anything. Trouble is everywhere. I think he is afraid Bubbeh will die and he will be all alone in America.

I think we should move to Brooklyn and we will be luckier. Shmuel can't get a job here and seems sad. Ava is worried because Len has introduced Shmuel to some friends that are "bad." Ava says they are criminals, but she thinks anyone who comes into the pool hall is up to no good. Shmuel plays pool, too, and hardly ever talks to me.

Last week the police were in our building. Mrs. Ratner, who lives across the hall, was making whiskey in her bathroom, and someone told on her.

Please God, let Bubbeh get well. Let Papa feel better. Let Zayde stop shaking. Let Mama rest. Let Musetta be kind to Bubbeh and not so mean to me. Let the world be nicer.

1923

FORTY-ONE

The one thing Musetta could not stand was stupidity. Yet wherever she went stupid human beings surrounded her. Here in Roosevelt High School she was a hundred times smarter than every teacher she had had so far. Today Mrs. Vicci was droning on about the short forms of the Gregg shorthand method. Musetta had learned them from the book in one evening and in a few days could write them with lightning speed. But in school Mrs. Vicci would select five each week and drill the class in them for two hours every morning.

Musetta felt herself grinding her teeth. In the seat beside her Rozzie was bent in concentration over her desk, dipping her pen in the inkwell carefully, writing the forms over and over on her notepad.

Rozzie was energetic and sweet, but she was also stupid. Musetta had followed her to Roosevelt High School because Rozzie had begged her: "Don't go to Hunter and be a schoolteacher for a bunch of brats. Come to Roosevelt with me, and when we graduate we can get glamorous jobs working for handsome men."

Something about this reasoning appealed to Musetta. Although Roosevelt was the commercial high school where less ambitious students ended up, it seemed more attractive than Hunter, where so many girls went to become teachers. Everyone expected Musetta to go to Hunter, and Papa had protested when he heard her decision.

Mama had interrupted his tirade: "Leave her! Leave her! You can't tell a child like her what to do! She has a strong will."

Musetta knew Mama was criticizing her more than supporting her, but what did it matter if it helped her to achieve what she wanted. Maybe Mama realized that Musetta would be happier working with accomplished professional men than being around noisy, demanding children. The only trouble was that to get anywhere in life she would have to tolerate hours and hours of boring drudgery.

Her plans to be a concert pianist had become doubtful when what she would have to do became clear to her. Scales! Scales and chords, when all she wanted to do was play like a dream and play only music she loved—Chopin waltzes and Schubert songs. Her teacher would rap her knuckles and say, "Keep to strict rhythm, Musetta! Count! Count!"

But within seconds Musetta would forget to count and sway dreamily about on the piano bench, drawing out long romantic passages and hurrying through less interesting parts. How she hated Bach! It was all up and down with her fingers as if she were working on Papa's sewing machine. But her teacher assigned her one two-part invention after the other, leaving her at the end of the lesson with the command to count!

In a way it was really quite convenient that Bubbeh had had her stroke when she did because Musetta was finding it impossible to keep her attention on Bach and dreaded her music lessons more and more. It even made her seem generous and thoughtful when she suggested that she stop her music lessons for a while. Since Bubbeh's bed was pushed right up against the piano bench, it would be inconsiderate, Musetta suggested, to have to move her bed away while Musetta practiced.

And then, when Bubbeh finally died, no one suggested that they rehire the music teacher. That was fine with Musetta—it meant she could play her music any way she wanted to, and she would never again have to practice scales and chords. Though she knew she would never be a concert pianist, she was attracted to the idea of working in an office with smart and accomplished men. So she had come to Roosevelt High School with Rozzie.

She felt a tug on her hair. She whipped her head around and felt a cool spray of liquid fly against her face. When she raised her hand to wipe away the drop, her fingers became smeared with blue ink. The fat girl behind her giggled and held her hand over her mouth. "Mrs. Vicci," Musetta called out. "Tillie just dipped my hair in her inkwell."

"We mustn't, mustn't, mustn't do things like that, Tillie. We know better. Musetta, you may be excused to wash your hands and face."

Musetta stood and carried her notepad to the front of the room. In clear view of Mrs. Vicci and the entire class she calmly ripped it in half and dropped it in the garbage can. "I won't be back," she announced. "I'll never come back here."

As she walked quickly down the hall, she heard footsteps hurrying after her. Rozzie cried, "How can you just leave? Think about it, Musetta! You'll be sorry."

"I won't be sorry. I can't stand it here another minute."

"Just because of Tillie?"

"Because of everyone," Musetta said fiercely.

"But what will you do?"

"I know exactly what I'll do. I'm going to Bird's Business College."

"But that's expensive!" Rozzie said.

"I'll borrow money from Shmuel or from Ava and Len. They say you can progress there at your own speed, so I won't have to stay very long. And then—when I'm the world's most efficient secretary, I can get any job in the city."

"Would you really do it?" Rozzie said.

"Would I?" Musetta said. "I'm going there right now, this very minute, to register."

FORTY-TWO

November 28, 1923

Secret Heart

Mama is so insensitive! Yesterday I told her I badly need new shoes and a dress, and she said, "What for? You never go anywhere!" Musetta says she is of peasant stock, and we can't expect her to have a delicate heart and soul. But can't Mama see that is exactly the point? It's true I never go anywhere— How could I with this face? But I need some new clothes to cheer me up. Mama has flawless skin anyway (like Musetta!) and has no sympathy for my pimples, which she tells me to ignore. Ignore! Can one ignore a snake that sits on one's head? Dr. Schwartz says my trouble is a normal inflammation of the glands of the skin, common in adolescents, but he cannot explain the nausea that makes it impossible for me to go out in the street. How can I tell him that the nausea comes only after I look in the mirror and consider how my face looks to others?

At the party last night, in honor of Thanksgiving and of Musetta's sixteenth birthday, it was all I could do to appear at the dinner table. I was sure the guests would lose their appetites at the sight of my blistered, oozing skin.

As usual, Musetta threw a fit about some silly matter. Aunt Rose and Uncle Hymie brought her a wonderful set of perfume and bath powder, and she immediately opened it and primped and posed and looked glamorous, patting the powder puff to her beautiful smooth skin. She loves to be the center of attention and is happy only when all eyes are on her! But the trouble started when Shmuel gave her his present—a chocolate turkey (because Musetta loves chocolate and because it was Thanksgiving). But he also had a chocolate turkey for me, not even smaller than Musetta's, but identical to hers.

Well, the famous pout appeared and that cold angry look she gets in her eyes and that sour expression about her lips! "But it isn't Gilda's birthday!" she protested. That smallness always gives her away, that jealousy! She hasn't one generous, giving bone in her body. She could be someone I would admire so much if only she didn't have to prove that she deserves more than anyone, all the time. Of course, Shmuel, sweet good man that he is, said at once, "Ah, but it is Thanksgiving for her as well as for you! Your birthday present I will bring home tomorrow night —and it will be something special for you alone." Musetta was appeased, but only for the moment. She is so sensitive to being ignored or—worse—to being unpraised. She thinks home is like school, where she must be at the head of the class, where she ought to get an "A" for setting the table, an "A" for helping Mama to knead the dough for the *chalah.*

Last week when I brought my sewing book home with a silk flower pinned to it by Miss Richmond because I had made such wonderful samples of the hardest stitches, Musetta glanced at it and said, "Sewing! Anyone can push a needle in and out, Gilda! Why don't you read more and improve your mind?"

I am not such a dummy as she thinks. I do read, poetry and romantic stories—and I love the moving pictures. She can't see that anything anyone else does is of any value. Tomorrow I am going to stay with Ava's darling boy Richard while she and Len look for a house in Brooklyn. Papa wants to move there very soon, but Mama says we must wait till Zayde dies. He is so frail now, without Bubbeh, that he is like a ghost. He hardly eats, and Mama says he could never withstand the move. Also, she is thinking that there would not be room in a new house for him unless they squeezed him in with someone, probably me. Mama is tired of being inconvenienced. She doesn't want to have to think about him when we move. She is right in saying that she does all the work and Papa gets all the credit for taking in the old man. Zayde used to play with me, but he is much too weak now, his cheeks are like puckered apples. I don't think he wants to live very much longer.

Well—here's to Brooklyn and the flowers and the sweet air of the country. Here's to health and babies! Maybe someday it will be my good fortune to have a beautiful baby like Ava's. And a loving husband as well. But it can happen only if my face clears, if the boils go away, and if I am not disgusting to look at. All the lace blouses and all the flowers in the world can't hide this face. God help me.

FORTY-THREE

"You will not get Shmuel mixed up with those boys!" Ava said to Len as they stood in the pool hall. Len had just closed up for the night, and they stood in the greenish glow of the still-lit neon sign.

"I'm doing him a favor," Len said. "They have work for him to do, and he needs work. Since he got out of the army, he's been a lost soul. They pay him nothing at that factory, making fireproof doors."

"It's better than his getting in trouble!"

"What trouble?" he said, coming around the counter to where Ava stood, holding Richard in her arms. "And why did you come here at this hour of the night, anyway? Dragging our little boy out in the cold for what? To have a fight with me?"

"Shmuel just stopped by to tell me he's going to work for some of your 'boys.' He wouldn't tell me what he would be doing; he said he didn't really know, but that it would pay him good money."

"So isn't that good?" Len said calmly. "You want him to make bad money?"

"From gangsters it has to be bad money."

"Ava, Ava, darling. Would I ever do anything to hurt your brother Shmuel you love so much?"

Len leaned toward her and kissed her cheek, then kissed Richard's. The boy threw his arms around his father's neck and cried, "Get me ice cream, Daddy."

"Take him," Ava said, letting the boy slide into Len's arms. "He's too heavy for me, already." She smoothed back her hair. In the mirror above the bar she saw her wide face, her round shoulders, her large soft breasts. She saw that she looked much older than her twenty-seven years.

"I'm tired of arguing, Len," she said. "You promised me you'd give up this place when we were married, and look—I'm still waiting."

"The time is just around the corner," Len said. "The minute we find the right house in Brooklyn, I'll sell this place in a flash."

"And then?"

"And then—there are other ways to make a living. Don't worry. Have I ever not given you money for food and rent?"

"No—never," Ava agreed. "Only I want you to make clean money. Not all this dangerous money, bookie money, betting money."

"Am I not careful?" Len said, kissing Ava's cheek again. She shrugged him off. His heavy beard was bristly by this time of day, and she hated when his whiskers scratched her face. Richard was playing with a pool cue; he could hardly see over the edge of the pool table. Standing on tiptoe, he tried to hit a red ball on the green felt.

"See?" Ava whispered. "You want him to grow up here? You want him to hang out in pool halls?"

"My son . . . " Len said, "he will be a doctor. He will own a diamond mine!" He kissed the boy with a hard smacking noise on his soft cheek.

"Don't scrape his cheek like you do mine," Ava said. "Be careful, will you?"

Richard, with a face sweet as an angel, smiled up at his mother and father. He had soft brown curls that fell over his forehead and delicate pink cheeks. His lips were like rosebuds. Whenever Ava looked at him, a passionate weakness would sweep her body so that she would sometimes gasp aloud.

She felt, in some way, as if she still contained him, as if he still grew within her, moving and swimming in her dark silent places while her heartbeat was the music in his ears.

Sometimes, late in the afternoons when he was tired, he would still climb into her lap and nestle there, his head against her breast, and fall asleep. She would sit there in the dusk, feeling the pressure of his sweet head against her and imagine that he was a tiny baby, that she could unbutton her blouse and direct his round little mouth to her breast.

In her reverie a sweet sharp feeling would fill her, and she would rest there, content, aware that Len would soon be home, that she should be making his dinner, but not moving, not stirring till Richard woke himself, rubbed his eyes, and asked to be fed.

Late at night, when Len was already in bed, she would often sit beside the crib and hold the sleeping child's hand. The sound of his even breathing soothed her. She did not want to go to her bed and listen to Len snoring or feel his hairy legs entangle with hers.

"Shmuel will be glad to have this chance," Len said, coming back to the subject. "It's a struggle for him to earn a dollar—and it's time he had enough income to look for a wife already."

"In jail you can't find a wife," Ava said, "—and I'll tell you something, Len. He was always willing to take a chance. In the orphanage he did illegal things to get money for Mama. He has a wild streak."

"What is this with illegal?" Len said. "Did I ever suggest to you my business was not legal?"

Ava banged her closed fist against the wooden side of the pool table.

"Be nice, Mommy," Richard said, wrapping his arms around her knees. "Smile, okay?"

"Ava, darling," Len assured her. "We'll be in Brooklyn by next summer. We'll help your mama and papa find a house nearby. We'll have a swing in the garden for this precious boy of ours; we'll have a rocking horse in the backyard."

" . . . and a big airplane!" Richard added. "Zoom, zoom."

"Well, why not?" Len said. "Instead of a sandbox, I'll buy you an airplane."

"Oh my," Ava said, "my big boy, wanting to fly an airplane."

She looked up at Len, and her feelings softened. Len had given this child to her. "He's getting so grown up," Ava whispered. "I loved it when he was little."

"So—" Len said, "we'll get you a brand new baby. Yes? Tell me yes, Ava, my beautiful girl."

Ava smiled shyly. "We'll see," she said, feeling her heart pound in a sudden rush of pleasure. "We'll talk about it later."

PART TWO

Brooklyn, 1925–1945

1925

FORTY-FOUR

June 10, 1925

Secret Heart

Lilacs! Lilies of the valley! Roses and violets! Trees and birds and fruit trees and a grassy backyard. I never knew Brooklyn would be like heaven! I am sitting here at the back window, writing on my desk, and I can smell the perfume of the flowers rising up from the garden. It is my fifteenth birthday today; Mama is making *kreplach* for dinner—my very favorite dish—and later we are going to visit Ava in her new house, just Mama and Musetta and me, since Papa never wants to see Ava.

Ava is pregnant again! She is so happy; she walks around singing and patting her belly. Richard is so big now—he says he wants a little sister. Ava wants another boy—she has told me so in confidence. She says that boys have an easier life than girls; I don't agree. I like being a girl because it means someday a man will take care of me and make a home for me and be in charge of everything so that I don't have to worry.

I have hopes that life is going to get happier now—in this new place, in this beautiful house. The house cost a great fortune: $9,999! Papa put all his savings into the down payment, but he says the house will be ours in thirty-five years!

In thirty-five years I will be a woman of fifty! Perhaps even a grand-mother! I can't imagine it. Will I still be so skinny? And will my face still break out whenever I am upset or nervous about something? Perhaps I will meet my handsome prince right on Avenue O, in front of the house. There are young men everywhere—I see them walking to the Culver Line and riding their bicycles down the street. Someday I am sure I will meet one of them, especially if I sit outside on the bench in front of the house and read or embroider. Sooner or later someone is bound to stop and talk to me. Musetta says I am a fool, thinking some man will find me while I am putting out the garbage. She says that if I want to do anything in this life I have to go after it, not just sit mooning around. What I don't understand is why she never "moons around"—as she calls it. She never sits quietly in the backyard unless she's decided to get a suntan, and then she does it with a vengeance, turning her face upward tensely as if she dares a cloud to cross the sun and defeat her purpose. There isn't a bone in her that ever relaxes or seems to enjoy or appreciate anything for its own sake.

We are sharing a bed in the new house, a big double bed that Uncle Hymie got secondhand, very cheap.

I know Musetta hates sleeping with me—she cringes if our arms brush under the covers or if I accidentally move my leg too far and graze her calf. We had hoped that in the new house each of us would have a room of her own, but after much discussion, Mama and Papa decided that we would have to take in a boarder in the third bedroom in order to help pay the high mortgage payments. (The interest is 4 percent, which Papa says is very high!) They have not found the right roomer yet. He has to be clean and reliable and have a good job, Mama says, and such a man isn't easy to find in a hurry. So, although the room is still empty, Musetta and I have to share a bed now.

Shmuel doesn't get a room at all; Papa thinks he should not even live here. He is old enough, certainly, to be out on his own, and he spends time with people Papa doesn't like, men who are friends of Len's. He keeps odd hours and is very secretive about what he does, though he is generous about giving Mama lots of money. So—he is living in the basement! Down there, with the furnace and the washtubs and the motor that runs the refrigerator in the kitchen. He is so agreeable, he doesn't seem to mind, and since there is a basement door, he can come and go in privacy and not disturb the rest of the family.

Mama is very unhappy about the women he sees, who are *shiksas*. Papa says, "What else would you expect from him?" (which makes Mama very unhappy). Papa likes everyone to behave the way he thinks is "right"—and is very bitter toward those who don't fit his ideals. However, Papa generally seems to think I act "right"; he tells me I am his favorite girl. He hates me to tire myself or do anything dangerous. He is afraid I will be kidnapped if, when I am at the movies at the Claridge on Avenue P with Mama, I go to the bathroom alone without her. It's very safe at the theater—I love to go to see love stories. Papa never goes to the movies—he hates entertainment of any kind, except for the opera, and now that Caruso is dead, he never goes anywhere. Papa keeps saying that Caruso died at forty-eight, and he thinks that he will die at that age, too. He is always having stomach pains and heart flutters and sore throats. He looks much older than a man of forty-four should look—he even looks older than Mama, and she is fifty-four, ten years older than Papa!

I could go on writing here forever. It's so much pleasanter to write and dream than to do ordinary things in the world. Right now I have all kinds of work waiting for me: my undies to rinse out, and cookies to bake, and the bib I am embroidering for Ava's new baby. In the fall I will be going to Madison High School, and I want to shop for some new clothes.

If only I were as beautiful as Musetta! I do admire her! I simply can't understand where she gets the courage and energy to go charging into the world. She is trying to get a job. She graduated from Bird's Business College last year with the highest grades of anyone! She graduated in only three months, a record, but Mama would not let her get a job till we were all moved and settled in Brooklyn. Now she goes into the city every morning, dressed like a fashion model, and answers ads for secretaries.

I could love her so much if only she were not so critical of me and the things I like to do. She hates it when I sew or knit, saying that I am just wasting my time when machines can do all that faster and better than I can. If she finds me cutting poems from magazines and pasting them in my scrapbook, she sneers, saying I am playing with paper dolls in a dream world. What, I wonder, does she dream about? She's vain enough, that is certain. I see her standing before the window with her hand mirror examining her flawless skin for faults (which she never finds!). Her hair is a tumble of burnished gold, while mine is stiff and dull brown, without any sheen. Even Papa has urged her to relax a little, not to drive herself so hard, but no; she has to be the best, she can stop only when she is convinced that no one has gotten ahead of her.

Well—enough about Musetta. It's time to go downstairs now to have Mama's *kreplach*—and then on to Ava's, where I can play with Richard and kid around with Len. Len is really prospering these days—he wears a diamond tie pin and smokes the best cigars. He loves Ava so much—and the fatter she gets, the more he loves her. Her hips are like wide pillows these days. And Len slaps her on the backside whenever she passes him by.

Musetta, of course, thinks Len is vulgar and animal-like, but I think of him as a man rich in lusty appetites and good humor. (Of course, his friends are not the "upper crust"—but he never brings them home, so that's a good thing.)

I can see lots of little peaches on the peach tree from my window! Just the view alone is magnificent, after those ugly tenement buildings. I know we will be happy here in Brooklyn and that life will get better and better!

FORTY-FIVE

Musetta caught a glimpse of herself reflected in the window of the elevated train. Her hat was perfect for the heart-shaped curve of her face. The material was soft gray felt, accented by a touch of color from the egret feathers.

Arranging her face into a pleasant expression, she crossed and uncrossed her legs, aware of the light shining on the roundness of her calves, aware of the sheen of her silk stockings. She pursed her lips into a pretty round "O," admiring the hollows that formed in her cheeks, wondering if that gaunt look gave her a dramatic or an ethereal appearance.

This morning she was to have an interview at the Stenographic and Translation Bureau in Manhattan. As a star graduate of the Bird Business College, she was given a recommendation for several jobs she wished to investigate. So far she had turned down three—one in the grim, bare office of a coal company, another in the clothing district keeping the books for a fat Jewish businessman, and the third as a secretary for a diamond importer in the jewelry district. In each place she could see at a glance that these jobs were not for her.

She wanted to meet important people. She wanted the admiration of successful and wealthy men. She had no regrets about dropping out of high school. If anything, her education would continue at a faster pace, focusing on more important subjects. Poor Rozzie—she was still struggling along at

Roosevelt and was engaged to marry Milton Goldberg, a boy with buckteeth and large round eyeglasses. She would probably never see Rozzie again— Brooklyn was continents removed from Rozzie's life in the city. Besides, how could she further her own ends by seeing Rozzie? It wasn't likely.

The train rocked and shook as it clattered through the dark murky underground. The lights flashed and dimmed. Musetta wished she had had less breakfast. The food Mama cooked for her lay heavy in her stomach—the grainy taste of cornmeal and sour cream. She gagged now, remembering how hard it had been to swallow. She was never hungry—mealtimes seemed an ordeal. Mama was always pushing food on her: have another peach, have a slice of honey cake, eat, eat. When Bubbeh and Zayde had been alive, eating was their only activity. Slurping tea, dipping *mandelbrot* in it so that the crumbs floated out in a greasy circle on the surface of the amber fluid: Musetta shuddered. Ugh—she caught a reflection of her ugly expression in the window of the train and quickly replaced it with a pleasant smile. A man across the aisle was watching her. She lowered her eyelids and fluttered them gracefully.

But her mind came back to old people and their smells, their belches, their fingernails and toenails like claws. How odd that Gilda had been able to tolerate them—how kindly she had behaved when she trimmed Zayde's beard for him and cut his thick curved toenails! Was her sweetness an act? Musetta could not believe it was sincere; surely she got something out of it, extra gifts or sweets or something. Gilda was sugar coated, always pretending to care about people, always pretending she wanted to help them out of the goodness of her soul!

Between Mama's pushing food on her and Gilda's constant concern ("Aren't you getting too much sun on your face, Musetta? Don't you think you ought to come in?") she felt suffocated in that house. Papa was nearly invisible these days—he was either off at work in the city or pumping away on his sewing machine or groaning in bed about his stomach or his sore throats.

The whole environment at home was a constant irritation. She still kept in her mind the image of Miss McGinley, her first grade teacher: elegant, well mannered, perfectly dressed, not a hair out of place. Soon Musetta would get a job and remove herself from her origins. She would go as far as she could go—and someday no one would ever know that she was a child of Rachel and Isaac Sauerbach of the old country.

FORTY-SIX

"Good Yontiv, Good Yontiv! Come in quickly, out of the rain!" Ava greeted Mama at the door of her new house and hugged her. "I'm so glad you all came." Isaac walked slowly behind Mama, head down, his face unshaven. "You, too," Ava said, "I'm glad you are here." Isaac nodded, but kept his eyes down. Behind him came Gilda, who hugged Ava tightly.

"Be careful you don't hurt the baby," Mama cautioned.

"Don't worry," Ava said, thumping lightly on the drum of her swollen belly. "It's safe in there. Hurry, Musetta, you'll be soaked."

Musetta came up the walk, holding her face up to the dark sky. "I love the fresh smell," she said. "After the shul and everyone's sour breath, this is a relief. I can't understand why you're not allowed to brush your teeth on Yom Kippur. Jews are so worried about hygiene and germs; the least they could do is let the people who fast brush their teeth!"

"Don't argue with me," Ava said with a smile. "Go find the rabbi and argue with him."

"I've had enough of rabbis today to last me all my life," Musetta said sullenly. "Mama and Papa made me go to the Avenue N shul. Because we're new in the neighborhood, she said it wouldn't be right for the whole family not to go on such a holy day." Musetta made a face. "All that droning and moaning, I can't stand it."

"Dovening," Gilda corrected her. "I love how it feels in the shul on Yom Kippur. It's so solemn and so . . . holy. The sound when they blow the shofar shakes me down to my toes."

"Blowing into a ram's horn seems so primitive," Musetta said. "Why don't they just blow a trumpet or something?"

"Come and eat," Ava said. "I have nice food ready—pickled herring and lox and cream cheese and noodle pudding, nothing heavy to upset your stomach." She addressed the last comment to Isaac, who nodded slightly, still not looking at her. Ava could not call him by his name, Isaac, and she would rather have bitten off her tongue than call him Papa. She had said to Len earlier in the day, "It's a miracle that he's coming here," and Len had said, "It's a miracle that you asked him."

"Well," Ava replied, "He's getting older, he's not well. And Mama is so sad that he doesn't come over to see Richard. And with a new baby coming, we might as well be civil to one another. Grandparents are good for babies to have."

Now, as Len came down the hall, he said heartily, "Good Yontiv! We're happy to have you all here in our new house, to break fast with us."

"Where's little Richkala?" Mama asked. "For him, only for him would I come out in such rain."

"He's napping, Mama," Ava said. "He'll be up soon. Come in, come and sit down at the table. You must be ready to faint with hunger."

"I'm ready to faint," Gilda said. "I'm desperate."

"Not me," Musetta said. "I didn't fast. It's so ridiculous not to eat. Look at Papa, with his terrible headache. He's dizzy. He didn't eat all day to atone for his sins! What sins? Atone to whom?"

"Sha," Mama said to Musetta. "I told you, don't carry on like that. Not today. Today we have to be respectful. Today is the most important holy day we have. It's the start of a new year for all of us."

They followed Ava into the dining room, where the food was laid out on a white linen tablecloth.

"Such exquisite silverware," Gilda cried. "Oh, Ava—when did you get it?"

Ava smiled. "Len bought it for me on our anniversary."

"It must have cost a million dollars," Gilda breathed.

"Not quite," Ava said. "We don't have a million dollars."

"Yes—" Len said, "we do, indeed. At least I do!" He came and put his arm around Ava. "This is my million dollars. This woman!"

Ava shrugged him off in embarrassment. "You sit here, Mama. And you," she said to Isaac, "you sit here. And Musetta is here, and Gilda is here . . . and . . . " Suddenly Ava cried, "But where is Shmuel? He was to come, too! He promised he would come!"

Mama and Papa looked at one another. Gilda frowned, and Musetta scowled. "You should have heard the fight that went on this morning," Musetta said finally. "Papa said if Shmuel was going to behave that way, he didn't deserve to live even in the cellar!"

"Behave what way?"

"He went fishing!" Gilda cried.

"Fishing?" Ava said in astonishment. "Today? In this weather?" She spun around to look at Len, to see if he might know anything of this, but he was busy reaching for a black olive, and his eyes did not meet hers.

"I don't know what's going on in his head," Mama said. "To go out in such a storm, on such a day, fishing! His friends needed him, he said. They had fish to catch, today it was important to catch fish. I don't know."

"Sit, sit," Len advised. "Let's eat." He sat down himself and passed a plate of whitefish around to Isaac.

Mama went on, "And he can hardly swim. Once we took him to Coney Island, and what did he do? He ran so fast that the waves shouldn't touch his toes! Never once, when he was growing up, did he like the beach. Or the water. But tonight, on Yom Kippur, fishing!" She shook her head.

Ave passed behind Len's chair and, pretending to bend over him to get a plate of rye bread, whispered, "Do you know anything about this?" Len let his mouth and eyes fly open. Me? he seemed to say. What would I know?

A blast of thunder shook the house. Ava shivered.

"So let's all eat," Mama said. "What's the sense of this talk? We'll eat, and then Ava and Len can show off their beautiful new house."

FORTY-SEVEN

"Please, Mama—try not to cry on the train, people are looking at you. Here, blow your nose on my handkerchief," Musetta said. "You can't cry every minute, you have to try to accept what happened. We all have to go on living."

"What did I do . . . ?" Mama sobbed, "that God should do this to me? Didn't I suffer enough in my life? Didn't I leave my family when I was a young girl? Didn't I have to give up my son to an orphanage? And didn't Shmuel suffer enough, living like that in such a place? Why should God want to punish him?"

"It isn't punishment, Mama. You sound like Papa when you say that. There was a terrible storm on Yom Kippur night. Shmuel's boat sank. It disappeared. They think everyone drowned—all the men Shmuel went with, not just Shmuel. It isn't punishment. It's nature."

"Papa says it's punishment. His eyes are still dry. He didn't shed a tear. To him it's clear as day—punishment. God took revenge on Shmuel for going fishing on Yom Kippur." Mama began to cry again, her shoulders shaking. Musetta put her arm around her and rocked her, whispered to her, tried to avoid the stares of the other passengers on the Culver Line.

The past few days had been a miserable blur—since the breaking of the fast at Ava's after sundown on Yom Kippur. The evening had gone well—they had eaten good food and had fun with Richard, and Musetta had played a Chopin waltz on Ava's shiny new piano. Even Papa had relaxed a little and let himself be taken on a tour of Ava and Len's beautiful new house. He still would not call Ava by her name or even look her in the eye, but he was willing to hold Richard on his knee and even hum a little song from the old country to him. Even if he didn't like Len, he couldn't help but be impressed by Len's ability to make money.

Only Ava had seemed uneasy; she was nervous and kept questioning why Shmuel had not come. After dinner, when Musetta had walked into the kitchen to bring in some dirty dishes, she heard Len and Ava arguing.

"Do you have any idea why my brother would have gone fishing in such terrible weather? He wasn't an idiot, you know."

Len shrugged his big bearish shoulders and said, "Am I a mind reader, Ava? What do I know what weather is good for fishing? A sportsman I am not. I always thought whitefish grew on ice in the fish market. And lox came on a bagel. To catch a fish must be slippery business—don't bother me about it, Ava. Your brother didn't come, so he didn't come. He's a young man, he has other things to do besides sit with relatives. Don't be insulted. So he missed your noodle pudding. Don't *shrie* about it."

"Shmuel would never disappoint me," Ava had said. "Not if he could help it." Then she had noticed Musetta in the doorway and said quickly, "Coffee and strudel for dessert. Come, Musetta, you can help me set it out."

Then, long after they had gotten home and gone to bed, there was a pounding on the door downstairs. At first Musetta had thought it was thunder, but it went on and on in a rhythmical way. Gilda had sat up in bed. "Do you hear that?" she said to Musetta. Then they saw Mama in the hallway, in her robe, going downstairs.

Musetta had jumped out of bed and followed Mama down. "Who is it?" Mama yelled through the closed front door. "Who is it?"

"Open it, open the door!" came Len's voice. He stood there on the brick stoop, his hair flattened with rain, water streaming down over his face.

"Sit down, Mama," he said. "I have bad news."

"Oh no, oh no, my Shmuel," Mama cried. "Not my Shmuel."

"The fishing boat disappeared," Len said. "The police came just now to my house. The Coast Guard heard an SOS, but they couldn't find the boat. They believe it sank, and everyone on it was drowned."

"God is punishing us all!" Mama screamed and fell onto the floor, pounding it with her fists.

"Sit quietly, Rachel," Papa said, coming down the staircase, his eyes hard and cold. "I told you what would be."

"You told me! You told me! What are you? God?" Rachel cried to Isaac.

"I can't stay here long," Len said. "Ava is collapsed on the bed. She's hysterical. Look—" he said to Musetta. "You're the sensible one around here. Do what you can for Mama."

"At least he's at peace," Gilda murmured.

"What peace?" Musetta asked furiously. "To be dead is not to be at peace. It's just to be dead. It's nothing."

"I've got to go," Len said. "In the morning I'll come back with Ava. I have to go right back to her now."

"My son, my precious son," Mama moaned.

Mama had cried all night and all the next day and all the next week. Now Musetta helped Mama off the train. "You have to be calm here, Mama. This isn't going to be easy."

"Then let's go home. I don't have the strength to do this. What if I see his face there?"

"It has to be done. If you can identify his body, you will get the money sooner."

"What do I care about money?"

"Shmuel bought the life insurance to protect you, Mama. He didn't know this would happen, but now that it has, he would want you to collect. It's five thousand dollars—a huge amount. It will help pay off the house."

"It will kill me if I see him," Mama said. "This my heart could not stand."

"But if we don't see his body at the morgue, then you will have to wait seven years to collect the money. If his body is here, and we can tell them it's him, then you get the money now."

A fresh flood of tears burst from Mama's eyes. "His beautiful curly hair—I can't believe this!"

"Come, walk faster," Musetta said. "The morgue is in that tall building there, at the end of the street." As she opened the heavy door to let Mama pass through, something closed in her throat. There was a strange smell here, an unnatural odor, and a chill in the air.

Musetta explained their errand to a woman at a desk; she and Mama were directed through long halls and many doors. They came to the door marked "Morgue."

"He is a drowning, am I correct?" a woman at another desk asked Mama. She had just put down a phone and seemed to be waiting for them. Mama nodded and leaned on the desk.

"Some of their faces are hard to recognize," the woman said kindly. "Water blows them up, and then there's fish—they eat at the flesh. I'm sorry, but I want you to be prepared."

"How . . . many drowned boys are there?" Mama said weakly.

"We have four unidentified drownings brought in yesterday afternoon. Will you come this way?"

Musetta and Mama clutched one another's hands. The room was dim, very cold. There was the sound of running water. Long green marble tables stood in rows. Most of them were empty, but at the end of the room four tables had bodies on them.

"Oh my God," Mama sobbed. "I can't look, Musetta. I don't care about the money."

"Mama, it's not only for that. It's so we can claim his body, bury him. So we have a place to go to visit him."

"You do it, please, Musetta. Spare me this. I can't look on the faces of these men."

Musetta glanced at the woman, who was waiting patiently for them to move along. The woman nodded at her. Musetta detached her hand from her mother's and moved toward the bodies. One by one, the woman lifted a sheet from the face of each man. What Musetta saw laid out on the tables were horrible frozen statues. Their flesh was gray, and they had paper labels strung on their toes. None of them was her brother, Shmuel.

"He's not here, Mama."

"Oh thank God, thank God. Maybe he is alive yet. Maybe he swam to another boat. Maybe he is still floating to a beach, and he'll come home soon."

Musetta and the woman exchanged glances.

"When shall we come back?" Musetta asked.

"Leave me your number," the woman said. "When we have other drownings, if a body seems to be a possible match, I'll call you."

"DEWEY 9-3852," Musetta said. "We live in Brooklyn. We just got a telephone."

"You'd better take your mother home," the woman said. "She's suffered a terrible shock, just being here. She needs to rest."

FORTY-EIGHT

"Don't touch me, Len," Ava said into the darkness of the room as she felt Len reach for her under the blankets. "I don't want to be touched."

"It's not bad for the baby, you told me so yourself."

"I can't. I'm too nervous. I'm sick to my heart. What do you think?"

"I don't think anything. Try not to go over and over it. We have to go on with life. With this new baby." He patted her belly and let his hand lay on the curve that lifted her nightgown high above her thighs.

"I sometimes wish I were not bringing new life into the world," Ava said. "Life is too hard."

"For our children it won't be hard," Len whispered to her, leaning close so that his hair scraped the side of her face. "Haven't I given our little Richy everything already? Doesn't he have a make-believe airplane in the backyard that all the kids from around here come running to see? Doesn't he have a silver bowl to eat his cereal out of? A piano—soon he can have lessons. What don't I give my boy?"

"It has nothing to do with you or what you can buy, Len. It has to do with what life takes away. Look at me—first my papa disappears, and I'm still waiting for him. Now my brother is also gone. They both could be alive, or they both could be dead. How can I live this way much longer . . . looking in crowds for my papa, for Shmuel? I think maybe Shmuel got hit on the head with a log in the ocean and washed up somewhere on shore, and then he forgot his name. So now he could be walking around the city, and I'll see him, and I imagine I'll take him home and take care of him."

"You sound like your mama," Len said with annoyance. "He's dead. The Coast Guard said their boat went down."

"How could they know for sure?" Ava asked. "Were they there?"

"They were there! They were there!" Len said. "You're not going to bump into your brother, Ava. So stop making stories in your head. Try to live here, with me, now."

"Why did he go fishing that night, Len?" Ava asked, feeling her voice turn icy. "I know he went with your buddies, the boys from the pool hall. Don't tell me you don't know about it, Len. I know you know about it. So this is the time to tell me. I have to know the truth. There was a terrible storm that day—no one in his right mind would go fishing. Something else has to be involved, something else was happening."

"You don't want to know about it, Ava. Better to think that he was fishing."

"I knew it!" Ava suddenly took a piece of Len's flesh on his upper arm and pinched it hard between her fingers. "Tell me!" she said. "Or you will never sleep in this bed with me again."

"You'll be sorry if I tell you. But don't hurt me like that. Your nails are sharp as ice picks."

"So I'll be sorry. But I'll have the truth."

"Well—there was an operation going on among the boys," Len told her reluctantly. "Shmuel wasn't involved in that particular operation. Four of the other boys were—they were rum running."

"What do you mean?"

"Well, it's complicated. You know about Prohibition. Once a week this boat came in from Canada—it anchored a few miles out, off Coney Island. The boys had a boat—they had an outboard motor, a big one. They went out there and picked up the liquor. It was very good money, Ava—very good."

"What did you have to do with it?"

"Me? Not much. I let them meet in my place, I lent them a little money for the boat, that's all. I got a small cut, very small."

"What has this got to do with Shmuel?"

"Well—on Yom Kippur they were short a man. One of the boys couldn't get away from home. His parents would have thrown him out if he'd gone away on that day. So he asked your brother to sit in for him. They needed at least four men to carry the boxes, to make the transfer from the big boat to the little one. Shmuel had done a few other things with them, nothing big, nothing dangerous, but they knew they could count on him. He was decent, he was reliable. And they knew he needed money to help pay for the house, to help your mama."

"So what happened, Len?"

"The Coast Guard spotted them, Ava. They knew what they were out there for, and they shot them down. They shot the boat full of holes, and the boat sank. They weren't fishing, Ava. You are right. Only a crazy man would go fishing on such a night."

"Oh my God," Ava said. "So you are the cause of it. You are the cause of my brother's death." She took her nails and dug them into Len's arm. "How could you do this to me!" she screamed. "Don't you know how much I loved him? Now I have no one left! No one!"

"He had the choice not to do it, Ava. You have to blame him, not me. A man does what he wants to do."

"You make me sick," Ava hissed. "Get out of this bed. Go sleep on the couch downstairs. If I tell Mama your part in this, it will kill her."

"Don't be a fool, Ava. What's the point of telling your mother, is there any point? Or Musetta? Or Gilda? It will just make Isaac more smug—don't you see? He already has no use for you or your brother. If you admit your brother was doing crooked things, he'll make your mother crazy, day and night, about it."

"Crooked things? My brother? What about you, Len? You!"

"You think Isaac is a fool? You think he doesn't wonder how we make our money?"

"I hate Isaac," Ava sobbed. "I wish I could see some good in him, but I can't. I hate him! Oh God—where is my papa? Oh, if I could only see him again."

FORTY-NINE

December 25, 1925

Secret Heart

It is snowing outside. The yard is soft with powdery snow, and I think of the snow falling over the land and over the sea, where my dear Shmuel rests. I have strange thoughts; I think of him floating in the midst of a glassy gray ocean, his hands crossed over his breast, looking up gratefully at the snow as it sifts down and lands gently on his face. He is so peaceful. His eyes are the same blue as Mama's eyes, but they are perfectly calm.

Mama is not calm. She does not eat or sleep. She bakes bread and mixes her tears in the dough. She spits out the sugar cube she sucks with her tea, asking why it should be bitter. When she singes the feathers from the chicken's skin, she burns her fingers on the stove. The other day she gave Papa sour cream to put on his flanken instead of horseradish. She actually dropped a spoonful of it right on his meat. He jumped up shouting, "Are you crazy, Rachel? Milk with meat? Have you lost your mind?" He ran to the garbage and threw in everything, his meat, his plate, his fork, his knife. He was beside himself. He went immediately to his room and put on his tallis and began dovening. He frightens me when he acts like that—as if he thinks God will strike him dead for a sin he committed.

If he knew that I wrote the word *God* in my diary this way, and not "G-D," he would be furious. He never speaks gently to Mama now, when she most needs it. He has decided to buy a Ping-Pong table and put it in the basement where Shmuel used to sleep. He has called the I-Cash-Clothes man to come in and take away Shmuel's clothes and shoes. Mama wanted to keep Shmuel's wool cap, but Papa said there was no sense to keep a hat to cry into.

Musetta is with Mama all the time now. They go into the city to check the morgue every week. They never let me go, saying I am too young to see such things. When they come back, Mama goes right to bed and puts a cold cloth on her head, and Musetta goes to the piano and plays crazy music without a melody. She says it is "modern," but I think it is worse than living under the "El." It makes me feel my heart is about to jump out of my breast.

I wish we could celebrate Christmas. Papa would kill me for thinking this, but I see the goyim pass in the street on their way to the church on Gravesend Avenue. They are all dressed up, in fur coats and fur muffs. They seem so happy and in harmony with one another. At the end of our street lives the Carlucci family—Tom and Joe Carlucci, and Teresa, who is married to Tom. They have no children, but they have a farm in their backyard. Papa says they should have stayed in Italy, but I love to walk by there. Teresa always calls me in and gives me fresh eggs her chickens have laid. Or vegetables from her garden. In the summer she gave me grapes from the vine arbor that grows over the two benches on their front walk.

They have a picture of Jesus over their sink; he looks like such a sweet man, full of tenderness. He has eyes that seem to shine light right into your soul.

Papa has forbidden me to sing Christmas songs in school, and I must never ever say the words "Jesus, my Lord" or "Jesus, my savior." He doesn't even want me to move my lips. He hates angels and shepherds and all the things that go with Christmas.

Ava accidentally slipped and told Mama that Len had bought Richard an aviator's outfit "for Christmas," and Mama nearly fainted. It doesn't mean anything—only that Len buys Richard presents for every possible occasion. The poor child has only one birthday a year—so Len gets him gifts on Thanksgiving and at Passover and at any other time he can call an occasion.

It's so funny to see Richard wear his flying costume—he has a helmet and goggles and a suit like an American ace. He draws pictures of planes all the time and spends hours in the yard, sitting in the contraption Len built for him—it has wooden wings and steps up to the cockpit.

Well, it is getting dim now, and I can hardly see the snow falling. Lights are going on up and down the street, and dinner is probably waiting for me. Dinners are sad affairs these days; no one talks, sometimes Mama just gets up and runs to her room, wiping her eyes on her apron. Musetta is sullen; she got a job with a translation bureau, but she had to quit because she has to be free to take Mama to the morgue and other strange places.

Tomorrow they have a secret errand, which they discuss in whispers, locked in the bathroom. Mostly I hear Musetta trying to persuade Mama to stay home and not go to wherever she wants to go. Apparently it is a secret from Papa, too—because when they come out of the bathroom, they make a great fuss of pretending that they aren't hiding anything. I suppose I could make a fuss and beg to know, but it seems pointless. Nothing they do or plan will bring Shmuel back.

I don't know what death is like. There must be a terrible moment for everyone, for all of us, when we realize we are finally dying. Maybe Shmuel, breathing water into his lungs, had that panic that I imagine. Maybe he thought of us. Maybe he asked God to forgive him that he went fishing on the highest of holy days. Maybe he had no thought except that he didn't want to die.

Musetta says that death isn't peaceful, that it's nothing. But when I think of the snow falling, of Shmuel floating in the water, gently rising and falling on the waves, letting all the forces of the universe carry him along—then I don't feel so bad.

FIFTY

"Let me warn you again, Mama," Musetta said. "You can't take seriously whatever this woman says—she probably just makes it all up."

"Aunt Rose says she's a very good, very powerful fortune-teller. People rave about her."

They had made their weekly trip to the morgue, and now, instead of going right back to Brooklyn, they were looking for an address on the Lower East Side.

"This is our last trip to the city for this purpose, Mama; I can't spend any more time on this wild-goose chase. The lady at the morgue said there's no point coming. After two months there's no way we'd be able to recognize anyone they fish out of the ocean."

"I don't need to go to the morgue anymore," Mama said, "I know he's alive. Why do you think you never recognized him there? Because he didn't drown. He's alive. The gypsy will tell us how to find him."

"I don't think she will, Mama. If you want to throw away five dollars, you can throw it away. But what can a gypsy know?"

"Gypsies know . . . " Mama said. "It's something in their blood. You know what happened to me in the old country, don't you?"

Musetta sighed impatiently. Her breath made a scroll of vapor in the freezing air. The words *old country* stood her teeth on edge. It meant a long story with no relevance at all to whatever was going on in her mind. It meant a rambling reminiscence that bored her and angered her. Couldn't these people from the old country just get used to the new country and live in it, in the present?

She glanced at Mama, and her heart softened just a little. Mama looked weary, older than her years. Her hair was completely white and soft as a baby's. Strands of it hung out from her babushka and flew around her face in the cold wind. Her skin was soft; her blue eyes always looked moist, on the verge of spilling over.

"If your story is about the time you met the gypsy, I already know about it." She knew that Mama would tell her again, anyway.

"Well, I was crossing a field in my village in Poland—a big field. And I saw coming toward me through the tall grasses a gypsy. My mama had warned me to have nothing to do with gypsies—they were thieves, all of them—but this one caught up with me and took my arm. 'How much money do you have?' she asked me. 'I have no money,' I said. 'But I have something important to tell you,' she said. 'Give me your earrings and I will tell you.' I was so afraid—I was afraid not to do what she said. So I gave her my earrings. She was a beautiful woman, wild, dirty looking, with long black hair, a large nose. She put my earrings in her bosom; then she leaned close to me and said, 'You will cross a big water. You will marry a handsome and dangerous man. It will be a bad marriage. He will leave you for another woman. But much later you will meet a dark haired man who will be kind and marry you and save you from misfortune.' Musetta—can you imagine how my heart pounds when I remember this? It all came true! I believe those gypsies really know something. That's why I have to find this woman who can tell me where Shmuel is!"

"It all came true?" Musetta said mockingly. "What are you talking about, Mama? Your first husband died young! And you had to go and work as a midwife! What do you mean—the gypsies know the truth? That wasn't the truth that your first husband left you for another woman."

Mama stopped walking and paused to catch her breath in the icy wind. She leaned on Musetta, gasping for breath.

"No, no," she said finally. "Of course it wasn't all true—you are right, you are right, Nathan died young. But the rest was true," she said, "—crossing the big water."

"Mama—everyone who left Europe 'crossed a big water.'"

"Never mind," Mama said, suddenly looking down. "Let's just walk fast and not talk so much now."

The gypsy lived in a tenement like everyone else in the neighborhood. She held aside a curtain of glass beads to allow Musetta and Rachel to pass through. Musetta was certain she could smell chicken soup cooking somewhere in the apartment. The gypsy said her name was Fantasia.

"Would you take a seat here, please?" she said to Musetta, showing her a worn flowered couch against the wall. "And would you come to the table,

Madam?" she said to Mama. "It is you who has come for a consultation, is it not?"

Mama was busy taking off her coat and putting it over the back of the wooden chair. The gypsy walked about, rattling the necklaces and bracelets she wore, her long gown dusting the floor as she swept around the room adjusting the curtains and the one dim lamp.

"Would you like me to tell your fortune with cards, with tea leaves, by reading your palm, or by my crystal ball?" the woman asked Mama. "They are equally reliable."

Musetta leaned back and saw that there was a *mazzuzah* on the doorway to the next room. Should she point it out to Mama? Should she reveal that this woman was no more a gypsy than Musetta was?

The crystal ball was brought forth. The woman placed her hands upon it, tapping the surface with her long red fingernails. Musetta sighed with boredom. For weeks she had done nothing but take Mama to the morgue or to Coney Island, where they would walk in the freezing wind on the deserted boardwalk, looking for men who might be Shmuel, men without homes wandering about and looking in garbage cans for food—a piece of uneaten Nathan's hot dog or a bag of cold fried potatoes.

If Shmuel had not disappeared, Musetta would have had a good job by now, with good pay, at the translation bureau. They had tested her and found her to be quick and efficient. On the first day she was given an assignment—to take dictation for a judge in his office. His praise for her had been so effusive she had almost blushed with embarrassment.

But then Shmuel had drowned, followed by Mama's endless grieving and her obsession that Shmuel was still alive and would one day walk up the steps at 405 Avenue O, bang the knocker, and be home with them again. The gypsy was now chanting some gibberish. From the back of the apartment Musetta could hear a baby wailing. At least if Mama had been directed to a real gypsy! But Fantasia, stripped of her disguise, was probably like any of the Jewish women Musetta knew.

"You have had a loss in your life," she intoned, and Mama nodded, breathless, sitting on the edge of her chair.

"You are in mourning," the fortune-teller said.

Musetta was tempted to ask, "How did you guess?"—but she held her tongue.

"Yes, I am," Mama said.

"But you have hope this person is still alive. It is a man, am I correct?"

"Yes," breathed Mama. "Yes, yes."

"Could it be your son?"

"Oh yes!" Mama cried out, tears pouring suddenly down her cheeks. "It is my son, my darling boy."

"I see . . . that there is a chance . . . he is still with us. I see an image, an image of curly hair, a handsome face. The man is in a distant place, he is on a mountain . . . he is in a meadow of flowers, high on a mountain."

Oh no, Musetta thought. Now Mama will make me take her to the mountains! We will have to find a meadow on a mountain. I will never be free of this, I will never get a job.

"Mama!" Musetta said loudly. "Do gypsies put *mazzuzahs* on their door posts?"

"What?" Mama said. "Shh, Musetta. Don't speak now."

"Do gypsies have menorahs on their bookcases?" Musetta said, standing up and reaching for a bronze candleholder that was behind a set of books on the shelf.

"Don't touch that!" the gypsy cried out. "Don't handle my decorations."

"What is your real name?" Musetta said. "Mrs. Goldstone? Mama, this is just an ordinary woman. Someone just like us. You don't want to listen to her."

"She says Shmuel is in the mountains!"

"Shmuel is not in the mountains! He is not anywhere, Mama! We have to get used to the fact that Shmuel is not anywhere and that we will never see him again!"

The woman was rushing around now, waving her arms. "Go, please—you have disturbed my special powers. Go—I don't want you here."

"I'm sorry, I'm sorry," Mama said. "I apologize for my daughter. She is crazy with sorrow, like I am."

"He's gone," Musetta said. "Just face it, Mama. If I can face it, you can, too."

1926

FIFTY-ONE

February 17, 1926

Secret Heart

The strangest things are happening here. First—the séance Mama held here Friday night while Papa was in shul, and then yesterday the old man coming to the door while no one was home! My mind doesn't want to think about all these peculiar happenings; I yearn to be left alone to do my schoolwork and embroider handkerchiefs and consider how the snowfall sits in the "Y" of the maple tree in the front yard, how the snow builds up a delicate bridge between the two arms of the tree. When I begin to reflect on the strange things that are going on, my heart begins to pound and skip, and I can feel my fear in my throat. I hate lies and secrets—and Mama taught me always to be honest. Why is it now she tells lies to Papa and rushes off with Musetta to secret meetings? Last Friday was the worst—because she had to hurry Papa out the door to shul even though he didn't feel well and thought he might not want to go in what turned out to be almost a blizzard. But she said it was good for him, that he always felt guilty if he didn't go, that his stomachache would be soothed if he went to pray. So she sent him out, watching him slipping around on the ice, to walk to the Avenue N shul, and no sooner was he out of sight than the medium came, wearing a turban and a fringed shawl over her heavy winter coat.

She smelled of cheap perfume and carried a huge carpetbag. Musetta warned me to keep an eye on Mama's silver teapot and to lock away any-thing of value that could be stolen. The séance took place in the cellar, where Shmuel's spirit would be strongest since he used to sleep there. To me it smelled of camphor and bleach and dampness.

There were only the three of us; the medium said it might not be enough, four would be better, but she would do what she could. She said there would be no visitations in the cellar, that this was only a preliminary exercise to get a feel for Shmuel's attitude. If we wanted a visitation, we would have to come to her house. I felt nauseated when she turned out the lights and took my hand. Hers was cold and clawlike, and I felt I was being buried alive by the snow that was piling up on the sills of the cellar windows. I didn't want Shmuel to come back to us through a woman like her; I would rather he didn't come back at all, but lived, warm and cherished and precious in our memories.

Musetta says we must humor Mama till her grief subsides, that we have to put up with her craziness. Mama has been to see a Christian Scientist practitioner, a Catholic priest, a fortune-teller. And now . . . the medium.

Of course Shmuel didn't come back or sing or whisper or touch anyone. In the darkness, feeling the fierce hand of that woman clutch me, I thought I might die myself and go to join Shmuel.

We had to hurry and be done before Papa came back, so that it didn't take as long as I feared. Mama was trembling as the medium moaned and hummed and made little mouselike noises. Musetta, sitting across the card table from me, had her eyes open the whole time. I could see the glow from the window of the furnace reflected in the whites of her eyes.

I've never been a mother, so I don't know the pain of losing a child, but I believe Mama is in true agony. When Aunt Rose comes to visit, all Mama does is cry and sob. Aunt Rose told me privately that she could carry on this way for a year or more, but that eventually her grief would settle down and the pain would reduce itself.

Mama paid the medium from money she keeps hidden in a box that used to hold tea leaves. I could hardly wait to get upstairs and wash my hands afterward. I heard Papa get in from shul; he was nearly frozen to death, and his stomach pain was worse. He was angry that Mama had pushed him to go. She had no sympathy for him. She has become like a brick wall.

And then . . . yesterday, the visit from the old man!

I was alone in the kitchen baking cookies and my hands were full of flour. Musetta and Mama had gone to the bank on Kings Highway. My heart jumped when I heard the harsh bang of the knocker on the front door. No one ever uses the knocker; it is only for decoration. Everyone uses the door-bell. So I hurried to the front door and looked out through the colored glass panes that are set into the little arched window in the heavy wood. On sunny days the sunlight streams through the glass, making rainbow patterns on the rug. Yesterday, it was cloudy and glum. When I looked out, the man's face was distorted and a sickly blue color.

"Who is it?" I called.

"I am looking for a woman named Chaveleh," he said.

"Oh, she doesn't live here," I said, before I could think. "She lives on Quentin Road."

"Do you know the number?" the old man called through the door.

Suddenly I remembered that Mama had warned me never to give out Len and Ava's address to anyone. The precaution had to do with the gangsters Len knew.

"No, I don't. I don't know her address." Again I found myself lying, as I had had to do on Friday about the medium's visit.

There was a pause. "Do you think you could open the door so we could talk?" the old man finally asked. He seemed harmless and sounded tired. I opened the door and wiped my hands on my apron.

"You are Chaveleh's sister, am I right?" he said. "Don't bother to call your mama to the door; I don't want to trouble her."

"She isn't home."

"Ah—yes," he said. He was wearing a heavy black coat with a velvet col-lar, badly frayed. His eyes were piercing and dark, shaded by heavy eyebrows. His face was old, yet powerful looking and quite handsome. It seemed I might almost recognize him or remember him, though I knew it was an illusion.

"I am just an old family friend," he said awkwardly, "and I want to see Chaveleh."

"Ava—we call her Ava," I said. I was wondering if I ought to ask him in and offer him tea and cookies. It was so cold outside; the wind blew up the steps and flew under my dress.

"You don't know your sister's address?" he asked, not unkindly.

"Well—" I smiled. "Why don't you tell me your name, and I'll call her and say you want to see her. We both have phones now," I said proudly. "You could even talk to her."

"No, no—thank you just the same," he said, beginning to walk backwards down the stairs, one step at a time. "Never mind, sorry to trouble you."

"I'll tell you one thing," I said. "She often takes her little boy to the park on Quentin Road near East Eighth Street. You might find her there one day."

"Thank you, thank you," the old man said. "A blessing on your head." And then he hurried away down the street, his head bent into the wind. When he left, I phoned Ava and told her an old man had been looking for her, an old family friend.

"Did he say his name?" she asked instantly.

"No."

"What did he look like?"

"Don't sound so worried," I said. "I don't think it was that important. He probably had regards from some relatives."

"What relatives! What relatives could he have regards from?"

"I don't know," I said. "Everyone has relatives."

"What did he look like?" she demanded again.

"Well—he was old, and he had a coat with a velvet collar, and he had bushy eyebrows."

"Did you tell him where I am?"

"Of course not. You know I'm not supposed to tell anyone where you and Len live. All I said was that you sometimes take your little boy to the park on Quentin Road."

"Did you say I'd be there today? In this bad weather?"

"I didn't say anything."

"All right, Gilda," Ava said. "Thank you."

"I'm baking cookies, with raspberry centers," I told her. "Would you like me to save you some?" But the phone had already gone dead; she had hung up. How strange everything is these days. Perhaps it's because her baby is due to be born so soon. Everyone seems afraid, somehow, that more bad things will happen. Maybe the baby will be born crippled. Or born dead. Ever since Shmuel drowned, we all feel that anything terrible could happen. Mama could die. Papa could die. I could die. I could die and never write in this diary again. This would be my last word.

FIFTY-TWO

"Hold my hand, Richard."

"I won't run in the street, Mama."

"I'm not worried about that. Hold my hand so I don't slip on the ice."

Richard took Ava's hand and pressed his gloved fingers between her bare ones. She had run out of the house so fast that she had forgotten her gloves.

"Why are we going to the park when the sky is so dark?" Richard asked. "Papa will be angry. He said you must stay home."

"We won't tell your father," Ava said. "I can't stand being cooped up, I need some air. I need some space around me."

"Can I swing as high as I want to?" Richard asked. "I like to feel like I'm flying."

"Not so high you fall off."

"I won't fall. I never fall."

"I don't like you to let go and jump off while the swing is still moving," Ava said. "You could get hurt."

"I don't jump off. I *fly* off. I'm learning how to fly."

"Yes, yes," Ava said. It was hard to walk. The growing baby was like a leaden egg inside her; it pressed on her bladder and bowels, it pressed on the nerves of her legs, sending shooting pains down to her toes.

"I wish humans could fly," Richard said. "Aunt Gilda said that birds have a brain the size of a pea and have no sense at all. I'm much smarter than a bird, so why can't I fly if I want to?"

"Someday you can fly if you want to, in an airplane," Ava said. "Humans are very smart—they invent ways to do what they cannot seem to do at first."

"I once dreamed I was flying," Richard said. "I went up on the roof of our house and I held my hands together over my head—like this, look at me, Mama—pointing up, like you said the goyim do when they pray, and then I just zoomed up, way up between the houses and over the rooftops. Mama—you're not listening."

"I'm listening, Richard. Walk a little faster, though. I want to get to the park to sit down."

They hurried along the slushy street; Ava peered at a figure in the distance that seemed to be coming toward them. She could not tell if it was a man or a woman. Perhaps she was insane to come rushing out in such weather, under such heavy gray clouds, in the freezing wind. Len had warned her not to go to the park at all. "Why do you need to take the boy to a public playground when we have a park fit for a prince right here in our own backyard?" he had said to her. "What does my son need with ordinary swings when here he has a wooden airplane and a hangar and the tree house for his officer's quarters?"

"Children need to see other children, Len," she had said to her husband. "We can't lock him up here. Our backyard isn't the world."

"Soon enough the world will have him," Len said. "Let's keep him as long as we can. That's all I'm asking."

But Ava didn't agree with Len. She felt the boy ought not to be isolated, that he ought to be treated like an ordinary child, not like royalty.

"Don't run!" she called after her son. "I told you—I want to hold your hand. I'm like an elephant—I can't balance so well. I'm such a fat lady, you know."

Richard laughed. Ava could see that the figure in the distance was an old man. He was coming toward them. "Hurry and take my hand," Ava said. "We'll be the only ones in the park." She turned into the gate of the playground and walked carefully over the cobblestones toward a bench while Richard flew away to the swings. Ava's heart was pounding as it had been since Gilda had phoned. The old man who had been looking for her was probably an old neighbor or a friend of Len's family. Who else could it possibly be? She shivered at the thought that kept flashing through her mind. Impossible, she told herself, impossible. Yet, she sat stiffly, keeping her eyes on Richard, refusing to look toward the gate of the playground to see if the old man was walking by or turning in.

Her son held tight to the chains of the swing and kicked his legs upward toward the gray sky. She saw his boots draw a black arc as he swung higher and higher.

"Be careful," she called. "Please, Richard—if you fall and break your head, who will run to pick you up?"

" . . . I will run to him," said a deep voice behind her. "His grandfather will lift him up if he falls."

The sound of this voice let loose a vibration in Ava's head. Something wild and tight was uncoiling behind her eyes.

"Chaveleh?" the old man said.

"What is it?" she cried, covering her belly with her arms as if to protect herself. "What do you want?" He was coming toward her, his arms out, walking with a slight unsteady sway over the uneven cobblestones.

She could not look into his eyes, but instead looked at the velvet collar of his coat, at the uncombed tangle of his gray hair blowing in the cold wind.

"It is you, Chaveleh? Tell me it is you."

"It is me," she said. "Oh my God, yes, it is me."

"So," he said. "So . . . " He held out his arms.

"I don't know . . . " she said.

"Please. First let me hug you . . . then we will talk."

"Oh God, Papa!" she cried, pushing herself from the bench and moving into his open arms. "Oh, Papa, how can it be you after so many years?" She buried her face in his shoulder, and he rocked against her, moaning, "God forgive me, God forgive me."

"Oh God, Papa, why didn't you come back?"

"Why, why—only God knows why."

He guided her to the bench where she sat heavily, feeling the child inside her shift and float up to constrict her lungs and make it almost impossible to breathe.

Rushing through her mind were wild images: a carved rocking horse, a doll carriage, a mansion with a curving staircase, a fierce huge dog who would forever keep her from harm. "How did you find me?" she whispered.

The old man began to cough and turned his head away as his chest was racked with convulsions.

"You're sick."

"No, no—it's nothing," he said, turning back to face her. His eyes, now that she could look at them, were watery and bloodshot. "I'm glad you have a good life," he said.

"Well—what do you know of my life?" Ava asked.

"Oh—I asked everywhere. I heard that you married well. That you moved to Brooklyn. And I see you have a fine son."

Richard was waving to her now from the swings.

"Hold on with both hands," she called to him. "I told you, both hands, always, when you go so high."

"Who is that?" Richard called over the scraping of the metal chains. "Do you know that man?"

"It's okay, yes I know him," Ava called back. "Yes—I knew him a long time ago."

FIFTY-THREE

"I wish you wouldn't light your cigar till you leave the house," Ava said, handing Len his coat and a knitted scarf as he came down the stairs. "Lately the smell makes me want to vomit. I wish you would smoke a pipe. The cigar reminds me of Uncle Hymie, it's horrible."

"I like the feel of a good cigar in my mouth," Len said, putting on his coat, "now that I can afford good cigars."

He patted his jacket pocket, where the gold rings of three cigars were visible. "Don't give me that scarf," Len said, "it makes my neck itch."

"Can't you wear it just today? Gilda is coming over this afternoon to stay with Richard, and she'll probably be here when you get home tonight. I'd like her to see you wearing it. The child spent weeks knitting it for your birthday—I'd feel happy if she thought you liked it."

"But I don't like it," Len said. "I have to be comfortable. I can't help what your sister will think or, for that matter, what the rest of your family will think. I would never get anything done if I tried to please everyone all the time."

"Let's not argue," Ava said. "All right, wear this one. You like this one." She leaned her body heavily against the wall. "Give me some money before you go, will you? I have to shop today."

"You shouldn't be going out when the baby is so close," Len said. "If you want me to pick up some food on my way home, I will."

"I don't need food. I'm planning to buy some baby furniture."

"I thought you were going to use Richard's crib for the new baby."

"It's too rickety," Ava said. "Will you give me the money?"

"Do I ever deprive you of anything?" Len said. He pulled a roll of bills from his pocket and peeled off two fifty-dollar bills. "Is that enough?"

"Give me a little more," Ava said, looking away, careful not to meet his gaze.

"What kind of a crib is this? Solid gold?" Len asked. He touched her arm. "What's going on, Ava? Something's fishy here. For you to go out in this weather to buy a crib we don't need when the baby could be born any minute is not like you. What's going on? Is something wrong?"

"No," Ava said shortly. "Go to work already—I have to sit down. I'm not feeling well."

"Maybe I should stay home then."

"No!" Ava cried. "No! Go to work!"

"What are you hiding?" Len asked. "What are you planning to do that you want me out of the house so fast?"

"Nothing!" Ava protested. "Why do you say that?"

"Because you're not a good liar," Len said. He took off his coat and scarf and threw them over a chair in the hallway. "Come sit down with me in the living room and tell me what's going on."

"Please, Len, just go. Why should something be going on?"

"Tell me. I know you too well." He drew her down on the couch beside him and faced her. His round face was earnest and kind in expression, yet his hand on her arm was demanding and strict. "What is it?"

"I saw my papa in the park yesterday."

"Isaac was in the park? What was he doing there?"

"Not Isaac, Len! My *papa!* Would I ever call Isaac my papa?"

"I don't understand."

"My papa! My real father! Nathan! He was in the park."

Len looked at her as if she might be crazy.

"This is true, Len," she said, hearing her voice quiver. "Don't ask how he found me. Somehow, he did. He made inquiries in the old neighborhood. He talked to Gilda at the house, and she told him where to find me."

"Did he tell Gilda who he was?"

"No, of course not. He said he was an old friend."

Len shook his head. "I would have thought he was long dead by now."

"He soon will be. He's very sick, Len."

"And he wants money?"

"He needs money."

"But he didn't ask for any?"

"Well, yes, he did ask. He heard you were a rich man."

"Not rich enough to be blackmailed, Ava."

"There's no need to call it that! He knew if he could find me, I would help him. Who else would help him? He's old and sick. He needs money to rent a room, to buy food."

"And if you don't give it to him?"

"Well—he might go to Mama."

"He threatened to do that?" Len said. "And you don't want to call it blackmail?"

"He didn't threaten anything, Len, but I have to help him. He's my father."

"And does that mean we'll have him for Shabbos dinner every Friday, so he can teach his grandchildren how to become philanderers and gamblers?"

"That's all over. He's had a very hard, sad life. The girl he was in love with—the young red-headed girl, you remember I told you about her? After he left, he learned that she killed herself. And that was only the beginning of his misery; he married another woman in Cleveland who died in childbirth. His business plans turned to smoke. He has no children—only me now that Shmuel is gone. And I can't let him go to Mama for help; it would kill her. Isaac to this day doesn't know Papa is alive. He thought Mama was a widow when she married him. We have to take care of him, Len."

"You have a good heart, Ava. Too good." Len got up from the couch and picked up his coat. "I'll do what you want me to do. You want money, you shall have money. You want me to keep secrets, I'll do it for you. You want to let the old man get to know our children, I give you permission. Only one thing I ask. That when the new baby is born, and you are feeling strong again, you smile at me sometimes. It has been a long time since you smiled at me; only Richard gets your smiles these days."

Ava bowed her head. She knew it was true. "I'm sorry, Len. I will try harder to be a good wife."

"I know, I know," he said. "You are a good wife, Ava. Believe me, I appreciate you. I adore you. Look—here," he said, "I'll even wear this scratchy scarf your sister knitted for me. Anything to please you. I'll throw away my cigars."

Ava stood slowly and came toward him, holding out her arms. Len received her gently. "You are a good husband," she spoke into the heavy cloth of his coat. "You are so good to me, you give me more than I deserve."

FIFTY-FOUR

"We're very impressed with your abilities, Miss Sauerbach," said Dan Dolan of Dolan, Gimelson, Shemesh, and Merkin. "You haven't had much experience working in law offices, have you?"

"Oh yes, I have," Musetta said, looking down at the leather gloves in her lap and smoothing them against her thighs. "I worked with many lawyers in my job with the translation bureau. I'm quite familiar with all legal procedures."

"Well, it's a relief to hear that," said Dan Dolan, "because I'm inclined to hire you on the spot. Your typing is extraordinary, and we've never had anyone take shorthand with such speed."

"Thank you," Musetta said, lowering her lashes and looking down. She smiled very slightly so that her dimple would be visible. She preferred not to smile with her mouth open since her teeth were not perfectly straight. She drew her feet together delicately, aware that her calves would look trim and neat in her nylons.

"You would be a lovely addition to our office," he added, giving Musetta a warm smile.

"Well then," she said, standing up. "What will my duties be?" Now that she was hired, there was no reason to go on smiling and showing dimples. There was something about Dan Dolan she didn't care for, arrogance in the way he held his broad shoulders. The pin stripes on his suit ran together before her eyes, making her dizzy for a moment.

"Come this way," he said. "I'll show you your desk and introduce you to Rosa Halley; she's been with us forever."

Musetta followed Dan Dolan through a large office and then through a doorway to a smaller room. A young man wearing glasses stood up quickly from his desk—so quickly that he knocked a marble pen holder onto the floor. "Oh, excuse me," he mumbled while Dan Dolan stood impatiently until he retrieved it.

"This is Miss Sauerbach, Miss Musetta Sauerbach," Dan Dolan said. "And this is Arthur Eslick, one of our junior members."

Arthur stood up, holding the pen. "H—, h—, how do you do?" he said to Musetta. "From your name I would guess your mother is an opera lover."

"My father," Musetta said.

"That's *La . . . La . . . La Bohème*, isn't it?"

"Yes," said Musetta. Aside from his stutter, she noticed that his skin was not good.

"Maybe you and I could go to the opera someday?" he said. "I rather like it myself."

"Let's not socialize on office time!" Dan Dolan said. "Come this way, Miss Sauerbach."

Musetta followed Mr. Dolan's brisk step into another room. A tall thin woman with a twist of dark hair piled on her head rose to greet them.

"Meet Musetta Sauerbach," Mr. Dolan said. "She'll be my number two girl after you, Rosa." Rosa smiled sourly. "Glad to meet you," she said, extending an icy hand to Musetta.

" . . . And come in here, this is your desk," Dan Dolan said, stepping into another room. "That door over there comes in from the outside hall, so you'll also act as receptionist. This is your typewriter, here's the phone. However, phones are for business only, not for personal calls."

Musetta put her gloves on the desk. "Thank you, I'll remember that," she said. "Will you have some work for me this morning?"

"Make yourself comfortable. I'll have some dictation to give you in about fifteen minutes. Till then, get acquainted with our supplies, with the office layout. Glad to have you with us. May I call you Musetta?"

"Certainly, Mr. Dolan." He nodded, smiled again, and left her alone at her desk in the reception area. She sighed. She hadn't asked him about pay. She should have bargained. But she was terribly anxious to get the job and get out of the house. Life was oppressive at home since Shmuel had disappeared, and finally, now, Mama was willing to let her out into the world again. They had run all they could run, visited the morgue till there was no longer any chance Shmuel would turn up in recognizable shape.

Mama had gone to the ends of the earth to find answers; fortune-tellers, gypsies, priests. Oddly, she had not wanted to see a rabbi. "What can they tell me, a bunch of *mishigoss*? What do they know?" Mama was tired out. She still sat for hours at the window and stared at the street as if she expected Shmuel to come striding along in his dark coat, his curly hair blowing in the wind.

Then of course at home was Gilda, frail and sensitive, swooning at the beauty of every weed in the yard, puttering in the kitchen with making dainty cookies and perfect strudel. She annoyed Musetta with her constant chatter about whatever she was knitting or embroidering. Her hands were delicate, dainty. Musetta felt her own hands were like mallets beside Gilda's. Gilda behaved like a little fairy-tale princess, prancing and tiptoeing about the house, oohing and aahing about how beautiful dogs and trees and babies were.

Now that Ava had given birth to a new baby, Gilda carried on about him, too. "Oh, just look at his tiny dimpled fingers and his beautiful ears. His toenails are no bigger than raindrops. And his eyelashes, they are barely filaments of gold." What Musetta saw about the baby—they had named him Sam in memory of Shmuel—was his drooling mouth, the eczema on his scalp, the curdy white stuff that poured out of his mouth when he spit up after being nursed by Ava. Even worse was the stink from below—when he squeezed and strained and turned red in the face, followed by a bubbling sound in his diaper region, and the awful stench that rose around them till Ava hurried him away, smiling and kissing his brow, to clean him up.

Babies! You'd think there would be a neater way to come into the world, without all that blood and pain and mess. Even though Ava had spent three months vomiting early in her pregnancy, she had taken it all as if it were a blessing. Musetta hoped if she ever had children, she would be able to separate herself from all that fleshy, bloody, physical part. The idea of what had to be done to conceive a child was quite disgusting to her. When she thought of Len and Ava, together, in bed, doing *that*—she thought she might never marry. And yet she loved the approving glances of men, loved the power she felt when they looked at her long shapely legs or at her glowing hair when the sun shone on it. What a waste it would be—her dimples, her slim body, her legs—if she didn't put them to good advantage and marry well. What she loved was the admiration of men, their praise of her. As for their companionship, they were as dull and boring as anyone else. She would rather be alone.

She busied herself at her desk, putting loose rubber bands into one compartment, arranging the pencils neatly in the wooden tray. She knew nothing about working in a law office, but she could learn in no time. They would soon be astonished by her quickness, intelligence, her capability. Whatever they would pay her, she would ask them to double it in three months.

The door from the outer hall opened and a distinguished-looking man in a dark suit stood in front of her desk. "I'd like to see the process server," he said.

"Oh—yes, of course," Musetta said, bending to open the lower drawer of her desk. She shuffled through some folders in the drawer, feeling her face turn red. What did a process server look like? Was it an implement? Would it be in a folder, in an envelope?

"What are you doing, young lady?" the man asked.

"Just one moment," Musetta said, "I'm looking for the process server." Just then Arthur Eslick came into the room. The tall man said to him, "Your secretary seems to be looking for the process server in her desk drawer!"

"Oh! I see!" Arthur said. "I'm sure she misunderstood. Come with me, please," he said to the man. "I'll get him for you." Musetta covered her face with her hands.

"Don't worry," Arthur whispered to her as he followed the man out the door. "I'll be with you every step of the way, and no one will be the wiser."

FIFTY-FIVE

June 23, 1926

Secret Heart

Two humiliations in one day! And just as I was beginning to feel a little kinder toward myself. I must blame it on Musetta, who has been nagging me to get a job, get a job. When I see her face, I think of a parrot who has one line to say. "Get a job"—the only words that come out of her mouth. Why she is so worried about my not working I will never know. We are hardly starving here; Papa earns a good wage, and if Shmuel's body is not found within seven years, Mama will get five thousand dollars from his life insurance. (Sooner if his body is found and they can prove he is dead.)

But now that school is out, Musetta buzzes around me, giving me tips on how to get jobs. If she only knew how fearful I am, how my stomach turns over when I contemplate such things. I'm not like her. Oh no, not at all. She can prance down the street in her leather shoes and toss the feather in her hat at the wind. She has the confidence of a princess. She could get a dozen jobs and not blink.

I offered to work at home—and even tried it for the last week. I baked butter cookies and packed them beautifully in boxes, with paper lace doilies under them—and Musetta grudgingly agreed to bring them to her office and try to sell them for me there. But she hated it! She got grease on her good blue suit from the butter in the cookies, and she said, "I am not a delivery girl, Gilda." Well, it was she who suggested I try to find a way to make money, and it seemed a reasonable way. She said a young lawyer in her office, named Arthur, raved about how good the cookies were. She speaks of him as if he is an annoying mosquito. I hardly know any men at all. I wish Arthur would come here and rave about my cookies to my face. God knows I could use a compliment, sometime, from someone.

Well, since baking is one of my skills, I walked down to Spiros' Greek Bakery on Gravesend Avenue and asked them if they could use a worker. They took me on, for a day, not baking, but wrapping cookies by the dozen, in wax paper packets. I wrapped till my fingers were falling off, and the owner, Spiros Antanopoulos, kept breathing down my neck, "Faster, can't you do it faster?!" Finally I straightened my back and said, "I am not a machine that you can rush me along so fast, Mr. Antanopoulos," and when he said, "Yes, yes, I can do anything I please," I said to him, "Well, I am only a human being."

Good night. He fired me on the spot. I still can't believe what he said to me: "We couldn't hire you anyway, Miss Sauerbach, not with your face. Anyone looking at you would threaten to call the health department if they saw you handling the baked goods."

I ran out, crying, and on the way home a perfect stranger stopped me, an old woman, who said, out of the blue, "I have a cure for your face, young woman. Soak washcloths in your urine and hold them on your face before you go to bed."

My face, my face! What shall I do with my face! I would tear it off if I could and go around with only my neck showing! I can't bear any more humiliations!

"You will outgrow it," Mama said when I told her how I was feeling. "When you get married, your system will get calm, and the pimples will go away. You'll see, you'll get fat and satisfied when you're married."

Married? What can she be thinking? Who would ever marry me? And what will I say to Musetta tonight when she comes home and asks me if I got a job? I won't give her the satisfaction of knowing how wretched I am; she would only press her lips together, and dimples would appear in her beautiful cheeks, and she would toss her long hair and go upstairs to our bedroom.

Is it fair that God should make some people beautiful and capable and others weak and hopeless?

FIFTY-SIX

"I wish they would stop giggling in there," Musetta said irritably to Papa, who sat reading the *Jewish Daily Forward* in the big armchair across the room from the piano. "I can't hear myself play."

"Your playing is beautiful," Isaac said. "Just go on. Play that Russian melody again . . . "

"Not with those girls in there sounding like a barn full of cackling hens," Musetta said, closing the lid of the piano keys with a thump. "How often is this going to go on?"

"Musetta, please, Musetta," Papa said. "This is the first time Gilda has a little party of girls meeting here. She's so excited tonight, she threw up after dinner trying to get everything right."

"Why would anyone throw up just because a few girls are coming over?"

"She has a delicate nature, your sister," Papa said. "She wants this meeting to go just right, everything to work out, the cookies she baked, the cocoa she made . . . everything to her is a crisis."

"I know, I know," Musetta said. "She has a crisis putting on her apron every morning. She makes me sick!"

"Can't you be a little tolerant?" Papa said.

"Tolerant? What about you, Papa? Are you tolerant when things don't go your way?" Papa shrugged and picked up his newspaper again. Musetta could see several of the girls in the sun porch. They all were from Gilda's high school; they all had shrill voices and raucous laughs.

"When I come home from work," Musetta muttered, "you'd think I could have a half-hour of peace to play the piano. I work all day, and Gilda sits home and files her nails and pulls petals off daisies. If she knits one square of her quilt, she has to lie down for an hour to rest. How come Mama allowed her to have her meeting here, anyway?"

"It's her home," Papa said over the edge of the newspaper. "She's entitled, just like you are, to entertain here."

"I never entertain here," Musetta said.

"Well, no—" Papa said, "but you could. Instead you go out every weekend, with this lawyer, with that lawyer."

"Can I help it if I get asked out?" Musetta said.

"If Gilda got asked out, I am sure she would go," Papa said.

"No, she'd probably throw up, Papa. The excitement would kill her."

"Why are you so angry tonight?" Papa's face was yellow in the light from the standing lamp.

"Oh—I don't know," Musetta said. "They don't leave me alone at the office. Dan Dolan is always after me to have dinner with him, and Arthur follows me around like a puppy dog. I can hardly get my work done."

"You should be flattered," Papa said.

"For what?"

"For being talented. For being a beautiful girl. They pay you compliments. For a girl with such gifts, maybe you could try to be more cheerful. More thankful. You should thank God for all you have."

"You thank him for me!" Musetta said. "I'm going up to bed." She rushed up the stairs, and as she passed the bathroom, Mama called out to her, "Musettala, you have time to come in and scrub my back with the brush?"

"Not now, Mama. That's Gilda's job."

"Tonight Gilda has company."

"You don't have to tell me. I can hear them giggling and screeching even up here."

"I like someone to scrub my back."

"Oh, well, just for a minute, Mama." She pushed open the bathroom door and felt a cloud of damp air swirl around her face. Mama sat curved forward in the claw-footed tub, a few inches of grayish water sloshing around her hips. Compared to Papa, Mama was a mountain of flesh. Her breasts hung like doughy pendulums nearly to her waist. Musetta looked away. She hated that Mama was human and fleshy; she hated that she herself was. They all would rot away and die someday. Papa seemed to be turning yellow before their eyes. The only pink healthy things were Ava's boys, Richard, and the new baby, Sammy, who was just a few months old. When she looked at them, she did not think of everyone's sad miserable end. But here with

Mama in the bath she could think of nothing else. Flesh and blood. That's all they were.

Today at work she had been humiliated by blood—her own blood. She had come in to the office this morning, as usual, taken off her gloves, put her hat and purse in the bottom drawer of her desk, and sat down to her work. A gardenia was in the middle of her desk, already turning brown at the edges. She tossed it in the wastebasket. She found a gift from Arthur every morning—a rose, a bunch of violets, an arrangement of fall leaves. Later in the morning he'd come smiling and stuttering toward her, and she'd have to thank him for the offerings left for her with the occasional spider or ant that came with them.

This morning she hadn't even bothered to smell the gardenia; she had already smelled it from halfway across the room. Even from the wastebasket, its strong scent assailed her nostrils. She got up from her desk chair, knelt to retrieve it, and was carrying it toward the window, to throw it out, when Rosa Halley came through the doorway with a pile of papers and said, "My dear, whatever is it all over your white skirt?"

Musetta looked over her shoulder, trying to see the back of her skirt. "I don't know, I must have sat in something," Musetta whispered, backing up toward her chair, sitting down firmly. She knew immediately what it was Rosa saw. She hurriedly began to look through some letters she had typed the after- noon before. Musetta felt tears of embarrassment and rage on her face. Wasn't it enough to be victimized by monthly cramps, by the grinding discomfort of her female organs? Did her involuntary biological state also have to leave her open to humiliation? Men didn't have to put up with this kind of embarrass- ment! They didn't have to keep calendars with check marks and X marks to record what Gilda always called her "D. C." for "delicate condition."

"D . . . d . . . did . . . you get my flower, Musetta?" Arthur asked, approach- ing her desk.

"Yes. Thank you," she said shortly.

"Oh good. Do you have a minute? Mr. Dolan would like to see you in his office."

"Oh Arthur!" Musetta cried in exasperation. "I can't go in there. I've sat in something. I—I have a stain all over my skirt. I don't know what to do!"

A look of comprehension flashed on his face. "Maybe I can help you, Musetta. Tell me, what size is your waist?"

"My waist? It's twenty-three inches."

"All right," he said. "I'll tell Dan you're busy right now, but you'll come in to see him in a little while. In the meantime just sit tight. I'll be back in a few minutes. I'm going across the street to the department store."

Musetta knew there would be a price to pay for this favor. He returned in twenty minutes with a box. Standing at her desk, he took off his suit jacket and held it for her while she placed her arms in the sleeves. It was just long enough to cover the back of her stained skirt. They said nothing to each other. She took the box and hurried down the hall to the bathroom. There she exchanged her bloody skirt for the black wool skirt he had bought for her.

She did not see him again till the afternoon, when she sought him out at his desk. "I would like to pay you for the skirt, Arthur. How much do I owe you?"

"The only way you could repay me, Musetta, is to let me c-c-come and call on you at your house."

"Well, of course, you're welcome any time," she said.

And now there was that to look forward to. The steam in the bathroom made her perspire. The giggles of Gilda's stupid friends were giving her a headache. She rubbed the brush impatiently over the soft skin of Mama's back, wishing she did not have the family she had or the job she had or the destiny she had.

She always felt as if something heavy sat on her back, pressing on her, keeping her from having pleasure, preventing her from enjoying anything. If she was so good, so superior, so special, why did she have to put up with aggravation every minute of the day?

"You're hurting me, don't rub so hard," Mama said.

"Then let Gilda do it," Musetta said. "I'm not good at this sort of thing. Good night, Mama—I'm going to bed."

FIFTY-SEVEN

November 28, 1926

Secret Heart

To celebrate Musetta's birthday, Papa and Mama have taken her to see the new musical show *The Desert Song*. Even if they had invited me, I couldn't have gone since I am having an attack of "nerves" this week—diarrhea and heart palpitations and trouble taking deep breaths. But the fact is they didn't invite me. Papa took me aside and said, "You know how Musetta is—she's so touchy—when it's her birthday, she feels it's her privilege to celebrate it herself." I told Papa, "Don't worry, it's fine with me, I don't like musicals anyway," but the truth is I love musicals and movies and shows, and I really can't believe a grown-up woman would carry on that way if another family member came along. I think Papa should not indulge her that way. The last thing Musetta needs is to be taken to a show since she goes to a play or concert almost every weekend with some young lawyer or other from her office building. Even if I'm right there in the living room when her date arrives, she never introduces me; she just pretends I'm less than a picture on the wall.

I hate those nights when she's getting ready to go out. She gets furious if anyone is in the bathroom when she wants to fix her hair, and she snarls if I so much as make a suggestion about what dress she might wear. She can snap at me one moment and then the next demand that I help her fix the wave in her hair. She knows I'm very good with hair and nails and things that take patience and care—so she uses my services when she wants them. But she never says "thank you." Then when the doorbell rings, a transformation occurs. A mask comes over her mean expression, and she goes flying downstairs to open the door. Then I hear peals of laughter and this sweet girlish bubbly voice that is at once charming and seductive. How she can be so two-faced is a mystery to me. (The same thing happens when my sorority sisters are here; though she calls them stupid and crude behind their backs, she loves to have them compliment her on her piano playing and is so cordial and gracious that my stomach heaves.)

She has so many suitors; if only she could spare me one! Poor Arthur Eslick comes mooning around; he adores her, his face is like a gray bulb till she comes into the room, and then he is radiant. (No man will ever feel that way about me. I know it. It breaks my heart to think that I will miss all that in life.) He brings cakes and flowers to Mama (because if he can't have Musetta, at least he can visit us and breathe in Musetta's aura, I suppose.) He brings me things as well; embroidery thread his mother was going to throw away, some extra yarn of hers. I wonder if he sees me as the little mouse who sits in the corner and sews. Well, what else am I? He could ask me to the movies. I would go and thank him all the rest of my life. But all he wants is my sympathy that Musetta is not wild about him. "Do you think she might grow to like me?" he asks. "Do you think my approach is wrong? What would please her?"

The answer is that nothing would please her. She is like the fisherman's wife in the fairy tale "The Fisherman and the Sea." If you gave her a house, she'd want a bigger house; if you made her a princess, she'd want to be queen of the world.

Mama has hopes that Arthur might grow to like me. After all, he has a stutter and I have bad skin. We could be a pair!

This is pointless; stewing about Musetta will make my skin break out in another explosion of monstrous volcanoes. And will it do me any good? Being angry at the world and my sister and myself will serve to keep me busy for a short time, but in the end I have to move forward and in some small way find some satisfactions.

Well, that is enough philosophy for tonight. Since I am all alone in the house, I will have a long hot soak in the bathtub and sing as loud as I please and make my own musical right here at home.

FIFTY-EIGHT

"It's too windy here for Sammy," Ava said, tucking the wool blanket snugly around the baby's chin. "He'll catch something for sure."

"It's only a little wind, Ava," Len said. "And he's tough, like his daddy, like his big brother here."

"Look!" Richard cried. "Look, the plane's taking off now. Look at those props go!" Richard pressed his face against the fence, pushed against it as if he would break it down and run onto the landing strip. "Please, Papa—please let me go up!"

"Stop begging, Richard!" Ava said. "We said we'd bring you here to watch the planes land and take off. That's all."

"But I want to go up in a plane so badly!" he cried. "I'll do anything. I'll help pay for it. I'll work in the pool hall. I'll clean the house for you, Mama."

"No."

"I'll die if I can't go up," Richard said. "Look—there are some people lining up for the next ride. There's a boy my age!"

"They may well be millionaires," Ava said. "We don't have twenty-five dollars to throw away like that."

Richard flung his head against the fence. Ava thought he might be crying. Len stood in the wind and puffed on his cigar. On the runway a wind sock billowed and blew straight out. Ava walked to where Len stood, pushing the stroller along the rocky tarmac. "You're not considering it, are you?" she asked.

"I'm considering," he said.

"It's not just the money," Ava said. "It's too dangerous. All those tons of metal, and nothing to hold it up but a few spinning propellers."

"Ava—don't talk like a silly woman," Len said. "I'd like to go up myself."

"So . . . go," she said. "Both of you go. Why not take the baby, too?"

"When he's older, he'll get his chance." Len leaned down toward Sammy and kissed the baby loudly on the face. The baby pushed him away with mittened fists. "Richy!" Len called suddenly. "You can have a ride! Mama and I decided you're a good boy, you deserve it!"

"Oh Papa, Papa. Oh thank you, thank you. Oh Mama, thank you!"

"All right, don't make such a fuss," Ava said. The boy's face was flushed; his eyes were shining as if candles glowed in their depths. She suddenly pressed his head against her breast, crushing his face into her heavy coat. To let him go up like that, without her, into the sky. . . .

"It's coming back," Len shouted. "Let him go, Ava, let him watch it land." The small plane was circling in the distance, getting ready to come in for another landing. Ava released her son and watched him rush back to the fence. His sturdy body seemed electrified by excitement and joy. She felt a corresponding expansion in her chest, her heart. How she loved that boy! His dark curls reminded her of Shmuel; his serious intelligent eyes reminded her of Papa. He seemed all good things to her, a mixture of the best in all of them. He had Len's strength and good nature, he had patience and determination like Mama, and from herself . . . What did he have from her? She thought about this as the buzz of the plane vibrated in her ears and shook the very ground upon which they stood.

Richard ran to the gate where Len was now buying him a ticket for the flight. His smile, as he turned to wave to his mother, was luminous.

Go, she thought. Fly like a bird, go into the sky. What he had inherited of hers was her soul. If she would ever fly in this life, it would be through him.

1929

FIFTY-NINE

"The train is coming Arthur," Musetta said." You better come over here."

"I'm g-g-getting some g-g-gum for us," Arthur called over the rumble of the approaching Culver Line train. The wooden platform shook and vibrated under their feet. Musetta sighed impatiently. She would rather be home doing almost anything than have to spend this evening with Arthur. But she owed it to him. He saved her life in some small way at work nearly every day; he was helping Mama with legal matters surrounding Shmuel's death and not charging a penny. He was always offering Gilda advice about her garden and what flowers would do best in what kind of soil. Musetta simply hadn't the heart to tell him the truth, that he bored her and made her want to sleep.

"I g-g-got the best seats in the theater," Arthur told her, handing her a penny box of gum. "Did you read it? I mean, *Henry the Fifth*—did you read it in the book I gave you?"

"Well—I tried," Musetta said.

The train roared to a halt, and they stopped speaking till they had taken their seats. Last week Arthur had brought Musetta a leather-bound copy of the *Complete Shakespeare*. He had inscribed it with some flowery words, a quote from one of the plays. Gilda had read the inscription and sighed. "Oh, he's in love with you, Musetta. And he's such a sweet young man. Can't you be nicer to him?"

"You be nice to him for me," Musetta had told her. "I can't be bothered." The truth was she didn't mind the gifts, but there was always some obligation attached. Now he would be asking her forever if she had read this play or that play. One day she might get around to reading them, but did he think she had all the time in the world? Her hands were full! Working in the city all week and on the weekends helping Mama with various things and going shopping for shoes and coats and suits for herself. It wasn't easy keeping up her wardrobe; Mr. Dolan expected her to dress in the most fashionable clothes. Papa still made her dresses now and then, but he was not well much of the time and didn't have the energy that he used to have. These days, Musetta was going to court with Dan Dolan in order to take dictation at various hearings and later transcribe her notes for him.

"You are the best girl we have ever had in this office," he told Musetta. She was pleased enough at that, but Dan said other things to her, suggestive things that worried her—and at those times she was more than grateful to have Arthur trailing after her in the office.

"I love the scene in *King Henry* where the young prince is wrapped in his friend's cloak by the fire, and no one knows his true identity," Arthur said. "Don't you?"

"Yes, it's a fine scene," Musetta said, arranging her dress carefully about her knees. It was made of brown silk embroidered with tiny seed pearls and had cost her two weeks' salary to buy. She admired it now, and the sheen of her silk stockings and the elegant pointed toes of her suede shoes.

"We'll s-s-see it tonight," Arthur said. "We'll have dinner on Mott Street first. We'll have a lovely evening." He smiled at her.

The train rocked along; it was in a black tunnel now. Sparks flashed in the darkness and the lights in the car dimmed and came on again. Very cautiously, Arthur reached for her hand. She pulled it away and patted the bun into which she had twisted her hair. She could see his profile reflected in the glass of the window beside her. His sallow skin, his rather beakish nose—he was not a man she could bear to touch.

"Your mother is a wonderful woman," Arthur said. "She has such a good heart."

"Yes," Musetta said. She was thinking how proud Mama would be if a man like Arthur, a lawyer, were to be made part of their family.

"Gilda is wonderful, too," Arthur added. "She's a sweet, sensitive young woman."

"Too sensitive," Musetta said. "Scared of her own shadow."

"She has many insecurities. She's not like you, Musetta. Beautiful and confident."

Musetta smiled and saw her dimple reflected in the window of the train.

"You know you are very b-b-beautiful," Arthur said. His stutter was explosive; when he finally said the word he was trying to say, he would sometimes spray saliva at Musetta. She tried not to think the word *disgusting.*

"Thank you," she said.

Arthur pulled something from his pocket. "I was going to give this to give you in the restaurant," he whispered in her ear, "but I feel this may be the p-p-proper moment."

"I don't think it is, Arthur," Musetta said. She felt a ringing in her ears. The lights went black for a blessed moment. When they came on, Arthur had opened the box, and a small brilliant diamond ring flashed at her from the blue velvet lining. "W-w-would you m-m-marry me, M-M-Musetta?"

"Oh Arthur," she said, feeling a flush come up all through her body. "You're very sweet, you're a very kind man, but please try to understand that I don't feel that way about you."

"Oh, please don't s-s-say no, Musetta. Maybe you c-c-can come to feel that way. For two years I have been planning this. You have been such a joy to me. You are my greatest h-h-hope."

"Arthur, I think of you as my very good friend, but please, put the ring away. People are looking at us. Close the box and put it in your pocket now."

With a sudden deft movement he dropped the box lightly in her lap so that it sank slightly in the delicate silk covering her thighs. "I want you to have it," he said, almost fiercely.

"I can't accept it, Arthur. I don't want to marry you." She set the box firmly on the seat between their legs.

"If you don't want it, I don't want it either."

"You must take it, Arthur. We're almost at our stop." She grasped the box and reached to place it in the pocket of his coat. He removed it at once and tossed it toward her so that it landed on the window ledge beside her.

"Arthur! I can't take it."

"I chose it with your face in my mind! It's for your beautiful hand."

"Return it to the jewelry store, please, Arthur."

"No," he said. "I don't want it."

"Then give it to my mother! Give it to Gilda! Don't waste it."

"My life is wasted if you won't have me," he said.

The train was slowly coming to a stop at their station. Musetta stood up. "Take the ring with you, Arthur!" she begged.

He stood up beside her. "Let's go," he said.

He ushered her a little roughly to the door and out onto the crowded train platform. Slowly the doors closed behind them. For a moment the train didn't move.

They both stared at the little black box, still on the windowsill beside the seat where they had sat a moment before.

"Arthur, that is a sin," Musetta said.

"Not my sin," Arthur said sadly as the train pulled away. "Yours, Musetta."

SIXTY

Ava carried a jar of chicken soup, a bag of bagels, and two packets containing cream cheese and lox into Mrs. Fishman's home, where her father was living as a boarder. Mrs. Fishman wiped her hands on her apron and said, "He's doing a little better, but he has no *koyech*."

"Thanks for keeping an eye on him. I brought him some food to tempt him."

"He eats good here," Mrs. Fishman said. "Pot roast and kasha last night."

"Oh—I know you make wonderful meals, Mrs. Fishman," Ava said. "This is just extra." She made her way up the stairs, calling out, "Papa? Are you dressed? It's Ava. I'm coming up."

Nathan was sitting in a chair by the window, his knees covered with a knitted blanket.

"You're such a good daughter to me," he said. He turned his head away and coughed. "Without you, I'd be dead by now."

Ava unwrapped the lox. "Could you have some, Papa?" She waved the slices of smoked salmon under his nose. "I could make you a little sandwich right now."

"No—wait a little. I've been thinking, Chaveleh . . . I would rather come and live with you than stay here."

"Papa! I've explained it to you. Len and I have talked about this. It's just too dangerous. One of these days Mama would drop in, and you would be sitting there. That's why I can't even let you visit at the house."

"Your Mama—I would love to see her. I would ask her to forgive me."

"But you can't. You can't just disrupt her life like that. Her husband, Isaac, thinks you died before they got married. I've told you this many times."

"But I'm tired of living here. Without the boys. Your boys . . . I would love to be near them."

"I bring them to see you. Didn't we all go to the zoo together last week?"

Nathan shrugged. His cheeks were gray with stubble. His flesh hung soft and pale, his once strong facial bones softened now by jowls. "I get lonely here," he said simply. Tears of self-pity welled up in his eyes.

"I think you're just bored," she said. "I will bring you more things to do. Maybe you can build toys for the boys. I'll have Len bring over some tools, some wood."

"Mrs. Balaboosta here would throw me out. If I get a crumb on the floor, she has a fit."

"I'll try to get here to visit you more often. It isn't easy—I have to make excuses to Gilda when she drops in and I'm about to come here. I tell her I'm going to the bank, to the fish market. She wonders how come I go shopping so often."

"Chaveleh . . . " Nathan said, "my conscience is heavy like lead. I don't know how long I'll live, but I really want to see Rachel again. I want her forgiveness."

"No. That is impossible, Papa."

"Once I walked by the house . . . "

"You didn't!"

"No one was there."

"She could have come out! She could have opened the window to shake out her dust rag. Don't take chances like that."

"I want to lay my eyes on her just once more."

"I forbid you to do that, ever again."

"They have a sign in the window. Boarder wanted."

"But not you, Papa! What are you thinking?"

Ava suddenly wondered if her father's mind was failing. Would she have to hire a nurse for him now? Len would be furious. He didn't like her to waste money. He was generous enough with the rent for Nathan's room and with his board, but a full-time nurse would be too much. "Look, Papa," she said. "I have to go now. Richard will be home from school soon, and Sammy is with my neighbor. But no more trips to Avenue O. Promise me."

"How can I fight you?" Nathan said. "I'm not a fighter anymore. All the fight has gone out of me."

"Good then," Ava said, bending to kiss his forehead. "I'll give the food to Mrs. Fishman, she'll put it away. It will be downstairs, keeping cold. So if you want it, just come down."

"A blessing on your head," Nathan said. "You're good to me."

SIXTY-ONE

May 22, 1929

Secret Heart

Things are definitely looking up! For one thing, Musetta and I are growing our hair very long. "Our crowning glories," she calls our long locks. The other day I was drying my hair in the sun, sitting in a beach chair in the backyard, when I felt as though I were being watched. Sure enough! There in the alley, leaning his elbows on the fence, was Marty Carp, Rose Rubin's friend.

"Don't stop brushing your hair on my account!" he called. "You look like a mermaid sitting on a rock."

"What are you doing here?" I cried. I could feel my face turning red (and I was already flushed from sitting in the hot sun).

"Rose sent me over to ask if you could lend her a half-pound of butter."

"Maybe not a whole half-pound," I said. "It depends how much Mama has."

"Well, no rush," Marty said, opening the gate and coming in. "Mind if I sit and talk for a few minutes?"

Mind! I could hardly catch my breath. Marty has dark blue eyes that look right through your skin. I think he's a Galitzianer. They're supposed to be especially passionate and not all that trustworthy. He sat down right at the foot of my beach chair, actually moving my legs over a little to make room for himself. As he talked to me, he kept touching my leg for emphasis, and one time he just rested his hand lightly on my ankle. My foot felt as if it were going up in flames.

I can't remember what we chatted about; I was thinking how wrong Musetta was, how she always said if I wanted to meet people, I had to get out of my own backyard, that I would never meet the man of my dreams while I was putting out the garbage or watering my violets. And there I was, in my own backyard!

When my hairbrush got caught in my hair, Marty said, "Here, let me do it," and he stood up and began brushing my hair for me, in long slow strokes. He didn't do it right, he pressed too hard, and, if anything, he put in more knots than he got out, but I loved every minute of it!

After a while he said he had to be getting back with the butter, so I went inside and gave him half of the block of butter Mama had in the refrigerator. (She was in the city, visiting Aunt Rose.) He just leaned against the wall in the kitchen, angular and monkeylike, and said in this cajoling tone, "I sure hope you make me some of your famous butter cookies sometime. Rose says they're heavenly."

"Oh, I will, Marty," I said. "Come back tomorrow, and I'll have them for you." I hope I didn't seem too anxious. I baked them right after he left, glad that I hadn't given him all of our butter, but he hasn't been back, and I don't know whether to let the family eat the cookies.

I know Rose won't care; she has so many boys flocking to her door that she will hardly miss Marty. She told me—anyway—that he's too skinny for her, there's not enough meat on his bones. (I'm skinny, too—maybe that's why he likes me.)

Is it *possible* he likes me? I had given myself up for lost. But the way he touched my ankle? I shiver just remembering it. Maybe the tide is turning, and I'll catch up to Musetta. She seems a little less cranky lately; poor Arthur Eslick has come to cry in Mama's lap (and mine) and tell us about the engagement ring left on the train. He knew Mama would be angry about that—and I guess he was hoping she would make Musetta feel guilty. But no one can make Musetta feel guilty about anything. "It was my right not to accept it," she said, "and he had no right to try to force it on me."

I doubt I'll see the day anyone wants to marry me so badly they will force an engagement ring on me, but at least I don't feel so hopeless right now. I am starting to knit a muffler for Marty—though I don't have to give it to him or even tell anyone what I'm making. It's just in case . . . something comes of this.

I know it isn't sensible to daydream about such things, but how I wish Marty Carp could be our boarder! Mr. Ricci, the insurance salesman, didn't work out (Mama said he didn't keep his room clean), and he went back to live with his sister in the Bronx. So the room is vacant now. I rather like not having a boarder (the bathroom was always occupied!), but sometimes I think of how special it would be if Marty lived in the house. Then the two of us would be alone sometimes, if Mama and Papa were out, and Musetta were on a date. I could be in the kitchen baking, and he might be home for the evening, and he would sit with me and maybe offer to brush my hair (prickles are running down my back at the thought!), and maybe if we were alone, he might kiss me. . . . Well, no point in going on this way. Marty already lives in a perfectly nice house with his family, and he's not going to be our boarder. We'll probably get some Italian who smells of olive oil and garlic. To bed now . . .

Later! Way past midnight. I must add this. Around ten I heard a tiny knock on the front door and ran downstairs. Everyone in the house was upstairs asleep. There was Marty on the doorstep, with his seductive grin. "Busy?" he said. Busy! I was in my robe already. He was carrying a brown bag, which he handed to me. I thought it was a present! Actually, it was a cashmere sweater of his that needed washing! He asked me if I knew what to do with a fancy sweater. He didn't know how to get it clean. Well, I volunteered to wash it for him (that means he will come back!), and he seemed pleased. I gave him the cookies (he ate half and took the rest with him), and we had some hot cocoa and sat and talked in whispers in the kitchen. He said there was something poetic and dreamy about me. He said I had delicate hands. My heart is turning over with excitement. It's almost too much for me. I must go to bed now.

SIXTY-TWO

"Maybe I shouldn't go to work today, Mama," Musetta said. "Papa seems worse, don't you think? I can't understand why a sore throat should hurt him so much. I'm going to call Dr. Rittenberg again."

"He won't like to be bothered. He's a busy man. What can he tell you? He was already here last night."

"I don't consider it 'bothering him' with Papa moaning out loud every few minutes. I think he should come again. Besides, we pay him. You don't need to feel guilty, Mama."

"He said it was just a bad cold." Mama pressed her hands against her chest. "Though in all my years of nursing I never saw such a cold. Even the worst sore throat was never like this. And your Papa is not a sissy."

Musetta stood uncertainly in the kitchen. "I have so much to do at the office . . . "

"Go, go," Mama said. "I'll call Dr. Rittenberg to come again."

"All right," Musetta said, "but first I'll go up and say good-bye to Papa."

Upstairs in the front bedroom Papa lay in bed like a bundle of rags. His head was turned limply to one side, his hand dangled off the edge of the mattress. "Are you awake?" Musetta whispered.

"Uh," Papa grunted.

"It's really bad, isn't it?" Musetta asked.

"Can't talk," Papa mumbled. "Pain."

"Mama is going to call the doctor again."

Papa made a motion with his hand, as if swatting away an insect. Musetta sat beside him on the bed and took his hand between hers. It felt damp, almost chilled. She realized she had almost never seen him this relaxed, with all the tension gone out of his body. He usually vibrated with nervousness, a kind of painful energy that never let him rest.

"Do you have an earache?" Musetta asked. "Does your chest hurt? Can you tell me what else you feel?"

"Swollen," Papa whispered, withdrawing his hand from hers to point at his throat. "Closing up."

"It only feels that way," Musetta said. "Sore throats always feel that way."

Papa shook his head weakly. There was a sound from the doorway, and Gilda appeared there, leaning into the room. "I better not come too close," she said. "I might catch it from Papa."

Musetta made a face. Always coddling herself. Her sister was afraid of the wind. Musetta stood up. "Make sure Mama calls the doctor, will you? I'm going to go to work now."

Gilda scurried down the hall. "And you, Papa—just rest. I'll call from work a little later." Papa nodded slightly. "You'll feel much better soon," Musetta promised.

At work she typed four letters for Mr. Dolan and took dictation from a junior member of the firm. Mr. Merkin called her in to compliment her on a long contract she had typed the day before. "Not a single error, Musetta. Not an error in twelve pages."

"Thank you," Musetta said. She smoothed her brown wool skirt carefully around her hips. "I like to do accurate work."

"We are very pleased with you," Mr. Merkin said. Just then Dan Dolan passed by in the hall. "Come into my office, Musetta. I want to discuss something with you."

She followed him down the hall and stood in his office as he walked around his desk and sat down in a large armchair. "I'm taking the train up to Albany on Friday. I'd like you to come with me for the weekend. There's the Winfred Case coming to trial, and I'd like to have you with me to take it down."

"The weekend?" Musetta said. "The whole weekend?"

"I would of course get you a room in the hotel, and the firm would pay for it."

"I'm afraid I can't, Mr. Dolan. My father is ill and . . . "

"If you can't do your job properly, just say so," Dan Dolan said, suddenly irate. "I told you when we hired you that there might be work after hours."

"You said there might be overtime," Musetta said coldly. "You didn't say full weekends."

"Well, this just happens to work out that way."

"I really can't," she said. "My father . . . "

"Never mind," Mr. Dolan said. "You may go back to your office.

As soon as she was at her desk again, Musetta dialed home. "Mama—it's me. Did you call the doctor yet?"

"Papa doesn't want him to come again, what can I do?"

"How does Papa seem?"

"Very bad . . . worse, maybe."

Just then Dan Dolan came into the room. Musetta said, "Don't wait, Mama. Call the doctor now. I'll speak to you again in a little while. Good-bye."

" . . . Miss Sauerbach," Dan Dolan said, placing his fist on the edge of her desk. "Was that a personal call you were making?"

"Yes, but . . . "

"Do you recall office rules? That business phones are not to be used for personal calls."

"Yes, I do, but . . . "

"And was that a personal call?"

"I was calling my mother," Musetta said. "My father is very ill."

"I think you know better than to break the rules, Miss Sauerbach. I will have to discuss this with my partners to see in what way they wish to deal with your behavior."

"But Mr. Dolan . . . " Musetta said, as he walked out of the room. She sat stunned in her chair. Arthur Eslick walked past her desk, and she averted her face from him. Heaven knew she didn't want to look into his accusing eyes just now. As far as Mr. Dolan was concerned—what was that all about? He had been trying to make passes at her for months now, and she had always skillfully warded off his suggestions that they lunch together or have dinner together. But now this. Just thinking about it made her shudder. With Papa home so sick, and her worry about him . . .

Furious, she stood up, grabbed her purse from the bottom drawer and marched into Mr. Dolan's office.

"I didn't call for you . . . " he said, but she cut him off and snapped open her pocketbook. Pulling out her change purse, she opened it and took out a nickel. She flung it at Mr. Dolan. It bounced on his desk with a dull clunk and fell into his lap.

"That," said Musetta, "is for the phone call. Good-bye!"

She turned on her heel and ran out of the building, down the street, and into the subway station to take the train home to Brooklyn.

SIXTY-THREE

June 10, 1929

Secret Heart

I am a fatherless child. My dearest Papa is not on earth to see me turn nineteen today. Oh God, when I think of how he suffered that night. If only I had forced Dr. Rittenberg to come in the morning, as Musetta made me promise to do. But when I called him, the doctor said he had an office full of patients. What was I so hysterical about? All Papa had was a cold. Such a fuss about a sore throat! So I apologized to have bothered him, and I hung up.

When Musetta came home from work, she was wild with worry. She had left work early and had run home all the way from the train station on Avenue P. "How is Papa?" she cried as she tore into the house. She didn't wait for an answer but took the steps two at a time, and I followed behind her. Mama was sitting at Papa's side, wiping his brow with a washcloth. His breath was neither going in nor coming out. He shook with effort trying to breathe. His cheeks sucked in as if he were drawing on a straw. His whole chest strained and shuddered as he labored to find a way to get air. I began to cry. Musetta threw me a look of such disgust that I tried to stop myself. Why should I have had to stop myself from crying! My beloved Papa was in pain, suffering. I had a right to cry.

"Call Dr. Rittenberg," Musetta said. "Tell him he must come immediately."

"I can't," I said. "I have to go to the bathroom. My stomach is upset." It was true. I ran to the bathroom and sat there, doubled over with pain, wracked with diarrhea.

In a minute I could hear Musetta shrieking into the phone at the foot of the staircase. "Don't tell me it's only a cold, Dr. Rittenberg. He's choking! No, no, we can't bring him over there! He can't move! You come here. Come over here right now."

She slammed down the phone. I could hear her galloping back up the stairs. I could hear Papa gasping for breath, drawing in air as if it were thick as coal dust, breathing with a grating, rasping, desperate sound.

I couldn't help it. I began to throw up. It was as if my body didn't want to witness such suffering. I cried for Mama. No one came.

"Gilda! Call for an ambulance!" Musetta shouted down the hall. When I came out of the bathroom, Papa was reaching crazily into the air, trying to grab something, anything. His hands were clawing at thin air, as if he were trying to climb out of a deep pit.

"Papa, don't die!"

Musetta came past me and slapped me on the face. I heard her half-falling and sliding down the stairs to the phone. Mama says that I fainted because the next thing I remember was two men in the bedroom, lifting Papa onto a stretcher. Mama dragged me out of their way so they could get through the hall.

I watched them carry Papa down the stairs. His face was like a little yellow marble, shiny, hard, his eyes like deep black holes in the marble. His hands had stopped flailing. Musetta was at the bottom of the stairs; she stopped the men long enough to lean over and kiss Papa on the forehead. "I'll come with you in the ambulance, Papa," she said. And I heard him say, in a weak fading voice, "Take a sweater so you don't catch cold."

And then he was gone. He never said a word to me, only to Musetta.

Musetta and Mama went in the ambulance; they left me home to imagine the horrors that were happening. They told me he died in the ambulance; his throat closed up. It simply choked him, a disease called Ludwig's angina that caused the floor of his mouth to swell up and cut off his air.

When Musetta and Mama finally got home, Mama went to bed. Musetta picked up the phone, though it was almost midnight, and she called Dr. Rittenberg at home.

"This is Musetta Sauerbach. My father died on the way to the hospital. You are a murderer! If you had come this morning, my father might have lived. I want you out of this neighborhood, Dr. Rittenberg. I swear, if I ever see you again on the street, anywhere near here, I will kill you myself."

Mama tried to calm her, but she only slammed down the phone and pushed Mama away. Her eyes were on fire; she was snarling like a wild animal. "I swear I will kill him if I ever see him again," she said.

"You need to rest," Mama said.

"Rest I will get in my grave," she hissed. "Just like Papa."

SIXTY-FOUR

Like a mechanical doll, Musetta moved her legs to get herself to her office building in Manhattan. Her head felt numb, her body parched. Wherever she looked, her eyes saw Papa's face in those last moments. As a child she had seen horses burn to death in the country, and she had always felt as if that moment, just before a living being died, must be the worst moment in all existence: when life was leaving the body and the mind comprehended its own end.

Had Papa believed in God? He talked enough of God. He went to shul, he prayed, he obeyed the Jewish laws. But did he really believe? Was he now, as the rabbi had said to Mama, in a better place? What could be a better place than their house on Avenue O, smelling of Mama's *mandelbrot* and full of the beautiful music that Papa loved?

Papa died at the age of forty-eight, the same age his beloved Caruso had died. Gilda had pointed that out to Musetta. At least she was good for something, with her annoying attention to detail.

Now there were all the rest of her days to look forward to without Papa. Without his stern glance, without his proud smile as she played the piano, without his shoulders hunched over the sewing machine as he made some beautiful dress or coat for her or Gilda or Mama.

Ava went with the family to the funeral at Mt. Hebron Cemetery but did not shed a tear at Papa's grave. She stood in her wide coat at the graveside, her face as stony as the tall gravestones around them. Richard and Sammy clung to her, and Len stood at a distance from the grave. But Ava's face was set in bitterness. What did she have against Papa? And why hadn't he shown even the slightest affection for her during all these years? She was a good, sweet woman. She was a wonderful mother to her boys. She kept an immaculately clean house (something that Musetta herself felt she could never be bothered to do). And she was loyal to Mama, calling often, bringing her gifts, inviting them to come to dinner.

Papa had gone to Ava's once or twice, but he hated to visit, and Mama did not press him about it.

Musetta wished she had made Papa more proud of her. Tears stung her eyes; she was not a concert pianist. She was just a secretary. A good secretary, but still . . .

And now one without a job. She hastened her steps on the pavement. She would clean out her desk this morning and leave. She would not even say good-bye to the other law partners—Mr. Merkin, Mr. Shemesh, and Mr. Gimelson. As for Arthur—he barely glanced her way now, so that was settled. It would be a relief not to work near him, not to have to feel guilty that she had caused him such grief by refusing to take his engagement ring.

She turned into the doorway of her building and hurried up the marble steps. She kept her head down; she didn't wish to explain her absence of the last week to anyone who didn't know why she'd been gone; she didn't want to accept condolences from anyone, didn't wish to talk. Her heels clicked across the polished wooden floor. She had brought a little satchel with her to take home her personal papers, a few books, the extra skirt she kept in the bottom drawer so that she would never have to experience again the kind of humiliation she had felt on the day Arthur had to buy a new skirt for her.

Some woman was already at her desk! My God, they hadn't waited very long to replace her, had they? Her tears were close to the surface; they hovered on the inside of her eyelids, ready to spill.

"Ahem . . . " Someone cleared his throat. "Miss Sauerbach . . . " Mr. Merkin, a dignified and imposing older man, came toward her.

"I—I just came in to collect my things. I won't be long. I wonder if that young woman has already emptied my desk . . . "

"Would you come into my office, please? Do you mind if I call you Musetta?" She wondered why it mattered what he called her—he would never see her again after today. She followed him down the hall.

She understood soon enough why he wanted to see her. "Mr. Dolan made a complaint against you last week, Musetta . . . "

"I know," she said shortly. "I was making a personal phone call to my mother. My father was dying that day; in fact he died that night—" Her voice broke. She lowered her head and fumbled for a handkerchief in her purse.

"No apologies are needed," Mr. Merkin said. "We have considered the matter carefully. We were planning to call you."

"That's all right, I understand," Musetta said. "But I can't apologize for my behavior to Mr. Dolan."

"No need, no need. Look at me, Musetta. We have let Mr. Dolan go. He is no longer with this partnership. Mr. Gimelson and Mr. Shemesh and I have been displeased with his behavior for a long time; we felt you were our most promising employee in years, and when he asked that you be dismissed . . . well, we dismissed him instead."

Musetta stared at Mr. Merkin's smiling face.

"He wanted me to go with him on a weekend trip," she said. "When I refused, he was very unhappy with me."

"There are never weekend trips with this firm," Mr. Merkin said. "We want you to stay on working for us."

"But a woman is already at my desk."

"We'd like to offer you a promotion, Musetta. I'd like you to be my private secretary. There's a desk for you in the small office just outside this one. And we've bought a new typewriter for you!"

"Really?"

"And that isn't all. We'd also like to offer you an opportunity to advance your position in the world. Mr. Shemesh and Mr. Gimelson and I think you would make an excellent lawyer. We would like to offer to pay your tuition to law school at night, if you think you could manage it."

"Law school?"

'You have a fine mind, Musetta. Why not?"

"I never thought of it."

"It wouldn't be easy. You'd have your work here and classes in the evening. It will not be easy to find time to do your homework. Take a while to think it over. There's no hurry. You've been through a shock with your father. Wait a while and consider it. You'd have a place with us in this firm if you got a law degree, of course. But if not, you may always have a job with us."

"I'm overwhelmed, Mr. Merkin."

"Don't be." He smiled again and patted her shoulder. "Go home and think about it. And remember, you may call your mother anytime you want to. Anytime."

SIXTY-FIVE

Thanksgiving, 1929

Secret Heart

No one has even made mention of Musetta's birthday this year. Mama is not planning a family dinner, Papa is not here to buy tickets to a show or concert, Ava has dropped out of sight with her babies, and even Arthur Eslick, the poor fool, has stopped wasting money on useless gifts for the Queen of Sheba.

So I feel a little sorry for Musetta. She works hard; she works late at her office to earn overtime money now that Papa is gone. We are lucky we had almost no money in the bank on the day all the banks failed. (We had a little money in the bank on Kings Highway; Mama and I rushed down there as soon as we heard the terrible news on the radio. A mounted policeman was there, trying to keep back hundreds of people who wanted to get into the bank. "Hold on, it'll be all right," he kept saying, but people were pushing and screaming. Finally, when it was evident we would never be let in, we walked home. But the bank people say we will get our money eventually.

Most of our money is in the value of our house, so we're not desperate, like the richer people are, who have more to lose. I don't understand Wall Street and the stock market, and what it means that it crashed, but luckily I don't have to.

On our way home we stopped into Woolworth's, and although this may be hard to believe, a salesgirl there nearly put out my eye. Some lady was asking the salesgirl where to find knitting needles, and, without looking, the salesgirl simply thrust out her arm to the side where I stood and, pointing the way for the woman, stuck her finger into my eye! Just my luck! She screamed and kept wiping her finger on her skirt as if she had stuck it into some disgusting mess. I was nearly blinded, tears rolling down my cheek. The manager came running and took my name and address.

When we got home, Mama called Arthur Eslick and asked him if we ought to sue Woolworth's. He was very cold to her; he said it was our business what we did. Mama, so dense in matters like this, asked him if he would be our lawyer. (She doesn't see that what occurred between him and Musetta should have anything to do with his willingness to serve us . . . and without charge.) He set her straight, saying that he would rather not represent us, but if she were adamant, he would charge his usual fees. Mama was puzzled—she even had the nerve (or stupidity) to ask him why he didn't come around anymore, and he told her he was busy these days. To top it off, a bill came in the mail a few days later for eighty-five dollars for work he had done in trying to get Shmuel's life insurance paid to Mama sooner than the seven years we are supposed to wait from the time of his death unless his body is found. Imagine! Either he is truly nasty or is so badly hurt by Musetta that he will do anything to strike back at us. But why all of us? We can't afford to pay his bill; Musetta said we absolutely won't. If he makes trouble, she will speak to the head of the law firm, Mr. Merkin, and he'll make short work of Arthur!

In the meantime my eye aches like the dickens, and we have been to the doctor twice (not so much because it is necessary but because Musetta said that if we decide to sue Woolworth's we should have documentation—her word—that I had to have medical care).

Now that Musetta feels she is "head of the household," she seems less cranky. I don't suppose a leopard ever really changes her spots, but she seems to have decided to be less childish about everything. I almost admire her sometimes. Which makes me think I ought to make her some kind of birthday present. A scarf? A sweater? A pair of cozy knitted socks? I'll have to think about it.

Speaking of socks, Marty Carp came by (he always brings something for me to wash and then has an excuse to come back to see me!)—this time he brought his dirty socks! They were argyle, beautifully hand-knit. I asked him who gave them to him, his girlfriend? And he just smiled shyly. Well, I don't know what to make of it. If he has a girlfriend, he's the biggest louse that ever lived. Bringing me his dirty clothes to wash! But if he hasn't a girl friend . . . then why doesn't he make some kind of pass, at least? Who can understand men?

I heard today from my sorority sister Linda Levine that Dr. Rittenberg's office is for rent! He moved! Afraid of Musetta's threat! I don't blame him. When my sister is angry, I'm sure she could kill. She has good reason to want to kill him. I'd like to myself, but I'm not the hating kind.

The house without Papa is lopsided. When I pass his sewing machine, I break into tears. Sometimes I wonder if life is worth living. There's so much pain and so many hard things. Already in my life I have lost my father and my brother—and I am only nineteen. If I live to ninety, what pain I will have to suffer through! If only there were some joy to offset it. I know—there is the sight of the new moon and the smell of the ocean and the dark knowing eyes of newborn babies. But to have real joy, there must be someone to share it with. And that I may never have.

1930

SIXTY-SIX

"What do you mean, he moved out?" Ava cried. Mrs. Fishman was singeing the feathers off a chicken. She held the pale bird over the flame as each feather zapped and shriveled to nothing, leaving only an acrid shimmer of smoke in its wake.

"What do I know?" Mrs. Fishman said, shrugging her shoulders. He got up early, he came down, he boiled himself some *mamalega*, he said, 'You got a sign you could put out? Because now you could rent my room, I'm moving to another room.'"

"He said that? You didn't ask him where he was going?"

"Is it my business? A half-hour later he came down, carrying a suitcase. He thanked me for keeping such a clean house, and he left. No notice, no warning. If I'd had some warning, I could have put a card up in the butcher store that I'm taking in a boarder again."

"Don't worry about that," Ava said. "I'll pay you two weeks more. But do you have *any* idea where he was going?"

"What am I?" Mrs. Fishman said. "A mind reader?"

"Is it okay if I run upstairs and see if he left anything in the room?"

"Go. You know the way."

Halfway up the stairs, Ava had a sudden thought and turned around. She called good-bye to Mrs. Fishman and let herself out.

She half-ran all the way to Avenue O. Her heart nearly stopped when she saw the "Boarder Wanted" sign no longer in the window of her mother's house. She leaned against the wishbone tree in front of the house and tried to collect her thoughts.

A month after Isaac died, her mother had taken in two bachelor brothers who rented the big back bedroom. Musetta and Gilda had moved into the front bedroom with Mama—Gilda sleeping with her mother, and Musetta sleeping on Shmuel's cot brought up from the basement. The tiny middle bedroom, which they had always talked about renting to a boarder, had housed Isaac's sewing machine for the past five years.

Mama had told Ava that now it was time to rent that, too. The bachelor brothers, Willy and Izzy Nachman, paid fifteen dollars a month each, money that Mama felt was a great help to the family.

Paying bills was a struggle without Isaac's income, but Musetta's firm had raised her weekly salary to thirty-five dollars a week, an amount more than a man might earn. With that and money from the boarders (and the hope that Gilda soon might find some kind of job) they would manage.

Now the missing sign indicated that Mama had rented out the little middle bedroom. But to whom? There were two terrible possibilities: one that Nathan had decided to move in there, the other that he had simply run off and Ava would never see him again. How could he survive, in bad health and without money? But what if he were here? What if right now he was revealing the truth to Mama? Mama might have a heart attack, Gilda would certainly collapse in hysteria, and Musetta, fiercely loyal to Isaac's memory these days, would stab him in his sleep for all the harm he had done to Mama.

Ava shivered in fear. The girls had always been told Rachel's first husband had died young. No one knew the truth.

Ava went to the front door. She had a key to the house in case of emergency. She used it, hoping against hope that no one was here but Nathan, hoping that if he had rented the room he had not yet told Mama who he was, hoping that Gilda was out on some errand. Musetta would be at work.

It was silent downstairs. No one was in the sun porch or the living room. The kitchen was warm and smelled of a pot of bubbling flanken soup.

Upstairs there was a murmur. Ava went to the staircase and held herself perfectly still. She could hear voices, low and gentle. Her father. Her mother.

Looking up, she could see his suitcase on the top landing. She tiptoed very slowly up the stairs, almost holding her breath. In the upper hallway she felt suddenly faint. She was trembling and her lips were quivering.

The sound of her parents' voices, whispering softly in Yiddish, took her back more than thirty years. Her heart felt as if it might burst.

They were conspiring together. Her mother was softly crying, her father was explaining . . . coughing and explaining: his sad life, his many mistakes, his sorrows, his regrets. Rachel was telling him of her hardships, of her twenty-three years of marriage to a man who never could love her children by Nathan.

Rachel's voice was tender. Just as Ava had not been able to hate him, Rachel, it seemed, could not either.

Unable to help herself, Ava heard a sob escape her lips.

"Who is there?" Mama called fearfully. "Willy? Izzy?"

She came to the door of her bedroom, tears still on her cheeks, her white hair disheveled. "Oh my God," she cried. "It's Chaveleh." She looked over her shoulder into the room. "Chaveleh, you will never believe this, a man came today to rent the room, it's God's miracle."

Ava walked into the bedroom. Her father sat on Shmuel's cot, his face soft with emotion, his cheeks wet with tears.

"Papa," Ava whispered. "You came here!"

"You know?" Mama asked her. "You know who this is?"

"I know," Ava said. "I know who it is, Mama."

"God works in strange ways," Mama said. "For years, if I'd seen him, I would have murdered him. Now—it's strange—it's like a dream what happened so long ago. I don't care now what was in the past. A whole lifetime passed. Isaac died and left me alone, and God sent Nathan back to me."

Nathan held out his hand, and Rachel went to him, sat down beside him, put her hand in his.

"Come, darling," Nathan said to Ava. "Come sit by us, our little Chaveleh."

"I thought I would be alone all the rest of my life," Rachel said.

"And me," Nathan said. "I thought I would be."

They were still, absorbing the moment. There was a noise downstairs.

"It must be Gilda," Mama said. "What will we tell her?"

"The truth," Ava said. "What else is there to tell her?"

"Maybe . . . " Rachel said in a practical voice, " . . . maybe the girls can move into the little bedroom and . . . "

"Mama, what are you saying? You and Papa are divorced."

"So?" Nathan said. "So we could have a wedding again, no?"

"A wedding?" Mama said.

Gilda came rushing up the stairs and into the front room. "Oh—excuse me," she said breathlessly, coming upon the three of them. " . . . Are you the new boarder?"

Papa began to laugh, then Mama, then Ava. The three of them sat laughing as Gilda looked on in bewilderment. Finally Ava struggled to her feet.

"Gilda," she said. "Hold onto your hat while I tell you something amazing. This man is going to be your new papa."

SIXTY-SEVEN

October 22, 1930

Secret Heart

It is all too much for me. Papa is dead, and Mama has gone off on a honeymoon with a man who was supposed to be dead twenty-five years ago. Musetta and I have been moved into the tiny middle bedroom, and the house is crowded. The real boarders, the Nachman brothers, use the bathroom for hours at a time, not to mention how long Mama stays in there these days combing her hair, or Nathan, coughing and clearing his throat and spitting.

Mama's first husband seems a harmless sort of man, hardly the villain who could have deserted her so long ago. He is neither handsome nor romantic nor interesting. Papa, my poor dead Papa, was by far a better husband for her, at least in my view. This story is full of mystery. How can Nathan be alive if he was supposed to be dead? Mama says now that she only told us he was dead in order not to upset Isaac, but why did Nathan leave her in the first place?

She says he went off to Cleveland to try to open a business and never came back. They won't discuss it further than that, and I suppose it's their business. What counts is that Mama is not so sad; she doesn't cry anymore, she laughs, and she doesn't talk about Shmuel and Papa day and night now. It's as if a pall has been lifted from this house, and all because of the presence of a little old man who seems so grateful to be here that he would kiss all of our hems.

Musetta is furious. She wants to know who is going to feed this new member of the household! She says she can hardly pay the bills as it is. Ava has promised to contribute money, but Musetta thinks Len will get tired of doing that, and then she will be stuck with all the responsibility. I guess in the end I will have to get a job myself. Nathan is too ill too work, and Mama is too old.

I know it is selfish to add this, but I'm jealous. At least Mama and I were at home together all the days Papa and Musetta were at work, but now it will be Mama and Nathan, and I will be the third wheel.

Mama and Nathan will be gone on their honeymoon for only two days; they went by train to Lakewood, New Jersey, to stay on a chicken farm that rents rooms. While they are gone, I will sleep alone in the big bed in the front room; when they come back, I will once again be squeezed into bed with Musetta in the little bedroom.

If only my fate would take a new turn! If only something would happen! I don't think Willy or Izzy Nachman will be the man of my dreams. They work in the butcher shop on Avenue P and come home with bloody aprons, which Mama washes without charging them extra. They're a little crazy. Musetta thinks they're not right in the head, either one of them. When the three of us were sleeping in the front room, she had a lock installed on the inside of the bedroom door, for fear they would come in during the night and attack us. I hardly think so, considering their timid ways, their hunched shoulders.

But you never know with men, I suppose.

What do I know about men anyway? My only male visitor brings me his dirty socks to wash! Linda Levine is disgusted with men also! She met a man on the bicycle path on Ocean Parkway, and he invited her for a soda. The next weekend he made a date to take her to the movies. When he arrived, he said to her, "I'm a little late because I went to see a certain lady of poor reputation, and she took care of my business. I knew I was coming to see a good girl, and I didn't want to get all hot and bothered. So you don't have to worry!" What a promiscuous lot men are!

My face is not as bad as it was (though plenty bad enough), and I'm filling out just a little. I am going to get false bosoms as soon as I get the courage to go and buy them. I bet they will make the difference—like between night and day!

I could fall in love with Ava's son Richard if I had half a chance. What a beautiful boy; almost a young man. He's tall now, with the sweetest, kindest face. He's almost unreal. Smooth brow, smooth cheeks, eyes that light up with pleasure when he sees me, the most exquisite smile, full of warmth and welcome. He calls me Aunt Gilda—it makes me feel a century old when actually I am only eight years older than he is!

He constantly talks about airplanes; how boring that is to me. It makes Ava impatient. She tries to direct his interests elsewhere, but always the talk comes back to airplanes. He reads books about them, he builds models of them, he puts pictures of them on the walls of his room. One day he may try to fly away.

Sammy, his brother, is sweet and round and pudgy like Len. He's also very strong like his father. Ava seems proud of them both, content with the offspring she has produced. She is getting heavy and matronly looking, but is still quite beautiful in her way.

What could a honeymoon be like for people as old as Mama and Nathan? Mama is nearly sixty, and Nathan must be sixty-five!

I blush to think of it. Someday, God willing, I will find out what a honeymoon is all about.

SIXTY-EIGHT

Musetta sat on a beach chair in the backyard, her head held at an unnatural angle toward the sun. She wanted some sun on her pale throat—she felt her neck was white and scrawny, like a plucked chicken's. She had to sit somewhere; the house was all taken up with people and their business. Gilda and her gaggle of girlfriends were in the sun porch, planning a party, and Mama was selling pots to the neighbors in the living room. A lady had come by last week, offering Mama ten dollars off a set of waterless cookware if she would hold a party at her house and invite the neighbor ladies in to witness the miracle of cooking in heavy aluminum. The lady said she would bring enough food to feed eight ladies and demonstrate how to cook it in the marvelous pots.

Mama agreed at once and began calling up and down the street to invite the neighbors over. So the entire Saturday was ruined, with all kinds of noisy strangers in the house. Musetta had been planning to relax and get some extra beauty sleep; the weekend was her only peaceful time, and now she had to put up with all this racket and annoyance in the house.

She sighed and crossed her long legs on the slatted beach chair. She stopped agitating her mind long enough to admire them—long and tan and shapely. She often thought she had the legs of a movie star, sultry and sexy. Sometimes she liked to lean back against things—trees, buildings, and rest her weight on one leg, thrusting her hip out, looking glamorous. No one ever noticed, she was sure. Besides, it didn't suit her professional image: intelligent, efficient Musetta.

Mr. Merkin asked her daily if she was considering his offer. She always answered that she was thinking about it. But she knew she couldn't manage law school; working all day, staying in the city at night to go to classes, coming home late, only to begin her studies at midnight! She wasn't superhuman. What did Mr. Merkin think of her, that she could do all the work he demanded of her and go to law school at the same time?

If he really wanted to help her and felt she would be an important addition to the firm, he could have suggested that she work only half a day and go to school in the afternoon. But no, he wasn't that generous! He wanted her services in the office, her efficient dictation, her high-speed typing, her courteous and brisk manner with visitors to the firm.

Her life seemed to be moving toward a dead end. She would work till she was ninety, avoiding the eyes of Arthur Eslick and making detours around the sour face of Rosa Halley, who for some reason had taken a terrible dislike to her from the beginning.

Musetta adjusted the beach chair to its flat position and turned over on her stomach, exposing the pale back of her legs to the sun. She could hear giggles and screams coming from the front of the house—that silly sorority! All those girls did was chatter and whisper about boys; Gilda was no exception.

It was time Gilda got serious, buckled down, and started thinking of what to do with her life. But no—she still mooned around at home, pressing flowers, reading poetry, baking adorable little cookies. She and Nathan were beginning to be buddies; she baked and cooked things, and he tasted them and praised her. What a combination!

It was too hot out here. Musetta couldn't stay in the sun any longer. But where could she go in the house? The Nachman boys always used the bathtub on Saturday mornings, so a long bath for Musetta was out of the question. Besides, she hated to find their curly black hairs sticking to the side of the tub when she wanted to bathe. Nathan was probably in the front bedroom reading the paper. He wasn't really any trouble; but he just made the house more crowded. Since Papa had died, it seemed there were strangers everywhere.

Grabbing her blouse and putting it on over her bathing-suit top, Musetta went down the alley and entered the house through the cellar door. Instead of going up the stairs toward the kitchen, where the miracle pots were sizzling away on the stove, she went down the steps to the cellar and blinked while her eyes adjusted to the dimness.

She always thought she could smell Shmuel's scent in the basement. His banjo was still there, leaning against one of the storage benches built into the wall. Musetta made her way carefully around boxes of wool sweaters and winter coats packed in mothballs and picked up the banjo. She sat down on one of the green benches and began to strum her fingers over the catgut strings. There was always pleasure in music. She would thank Papa for giving her that, for allowing her to learn the piano. But when did she ever get a chance to play it now?

The banjo echoed eerily in the cellar. The sound seemed to stop short at the low ceiling, bouncing down and around the dim, dusty room. At the far end of the room was a hole in the brick, opening into black dirt under the front of the house. It made her think of graves, of death. Shmuel and Papa were dead. Would it be less painful to think about death if she believed in God? God! Would a good God drown a sweet brother and choke to death a loving father?

Her father had prayed, gone to shul, believed in something. About Shmuel she was not sure. Like Mama, he accepted what those around him believed. If Mama had told him there was God, he probably believed there was God.

Musetta felt if she had a God, it would be Music. But she had no time to worship anything. Her life was work, work, and more work, to pay the bills, to pay the mortgage. When was there time for fun? What was fun? Fun was as hard to understand as God. Other people seemed to have it, believe in it. Fun and joy. She should try to find some, she knew. What was the point of having dimples and long lovely legs and a sharp mind and magnificent hair if one didn't get some joy in life?

1931

April 12, 1931

Secret Heart

I have just done my nails and my hair for tonight. The girls came over this afternoon, and we decorated the house with crepe paper and balloons. I made a special cake with seven layers and a chocolate butter-cream icing. I have a new dress, too—and, come to think of it, it has seven layers, just like the cake! But they're lacy layers, as if someone held up a bolt of pure lace and I spun around and around in it, wrapping myself up till it covered me! That's my new dress, pink lace. Mama says I look "gorgeous." Even Ava, who is not generous with compliments, came over this afternoon with the boys and told me I was sure to be a big hit. Richard stroked my dress very delicately, looked up to me with his wonderful eyes, and said, "Auntie Gilda, you look like a princess." How I adore him!

God must be with me because there are no new "hickeys" on my face, and usually when I am excited a dozen new ones break out. Best of all, I have hope this time. Usually at parties I know I am going to be a wallflower; I smile and stay cheerful, but my heart is usually down in my feet, knowing that the boys will flirt with everyone else, but not usually with me. Maybe I look too serious. Maybe they know I am a "good girl"—certainly not like Irma or Sadie, who give it away to just about anyone.

But tonight I know there will be someone there just for me. Linda's boyfriend, Harry, is bringing along a friend to be my date. Harry has told him all about me, that I'm shy and gentle and a stay-at-home type of person, and

Meyer (that's his name!) told Harry that's just the kind of girl he'd like to meet! Meyer is a quiet type, too. Harry told Linda that he's tall and gangly. (I always go for tall, skinny fellows, like Marty Carp. But Marty was a louse! He's engaged to be married now, and all he ever did was bring me his dirty clothes to wash. It took me a long time to get over him, and maybe I never will. I still have dreams where he leans close to me with those dark, knowing eyes and whispers in my ear.)

But back to Meyer—he's tall and has a big family that he helps to take care of; his father is in a hospital I think. Meyer works at Abraham and Strauss Department Store selling men's pajamas, and he smokes a pipe. That's all I know about him, but he sounds wonderful. Mama and Nathan are going to the movies tonight, to leave us alone in the house. The Nachman brothers are in Brighton Beach for the weekend, and Musetta has a date tonight with another lawyer. So the coast is clear for a wonderful time!

I am wearing April Showers perfume, which Papa gave me on my sixteenth birthday, and every time I take a breath, I think of Papa and how much I owe to him. I miss him every minute of the day, but I know he would want me to have fun and try to enjoy life, not grieve forever. So here I go downstairs. Someone has just put a record on the Victrola, it must be Roz—she always just walks in the front door. Maybe Linda and Harry and the man of my dreams are already right here in the house.

Meyer. Meyer Berger. Mrs. Meyer Berger. Better than Gilda Sauerbach, don't you think?

SEVENTY

Even through the trees, Musetta could see the house lit up like a jewel. Her heels clicked on the cement as she walked up East Fourth street with Arnold Kallman, a law clerk with whom she had been to a concert. She was glad to be at the end of a long dull evening. Arnold had a droning voice and no imagination. He had spent the entire train ride back going on and on about the superiority of combination locks over key locks, a subject that for some reason fascinated him.

He had wanted to stop with her on Avenue P for an ice cream soda, but Musetta said she had a headache and wanted to get home. She did have a headache. It wasn't going to be improved by the loud music she heard coming from the house or by the chatter of Gilda's sorority sisters and their dopey dates. As they approached the corner, Arnold slowed his steps and hooked his arm through hers. This was the moment he would ask her for another date—a movie next Saturday night or dinner. Musetta felt so tired; she knew in the next minute or two how miserable she would feel, either because she turned Arnold down or, worse, because she accepted his invitation and would then have to dread it all week.

"Musetta . . . " he began. "I have, well, a friend gave me . . . " He reached into his pocket and pulled out two tickets. "Ice skating!" he said. "What about that? Free passes to go ice skating." He waved the tickets so close to her eyes that she had to blink. She took them from his hand.

"How nice," she said. She held them tightly so that Arnold could not get them and wag them in her face again.

"Will you go with me? Next Saturday night?"

"That's a nice idea," she said, tucking the tickets into her pocket. "Why don't you call me during the week, or stop by at the office and we'll discuss it."

"Oh yes, oh good," Arnold said.

"Let's cross the street now," Musetta said firmly. "Before any cars come."

She hurried toward the house with Arnold behind her. If only she could get inside fast, get past Gilda's guests without too much sociable chatter, without introductions to all those silly people.

"I can't ask you in for a cup of tea," Musetta said, to forestall any suggestions. "My sister is having a party tonight, and the house is just creeping with strangers. I doubt I could even get to the kitchen to put up a pot of water."

"Oh, that's okay," Arnold said. He paused, as if to linger with her at the foot of the brick steps, but Musetta ran up them quickly and pressed the latch of the door.

"Good-bye, Arnold. Thank you for a lovely time."

With a spin of her foot she was in the house with the door closed behind her. She sighed. She flung herself down on the wicker chair in the dark sun porch and said aloud to herself, "Thank God that's over."

"Well—you must have had a wonderful time," a voice said from the darkness. She tried to focus her eyes in the dark room but saw only the momentary glow of a pipe. A rich mellow odor, like cream soda, circled her head. She inhaled the sweetness of the tobacco aroma.

"Who's out here?" she said, finally.

"Meyer," said the voice.

"I don't know you," Musetta said shortly.

"I don't know you either," he said and laughed. It was a relaxed, warm laugh. She liked the sound of it.

"I'm Musetta. Gilda's sister. Gilda is the one who's giving this party."

"Oh yes," the voice said. "I've met her. She's nice."

"You aren't the date Harry brought along for her, are you?" Musetta asked, turning toward the glowing pipe.

"Well, I believe I am," Meyer said. "But I'm not much for parties."

"So you've been sitting out here alone all evening?"

There was a silence. She heard him draw on his pipe. "I like to sit," he said finally. "It's quite pleasant."

"Shouldn't you at least make an effort to be sociable?"

"Oh—I did. Your sister and I had a nice talk," Meyer said. Musetta heard him rock back on the legs of the chair. "I thought I might even go back in there after a while to stretch my legs." In the darkness he moved his legs forward so that one foot touched the tip of Musetta's shoe.

"Sorry—" he said, but did not remove his foot.

Musetta stood up. "Well, I've had a long evening. I've got to go upstairs and put on something comfortable."

"Not on my account, I hope," Meyer said.

"I wasn't thinking of doing it on your account," Musetta said. "Look, it's been nice to meet you, Meyer, good night."

"Won't you come back down?" She felt rather than saw him stand up. There was almost a hot breeze moving between them. She hesitated.

"Do come down," he said calmly. "I'll be waiting for you. I was thinking of sitting out there in the garden under the lilac tree. Look for me there."

Flushed, almost blushing, Musetta ran up the stairs, careful not to look around at anyone and thus be detained by idle talk. In the little bedroom she tugged her dress over her head, kicked off her heels, and rapidly pulled the pins out of the bun in which her hair was coiled. She was exhausted but also exhilarated. She should just go down the hall, wash her face, and go to sleep. But instead she took from the closet her red silk dressing gown, which Papa had sewn for her, and put it on over her slip, tying the sash tightly around her waist.

As she slid her feet into her red satin slippers, she noticed that the tickets to the ice-skating rink had fallen on the floor. She picked them up and slipped them into the pocket of her dressing gown. She spun from her room and ran to the staircase, clattering down the steps and feeling her hair fly behind her like a horse's mane.

"Oh Musetta, are you going to join us?" Her sister stood at the foot of the stairs, holding out a tray of little rosebud cookies. In the center of each one was a red cherry; they looked to Musetta like the blemishes that flared on Gilda's cheeks and forehead. "But you shouldn't have taken off your street clothes," Gilda chided her. "That dressing gown isn't really appropriate for a party . . . "

"I'm not going to stay," Musetta snapped. "I just came down to get some milk. Then I'm going up to bed, so don't worry about it." Musetta swished past Gilda and flung open the refrigerator door. She pulled out a bottle of milk.

"You want to sit with us?" Mama asked. She and Nathan were sitting together on one side of the kitchen table, drinking tea. "We came home from the movies, but we don't know what to do with ourselves now."

"We would go to bed," Nathan said, "but who could sleep?" He turned to Mama and smiled, pressing her hand with his on the tabletop.

"No—thanks, I'm just going right up to bed," Musetta said, pouring herself a glass of milk and drinking it so fast she could feel her throat bobbing. "Good night," she said, and holding her head downward, like a bull charging, she rushed blindly through the living room and sun porch, and arrived outside on the brick stoop.

The moon was as white as the keys on the piano; the air was cold to her burning face.

"Over here . . . " Meyer said. "On the bench under the lilac tree. I thought maybe you'd decided to go to bed."

"I did," Musetta said. "I mean, I should have, that's what I decided." She came down the brick steps and walked around the hedge into the little front garden.

"Here, sit here," Meyer said, patting the bench. She sat down and stood upright instantly. She had sat on his hand.

"Oh, I'm sorry."

"That's okay," he said. He puffed on his pipe. The tobacco in the bowl glowed in a ruby haze. "Now you can sit down safely." He put his hand on her hip briefly to prove to her that it was no longer on the bench.

She realized she was breathing hard, as if she had run a long distance. When she finally sat down and leaned back, she wondered if was too cold to stay outside in just her dressing gown.

"Your long hair, that's quite a heavy load to carry around," Meyer said. Musetta didn't know what to say to that. It wasn't a compliment—she was used to being complimented on her hair.

"In the old days . . . you know," Meyer said, "women used to sell their hair." Musetta put her hand on the crown of her head as if to keep him from removing her hair.

"Pillows, pincushions, a kind of battle armor . . . "

"Armor?"

"Well, a warrior used to believe that if he went into battle wearing the hair of his beloved, he would not die."

"How do you know about this? Is it really true?"

"Who knows? It sounds good to me." Meyer chuckled. Musetta could feel the low vibration of his laughter run through the wooden slats of the bench and caress her tense back. She relaxed a little, took a deep breath.

"Why don't you like parties?" she asked him.

"Oh—talk, silly chatter, you know. Games. Look—was that a firefly? I wonder if they come out this early in spring."

She gazed into the darkness. A tiny glow appeared, like a signal in the night.

"So why did you come to this party?"

"Harry said, 'Do me a favor, come along.' Harry's a nice fellow. So I came along. Might as well sit here as in front of my house. A new view is always nice."

"I should probably go in," Musetta said, shivering slightly.

"I hear you play the piano," Meyer said. "Can you play for me?"

"Not now!"

"Oh, no—I didn't mean now," Meyer said. The light coming from the front windows illuminated his curly dark hair and the full, comforting shape of his face. "Soon someone will find out us here, so let's make plans," he said. "What do you think?"

"What kind of plans?"

"I don't know. We could go somewhere."

"We could go ice skating." Musetta said, to her surprise. "I have some free tickets to the ice rink on Ocean Parkway right here in my pocket."

"I don't know how to ice skate," Meyer said.

"Neither do I."

"Good. We'll go then," he said. "When?"

"Next Saturday."

"I'll be here to pick you up. How about noon?"

Just then the front door was flung open, and they were bathed in the bright light of the porch lamp.

"Oh, there you are, Meyer," Gilda said tremulously. "I wondered if you might want to dance, we have the Victrola going in there, you know. . . . " She stood uncertainly on the step. "Musetta . . . I didn't know you were out here . . . " and then her voice broke off in a sob. She stood there in her lace dress looking to Musetta like a pink cabbage wrapped in ruffles.

"Oh!" Gilda cried. She turned around and rushed back into the house, leaving the door open so that the noise and the music spilled out into the quiet garden. After a moment Meyer said, "People can't arrange other people's lives you know. You can't worry about it too much. They mean well, but no one is obligated."

"I will have to sleep in the basement tonight," Musetta said. "She will lock me out of the bedroom."

SEVENTY-ONE

April 13, 1931, 2:00 A.M.

Oh Secret Heart

I hate her, I hate her! I know it's wrong to hate this way, but I do, in my heart, in my bones, in the burning sockets of my eyes. My own sister, looking like a floozy in a red silk dressing gown, inviting gentle Meyer Berger to paw her in the garden! How could he resist her? She is a sorceress, a seducer, a hypnotist!

I truly don't understand it. She could have anyone in the world—with her face, her figure, her talent. She was already out on a date tonight, but could she have kept her face out of this precious event of mine, my once-in-a-lifetime party, kept her hands off this sweet man? No, of course not. She had to shimmy downstairs in those satin slippers with that hair of hers giving off sparks!

She cut through the room like a whirlwind. I was hoping Meyer didn't see her. He and I had had such a nice talk; he was so shy I wanted to reach out and touch his sweet face. I wanted to reassure him—me, the girl scared of her own ghost. He gave me such confidence—treating me so kindly, nodding his head, watching my face as I talked, really listening. Harry and Linda came early with him, so we stood in the kitchen and talked a while; he tasted my cherry-filled sugar cookies and said they were wonderful. I felt radiant. I knew I looked as pretty as I ever will, and I thought, This is going to be my lucky night. This man will be the man of my dreams.

But he went out there, out front in the garden, where she stalked him, my red devil sister, and I didn't realize it, I stepped right into the trap.

I had been planning to go out and find Meyer when someone put on a waltz. I was so glad someone else put on the record because I wanted it to seem accidental, fated. Then I went out front (I thought Musetta had finally gone upstairs to bed, having made her shocking impression on everyone)— and there they were, the two of them and I felt as if my heart would stop and I would fall down dead on the steps.

If only I had! If only I had! I don't ever want to see her face again! She hasn't dared come upstairs to bed. If she tried to come in here I'd scream—I feel so close to bursting, I didn't know I could ever feel this wild.

Perhaps she fell into the furnace. I pray she felt so shamed that she flung open the metal door and crawled into the fire. What am I saying? God forgive me! Papa, Shmuel, I am lost here, lost in the world. I know I will always be alone.

How can I live another day to face her dimples and her pearly skin? It was only an accident that she should have been born looking her way and me my way. Sisters. It could have been the other way around. But when men look at Musetta, I see in their eyes a rush of desire. When they look at me, I see nothing.

I should die before I write things like this, I should burn these pages! But I am pushed beyond my usual thoughts tonight. I will say what I please, and let whoever snoops here read and be shamed. I am beginning to cry now, so that the ink is smearing on the page. Let me hide in my pillow, let me die by morning.

SEVENTY-TWO

"I'm sick, Arnold, I'm really sorry about this, but I can't possibly go skating with you today," Musetta said into the phone. Out of the corner of her eye she could see Gilda standing in the kitchen, pretending to be looking at something on the stove, but clearly cocking her ear to hear every word.

Arnold was now offering to bring over some of his mother's chicken soup. "No, no," Musetta said. "You'd catch something, and I don't feel much like eating. I'm awfully sorry . . . but if you want to ask someone else . . . really, I wouldn't mind, you could come and pick up the tickets . . . well, all right . . . I'll just paste them in my scrapbook then, one of life's missed opportunities."

She saw Gilda in profile making a disgusted face. Musetta knew she was piling it on a bit heavily, but Arnold was such a silly man, he had to be manipulated before he would loosen his grip.

"Call me next week, all right?" she said. She stretched her legs out in front of her; she was wearing a pair of red-and-white cotton stockings and a red wool skating skirt she had bought downtown.

Though she had no idea how to ice skate, she knew how to look the part, and dressing up for it was as much fun as trying to skate would be. She had also bought a little woolen cap with a pom-pom at the top and a white fuzzy sweater.

She hung up the phone. Mama, who was also in the kitchen, came to lean in the doorway to the dining room. "Such lies, Musetta," she said, wiping her hands on her apron. "I shiver to hear you talk like that."

"It's necessary, Mama," Musetta said. "I have to handle things my own way."

She heard Gilda snort. What an ugly sound. Gilda had better toughen up and face the facts; there was no point in blaming everyone else for the way she was. Musetta had no patience with her and no sympathy for her. She ought to get out into the world! Meyer would never have been the right man for her. Meyer needed someone with a sense of humor. He needed someone full of life—like Musetta.

In the week since the party Gilda had not spoken one word to her. Musetta had taken to sleeping on the couch in the living room and entered their bedroom only to get her clothes and carry them to the bathroom to dress.

She was not guilty of anything; she was not responsible for Gilda's disappointments in life. Even Meyer had said so.

At the thought of Meyer a warm flow of blood started in her throat and moved up into her cheeks. He would be here soon! It surprised her that she was so delighted; no man had ever delighted her. And even more surprising was that he worked as a pajama salesman in a department store, and this did not dismay her. She had vowed only to date educated men, men with intellect, promise, status. But look at Arnold Kallman and Arthur Eslick. They were weak, humorless men, men without warmth, without confidence. They scurried about at her feet like little rodents.

But the thought of Meyer filled her with a warm light—the rich deep sound of his laughter, the ruby glow of his pipe.

"Go upstairs," Mama was now advising Gilda quietly. "What do you need to be here for when he comes? To turn the knife in your heart a little more? Go—go, go upstairs and wash your face. Nathan and I will take you to Avenue P for an ice cream soda in a little while."

SEVENTY-THREE

Meyer ducked his head coming in the front door. "Sorry, it's just a habit," he said. "When I don't do it, half the time I get whacked in the forehead by a low doorway."

"It's nice to be so tall," Mama said. "It's good for a man to be tall."

Meyer smiled at her. "Men should be tall and girls should be pretty?"

"Why not?" Mama said. "Could it be a bad thing?"

"And men should be smart and girls should be dumb?" Musetta asked Mama, casting a glance at Meyer.

"That I didn't say," Mama answered, blushing. "Can't I give a compliment to this young man if I want?"

"A compliment I will accept anytime," said Meyer.

He touched Musetta's arm. "Are you ready? You look like Sonja Henie today." At the curb Meyer untied some rope from the handle of his car door. "Excuse this," he said, "but the car is an old jalopy, and the door doesn't always stay latched. I wouldn't want you falling out on the way—though I know this doesn't look too classy."

"I can see that," Musetta said. She noticed a movement at the upstairs window. Gilda looking out at them? Musetta placed her hand gently on Meyer's shoulder. Pleased, Meyer looked back in surprise at her touch. Satisfied, Musetta let herself delicately into the car and waited, facing forward, while Meyer secured the door again. She stared at his curly dark hair, parted in the center, but flying in unruly spirals over his head.

"Ready to go?" he said, getting in and starting the motor. As they drove off, she was aware of the tense dark blot behind the upstairs shade . . . her sister, Gilda, steaming in her frustration and fury.

The ice rink on Ocean Parkway rang with music as brightly dressed skaters whirled in a circular stream around the ice.

"Hang on!!" Meyer laughed, "Hang on, here we go!" He pulled Musetta onto the ice with him and stood wavering and bobbing beside the rail while Musetta tried to steady her ankles inside the high, white shoe skates.

"I don't think mine are tight enough," Meyer said.

"I don't think mine are loose enough," Musetta moaned. "I have no circulation—you pulled the laces too tight."

"Let's just stand here . . . casually," Meyer said. He pulled his pipe from his pocket and hunted for a match. "Nonchalance is the key," he said. "Nice and easy."

The icy air spiked upward from the skating surface and rose into the swirls of Musetta's red wool skirt. Meyer tugged her elbow slightly and spun her around like a top. She heard herself giggle; it was not like her. She pressed her lips together and tried her usual enigmatic smile, sarcastic, amused, with just a touch of charming dimple showing.

But just then he rubbed his knuckles down her spine in such a way that she screamed in delight. It was impossible to be dignified with this man! His smile was infectious, his enjoyment contagious. He didn't know she made it a point to be composed and dignified; he didn't know how self-contained she was, how competent, how strong willed.

He pressed her close, and before she could protest that she hardly knew him, she realized the movement was not a caress, but a desperate grab to keep himself from falling on the ice. That also made her laugh; she felt he had found a hidden spring of joy within her, quite innocently, without conspiring to trap or seduce her.

"Come on, let's really get out there," she challenged him, tugging him away from the rail. The music was rhythmic and raucous; couples whizzed past them, arms entwined or hands knotted together. A few skated backwards, spinning, doing figure eights, pirouetting.

"Don't hold onto me," he said. "I am perfectly capable of skating backwards myself—just like that fellow there, see? Watch this." He took his pipe from his mouth and handed it to her. He spread his arms like a pelican's wings and flapped them vigorously. "Here I go . . . " he announced and with his long legs began to skate forward with grace, with style, until instantly he crashed into a wrestler-size bald man and went sprawling and skidding across the ice as a dozen skaters tried to stop him and instead ploughed into him and each other.

"Meyer! Meyer! Are you all right?" she cried, tiptoeing over the ice on the points of her skates till she thought she recognized the long gray arm of his sweater. She thrust his pipe into her own mouth, holding it between her teeth as she used both hands to tug him out of the pile of skaters.

He allowed her to extricate him from the mass of bodies. "Anyone else need a hand up?" he asked jauntily as he struggled to his feet. Several of the fallen stared at them with wonder, at Musetta with the pipe in her mouth and at Meyer beside her, thrashing toward the rail with great difficulty. Musetta took a deep breath and inhaled the bitter brew of cold tobacco ash.

"May we sit out the next dance, my dear?" Meyer gasped. "Would a hot chocolate please you just as well?"

"Anything you suggest would please me," Musetta said, thrusting the pipe toward him. "Here, take this, will you?"

He opened his mouth as if to grip the stem of the pipe between his lips but instead leaned forward suddenly to bite down hard on her outstretched wrist.

"Ouch!" she screamed.

"Here, you can bite me back," he offered. "Any part of me you want. You want my ear? My elbow? My big toe?"

"Never mind!" Musetta cried, laughing so hard that tears blurred her vision.

"I'll give you all week to make your choice," Meyer promised. "Any part of me you want. Any time of the day or night. Just call me, and I'll be there to be devoured by your pretty little teeth."

1934

SEVENTY-FOUR

July 4, 1934

Secret Heart

I live on crumbs, like the crusts I am feeding to the ducks on the lake, like the peanuts I am tossing to the squirrels. The lovers, out there in the canoe, feast on each other. Meyer likes to bite her; while they were here on the blanket with me, his teeth, like an alligator's, were everywhere on her exposed skin. He can make her laugh. No one else ever could. She sees him coming at her, and she laughs in advance. A miracle. They both are wearing white today; Musetta in a white cotton blouse and long white cotton slacks (she posed delicately for a snapshot I took an hour ago, holding a leaf up to shade her eyes from the sun. The shadow masked her face like a raccoon's disguise).

Meyer is wearing white trousers, but no shirt at all. His chest is muscular, slender, with thick curly hair growing on it in the shape of a cross. They are a charmed couple. What do they want with me? Yet a beggar can't refuse crumbs. They invited me on their Fourth of July picnic; I came. What then? To sit alone at home and listen to fire crackers go off all about me? (Mama and Nathan went to visit Aunt Rose and Uncle Hymie.) Tonight we all will go to Coney Island and watch the fireworks blaze over the ocean.

Meyer likes to have me come along. He pretends not to see Musetta's annoyance; I don't call it jealousy, since she is too puffed up for jealousy; she has no sense in her that anyone could ever be more desirable than she is. The fact is I am better suited to Meyer than she is. I think at times he feels that to be true.

For example, they were talking of the wedding, which is to be Saturday, November 10, at our house. I recommended that they use the services of Rabbi Hirschman of the Avenue N Temple. Mama began to talk about getting or making a chuppah and suddenly Musetta said, "A rabbi! Do we have to have a rabbi? I hate the idea of some old man with a beard babbling away in a foreign language at my wedding!"

Meyer looked as if he'd been struck by an arrow in the heart. Who else, I'm sure he was wondering, should marry them?! She is so righteous and insensitive when she says things like that, overlooking Meyer's respect for rituals the Jewish people have observed for centuries. She acts peeved, as if the world has conspired to annoy her by inventing old men who speak Hebrew and read out of ancient texts. Meyer is such a gentle man, though. He would never confront her; he always tries to appease her, as he did this time by suggesting that the service be half and half; half Hebrew, half English.

Meyer's family must also be considered. His mother lives as a widow in her brother's house, though she is not a widow. Meyer's father is in an institution (a mental hospital?), though Meyer prefers not to speak of him. All we know is that when a young man and working in a shipyard, he was hit on the head with an iron post. After that he was not right in the head and went to live in some mysterious distant place, an institution.

Meyer has two brothers and two sisters; one of the sisters (as well as one of the brothers) is older than he is, and the reason he and Musetta waited this long to set a wedding date was that the family has a rule: an older sister must marry before a younger brother may marry. How strange. Lucky I do not have a younger brother, or the poor soul would be doomed to be a bachelor all his life!

But luckily Meyer's older sister, Harriet, was married just this past June (she married a furrier), and now the road is clear for Meyer to take the big step. I can see them out in the canoe even as I write this. They are drifting along so peacefully . . . but Musetta can't relax and take it in. No, even from here I can see her mouth going a million miles a second, yap, yap, yap, she never shuts up, she always has something to explain to him or complain to him about.

He could have been mine. He was meant to be. If only they would marry and move away, but no—they are going to live right in our house, in the front bedroom, the room next to my bedroom. Mama and Nathan will take the back bedroom, and the Nachman Brothers, thank heaven, are moving to Philadelphia. Meyer, saint that he is, has offered to take on the support of the whole family.

Nathan can't work; he's barely able to breathe these days. So all the burden will be on Meyer and Musetta . . . and finally on me, too. I will have to get a job this winter. I will have to try, though the thought of it turns my stomach upside down. Now he is kissing her out there in the middle of the lake.

If God wanted me to be alone in this life, he should have made me pure, whole, without longing. He shouldn't have put that ivory-skinned sister in my house or the tall, sweet, handsome Meyer beside her. He should have let me be born to be a Catholic nun, with (forgive me, Papa) Jesus to love. I feel I was meant to do good on earth, but who can I do good for when I am locked into a house with my old mother, her old husband, and these newlyweds? I ought to work with the poor in some foreign land. I ought to work with lepers in India. So where am I? In Brooklyn, in the park, on the Fourth of July!

SEVENTY-FIVE

"Open your eyes, Chaveleh."

Through her lashes, Ava saw a handsome, curly-haired man silhouetted against the window shade. He seemed to be holding toward her a white figure in a lacy garment.

"Yes?" she said, propping herself up on her elbows. "What is it?"

"Wake up!"

"I am up, Papa! What do you want? Is that a new doll for me?"

"A doll, Mama? What are you talking about? It's me, Richard. I've brought you your breakfast! A Sunday morning surprise!"

"Oh. Is it you, Richard? I must have been dreaming. I thought you were my papa bringing me a new doll and that I was just a little girl."

Richard smiled, leaning forward to set the white tray over Ava's knees. "What a sweet dream that must have been, Mamaleh."

"But you did call me 'Chaveleh' a moment ago, didn't you?"

"Just for fun. I thought it would please you, my beautiful Mama." Ava reached for his hand and pressed her lips to his fingers.

"Everything you do pleases me, my precious boy. Will you look at this elegant breakfast? Do I really deserve to be treated like a queen?"

"Haven't you always treated me like a king?" Richard asked. He bent over the bed and kissed his mother briefly on the lips. "I hope you like it," he said. "Matzo-brie, juice, coffee, and a rose from the garden."

"I love it," she said. "Where is Sammy? And Papa?"

"Papa had business downtown. He told me to tell you he would be home late. And Sammy is playing with his trains in his room."

"Even on Sunday . . . " Ava sighed. "It's always business with your father." She drank a sip of juice from her tray. "Another long weekend at home."

"We could go someplace," Richard said. "You and Sammy and I . . . we could take the train to the airport and watch the planes come in."

Ava laughed. "You and your planes! One day, if you don't watch out, you will sprout propellers from your ears!"

"If only I could be so lucky," Richard laughed.

"Well, let me finish my breakfast. Maybe we will go to the airport."

Ava watched him walk out of the room, watched him duck his head at the doorway as if he were taller than the doorframe. At sixteen he was two heads taller than Len already—a tall strapping boy with eyes as clear and honest as glass. She flushed with love. She was blessed with this son. Not only was he beautiful to look at, but he had a beautiful soul—so gentle, so careful to do what others would like him to do. Even with his brother, Sammy, who had a temperament like Len, he was considerate, respectful.

She remembered her dreamlike state, just a few moments ago, when she had felt that it was her papa leaning over the bed. It never left her, that longing for her father, the father of her youth, the smiling, dashing, beautiful Nathan. Never mind the old man who had come back to her, the old man who lived with Mama in the house on Avenue O and tried to make up to Mama all the grief he had caused her in the past. What could he make up, now that he was ailing, weak, sick, sorrowful? Could he ever make up to her that Shmuel had to live in an orphanage? That Ava had had to live with Aunt Rose and take the abuse of Uncle Hymie? That Mama had been forced to marry Isaac and that Isaac had always hated Ava?

There was no undoing the past. What Ava longed for were the years she never had with Nathan, all the sweet good years, all the love she would have had from him had he stayed with them.

It was so strange to look at the two of them now, Mama and Papa, and feel that empty space between them, the life that never was, the goodness that couldn't be. Now she was grown, and Shmuel was dead, and it was over: their family life—the one they hadn't had—was gone.

There were moments she felt she would go to Nathan and demand an explanation from him, an apology, a pound of his flesh in exchange for what they had suffered. He was only human, full of failings, weak of spirit—a servant, like everyone else, to the demands of his flesh.

She began to eat the breakfast Richard had made for her. He had called her his beautiful mama. Beautiful. Well, it had been a long time since Len had told her she was beautiful. Her breasts and thighs were thick and heavy now, her waist was no longer narrowed by corsets. She set the tray aside on the bed and stood up. Pulling her nightgown over her head and tossing it on the bed, she moved toward the mirror to examine herself. There were pearly lines on her belly and over her hips, made by the stretching of the babies inside her. A dark line ran from her navel to her triangle of hair, almost as dark now as the hairs Len had all over his body. She rested her hands on her head and surveyed herself. She had not done much with this body other than nurture babies with it. She had not been generous with it toward Len. Of course, she allowed him use of it, whenever he wanted (which was almost never, now) but the truth was, she was a cold fish. What that meant to her was that she was not passionate. She was not like the showgirls who kick up their long legs and wink at men, promising secrets and thrills.

Some women had that capability; she had never felt it, never known it . . . except perhaps when Richard had been a baby at her breast. Then . . . aah, then . . . that had been something. She cupped her own full breasts in her hands and let the weight of them warm her palms. She had not nursed Sammy; she had developed a serious breast infection, and the doctor had said she must give Sammy formula. But those long months with Richard, rocking in the rocker with him in her arms, his tiny lips pulling at her nipples. A shivery convulsion went through her at the memory of it. She smiled and rolled her nipples now between the thumb and forefinger of each hand. If ever she had felt passion, it had been then.

"Mama—I've brought you some more hot coffee . . . " Richard said, coming abruptly into the room and stopping short at the sight of her. He lowered the coffee pot suddenly, and a stream of steaming liquid poured out of the spout and over his foot, scalding him through his sock. He fell back heavily on the bed, his teeth clenched in pain.

"Oh my God, Richard!" Ava cried, running toward him, kneeling to grasp his flailing foot, untie the shoelaces, and pull the shoe and sock from his foot.

Then she sat, still naked, beside him and pulled his face against her breast. "It will be all right," she said. "In just an instant, it will cool down, and then we will put ice on it. It will be all right, Richard." She rocked his head against her and saw, reflected in the mirror across the room, the sight of them, mother and son, bound together in pain. But it was not right, she knew it, and she hurried away from him to put on her dressing gown and pull the belt tight.

SEVENTY-SIX

November 11, 1934

Secret Heart

How I Spent The Wedding Night: His and Hers, of course, certainly not mine. At age twenty-four, with no prospects, this may well be my only one.

But—such a night! Hang on to your hat! The truth is I slept with a man just as truly as Musetta did last night! It was wild! The house was full of company, relatives and friends and landsmen (heaven knows where Mama dug them up!), and people were sleeping on the couch and in the basement, just about everywhere! Mama asked if I could stay with a friend so she could give my bed to Aunt Rose and Uncle Hymie, who didn't want to travel back to the city late at night. I asked Linda and Harry if I could stay at their place. After they were married last summer, they rented an adorable basement apartment on East Third Street, and I knew they would be glad to offer me their couch.

Well—after the wedding they were a little drunk on sweet wine (even I was!), and Linda kept telling me to pack up my trousseau and come along with them, and Harry kept winking and saying that he'd be "gentle" with me. I was in such a tizzy, my eyes were full of tears all through the ceremony.

Musetta looked so frightened (for her!) in a very chic brown silk dress with a corsage of gardenias that Meyer pinned on her. Her hands were like ice all day (I had done her nails earlier in the afternoon), and even during the ceremony she held a little white handkerchief all balled up in her right hand, as if she had to hang on to something.

Meyer had had his hair cut, and his big ears stuck out like handles. He was grinning all over the place (he has the biggest, kindest smile of anyone I ever saw), and the love in his eyes for Musetta made me sob so hard that I had to run into the pantry to cry till the spell passed.

I don't know why she deserves this reward here on earth.

I'm trying to be generous (I've been civil to her all these years that she and Meyer have been courting; I've never once accused her of her crime, of walking in and snatching him away from under my nose . . . and I never will). But in my heart I feel she is the luckiest woman on earth, to have a man that sweet, that generous and wise, to adore her.

The ceremony was fine. Rabbi Hirschman did it all in Hebrew, and Musetta didn't scowl once; she stood there like a marble statue, her lips pressed together primly, looking above it all (except for the hankie in her hand, crushed to nothing). Meyer, with a yarmulke on his head and a tallis on his shoulders, looked serious and almost like a man much older than he is. His mother and two sisters and two brothers were there, but none of them spoke to me. Only the mother, whose name is Fanny, spoke to Mama for a few minutes. I don't think they like the idea of Meyer marrying into a family that has no visible means of support.

Four men held up the chuppah (Nathan, Uncle Hymie, Len, and Richard). Harry was the best man, and Ava was the matron of honor. I was nothing, of course; I had secretly hoped that Musetta would ask me to be maid of honor, but I don't suppose she wanted to have her natural enemy stand with her under the chuppah. It wouldn't be right. I would never have her be my maid of honor if I were ever to marry.

After the ceremony I tried not to watch Musetta and Meyer every minute; I didn't want to have my eyes on them when they gave each other the signal that meant "let's go." (They were going to Niagara Falls for a few days.)

But of course I did see it happen anyway; I was standing at the far end of the dining-room table, chewing a slice of honey cake, when I saw him slip into the kitchen and make a high sign to her with his eyebrows. She lowered her lids and stepped sideways through the crowd in her delicate, pointy-toed leather shoes. And then he stepped behind the side of the refrigerator with her, and I could see nothing but the slender curve of her back, his long arms around her, his big powerful hands pressing her toward him. My heart stopped beating completely. To know about such a passion is one thing; to witness it is another. And the next thing, they were gone, and I had to wash down the honey cake with something, so I drank three glasses of sweet grape wine.

Then Harry and Linda took me home with them, all of us singing in the street as we walked, and Harry swinging my little valise with my nightgown and robe.

"We have a surprise for you," they said as Harry unlocked the door of their basement apartment. They dragged me, each holding one hand, down the few steps and pulled me into their bedroom. "In honor of you . . . " Harry said, motioning toward the bed where I saw the most garish set of purple silk sheets and pillowcases!

"What are you talking about?"

"These are really special," Linda said. "We used them only once before, on our wedding night."

"So?" I said.

"Well, since this is also a wedding night, we put them on the bed again."

"Well, good," I said. "I hope you enjoy them." I felt myself beginning to blush. "So now I'll go and lie down on the couch. I'm really tired."

"The couch!" Harry said. "We're all going to sleep in the big bed! On the satin sheets!" He laughed like a madman. "Linda will be happy to share me, right, Linda?"

Linda giggled. "Oh you silly. But he's right. "We're all going to sleep together. It will be perfectly safe, Gilda. I'll be in the middle. There's plenty of room; there's no reason for you to sleep on the lumpy old couch."

"You must be mad," I said. But then I started giggling, and Linda pushed me into the bathroom and undressed me, helping me get my arms into my nightgown. The next thing I knew we were all horsing around in the big bed, tangling our arms and legs together and giggling and tickling till I felt completely dizzy and totally not myself. As we got calmed down and caught our breath, no one could say a word for the longest time.

Linda was in the middle, and just as we were beginning to relax, Harry started the whole thing again, flinging off the bedclothes and pretending to bite my thigh and throwing the pillows in the air.

"Shh, Mrs. Slotkin upstairs will have a fit," Linda said, but she was just as crazy as Harry. Finally, in exhaustion, we all fell asleep piled on one another, and when I opened my eyes this morning, Harry was in the middle, and my forehead was resting against his hard shoulder, and I could see his chest rise and fall as he breathed. He had his arm around Linda (he was partly turned toward her), but my foot was against his leg, and I could feel his heat all through my body.

Such a pure animal pleasure! I stayed as long as I dared, but finally got up and tiptoed into the bathroom, where I put on my robe. It was then, as I stood looking at my face in the mirror, that I thought of Musetta and Meyer, and of what they had done during the night—how they, like Linda and Harry, were locked together in love, in sleep, in marriage, right at that moment. And then the party ended, and I faced up to myself again, to Gilda Sauerbach, in this age of her life, in this world, with this fate.

SEVENTY-SEVEN

"Are you awake, Mew?"

"Do you think I'm a cat?"

"Well, Moo, then."

"A cow? That's worse!"

"Well, I can't call you Musetta now that we're married. It will take up too much time. Let's say we're married seventy-five years; think of all the times I will be saying your name. I will spend years just saying 'setta' alone!"

"Well, how else would you rather spend the time?"

"Kissing you, my dear Moo." Meyer plunged his lips into the hollow of Musetta's neck and blew on her skin as if it were a bugle. She screamed and laughed all at once, too weak to push him away.

"You're crazy! Then I will have to call you 'My' instead of Meyer. 'My and Moo'—what a pair we'll make!"

"We've already made a nice pairing," Meyer said quietly, moving her hair gently off her cheek. "Don't you think?"

Musetta did not raise her eyes to his; instead she turned on her side, feeling the springs creak in the unfamiliar bed, and let him fit his body against her back. She preferred not to talk about last night lest she show too little feeling or enthusiasm for an activity that Meyer clearly relished.

The joining of their bodies during the night had not horrified her, but rather seemed an exploration of a side of human existence she didn't prefer to dwell on. She had been tired to the point of exhaustion when finally they had arrived at the Rustic Hills Inn. The hotel room had been chilly, and she had claimed a few additional minutes of privacy by telling Meyer she was going to take a hot shower. Then she had been jarred to the very marrow of her bones when he entered the bathroom without ceremony and tossed a glassful of cold water over the shower curtain. He quieted her scream with a kiss, jumping into the shower with her and letting the water stream over his face and hair and onto the tiled bathroom floor without regard to consequences.

He had such animal energy! In bed he trumpeted songs and distributed caresses on every surface of her body, even between her toes and on the rough curves of her heels. He seemed to accept her totally, while she would have been more comfortable keeping certain places private, places that were less than ladylike and less in keeping with her image of herself.

This morning Meyer had not tried to conceal his heavy breath from her face or closed the bathroom door completely when he urinated into the toilet. She both admired and feared his unabashed acceptance of himself in all his aspects.

There were things about lovemaking that were messy; there were wetness and slipperiness, strange squeaking and sucking sounds; there were all the embarrassing mechanics of rubber protection devices going on and coming off.

Musetta had kept in her mind an image of the piano in the lounge of the small hotel—of how in the morning, when this necessary night was over and she was clean and dry and dressed in her lovely beige linen suit, when they had eaten breakfast on a nicely set table with a single rose in a vase at its center, when other guests were pleasantly sitting around on the chairs and couches, she would sit down delicately at the piano and play a Chopin waltz.

But now Meyer was nibbling at the nape of her neck, his hand was skiing down the curve of her side and up over the rise of her hip. In her back she could feel the baton of his inner music rising for an encore performance.

"I would love some breakfast!" she said, bounding out of bed and letting a cold draft of air billow the sheet as it settled over his outstretched arms. "Wouldn't you?" Not looking back, she tiptoed barefooted across the wooden floor to the even colder tile of the bathroom. "A quick shower," she said to him over her shoulder, closing the door firmly. And this time she turned the lock very quietly.

As she hoped, after breakfast there were many admirers for her piano playing. Meyer sat alone on a couch at the far end of the room, his arm stretched casually over the back of it, his face like a mellow moon as he beamed his warm, continuous smile her way. When she finished playing, the hotel guests who had gathered around applauded energetically and urged her to play another piece. She demurred, smiling sweetly, and stood gracefully, saying that her husband was waiting for her.

In a dreamlike mood she swept across the room, where she took Meyer's hand, and exited with him to the outside of the hotel, where a chill wind was blowing.

"Let's go and see the falls," she said. "We do have to see them at least once while we're here."

"You'll need your coat, though," Meyer said. "Let's go back to the room first." Musetta hesitated. If they went back to the room, and he had her there alone, he might once again want to engage her in lovemaking activities. She hoped to limit them as much as she could without offending him.

Just then an old car came speeding down the street, jumping wildly over the curb and racing toward them on the sidewalk. Musetta felt Meyer fling her back against the building and at the same time saw him block her with his body, as if he could stop the car with the force of his outstretched arms. With its wheels spinning, the car butted into the front wall of the hotel. In the midst of the smoke and gasoline fumes, Musetta could see a man slumped over the wheel of the car. The motor roared and the wheels of the car continued to spin.

"Get back!" Meyer yelled to her. "Get out of the way!"

"You get back too!" she shrieked. Meyer was running toward the car, his jacket flapping about his waist.

"You'll be killed!" she cried.

But now Meyer was trying to open the door of the car. Unable to open it, he flung his foot at the window, kicking it till the glass shattered and he could reach inside to open the door. Musetta watched him climb into the car and struggle with the man inside. Others were gathering at the scene. Meyer dragged the man to the pavement and called out hoarsely, "Call an ambulance, hurry, I think he's had a heart attack."

Blood was running down Meyer's arm as he held the man's head gently. "He's breathing," he called out finally. "I think he'll live."

● ⟨◉⟩ ●

That night, as Musetta and Meyer lay in bed, she gently stroked the heavy bandage on his arm. "You must never do such a thing again," she said. "You could have been killed."

"I saved the man, Moo," Meyer said. "He'll be okay, the doctor said so."

"But what about me? I could have been left a widow on my honeymoon."

"I didn't think of you just then, Moo."

"I know," she said. "That's what I mean."

"The man's foot was wedged on the gas pedal," Meyer said. "I had to get him out of there. He could have killed other people. The car could have gone up in flames."

"But what if you'd been killed?"

"I'm fine, so don't worry."

"But you took a terrible risk," Musetta said.

"A man who doesn't take risks isn't living his life," Meyer said. "Look—don't worry about it. It's over. I'm only a little worse for the wear. And I promise you . . . tomorrow we'll go and look at Niagara Falls."

"Only if you don't jump in to rescue someone," Musetta said. "Swear to me, even if someone is drowning, you won't go in after him."

"Only if it's you," Meyer said. "Is that all right?"

"Well—only if it's me," she conceded.

1935

SEVENTY-EIGHT

January 17, 1935

Secret Heart

"Moo," he calls her "Moo"—and it's the perfect name for her. She hates it, she says it sounds like he's calling his pet cow home, but I soothed her a little bit the other day by telling her it was really an elegant French word. "Oh, what does it mean?" she said, perking up, already thinking it sounded classy.

"It has something to do with the expression of the mouth," I said. That seemed to please her, and for once she didn't go rushing to the dictionary to check, which is lucky for me since the word she'd find was *moue*, meaning "a grimace expressive of petulance or dissatisfaction." It's perfect for her, of course. *Miss Petulance of 1935*. Or should I say "Mrs."? Musetta, my married sister. How could I forget it? I hear them come up the stairs at bedtime, laughing softly. (Only Meyer can make her laugh, no one else!) I hear them in their bedroom getting undressed, hear the hangers slide and clink in their closet, hear Meyer's shoes clunk on the floor, hear them going down the hall to the bathroom, one at a time, and hear them finally close their door for the night . . . I try not to hear the rest.

What am I afraid of? Sometimes I hum myself to sleep, my heart pounding . . . but with what? Jealousy? Fear? Excitement? My mind does such strange things. I imagine Musetta in terrible unladylike positions. ("Intercourse is done with the woman on her back and knees flexed," our medical book says.) When I imagine that, I think of Musetta in the dentist's chair, her face screwed up tight, her eyes squeezed closed, her fingers gripping the arms of the chair in panic. She has always hated her physical body, as if it were an insult to her higher instincts, as if it were mortifying to have to chew and swallow and go to the bathroom. She never sweats! Never! It's as if she set her mind never to allow such a disgusting thing to happen to her. God only knows what she would do if she had a face like mine, with red angry pus pimples that burst and bleed and ooze! (I'm the one who knows what it's like to hate one's body!) But then—what is she thinking during those animal pairings that I know occur on the other side of my bedroom wall? I don't have trouble with Meyer; he's glad to be an animal. I think of the way he bites her and growls and sniffs her (even in front of me, at the beach, on picnics!). And I've seen him eat with great lusty appetite, swirling big chunks of bread around in delicious pot roast gravy, puncturing the yolks of his fried eggs at breakfast with a kind of ecstatic energy. Musetta practically gags breakfast down; she eats only the yolk of the egg, never the white (which, in its raw state, reminds her of mucous), and she chews with her eyes looking mournful and apologetic (as Bingo does when he has to "do his duty" outside in the mornings).

But how strange that Musetta doesn't even let her food touch her lips, but somehow takes each morsel off her fork with her teeth in order not to have intimate contact with any succulent matter. Well, never mind what they do at night behind closed doors. It isn't my business, is it? Better I should write about other matters.

Two subjects engage me much of the time, one happy (my dog Bingo!) and one horrible and sad. Hauptmann's trial is in the newspapers and on the radio all the time. What a grisly thing this is, and poor Anne Lindbergh, a little slip of a girl, a shy, delicate type (like me? she is about my age), has to live it all again, though it has been three years since her baby was kidnapped and found murdered. Whenever I envy her for her beautiful life (her handsome, sweet-tempered mate, the dimple in his chin!) and her second son, Jon (who looks so like the murdered baby it chills my heart), I think it is the same good luck and wealth and fame and beauty that have brought down on them this horror. At times, I thank God I am invisible, a tiny mouse crouching in a dark corner. Maybe I will escape certain miseries as a result of my insignificant life here. And I am not totally without love now. For I have my precious darling Bingo. Mama and Nathan were visiting Aunt Rose in the city, and a neighbor had a basket of puppies she was trying to find homes for. Mama, of course, could be talked into almost anything, and lo and behold, when she came home, she had this bit of brown and white fluff wrapped up in her coat, its adorable little eyes peeking out, its tongue flicking at me. Love at first sight! Mama isn't always silly—she has a sixth sense that's quite delicate. Some wisdom in her told her that I need something to love, to cuddle, some creature that will lick my face and never recoil from my scarred skin.

So Bingo is mine now. What a blissful mixture of Pomeranian and poodle. What trusting, kind eyes she has. What a soft, delicate underside—and beneath her tender skin, the vulnerable beating of her strong little heart. How she depends on me! For petting, for food, for long sweet talks, for love.

Musetta said Bingo smells, so I gave her a bath.

Musetta said she can't stand the sight of the dog licking herself, so I hide her when Musetta is around.

Musetta said it was disgusting to see her "mess" out by the curb, so whenever I take Bingo for a walk, I carry an old spoon and some newspaper to wrap her droppings in.

Musetta said the dog's nails tap on the floor when she walks and that it gives her a headache, so I said, "What do you want me to do? Cut off her feet?" And then Musetta was quiet.

I never tell Musetta what she does to me. I suppose I never shall.

SEVENTY-NINE

"It won't take long, maybe a half-hour," Musetta said. "The walk will do you good."

"I'm busy, I don't have time," Gilda said. She was sitting on her bed, clipping another poem from the newspaper and pasting it in the back of her photo album. Musetta could see an article just above the poem with the headline "Married Persons Happier, Columbia Survey Discloses." She leaned closer and read the first line: "If you're worried and aren't feeling healthy, get married."

"If you aren't feeling healthy," she said to Gilda, "a walk can do wonders."

"There's nothing wrong with my health," Gilda said. "I just have things to do here." She pressed the poem delicately against the black album leaf.

"What's this one about?" Musetta asked, in spite of herself. The last poem Gilda had shown her described a heart that was like a festered sore. The one before that was about a girl who wanted "to be a raindrop on my beloved's hand. . . . " It never ceased to amaze Musetta how Gilda's mind worked.

"Do you want me to read you the part I like?" Gilda asked.

"Will you go with me then?"

"What has one thing got to do with another? You're not doing me a favor by listening to the poem."

"Read it."

"Well—it's called 'Men Are Like Wild Horses.' This is the important part:

'They will not tolerate a chafing saddle,
and woe to any booted legs
that straddle their quivering backs . . .
But come to them with praise and honeyed words,
Reach out and pat their noses, touch their lips,
A lump of sugar in your fingertips,
Their rolling eyes will calm, their hoof beats still,
And they will take you anywhere you will.
Learn early; men cannot to pushed and shoved,
But, like fine horses, can be led and loved.'"

"Not so bad," said Musetta. "Better than some of the mush you seem to like."

"You would do well to heed that advice," Gilda said. "I heard you arguing with Meyer after dinner last night. Nagging isn't the way to get around him. If you want him to better himself, the way to do it isn't to browbeat him and tell him how he's belittling himself selling pajamas in a department store."

"And how would you do it, if you know so much about men?"

"Well, certainly not your way. I would be sweet, for one thing, I would be encouraging, I would stand behind him. What you do is discourage him by telling him that your salary is better than his. You should never do that. He's the man, Musetta."

"Well, that's just the point. If he's the 'man,' then he ought to be ambitious."

"Not everyone has your drive, Musetta."

"What do you mean by that?"

"I mean that Meyer is easy-going, he enjoys life, he doesn't always worry about what he doesn't have. The problem is that you always judge people by what they do, not who they are. You probably should have married Arthur Eslick or some other lawyer or a doctor—someone with a fancy education."

"Is that so?" Musetta asked, feeling her eyes narrow.

Gilda sat there prim and righteous on her bed, wearing a pink dotted-swiss blouse with a lace collar and holding her album possessively on her lap. It was filled with poems, some of them circled with red hearts.

"It says here in one of the articles I clipped . . . ," Gilda said, turning the pages carefully, " . . . here it is." She read aloud: "'These Modern Eves' is the headline. *'Dr. Paul Popenoe, director of the Los Angeles Institute of Family Relations, spoke on marriage last week before the American Home Economics Association in this city. He said very few men visited his Institute in search of wives, but the husband-hunting women were numerous.'* This is the important part," Gilda stressed. "*'In regard to marriage failures the superior education of wives is a frequent cause of breaks. No matter how successful the husband may be financially, the wife has, in general, a superiority complex toward him. Thus again, science verifies old folk ideas. The dominating female continues to nab her man and then to 'henpeck' him. And the only avoidance for the male of the species is to follow his grandfather's advice about women—either marry them young and dumb, or else don't marry at all.'*"

"How do you apply that to me?" Musetta asked. "Meyer isn't exactly financially successful."

"But you think you're so smart!" Gilda said. "If you had married Arthur Eslick, you wouldn't feel that smart because he would be a lawyer and you would be just a secretary. But with Meyer . . . well, you can be Queen of the Roost!"

"So you think he should have married someone 'young and dumb'? Who, exactly, did you have in mind? You?"

"Oh—Musetta, let's just forget all this. All I mean is that you ought to gently encourage him, not bludgeon him."

"Don't have such big ears if our private matters bother you so much."

"I don't have big ears," Gilda said, reddening. "If you and he shout, how can I help but hear?"

"Sometimes we whisper, and I have no doubt that you hear!"

"I also can't help that you have a room right on the other side of this wall," Gilda said, gesturing toward the front room.

"God only knows I wish we didn't live here! If only you earned money, Gilda! Meyer thinks it's his job to pay for everyone, for me and you, and for Mama and Nathan. All on what he earns at A & S! How can we ever save, or have a family or anything?"

"You know I've tried to get jobs," Gilda said.

"Not hard enough."

"Well, don't judge a woman unless you've walked a mile in her shoes."

"Is that some crap you cut out of the newspaper?"

"Crap?" Gilda said. Tears filled her eyes, and she turned quietly and closed her album. "Never mind. I won't bother you with my clippings."

"Oh—what's the point of all this?" Musetta said impatiently. "I only came in here to ask you to come with me to the beauty parlor. I still intend to go, I have an appointment in an hour."

"I told you . . . " Gilda said, sniffling into an embroidered handkerchief. "I will cut your hair for free."

"But it's a new cut, a kind of wavy bob. I want you to watch them do it, and then you can imitate it at home when my hair grows out and it has to be cut again."

"How do you know I could copy it?"

"Because you can do anything with hair! You're a genius when it comes to things like that!"

Musetta saw Gilda smile tremulously.

"Do you really think I'm good?"

"Yes—you're very good in certain things," Musetta assured her. "Sometimes you're a genius."

"Well, okay then; I'll come along with you."

EIGHTY

March 12, 1935

Secret Heart

I'm trembling so I can hardly write! I have Bingo in my lap right now, and her little warm snout is nestled way down between my legs, it's almost indecent. I don't know if I want to laugh or cry; my whole life is changing. Starting tomorrow morning I will have a job! Yesterday I went with Musetta to Cindy Lee's Beauty Parlor as a spy. The plan was for me to watch Musetta get a new-style bob and then be able to do it for her at home. Cindy Lee is no dummy; she saw me sitting there watching every snip, and she said in her loud, bleached-blonde way, "Hey, what're you gonna do, set up shop for twenty-five cents less down the street?"

I just smiled at her, and she said, "You got good fingers for holding scissors, you know? People say that about piano players, but I look for good cutters."

Musetta piped up and said, "That's my sister. She's a real talent, she can do nails and eyebrows and anything with her hands." Well, I was really flabbergasted. I don't often get compliments from Musetta. Cindy Lee (she's about thirty-five, big breasted, loud) started glancing at me in the mirror and finally said, "You here for a styling, too?"

"No," I said. "I'm just keeping Musetta company."

"Well—from the looks of you, you could use one," she said. At first I thought she was making fun of me, of my complexion, but then she went on to say, "With that thick hair of yours, I could do wonders if you'd let me get at it." Musetta (who is never talkative with shop people) was far too cheerful and chatty; I knew something was up. She said to Cindy Lee, "My sister needs a job;. Why don't you take her on as an apprentice? She wouldn't cost you very much, and I think you'd be surprised at her skill."

"Hey, kid," Cindy Lee said. "You want to try it out? I'll pay you two dollars a week!" All the while she was snipping and cutting Musetta's long gorgeous hair, and every shining lock that fell to the floor gave me a pang. I started to get a cramp in my stomach. Just the thought of working with this loud, brassy woman made me ill. Leaving home every day . . . and abandoning Bingo . . . and forcing myself to talk to the ladies who came in for a haircut! It was unthinkable.

"I'm not too well," I started to say, but Musetta interrupted and said loudly, "That would be grand. That's wonderful."

"You got plenty of energy?" Cindy Lee said to me.

Musetta said, "She's much stronger than she looks. She can work hard." Before I knew it, I had agreed to come back on Wednesday and start work. I can't believe it!

Since I was throwing all my usual caution to the wind, I also agreed to let her cut my hair off! I seem to be losing control of my life, the rug pulled out from under me, the sky whirling above my head. I know Musetta is doing this for her own gains, but maybe this is good for me in some way. It will force me to get out in the world and try to do the things that regular people do. Of course, you can't meet any men in a beauty parlor, but, even so, I might learn some tricks of the trade. Who knows? After a few weeks working in a beauty parlor, I might even be more beautiful!

EIGHTY-ONE

"You never should have urged Gilda to cut off her hair," Meyer said as he got ready for bed. It was already very cold in the house; snow was falling outside, and each windowsill had a little hump of white growing on it. Mama turned off the furnace at eight every evening to save oil, and by eleven the house was bitter with chill. Musetta pulled the knitted afghan up to her chin.

"Why not? She looks more modern now."

"She looks terrible," Meyer said. "Like a chicken without feathers. I'm surprised you didn't stop her. Her hair was her beautiful feature."

"And mine wasn't?"

"Your hair is only one of your beautiful features," Meyer said, turning back the covers and sliding into bed beside her. She felt an icy draft billow the sheet.

"Be careful, I'm just getting warm, don't let in cold air."

"But her hair was her only asset," Meyer said, intent on pursuing the subject. "It called attention away from her skin, and it gave her a frail, feminine quality."

"You don't like my haircut," Musetta said, challenging him.

"Your haircut is fine," he said. "Your face is lovely, and now your neck shows, and that's lovely too."

"I don't like you to compliment me in that tone of voice."

"I just think you did her a disservice, advising her to have her hair cut, that's all." Musetta lay in bed, waiting for him to roll over toward her, to reach for her as he always did. Instead he lay on his back, tensely, not moving.

"I'm sick of her," Musetta said. "I want to move away from here."

Meyer was silent.

"Right now she's just on the other side of that wall, trying to catch every word we say."

"I'm sure she's asleep," Meyer said. "And we should go to sleep too."

"I hate it when we, well . . . you know, when you make your grunts and groaning noises, and then in the morning she looks at me as if to say, 'I know what you two were doing last night.'"

"I never saw her look at you like that."

"Well, you don't notice things like I do." She felt Meyer reach for her hand.

"Don't touch me, your hands are like ice. I mean it—I want to move to a place of our own. I don't want to hear Nathan coughing and spitting when I pass the bathroom, and I don't want Mama picking up our underwear for the wash. I want privacy."

"Go to sleep, Moo," Meyer said. "Someday we'll have our own place. When your family can manage better on its own."

"When will that be? When Gilda is married? When Nathan discovers a million dollars in the backyard? When they're all dead?"

"Well, you said Gilda is just starting her new job. That's a good sign, isn't it? And someday, when I'm earning more money, we might be able to move and send money back here for them."

"And send money to your mother also, right? I mean, first we have to support everyone here and we have to help your mother and your sisters and brothers, and then whatever's left—left of your paycheck as a pajama salesman—that will be for us."

"I do the best I can, Moo."

"It's not good enough," she said bitterly.

"Then let your firm send you to law school at night. Do something yourself if you don't like what I do. In fact, you don't even have to go at night; quit your job and go to law school during the day. We'll manage somehow."

"How?"

"We could ask for a loan from my uncle Eddie; he does really well with his candy store."

"Let him give you a partnership then, and you work there, too. Then you'd have a future."

"I'll find something that's right for me, eventually, Moo. A candy store isn't what I want."

"You want to own oil wells?"

"No—I'm just sorry that you wish I did."

"Don't go making suggestions that I go to law school. I have enough responsibility as it is."

"I only meant that if you wanted to, you could. I want you to be happy, Moo. Maybe you want to take piano lessons again. We could manage that. Maybe you ought to finish school; you used to tell me you were an excellent student—the best!"

"Don't worry about my life," Musetta said. "Worry about yours, Meyer. Stop worrying about my little sister's hairdo and her delicate system, and think about me, think about what I need."

"I think about you all the time, Moo."

"I'm sure you do." She turned her back toward him and pulled the covers nearly over her head. She felt she was losing control of herself. Her heart had started pounding when Meyer urged her to do something with her own life.

Where had her future gone? She had wanted to do something great and important, but the moment to seize the opportunity had passed. She had lost her focus, her direction. Now she felt entitled to be taken care of and have children if she wanted them, to cook and bake in her own house. She hated cooking and baking, but she would never have her own house to try to get to like it, anyway! She would always live here, forever and ever, with Mama (who still left the outside lights on every night in case Shmuel might someday find his way home from whatever distant island he had washed up on so many years ago), and with Nathan (who was meek and grateful and always in the way), and with Gilda and her stinking dog Bingo. She and Meyer would never have their own living room, their own kitchen, their own garden. And she would never be a famous "anything"—never famous, never rich, never important.

Her life was cursed. Maybe she should have married Arthur Eslick! Angrily, she kicked Meyer in the shins under the blankets, startling him.

"Moo—try to relax. I don't know what's bothering you, but maybe it will just go away. We have to be realistic and do what we can. Don't attack me. You know how much I love you." She shrugged off his gentle touch. She should have married Arthur Eslick, and Meyer should have married Gilda!

1936

EIGHTY-TWO

April 4, 1936

Secret Heart

Last night Bruno Richard Hauptmann died in the electric chair for the kidnapping and murder of the Lindbergh baby. I think of how I would feel if Bingo were kidnapped, and then I think of Lindbergh's baby, with that mop of golden curls and that serious-looking dimple in his chin. Most of all I feel for Anne, who is so sweet and gentle, and has had to live four years between the night Hauptmann stole her baby and this final moment. I don't know why I think about this as much as I do—I don't generally give a hoot for the news or politicians or public figures (except for movie stars—I do like them), but for some reason I imagine myself in Anne Lindbergh's shoes, being at the side of that tall, decent, brave man who has had to go through this terrible time with her. (When I was seventeen, just after he flew alone in his plane to Paris, he was in a parade on Avenue P, and I saw him go by, waving out of a car. I will never forget his sweet boyish face. In some ways Ava's Richard reminds me of Lindbergh—that same kind of goodness and kindness in his eyes. And of course his love of airplanes!)

I can't believe that Richard will be eighteen this year! We are all getting so old . . . Mama will be sixty-five, and Ava forty, and Musetta twenty-nine! And I will be twenty-six, truly an old maid! Little Sammy is the youngest.

I don't know why I am taking this long view, but I feel things are changing and will soon be different. I worry about Mama dying—What if she dies and I am left to care for Nathan? What if Musetta and Meyer move away? She always threatens it, as if to make me behave. "Gilda, keep that miserable dog off my bed! I hate finding dog hairs on the afghan! I will have to move out of here if you don't keep Bingo out of my way!"

And Richard will be a man soon. I think Ava will die of grief when he leaves. Ava lives in the light of his eyes. She ought to be better friends with Len, for someday the children will be gone, and she will realize she has barely talked to Len in twenty years! (Len keeps busy; he is hardly ever home and is always out making business deals. He's getting fatter and richer every day.)

As for me, I see myself working at Cindy Lee's for the rest of my life, probably. She's paying me six dollars a week now, with work on Saturdays till after six—it's her busiest day. I am due there in half an hour, but am all dressed and ready to go, so I have some time to write here.

I like the ladies there. They like me. I know how to make them beautiful. I have a talent, a knack with my fingers. I can create wonderful clusters of curls from hair like straw.

From hands that are ragged and raw I can create soft graceful hands, with nails uniform and glowing with color. As if in return for the wonders I work, the women trust me with secrets. Maybe the hum of the dryer under which they must sit for thirty minutes creates a sense of confidence or trust. While I am combing out their sets, the women often tell me about their problems, their children, their no-good husbands or mothers-in-law.

Cindy Lee always says, "Give us some nice juicy gossip," but the women ignore her; she's too loud and stupid to trust with anything important. She only wants to know about illicit romances. She's got some strange fellow always waiting for her after work every Saturday. He wears a straw hat and white shoes and has a red, veiny nose. Whenever he sees me, he says "You remind me of Greta Garbo, sweetheart. Hasn't some guy got you yet?" He makes me shudder.

One of my customers, Mrs. Raspman, always squeezes my hand warmly when she leaves the beauty parlor and drops a tip into my apron pocket. Yesterday she put a letter in my pocket and said, "Don't be offended, darling, but my nephew is a medical student, and I asked him to write this up for you."

When I read it, my face was burning, to think that someone could dare to intrude in such a highly personal area! It was a long letter, which I will fold into the pages here. I would rather die than take this advice, but here is what he wrote:

Dear Miss Sauerbach:

My aunt, Gertie Raspman, told me of your difficulties with acne and asked that I make some general comments that might help you. The cure of one or more pimples is a simple thing of which nature takes care. The cause may be internal or external. If internal, it may be due to the secretion of putrefactive products from the intestine. These may get into the blood and destroy or impede the natural resistance that the body has under normal conditions. Another internal cause may be a weak condition of the skin of the face. Such a condition might cause eruptions of the skin due to foreign substances in the bloodstream or because of attacks by germs or bacteria from without. The face, being exposed, is assailed by the weather, dust, dirt, and other rough particles, and, if tender, is minutely scratched, thus permitting the invasion of the skin by bacteria, conveyed possibly by the hands to the face.

Most likely, the cause is external (dirt! foreign matter!), and the way to approach ridding yourself of it is to rid yourself of all possible sources of contamination and develop such habits as approach perfect cleanliness. You must conform to the following rules:

Do not touch the face except when you wash it.

Keep from handling dusty or dirty things, and if you do touch such, wash your hands immediately.

Wash your hands thoroughly after contact with the body, shoes, or after visiting the bathroom. Wash your hands after touching or holding plants. Never touch flowers! Don't touch your dog! In fact, give her away to someone to take care of. This is extremely important! There may be many things about the dog that affect your skin, even though you think them inconsequential: i.e., the smell of the hair, the sweat, the dirty and bacteria-laden fur. These things are conveyed to the face or to the hands and then to the face. You may not think that a dog is a dirty animal, but he is, even when well cared for, but let me explain why it is impossible to keep a domestic animal clean. Infection is brought in from the outside by the dog or by our feet and transmitted to the fur of the dog when he lies on the floor. Thus, the very things we step on in the streets are conveyed to our hands and thus to our face or mouth by patting, stroking, or fondling the dog even though the latter be a very clean animal. If you do ever by some careless accident touch your dog, rush at once to the bathroom, grasp your soap, and as quickly as possible scrub, scrub, scrub away the devilish matter!

In conclusion, I wish to advise you to wash your face often. This is your only hope. Lest you think I am somehow suggesting you are unclean, let me assure you this is certainly not the case. My aunt tells me you are a charming young woman, and I sincerely hope that someday we may meet and become acquainted.

Yours truly,

Milton Raspman

(soon to be Dr. Milton Raspman)

EIGHTY-THREE

"There," Ava said. "Again the phone is ringing, even at this hour." She flung the blankets back and felt for her slippers in the dark.

"It's probably Barney," Len said, turning on the bedside lamp. "I'll be right down to talk to him."

Ava hurried down the stairs, not wanting the ringing phone to wake the boys. "Yes, hello. Barney, yes, I know it's you. He's coming. Is it so important it couldn't wait till morning?" She handed the receiver to Len, who was behind her. "Tell him next time to wait till the morning."

Len nodded impatiently and waved her away. She went slowly upstairs, only half-listening to Len's voice; it was the usual—numbers, people, places, arrangements.

"Don't complain," Len had told her the last time they'd argued about it. "Not everyone has it easy making a living; you have what you want, the boys have what they want—who is it hurting?"

"Do you think the boys will be proud of a father who is a bookie? Is that what you want for them?"

"No—I want more for them! And this way they'll have it! Isn't Richard going to college now? Aren't you proud?"

Ava had had to nod her assent. The word *college* gave her a thrill; the idea that her son was there, at that special place, made her feel as if she wanted to bow her head and give thanks. But who should she thank? That little creepy man Barney to whom Len was always talking on the phone?

Now she heard Len put down the phone and come slowly up the stairs. Each step creaked under his weight. She could feel the thuds move through the floorboards and up through the headboard of the big bed.

He was wearing only pajama tops. She had more than once begged him, "Don't go around that way. God forbid the boys should come out in the hall and see you like that."

Len had said, "What is the big secret? They don't know what a man has? They are not men themselves?" And Ava had said, "That isn't the point. They should have respect for you, think of you as their father, not think of you that way."

"That's how I became their father, Ava! Did you forget?"

She had stopped talking about it; let him run around naked if he wanted to. She could not talk about it because then he might want to ask her why she would never let him approach her, why she would always turn her back to him in bed, tighten her shoulders, draw her thighs together, and pretend to be asleep. Could she say to him what she was thinking, even now, as she watched him walk to his dresser, take a notebook from his top drawer, and write some notations in it?

Some things were not to be talked about! It would be better not even to think about them. Could Len help it if he were not a young man anymore, if the skin of his buttocks hung loose, if the backs of his thighs were no longer firm and tight? She was no beauty now, either—God knew that was so!—but she kept herself covered, didn't parade around so anyone passing could see the fleshy thickness of her hips, the great doughy hammocks of her hanging breasts. But Len walked freely everywhere, undressed, like an animal. Perhaps all men were that way. But it wasn't only that. And it wasn't only that he was getting old, that his springy hair was thinning, that soon he would be bald, that he had loose folds now in his cheeks and dark bags under his eyes. That was the fate of them all, that they should grow old and lose their beauty. But the truth was that there was a young god in the house, their son Richard, and Ava had only to glance at him and her heart would begin to pound and her knees to weaken.

In the summer he would go with her and Sammy to Coney Island, and the sight of his young thighs in bathing trunks as he ran along the beach would strike her with dizziness under the bright merciless sun; she would stare at him till the ocean became black and spun over her face like a shroud. She was deeply ashamed to have such a love for her own son. But it was not a feeling she could control or dismiss; it colored her life. It was the reason for her rising in the morning, the source of the energy that moved her through the daily duties she had to face. Her son was her blessing in life, her single beautiful creation. Sammy she adored also, but he was different. She felt a distance from him; he was her son, but she understood it was a temporary arrangement. For a while he would be with her, and then he would grow up and leave. But when she thought of Richard's leaving her, her breath would almost stop; she would shut off the thought as if she were knotting a cord about a bleeding artery. To let it flow would kill her.

Len was mumbling now as he added up some figures. He looked like a fool, his private parts hanging there in full view. She could not look at him. When she looked at that part of him, she thought sometimes of a big mushroom and two boiled potatoes, sometimes of a hose and doorknobs. Yet when she thought of Richard, at eighteen now and much taller than Len, she thought of his penis as a long beautiful arrow.

Shame! For a mother to think such things! If only she were not such a cold fish, cold tomato, cold dame—things that men called women such as she. She had not been unfair to Len; she had for years been a patient wife, letting him do his business with her. He was never unkind or rough, yet he was not with her in any way, either, at those times. He was with himself, and with her only because her body had a place he wanted.

She knew of other women her age who were still sexy, who like floozies wiggled their behinds and winked at men. But she'd never had it in her, that wildness, that open hunger that men hunted for and loved and made jokes about. She wondered if it had been trampled out of her somehow. Perhaps Isaac had frightened her when she was young and had gone out dancing with Johnny Quinn, the Irishman. But with Johnny she had felt something, a little twinge of fire, a temptation to take a risk. His smile, his awareness of the chance to have fun in life, had been exciting. When they'd danced and he'd looked into her eyes, yes, she had felt something. But it never had a chance to come to life. When she remembered Isaac and his coldness, his tight disapproving face, she thought that he had trampled something to death in her, some soft open sweetness she should have had in life. But what was the sense of thinking like this?

"Hurry, can't you come to bed already? It's late. I want to turn off the light!" Ava grumbled.

"I'm done, I'm finished, Ava—I'm coming." Len tramped over the floor to the bed. "This will be a good week; we're having a run of luck these days." He sat his old man's bottom down on the sheets and swung his hairy legs into the bed. When he had shut the light off, he lay his head on the pillow and sighed. "Ava," he whispered, "I do this for you and the boys, to make you happy, to give you the things you need."

"I know," she answered, her lips pressed into the pillow, her back already toward him.

"Do you have all the things you need?" He tentatively touched her back with his hand. "Do you, Ava?"

"You give me everything I need, Len," she said. "You're a good provider, there couldn't be a better one."

EIGHTY-FOUR

At first there was only a tap-tapping sound in the radiator; every morning it began this way, a thin, insidious metallic tapping that seemed to come from far away, down in the bowels of the house. Musetta covered her head with her pillow and burrowed into the warm blankets. She could feel the blood begin to beat in her temples—her rest was over. Now the headache was starting. She would have to get up, feel the cold tile of the bathroom under her slippered feet, wait for the hot water to make its way up two stories so she could wash her face. Then the chilly struggle into her clothes and the attempt to swallow some breakfast. The long walk to the train station, the long ride into the city, the endless day at her desk, taking dictation, typing letters . . . I've been working too long, she thought.

I can't bear it anymore. She thought of Gilda snuggled under her quilt. Gilda could sleep more than an hour longer than Musetta. She had only to walk a few blocks to Cindy Lee's, and she was there. Even Meyer could sleep another half-hour; he could dress and eat in half the time it took her to get ready. Now the radiator pipes were beginning to shimmer and vibrate with steam. The tapping escalated into a hammering and then the hammering into a violent pounding until it felt as though the seams of the house would burst.

She knew she ought to be grateful to Mama for getting up early and turning on the furnace. But now Mama was bustling about the house, starting her cleaning, her cooking, her dusting—all the things she did every day.

I could pretend I'm sick today, Musetta thought. I could just go back to sleep and not go to work. She coughed slightly in Meyer's direction. She could pretend she was getting a cold. Soon the banging in the pipes would level off to a tolerable hissing sound, and she could snuggle down and go back to sleep. The decision pleased her, and she began to breathe slowly, trying to relax her body.

The doorknob rattled gently. Musetta opened one eye and watched it turn slowly. God damn it! She checked to be sure Meyer was covered by the blanket. She didn't want Mama to come in and find his naked parts staring her in the face. She closed her eyes and felt a breeze touch her face. Mama was in the room again, on her self-appointed laundry-gathering rounds. She heard Mama tiptoe along Meyer's side of the bed and then heard her knees crack slightly as she bent down and reached under the bed, feeling for Meyer's socks and underpants. There was a dull thud as she moved his shoes against one another, then the sound of her standing up and coming around to Musetta's side of the bed. She was looking for Musetta's nylons. Musetta had washed them the night before and hung them on the showerhead; she had told Mama there was no need to do this, to come creeping in at dawn looking for laundry!

Oh—it made her so furious! What if she and Meyer were . . . well, doing something! It could happen in the morning. If Meyer had his way, it would happen every morning and every night! Mama was impossible. She was insistent about being helpful, about doing what she could for Musetta to show how grateful she was that Musetta and Meyer were working and paying all the bills.

Well, thank God at least that Gilda was not in here, creeping on her hands and knees around the bed! She had to get away from here soon, or she'd die from lack of privacy.

Mama was quietly leaving now, closing the door with the slightest click of the latch. Meyer turned and yawned. Musetta was too aggravated to get back to sleep now, and there was no point staying home if she couldn't sleep. If only she could quit her job!

"Meyer," she whispered. "Are you up?"

"Yah, sure, why, is something wrong?"

"No, it's just time to get up. Don't you hear the pipes?"

"I'm coming," he said, but instantly closed his eyes.

"I may have to go away this weekend," Musetta said. She nudged Meyer. "Do you hear me?"

"Go away? What for?"

"Mr. Merkin is going to his cabin in Connecticut and would like me to come along to help him catch up on some dictation."

Meyer opened his eyes completely.

"Go with him for the weekend? I thought they never asked you to work on weekends."

"It's for business, Meyer. This is a special request. Lots of secretaries go with their employers to do weekend work. I'd get paid extra."

"I don't want you to go, Moo. Not unless I go along, too."

"Mr. Merkin wouldn't appreciate that. And don't read anything into it, Meyer. It's just something he suggested. I don't like to offend him; you know he's been very good to me. I make a very good salary and I can't just refuse."

"You ought to think about quitting your job," Meyer said, sitting up and swinging his legs out of bed. His hair was tousled and wild, the skin of his face bristly with stubble. "A married woman doesn't go off with her boss for weekends. Whatever the reason!"

"We need the money, Meyer. The oil bills are going up, the fish market charges you wouldn't believe how much these days. And the bakery, too!"

"I'm looking into other ways of making a living," Meyer said. "You know how you always urge me to quit my job? Well, I'm thinking about it seriously. I have some ideas . . . and as soon as one of them works out, maybe very soon, you can just tell Mr. Merkin you're leaving."

"So you don't want me to go with him this weekend?"

"Absolutely not!"

"Shh, you'll wake Gilda."

"Never mind Gilda. I won't have you going off to the country alone with some man."

Musetta smiled. "So you really do think I should quit my job soon?"

"Very soon."

"And if you get into a good business, do you think someday we can get a house of our own?"

"Of course, Moo, of course we will!"

"Good then," Musetta said. "Do you think the radiator is hot enough? I hate to get up until the room is warm, and I hate to put on my dress until I warm it up on the pipes."

"It's hot, I'm sure the radiator is hot by now," Meyer said.

"Well, good, I guess I'll get up then."

EIGHTY-FIVE

December 11, 1936

Secret Heart

Meyer is going into his own business! He says we may soon be rich! He came home last night with the machine that he is certain will make our fortune. As he set it up for us in the living room, he kept glancing at Musetta for approval. For once she was smiling, leaning back in the curve of the piano, her arms crossed over her chest in a smug, self-satisfied way.

Meyer explained it to us. "This is a crane machine," he said as Mama and Nathan bobbed around it like two curious birds. "Right here—in this glass box—are the little trinkets: dolls, small toys, rubber balls, whistles, pairs of dice, and then here on this platform is the one really good prize, the wristwatch. It's not that expensive, I pay about five dollars apiece for these watches—but still, it's a good prize when you only put in a nickel. Once the money drops in, this mechanical claw here starts roaming around the box—see how it goes back the forth? And then the player turns this wooden handle and tries to close the claw when it gets to the watch. Usually it misses, of course—and the claw picks up some other little prize and drops it in the chute."

"So where will you have these machines?" Mama asked.

"It's all worked out," he said proudly, smiling at Musetta. "Rube Frankel and I have bought ten machines as partners. We'll be putting them in bars and restaurants. It can't fail—we'll give a percentage to the owners, so it's to their benefit to encourage the customers to use the machines."

"Gambling . . . " Mama mumbled. "Gambling is the curse of this family." Nathan was hanging his head, and Mama was going on about Len and his betting, and about Shmuel and his getting in with a bad crowd, and all the while Meyer was smiling and moving that strange claw hand around in the box, and finally the claw dove down, gripped the cheap wristwatch, and slid it down the chute.

Meyer presented it to Mama. "Here," he said. "Let me put it on your wrist."

"*Mishuganah*," Mama said in Yiddish, waving him away, but blushing, really quite pleased.

"And if business is good," Meyer promised her, "I'm going to buy you a washer-wringer machine to put in the cellar."

"Don't make foolish promises," Mama said, but she was smiling by then.

"And I'll buy Gilda an electric hair dryer to have right here in the house, and she and Musetta will be the envy of Avenue O." I glanced at Musetta and saw her scowl; I didn't think presents for me were part of her plan. But she finally came forward and examined the machine, stroking the glass box as if it contained precious diamonds.

"How soon do you think they will produce a profit?" she asked Meyer.

"Oh—I hope very soon. In a month or two we might have the machines themselves paid off."

"Good," Musetta said. "The sooner the better."

1937

EIGHTY-SIX

Ava was coming out of Schwartz's Bakery on Kings Highway, a bagful of fragrant, warm bagels in her arm, when she became aware of a man staring at her. He was just getting into a car parked at the curb when his eyes fixed on her face and he became motionless. He stared hard at her. He was wearing a gray overcoat, a scarf, and a dark hat. She looked quickly away, feeling her heart lurch. He couldn't be someone she knew, she felt sure of that. She hurried on her way and turned into the appetizer store to buy lox and whitefish and black olives. Since her childhood, she had always comforted herself with these salty foods. She loved them more than she loved sweets; they made her saliva run, they gave her one of the few physical pleasures she enjoyed.

"Wait," she said to the salesgirl. "Before you wrap it up, let me have one of those olives." She was balancing the round black olive on her tongue as she left the store. Just as she let her teeth puncture the taut skin of it, just as it released a spray of salty, delicious juice, she felt an arm come around her shoulders and squeeze her energetically.

"I don't believe it! It's really you, Ava! Look, it's me, Johnny Quinn."

If his voice was unfamiliar after so long, the smell of his breath was not. "God help me," Ava said. "It is you."

She saw the thickly waved blond hair, lightened by gray, and the shape of his neck, thick, strong. "It must be twenty years," she said in wonder.

"More, more than that," Johnny Quinn said. "Ten lifetimes."

"It's so strange," Ava said, talking oddly because of the olive pit in her mouth, "but my first thought was, 'My God, if I talk to Johnny, I'm really going to get it from Isaac when I get home!'" She laughed, hearing the bitterness in her tone.

"And will you 'get it' from him?"

"He's been dead for years," Ava said, shifting the bags in her arms. "Besides, do you think at my age I would still be afraid of anyone?"

"What do you mean, your age? You're still eighteen to me. You still have the bloom in your cheek."

"Oh, you still have your line, Johnny Quinn," Ava said, hearing her laughter turn silvery.

"Say, come in here to the Chinese restaurant and have a pot of tea with me. Tea and fortune cookies."

"Oh—I shouldn't, I have fish to put away. Well, maybe just for a few minutes." She was aware of his height (much taller than Len) as they walked toward the entrance to the restaurant. She spat the black olive pit into her hand and then dropped it on the sidewalk without looking back.

They took a booth in the dim back of the restaurant; no one else was there but a Chinese man sitting alone at a table shelling peas. They could hear him snap each one open as he went patiently through the huge pile.

"So, anybody here?" Johnny Quinn boomed out in the shadowy quiet. "Could we get some tea and fortune cookies here, please?"

A small woman hurried forward and bowed her head. In a moment she was back with a pot of tea. "And fortune cookies with lucky fortunes in them," Johnny said. "Bring us good ones."

When the woman had padded away, he reached across the table for Ava's hand. "I wish you'd married me, Ava—and not left me to marry the shrew I got. I left her two years ago. We fought day and night."

"It never would have been good between us either, Johnny. You knew that. You know it now." Ava was sweating; she unbuttoned her coat and slipped it off.

"Who did you marry?" he asked.

"A good man," Ava said, not meeting his eyes.

"Rich?" Johnny asked, touching her hand lightly.

"He works hard," Ava said. She had sudden vision of Len, so dense, as if he had been compacted by a compressor. "So tell me—" she said in a conversational tone, "what kind of work do you do now and what brings you to Kings Highway in Brooklyn?"

"Work—did you ever think Johnny Quinn would work for a living?"

"I imagine we all have to do ordinary things after a while," Ava said. "I don't suppose you're still dancing your way through life."

"Ah, you've guessed it. Dry cleaning. I'm in dry cleaning."

"Not quite like dancing, is it?" Ava said.

"Not like dancing, no, my dear girl. And you?"

"Me? I'm a mother. I have two sons, one is eighteen, one is ten."

"And are you happy?"

"Who knows?" Ava said. "Who knows what that means?"

"Well, do you ever feeling like singing, like dancing?"

"Not like in the old days, Johnny."

"Maybe, you and me, we could make the old days come back."

"Johnny, look at me. Look how old we are now. My brother, Shmuel, you remember him? He's dead now. Isaac is dead now. My father, my real father, who disappeared when I was young, came back and tried to make up all his sins to my mother and now he's living with her on Avenue O. Unbelievable things have happened, good and bad. We can't make the old days come back. We can't go to Coney Island anymore."

"Why not?" Johnny Quinn asked. "We walk out the door here, go over to the Elevated, and we'd be at Coney Island in twenty minutes."

"That's not what I mean!" Ava said. "Tell me, how is your mother?"

"My mother is strapped in her bed, paralyzed by a stroke. I just came from visiting her. She moved to Brooklyn to live with my aunt. I was just picking up her medicine for her."

"And where do you live now?"

"The Bronx."

"Do you come to Brooklyn often?"

"Yes, and I could come more often knowing you're nearby, Ava."

"No, no—I don't think that would be a good idea, Johnny."

"We could have had beautiful children together, Ava."

Ava thought of Richard, of his beauty, and she wanted to say that no more beautiful son could ever have been born to her. The thought made her want to go home quickly. Johnny saw her reach for her coat.

"Wait, drink your tea first and let's see what our fortunes are. Here, take one."

She slowly cracked open a fortune cookie.

"Read it to me," Johnny Quinn whispered.

"It says, 'You will rediscover an old friend and be blessed.'" She felt herself flush.

"Well," he said, "you see? Fate has something in mind for us."

"I don't think so, Johnny. I am past all that."

"We are never past it, Ava," he said.

"I am."

Suddenly Johnny took the fortune from her, turned it over, and wrote a phone number on it. "Take this. Call me, Ava. If you ever want me or need me, if you ever feel I can help you in some way, call me at this number."

"Thank you, Johnny."

"I'll pray for you to call," he said.

"I wish you wouldn't," Ava said. "Then you will have reason to blame God for something he didn't do for you."

"Might as well blame God as anyone else for whatever doesn't work out. But please—call me, Ava. Call me soon."

Ava stood and got her coat, her packages. "Thank you for the tea, Johnny."

"Keep my number in a safe place."

"I will."

"Where?" he insisted. "Where?"

"I don't know. With my precious jewels!" she said with a laugh. "Will that do?"

"Promise. Promise me that the instant you get home, you'll put that number with your jewels."

"I will, I will."

He stood up. "Good-bye, my girl." He kissed her cheek quickly. "Someday I'll take you dancing again."

EIGHTY-SEVEN

March 8, 1937

Secret Heart

It is nearly midnight and I am too giddy to sleep. Bingo is curled in my lap, breathing softly. How I adore her! And to think if I had listened to (Dr.) Milton Raspman, I would have had to give her away! She is my one, loyal, absolutely true and loving friend. Imagine—tonight—when I was at the Purim dance (dressed as Queen Esther) at the Avenue N shul, a man came up to me and said, "Are you Gilda Sauerbach by any chance?" I thought, Who can this be? He was tall and fair-haired and didn't look at all Jewish, but rather like some movie actor. He had a crinkly smile and rosy-colored cheeks. "Well, yes I am," I said. "How do you know me?"

"My aunt told me you'd be here in a green nightgown!"

"Your aunt?"

"Gertie Raspman. You may have gotten my letter last year. You never replied. I hope it didn't offend you."

I'm sure I turned forty shades of red, there in front of Dr. Milton Raspman in my "green nightgown." Foolishly, earlier in the day in the beauty parlor I had told Mrs. Raspman while I was doing her hair that I was to be in the Purim play at the shul and that I would be wearing a homemade costume to play Queen Esther. I described it all to her (What else is there to do when you are cutting hair but talk and talk?). I told her about my green, hand-made nightgown, my silver slippers, my silver-beaded crown—I told her I would be regal looking. I described the cape that I would make out of the green velvet piano scarf, and the pleated standing collar I was going to make from silver paper.

And all the while she was plotting to have her nephew Milton Raspman ambush me at the shul! Oh, I can feel my blood boil, just thinking about it! How could he miss me as I stood there being queenly? And wearing the damaged face he was so eager to study in person! I felt murderous toward him at that moment.

"Excuse me," I said. "The play is beginning in two minutes." And so I hurried away and went backstage, and then the play began with Charlie Burk as King Ahaseurus striding out on the stage and saying his first silly line: "Aha, my stubborn, saucy Mrs. Ahaseurus, how dare you disobey your royal lord and master, the great king?"

Minnie Horowitz played Vashti, the king's first wife, and she kept losing her slip and forgetting her lines. It was just terrible. I don't know how I let myself be dragged into it in the first place. I struggled through my part, all the while aware of Milton Raspman there in the first row of the audience, beaming, smiling, obviously enjoying the spectacle. I wondered how his aunt had coerced him into coming.

I was as cool and indifferent as I could be. After the play I stood and talked with Linda and Harry. (Linda is now pregnant! And is so very happy and peaceful looking, so proud. I feel a pang of jealousy when I see her.) The "doctor" came and stood beside me for a while. I did my best to turn away from him—to hide a face that he obviously regards as nothing more than a medical challenge. Finally I managed to sneak away and exchange a few words with the rabbi; I agreed to sell raffles for the benefit of the building fund (the shul needs new seats) and promised that I would sell at least three books. The fact is, now that I am working at Cindy Lee's, I know dozens of women in the neighborhood, and I never go anywhere without seeing friendly faces, and I always stop to talk. So I should be able to sell the raffle books without any trouble. The job has really been good for me: the ladies all like "my gentle touch," and I know there's something special in my fingers—they seem almost separate from me as I watch them snipping and smoothing and fluffing hair. And I do wonderful manicures.

My own hands are very pretty—they set a good example for the work I do, with the dainty look of my oval-shaped nails covered with clear polish. Too bad men aren't all that interested in pretty hands; a scarred face and a flat bosom quite unbalance my luck in having pretty hands. Well, I wish I hadn't told Mama about the doctor's coming to the dance! I don't know what made me tell her; it's just that she was waiting up for me, and she always looks at me with pity, as if she knows that no one sought me out for dancing or anything else.

So—to make her feel less guilty—I told her that Gertie Raspman's nephew "the doctor" had been there. Oh, what a mistake that was! At once Mama was carrying on about what a good living a doctor makes, what a blessing it would be to have a doctor in the family. And if anyone got sick, wouldn't it be wonderful to have a doctor you could trust, who wouldn't charge you an arm and a leg!

"What did you and the doctor talk about?" Mama insisted, and so I said, "We talked about Mrs. Raspman's sister, who lives in Germany, and about all the trouble they're having there with Hitler."

The fact is I didn't talk to Milton Raspman at all, but left early, by a side door, and nearly ran all the way home to Avenue O. Some fearful feelings are in me now—I wish I hadn't been so rude, for one thing. After all, he said nothing to offend me, was simply pleasant. It's just that I don't dare hope for anything. Mama is already counting the money a doctor will make! How sad—but she has been poor so much of her life that she is frightened. I've told her to try not to worry; Meyer is doing well with his crane machines, and there's always Ava to go to—and her rich Len. (In fact, Ava has been tucking five-dollar bills into Mama's apron lately, whenever she stops by. Maybe she feels it's time they helped out. We have been very proud and have never asked her for money, though Len makes far more than Meyer ever could!)

Well, I must go to bed now. I think so much about my own personal fate, but all the way home from the shul I was thinking of Hitler and his crazy greed and hunger. Why must certain men always desire more land, more goods, more power? Why haven't they the gentleness of women? Of course, all men are not like Hitler. But in general they have something hard and cruel about them—all of them. Thank God I am not a man.

EIGHTY-EIGHT

"What?" Musetta said. "They did what? Where are you calling from?" She could hardly hear Meyer's voice and couldn't tell if it was because she had her hair as well as her ears covered by a towel or because the connection was bad. Gilda had given her a lemon and oil rinse, and she was supposed to leave the mixture on her scalp for an hour. Now that Meyer was making more money, she had left her job and had more time to pamper herself. "Talk louder, would you?" It was hard to move her lips. Gilda was also bleaching some dark hairs above her upper lip, and some cotton soaked in peroxide was balanced under her nose.

"What is he saying?" Gilda asked. "Something bad?"

"Shh," Musetta told her impatiently, "I can hardly hear him." She shook the phone. "Start over again, Meyer. You what? I should call Rube and tell him to come down to the police station? My God, is it serious? Are they arresting you?"

She heard Meyer clear his throat. "I'll be home in a couple of hours . . . or I hope I will. Don't worry." He hung up.

"His dumb luck," Musetta said to Gilda, putting back the receiver of the phone. "They took away all his crane machines. Confiscated by Mayor La Guardia. He doesn't like the idea of gambling."

"Took them away? How can they? Meyer owns them!"

"I'd better call Rube. Here, Gilda, take this towel off my head. I can hardly move."

She looked up Rube Frankel's number and dialed, telling him what she knew. She heard Rube yell to his wife, "Get my pants and shoes." To Musetta he said, "I'll try to save some of the machines before they get to them. If Meyer calls again, just say I'm on my way."

Mama came into the living room holding a dish towel. "I heard there's trouble. I knew it couldn't be so good for long," she said. She touched the wristwatch on her arm, one of the claw-machine prizes. "Trouble always comes."

"Never mind, Mama," Musetta said. "Don't get philosophical now." She shook loose her hair, which now smelled of olive oil.

"Gilda, rinse this out for me. I have no patience for this." Upstairs, with her head in the sink and Gilda beside her rubbing shampoo through her scalp, Musetta had a sense that she was falling through the darkness. What if the business were ruined? What if she had to go to Mr. Merkin, beg to have her job back? She had believed that she was through working forever. She was planning—as soon as Meyer got rich—to enter high society; she would dress well, vacation elegantly, go to the finest concerts and plays. She would sell the old piano and buy a Steinway. She would investigate the reputations of piano teachers and hire the most renowned. Instead of going to the library, she would acquire her own, a grand library, with floor-to-ceiling oak shelves and deep leather chairs in which to read. There was no end to the fantasies that came after the proposition "When Meyer gets rich . . . "

For some reason, as Gilda rubbed and massaged her scalp, the picture of Miss McGinley, her teacher, came into her mind, and she suffered a flash of shame. By now, if all had gone as planned, Musetta would have been a great pianist or a famous trial lawyer. After all, she was almost thirty now! Perhaps older than Miss McGinley was when Musetta was her student.

Soap was running down her face and burning her eyes. She felt tears of pain, then tears of anger, tears of regret. She didn't understand why she was unable to concentrate on anything. When she was in one place, she was thinking of being in another. When she was reading a book, she was wondering if perhaps she should be sitting out in the sun. When she was in bed with Meyer, she was thinking about the clothes she would wear in the morning.

And always she was dreaming of some better time in which she would be satisfied, content, fulfilled.

For weeks now she had been secretly planning the life she and Meyer would have away from Gilda and Mama and Nathan as soon as they had enough money to move. And now—where was that dream? The machines were being confiscated! The very claw that was supposed to lift her up out of this crowded, cluttered life and set her down in some sweet home with her husband had instead shredded her hope.

"You're blinding me!" she screamed at Gilda. "I'll never see again when you get through with me."

"Just relax," Gilda said soothingly. "The worst is nearly over."

EIGHTY-NINE

April 12, 1937

Secret Heart

It's all happening so fast I can't believe it. Meyer is already in Cleveland with Rube Frankel, and Musetta is packing to leave tomorrow! Mayor La Guardia threw all the crane machines in the East River and made a big stink about coming down hard on gambling in this city. All to get reelected, no doubt. A week ago Meyer brought me an atomizer for the brilliantine spray, almost as soon as I mentioned needing one. I've been knitting him a hat—and now he'll just be gone! I won't see him at breakfast, and I won't see him at dinner, and he won't be sleeping in the next room!

Musetta is jolly for once! Getting her wish! Moving away from us! It seems that Rube smuggled some of the machines out of the city, and since it's legal to use them in Cleveland, he and his wife and Musetta and Meyer are going to move to Cleveland and set up business there. I can't take it all in! Mama is wondering if we should rent their room, and Nathan is saying we should paint it first, and no one feels the panic I feel. Only Bingo knows . . . she snuggles up to me and licks the hollow in my neck to console me.

I know Musetta and I don't get along, and I know she hates me most of the time, and I know Meyer adores her, and I know all the troubles we have

. . . but still, those troubles are my life! And I need my life! I need people around here, other than the old folks, and I need things to think about and hope for. Even though I've always known I can't have Meyer, I love to think about him and pray for a man like him for myself. Musetta thinks I'm a permanent old maid—bloodless, a real Puritan. I think she's the bloodless Puritan. She's the one without hearty appetites and healthy dreams. She's so above all earthly things, so ethereal. She has skin like silk; it's as if she has no physical existence under that skin, no heart and lungs and stomach and bowels. Certainly no womb that longs to be filled. How can a person be sexy and sexless at the same time? Oh, what's the use! Tomorrow she will be gone, and I will live out my days setting the hair of women on their way to parties or weddings or dances and making them beautiful to celebrate life while I celebrate nothing.

I've really got the pip today, don't I? Full of self-pity and whining. Well, enough of this. I'll try to think of it this way: no more Musetta taking hours in the bathroom, no more sounds from their bedroom, no more envy, thinking of her snuggled close to Meyer every night. Maybe things will be better. You never know what the next day may bring.

NINETY

Musetta and Meyer lay together, looking at the slanted attic roof above them. Meyer, who had just come down the hall from the bathroom, said, "Guess what? Mrs. Schmidt took the white towels out of the bathroom and put in navy blue. She stopped me. 'You going to use the shower?' she asked. 'Well, you ruined four towels already with your dirty handprints, so don't expect white!'" Meyer laughed and dived under the covers, finding Musetta's stomach and blowing on it, making trumpeting noises.

"She's crazy," Musetta said, pushing his head away and smiling. "Be quiet if you're going to play."

"Why should I be quiet?" Meyer whooped. "You think we have to worry here in Cleveland, too? Do you miss your mama's coming in for the laundry? What—do you want to go home?"

"No, no, no!" Musetta whispered. "I never want to go home!" She felt Meyer's hands lifting her nightgown slowly above her knees, over her thighs.

"Don't you have to go to work?" she asked, pulling it down. "Don't you have to meet Rube?"

"We're meeting after lunch. He's doing the east side of town this morning, and I'm doing the west side. Then this afternoon we're going to shop around for stuff to refill the machines again."

Musetta pouted. "Then what will I do? I'll be here alone all day."

"You could bake me a honey cake," Meyer said, blowing gently on her ear. "You could make sauerbraten. When my mother made it, she would cook it for days."

"Oh—cook it yourself," Musetta said. "I'm no cook. If you wanted a cook, you should have brought Gilda to Cleveland."

"I only want you," Meyer said. "Only you, Moo . . . "

"I hate to be here alone all day. With nosy Mrs. Schmidt tiptoeing up and down in the hall, listening at the door."

"You could knit a baby blanket . . . " Meyer suggested. "At least you could start one . . . "

"Whatever for?"

"Well—in case we start a baby . . . "

"Is that your plan?"

"I don't have a plan, Moo. I just think, well, maybe it could happen. We've been married almost three years."

"I don't know," Musetta said. "Being pregnant would stretch out my stomach. Mama's stomach—it's got pearly blue lines all over it from having babies."

"So what's a few lines?" Meyer murmured, sliding his lips gently on the skin of her neck.

She relaxed back against the pillow. If she ever expected to get up and get dressed, to get Meyer sent off on his way, she had better let him get on with it. He traced a gentle line on her thigh. She noticed that the room was painted a horrible grayish purple color and that the closet door was warped and didn't close properly. She felt an old familiar feeling flood over her—her absolute knowledge that things were better, prettier, nicer elsewhere, that other people were in prettier rooms with fresh, light curtains instead of old dusty drapes, that other women had husbands who were rich because they were clever and calculating and not easy-going and kind the way Meyer was. She thought of Rube's wife, Hazel, and how right at this moment she had probably gone downtown to some department store because Rube liked to leave early for work, while Meyer liked to linger and nuzzle her in bed and waste valuable time during which he could be earning money.

Suddenly Meyer's head was above her, blocking out the view of the closet door, and his curly hair framed his earnest face. "Please, Moo, I want you to relax. Don't think of anything else, just think of you and me, here in this bed. Shh, shhh . . . " he placed his finger against her lips as she was about to speak. "Just be very still, and just feel me touching you, just feel how much I love you, how my hand goes up and down over your leg, over the curve of your hip. Close your eyes, don't let your eyes dart around, just keep them closed like that, that's right. Now don't think about Mrs. Schmidt. She's not important, she's just like another piece of furniture, and you don't have to worry about furniture. Don't think about your mama and Gilda, and don't think about Brooklyn, and don't think about crane machines or any worry at all. Just feel my hand . . . see, isn't that nice, how it warms you, how it touches you here . . . and here . . . and here?"

But she couldn't stop thinking. The more he whispered to her, the faster her thoughts flew: all the things she would never have and never do and never be. All the places she had never been and all the triumphs she had never felt! She had not had enough luck, had not been born in the right place to the right parents. If only she had been her own mother, instead of Mama, who was simple and not very talented. If only she had had the right head start, the kind of head start she would give her own child! Her own child.

The thought of a child of her own lifted a huge weight from her. She could sense it floating away, and her pain lightening. Her own child. What did it matter if lines would scar her belly if the baby she had was one of great beauty and intelligence? Already she could see her baby, fair-haired and blue-eyed, exquisite.

She felt some kind of barrier dissolve as she thought this, felt her body magically soften and then tense in a new and thrilling way, felt herself rise up toward Meyer and open her thighs willingly around his. She imagined herself as a hot balloon, rising up under the blankets to meet him.

He was gratified; he kissed her gratefully, passionately. She pressed herself upward, toward him, and cried out as if in a fit of madness.

When finally she opened her eyes, still breathing heavily, she loved the purple-gray walls of the room, loved the heavy private protection of the drapes. She would use this privacy to the fullest, use it as often as necessary to achieve her goal.

When Meyer moved carefully to disentangle himself from her, she stroked his back lovingly.

"Come home early tonight," she whispered, " . . . and we can do this again."

NINETY-ONE

May 1, 1937

Secret Heart

This is the first thing Mrs. Raspman said to me today after she came out of the dryer: "So I hear you met my nephew, Milton." She looked very nervous; she hadn't said a word to me all the time I was setting her hair, and it was her first time at Cindy Lee's in more than two months. I pretended not to hear her and got busy sweeping up the hair of my last two customers into a neat, furry stack.

"He said you weren't very friendly." I began mixing shampoo without speaking. I took a huge glob of green concentrated gel out of the ten-pound can Cindy Lee kept under the counter and began squeezing it into a snake-like form in order to get it down to a size that could be slid into a large bottle. Then I added water and began shaking the bottle with all my strength.

"He thinks you're very attractive," Mrs. Raspman said.

Finally I whirled around and faced her. "I don't appreciate what you did," I said—and my heart was pounding like thunder. "I think you even took . . . a liberty, telling him about my personal problem, and I think he took a liberty, daring to write me a letter about it. Do you know that his main piece of advice was for me to get rid of the creature I care about most in the world . . . my dog, Bingo?"

"I'm sure he didn't mean anything bad by it," Mrs. Raspman said. "He only meant well."

"No doubt."

"He probably didn't realize your dog meant so much to you."

"It doesn't matter," I said.

"He'd like to see you again," Mrs. Raspman said. She began to take out her pins, pulling the curls every which way. In a minute she would have ruined it all.

"Let me do that," I said. "If you want it to look decent . . . "

"Oh, you do it, darling, you have the Midas touch. Everywhere I go, people say, 'Who is the angel who did your hair?'"

"I'm glad you like my work," I said. "But who did your hair all last month?"

"Oh—that," she said. "Well, I was embarrassed to see you after you wouldn't talk to Milton. But today I came because he asked me to come, to tell you he was sorry if he embarrassed you. He thought you were charming in the Purim play; he wants to know if he can come by your house and talk to you."

"No," I said. "He can't."

"Why not?"

"Because—I am not a freak case to be studied for medical research!" I said, and I felt my face flame. Every blemish rose an inch higher.

"Oh! How wrong you are, Gilda!" Mrs. Raspman said. "Nothing, *nothing* like that is on his mind. He is a young man of fine qualities, and I told him what a fine young woman you are."

"So—you are a matchmaker?"

"Nothing like that either!"

"I'm really not interested," I said. "I have a busy life, and I have no time for outside interests."

"He would only come and take you for a walk on Ocean Parkway, maybe buy you an ice cream cone."

"I'm sorry, I really can't," I said. I combed out her set and fluffed it till it was perfect.

"Here," she said, sticking something into my apron pocket. It didn't feel like a coin, and later, when she had left, I pulled it out and found that it was a folded note. I read: "*Gilda, my dear, I swear we will have no professional exchange. You won't cut my hair, and I won't give you medical advice. Surely we can smell the lilacs without any friction. My dog is a beagle named Rabbi Cohen. What is the name of your dog? Maybe they could get along. Maybe we could take them both on our walk. I'll call you Sunday morning. Signed, Milton R.*"

The nerve of the man!!!!

NINETY-TWO

"He's meeting *shiksas* at City College," Len said to Ava at the breakfast table. "You meet them . . . and before long you marry them."

Ava did not look up from the *Brooklyn Eagle;* she was reading about Hitler and thinking about war. Richard had just gone out the front door, buttoning up his jacket, whistling. He had bent to kiss her, and the pungent smell of his shaving soap still lingered in his wake.

"Ava!" Len pounded the table. "Don't you worry about him?"

"I worry about war, not *shiksas,*" she murmured.

"So," he said. "So—you want granddaughters who go to church every Sunday morning wearing big hats with ribbons down the back?"

"It bothers you?" Ava asked. "That children on Easter Sunday get all dressed up? That they go to church to pray to a kind man who loves everyone?"

"What is this, Ava?" Len roared. "All of a sudden you're going over to the Christians? You're a Christ lover?"

"What has this got to do with anything? Richard hasn't even got a girl-friend. No one in this house is going to church as far as I know. What do you want to pick a fight for?"

"I don't know," Len said. "I feel angry."

"So go yell at your cronies," Ava said. "Leave me alone."

She sipped her cold, bitter coffee. Len pushed back his chair and took part of the newspaper; when he closed the bathroom door, she left the kitchen and went upstairs to lie down on her bed. It was true that Richard was going out a great deal. He was popular; he had boy friends and girl friends. She was proud of him—he was handsome, he was intelligent. And when she asked him about his "girlfriends," he always kissed her and said, "They're all ordinary, Mama. When I find one like you, then we'll talk business."

It wasn't the thought of girls that made Ava's heart close up and grow hard as a rock. It was airplanes. They were Richard's endless passion. In college he was studying a technical course about air currents and airplane engines, and on weekends he took flying lessons. He came home with his face flushed, his lips red and chapped.

"Someday, Mama, I'm going to take you up with me."

"Never mind!" Ava always said laughing. "I'm no bird, your mother." And when Len looked up at Richard, hopefully (he would have loved to be asked to fly), Richard would whack him good-naturedly on the shoulder and say, "Work on Mama. Let's convince her to go flying with me."

Well, she couldn't worry about Len. He had his disappointments, she had hers. Let him go to work and leave her with an empty house and time to think. When he was there, he filled her vision with his anger, filled her ears with his loudness, filled her soul with grief. What happened in a marriage? In the beginning there was some sweetness, some laughter, and for a while his total attention. He had been a kind man, good-hearted. And he still was.

But she was of no interest to him anymore. When she looked at him, she could see the blankness in his eyes and the busy-ness in his head as he plotted his moves or remembered whatever a man like him remembered.

When she tried to get his attention, she succeeded only if she discussed something urgent—the broken furnace, the cleaning lady who had stolen the candlesticks. But if she tried to talk about things in human life—about the kind of children they had, about Gilda's plight as an old maid, about how Mama and Nathan had somehow wiped out the horrible past and now were simply a devoted old couple—he would yawn and shift restlessly in his seat. What was it that held a man and a woman enthralled? In the early days of their courtship the excitement was not so much in what they shared between them, but in the change that would come about in their lives as a result of their marriage to one another. In Ava's case it had meant escape from Isaac. It meant peace and some degree of safety, of rest. In Len's case (she supposed) it meant her services: her warm body, her good cooking, her childbearing capabilities.

Now her body was not so warm; her cooking had made him fat; and their sons had replaced him in Ava's affections. She knew that was true; she loved both boys far more than she loved Len—and for Richard she would have given her life if he asked for it.

Now she heard Len coming up the stairs. He would get his jacket, take two cigars out of the box on top of his dresser, and say good-bye to her for the day. She could tell he was still irritated about something—the way he slammed the closet door. "So you don't care if he makes friends with *shiksas*," he said, "it doesn't bother you. Maybe you want to convert yourself?"

"What are you talking about?"

"How come you stopped lighting Friday night candles?"

"Sometimes I'm busy, Len."

"My mother asked me—'She still lights candles?'"

"What does it matter to your mother what I do?"

"She didn't see the candlesticks."

"Did you tell her the colored girl stole them?"

"So—we can't afford to buy another pair of brass candlesticks?"

"I didn't get around to it."

"We should have Shabbos in the house."

"We'll have it Friday night. I'll get candlesticks."

"Don't forget. We want the boys to know they're Jews."

"They have no doubt. Why are you feeling so guilty all of a sudden? You have a bad conscience? You think God will strike you dead?"

"Would you like that? For me to drop dead?"

"Oh Len—of course not."

"So—could we have a little smile once in a while?"

"When I have something to smile about, I'll smile."

"You don't have a fur coat? You don't have a big diamond? There's nothing to smile about?"

"Furs and diamonds don't make smiles," Ava said. "How you feel inside is what makes you smile."

"Why can't I make you feel good?"

"You do, you do," she said. She wished he would leave.

"How?"

"How! I don't know how! You're a good father. You're a good provider."

"And a good faithful husband?"

"Yes, of course."

"And you're a good faithful wife?"

"Certainly."

"So who is the man who is looking for you? Yesterday in the bakery, when I stopped to get a rye bread, Mrs. Schwartz said, 'A tall man was in here, looking for your wife. A *blondisha.*' Who is that, Ava? Tall and handsome, Mrs. Schwartz said. You know someone I don't know, Ava?"

"No!"

"So it's okay for Richard to have *shiksa* friends because you have *shaygets* friends?"

"Oh, go to work, Len. Don't make up fairy tales. Look at me. I'm getting old, I'm no bathing beauty! What's going on in your head?"

"What do you do here all day?"

"What do I do? I clean your house? I shop! I cook your meals! I wash your clothes! What do you think I do—go to see burlesque?"

"What a good idea!" Len said, rushing out of the room. As he ran down the stairs, he shouted, "I think that's where I'll go tonight! Don't expect me home early."

When the door slammed, Ava began to cry. After a while she went to her jewel box and lifted the velvet platform under her rings and bracelets. Very slowly she unfolded Johnny Quinn's phone number.

NINETY-THREE

Musetta leaned over Mrs. Schmidt's immaculate sink and felt another convulsion taking form. She braced herself, gripping the cold, white porcelain sides of the sink while the retching sound rose from her throat and made her shudder with disgust an instant before the hot flow of vomit poured up like a geyser and spilled from her mouth and nose.

Oh God, this is worse than death, she thought, gagging and coughing, smelling a vile smell, feeling the acid burning her delicate membranes. Punishment for the act of sex, she thought wildly, as another wave of retching gripped and shook her. Nature was so canny, tempting a woman into the act of sex for pleasure (though Musetta herself never really thought of the act as pleasurable) and then making her pay and pay and pay.

These days she would vomit at the slightest whiff of cooking onions, at the sight of a hair on her plate, at the sound of Meyer belching. Even a glance at her own long toenails made her gag. When she thought of her body, with its strange appendages, its convoluted passages, its symmetrical hills and valleys and gaping holes, she felt attacked and overwhelmed.

What she wanted was to hear a Chopin waltz or a symphony or a song. Sometime she imagined she heard her father singing some lovely airy aria from an opera.

She wanted to focus her attention on music and beauty and things of the mind and soul, not on the body's ugly pulsing, demanding appetites and functions. She detested the rumblings and gurglings of her bowels, the relentless bellows of her lungs, the urgent demands of her stomach. Even when she was deeply involved in the realm of art—as at a concert—she would suddenly look at the elegant, gifted woman playing the piano and imagine her in some ludicrous position, on the toilet, perhaps, or soaping her underarms in the bathtub. It seemed a cruel joke, combining in humans this taste for transcendent beauty and this other side—the hungry, sweating, excreting, instinctive side. Musetta retched again, feeling her rib cage thrust itself upward, tearing against the thin boundaries of her flesh.

Yet there was no way to her goal but through this, she thought. If she was to have her perfect child, if she wanted the opportunity to raise the baby with every advantage, every gift life offered, she had to do this every morning: vomit and retch and cling, sweating and shivering, to the porcelain sink. In a few months she would have to waddle, thick as a hippopotamus, through the days of her life until the child's birth required one last trial: the expulsion of the baby with its infinitely hard and bony head through her narrow birth passage.

Musetta raised herself up shakily on her weakened arms. In the mirror above the sink her face looked gray and drawn. How hard was it going to be . . . on the day the baby was ready to tunnel out into the light of day? Would she be able to tolerate the pain, the bloody mess? For an instant she wished that Mama were at her side, right then, as another wave of nausea swept through her, wished Mama could hold her hair away from her face as she convulsed, wished Mama could assure her that she had seen thousands of babies born and it would be all right—that hers would be healthy and perfect and that she would live through the labor.

Suddenly she missed Mama—miles away in Brooklyn. Did she even miss Gilda, with her gentle ways, her calm, deliberate, firm manner? She imagined giving birth with Gilda at her side, holding her hand, rubbing her temples. Gilda's hands were like delicate birds, fluttering and lighting with absolute certainty and grace. Musetta could see them in her mind's eye, as they tweezed almost invisible hairs from her eyebrows, as they clipped dead skin from her cuticles, as they massaged oil into her hair. At this far remove—Cleveland was indeed far from Brooklyn—she felt a wave of admiration for Gilda's skills, pride that her sister was so competent in certain ways. She had never said a word of this to Gilda—never! She had never told Gilda or Mama that she appreciated them . . . loved them. Funny that this feeling should occur to her now, as she swayed, nauseated, before the mirror in Mrs. Schmidt's rooming house.

There were long days to get through here in Cleveland. Meyer was out with Rube Frankel, servicing his machines, collecting money, buying trinkets to replenish the ones that the claw hand distributed to the customers. There was not much for Musetta to do.

Now and then she and Meyer went to the library in the evenings. But could she read all day? It occurred to her that she should write a long letter home to Brooklyn. So far she had sent only postcards, saying all was well. But maybe she'd write home and ask Gilda for some interesting recipes. The honey cake recipe. And she'd ask Mama for the stuffed cabbage recipe. She had kitchen privileges here in Mrs. Schmidt's rooming house. By the window in their room were chairs and a small table that she and Meyer could eat at; up to now they had eaten out almost every night. But perhaps she could spend a little time cooking. (After all, there was no piano here—she could hardly be blamed for cooking just a little.) Meyer would love it. And maybe . . . maybe she would write and find out from Gilda how to knit a simple stitch. She might be able to make the new baby a blanket. And make Meyer a scarf! Suddenly these tasks seemed almost a pleasure to anticipate. She began to plan the colors for the baby blanket! She was no longer so nauseated. Slowly she made her way back to her room and sat down on the wooden chair by the window. She took a pen and paper from the top of the rickety wooden dresser and began writing: "Dearest Mama and Gilda . . . I am feeling homesick today. I really miss you both . . . "

NINETY-FOUR

The smell of popcorn and pizza was in the air. Ava turned her face toward the sea, relishing the breeze on her flushed cheeks, and inhaled deeply of the salt air. She felt slightly sickened by the raw-cheesy smell of the pizza, a strange horrible combination of sausage and bubbling cheese on a slab of dough. She wondered how people could eat anything that smelled so much like vomit. She walked along the boardwalk hearing her heels clatter hollowly on the weathered wooden boards. She passed the Fun House; the insane spiraling laughter broadcast from within felt as if it were coming from her own throat. The breeze lifted her dress above her knees, billowing her black-and-white-checked skirt as if she were already in the Fun House and blasts of air were aimed directly under her clothes to embarrass her. She hurried along. She was to meet Johnny Quinn in front of the Cyclone. Already she could hear the shrieks from it, borne to her on the wind. They sounded like the cries of souls lost in hell.

She never should have come! Why had she come? For what earthly reason? She looked nervously over her shoulder. What if one of her neighbors had come with her children to spend the day at Coney Island? How could she explain her presence here? Could she say that she had come to win Kewpie dolls for herself? To relax on the Steeplechase ride?

It seemed everyone who passed her could read the guilt on her face. She had told Len she was going into the city to buy yarn at a wholesale house. He did not ask what she needed yarn for—it probably had not occurred to him that she had not knit anything for years. But if she came home without it, she could always say she had dropped it off for Gilda, that Gilda needed something to occupy herself with weekends and evenings now that Musetta and Meyer were living in Cleveland.

But what if Len wanted to know what color the yarn was, what Gilda intended to make with it? What if . . . ? She shook off these foolish questions. She passed the Municipal Baths, where she used to come as a child, where Mama would store their clothes in a locker and, after swimming, would make her wash off the sand in a public shower room. She remembered how odd it had been to see the pale naked limbs and soft doughy breasts of dozens of strange women. She had always hidden herself behind Mama, praying that she would never be so white and fat and sagging as those women seemed to be.

Now she was passing a hot-buttered-corn stand and saw herself briefly in the mirrored sign; she was as wide now as any woman in those shower rooms, hardly the girl she had been at ten. When had it got away from her—her graceful thin body, her hope? Some bathing beauty she was now! Thank God Johnny Quinn had not wanted to meet her on the beach for a picnic and a swim!

She could feel the breeze from the Cyclone now as a filled car swooped and dipped, getting ready for the torturous climb to the rickety top of the roller coaster. She had never been on it. Once she had come here with Mama and Isaac and Gilda and Musetta. Isaac had taken each of his own daughters on the ride, but not Ava. She had stood burning with envy, hearing the shrieks and cries of the riders, half-hoping Isaac's car would tumble off the track and fall like a flaming meteor at their feet. But then, when Gilda had stumbled off, white-faced and trembling, and threw up her Nathan's hot dog at the side of the boardwalk, she had felt remorse for her evil thought.

Ava stood now at the entrance to the ride and scanned the boardwalk for Johnny. She had called him in desperation, and now he was coming, gladly and willingly, to complicate her life. When she had dialed his number, she had thought only of getting some comfort, some kindness, some sweetness. Was that evil, to want some sweetness in life?

The boardwalk shuddered and trembled as the roller-coaster car came flying down the tracks, clattering and rumbling as its occupants screamed in abandon. She could see some of them throwing their arms over their heads to make the risk more shocking. The ride was like a life lived in fifty seconds, with all its fears, joys, turns, and dips. Now that the ride had stopped, now that it was over, she could see people leaving through the entrance—pale, stunned, all of them disappointed that it had ended so soon. She watched them file out, steady themselves, prepare themselves to face reality.

"Ava, my sweet flower, here I am," said Johnny Quinn, thrusting a handful of red roses into the crook of her arm.

"Oh! It's you," Ava gasped over the noise of another full car climbing once more to the heights.

"Let's get out of this thunder," Johnny said in her ear. "Unless you want me to take you up on it."

"I've never been," Ava said.

"Twenty years ago I would have said, 'I'll protect you, m'girl,' but I'm smarter now. Now you'd have to protect me."

"Let's just walk," Ava said. "That's risky enough for right now, don't you think?" Johnny looked dashing in a white linen jacket, yellow shirt, and light brown pants. He was tall enough to keep the sun from her eyes.

"We could try the Ferris wheel," he said. "We'd be closer to heaven."

"I'm not ready for heaven," Ava said. "Look at me, I called you up and here you are."

"You look like an angel," Johnny said. "To me you do."

Ava laughed. The laughter loosened the coil in her chest that had been choking her, and she breathed deeply as it unwound, allowed her to breathe in the sweet air and sunshine.

Johnny took her arm. "Let's promenade," he said. "Let's pretend we're back in 1915 and our souls are young as the new moon. Let's have some corn-on-a-stick and some chocolate custard, and then let's go in the Tunnel of Love. Let's not talk about our troubles, not this time. Let's go see if we can find some little dark café to dance in. Life is hard, Ava. Let's give ourselves the present of this day with no regrets." He tipped her chin up with his hand and looked into her eyes. "Can we do that, m'girl?"

"I'll try," Ava promised. "You help me and I'll really try."

Johnny kissed the tip of her nose. "Now let's you and I go in there to have a drink or two to get us started."

NINETY-FIVE

August 22, 1937

Secret Heart

So I'm to be an aunt again! How old that makes me feel! (Well, twenty-seven is no spring chicken, is it?) But I worry about Musetta for some reason—all alone in Cleveland, turning her guts inside out every morning. Of course Meyer is there, but a man is never much good at times like this. I feel so tender toward my distant sister, for some reason. Maybe I feel she's something of a victim now, following the lines of life just like everyone else has to, no longer such a special, snooty hotshot.

Her letters sound as if she actually misses us—she's lonely and has nothing to do and is asking for cooking recipes and knitting patterns! Can you imagine? Musetta, knitting? Musetta, making chicken soup! Incredible. When I think of the baby to come, my knees go weak. Maybe it will look like Papa or like Shmuel (if it's a boy). What a grand child it will be if it has Shmuel's goodness and Papa's fine voice and Meyer's handsome body! But, for myself, I would like a girl. I could teach a girl so much—how to be firm, how to keep her nails groomed and delicate looking, how to do her own hair, how to appreciate trees and birds and sunshine (something Musetta has never been able to do). I pray someday Musetta and Meyer will move back to Brooklyn so

I can have a hand in the raising of the new baby. What a joy that would be to me! I'm so tired of living with old people!

Something else I would teach a baby is how to be Jewish! Musetta is such a goy, such a witch! I still can't believe what she did to Meyer! (She thought it was a joke, a joke!) She wrote about it to us in a letter as if it were funny! (I didn't even read Mama that part of the letter; she has been having pains in her chest. If I told her what Musetta did, it might bring on a heart attack!) Musetta played a trick on Meyer—she made pork chops and told him they were having lamb chops! "He never knew the difference!" she wrote in the letter. "The man, with all his Jewish upbringing, can't tell a pig from a cow. What's more, I put butter in his mashed potatoes, instead of that awful white margarine that comes with a yellow pill to color it, and he didn't know the difference there either!"

So: Is Musetta not a witch? (All my tender feelings are gone again.) She gives her beloved husband pork, which is—to Jews—forbidden, and she gives him a dairy product, butter, with meat, which is also forbidden. And she thinks it's funny! But if I had some influence over the new baby, I would teach it what I know is important—always to light Sabbath candles, always to fast on Yom Kippur, to make *hamentashen* to celebrate Purim, to say Kaddish for the dead. And above all—always to marry a Jew. It's only a lucky accident Musetta married a Jew. She could just as soon have married an Irishman or an Italian or a Polack who goes to church every Sunday. She has no conscience, my sister, no loyalty to her people. So she'll need help with that baby; she needs my help.

Oh—I feel so cranky today. Milton Raspman came by again. Something in me freezes when I see him at the door. I feel he's examining every pimple on my face, though I swear he tries not to look at me. (Maybe he finds me too hideous to look at!) In any case I am never happy to see him, though his aunt continues to be my best customer at Cindy Lee's, and to please her and to have something to do (that isn't just sitting around with Mama and Nathan) I usually agree to go walking with him on Ocean Parkway.

It's always so awkward! He's such a good-looking young man, I can't imagine what he wants with an old maid like me. Yet how can I ask him what he's doing there with me! We talk about the weather and the color he is going to paint his new medical office. (He's opened up an office near the Botanical Gardens—on the ground floor of an apartment house. He's got only a few patients so far, but I'm sure he'll do very well. He has a very gentle manner. I think he would be good as a children's doctor.)

"Just say the word," he always says, "and I'll bring Rabbi Cohen along." I don't know if that's sacrilegious or not, calling a dog by a rabbi's name. But I certainly don't want to meet his dog, and I don't want him to talk to mine, not after all the cautions he once gave me about the dangers of owning a dog! (How come *he* has one if he thinks dogs are so filthy?) My only joy is Bingo: she's patient, she's accepting, she doesn't nag, she doesn't make demands. If I could marry a dog, I would. Well, a mood like this is best not harped on. Better to go to bed and try for a fresh start tomorrow.

NINETY-SIX

As in the old days, Ava rested her head on Johnny Quinn's shoulder and fitted her body to his as they waltzed together in the dark, smoky café. She could almost imagine Tony Angeloni and his girlfriend, Maria, dancing beside them (though Johnny had told her that Maria had eight children now and weighed two hundred pounds, and that Tony owned a restaurant in the Bronx and carried on an affair with every new waitress).

Ava closed her eyes in order not to see herself in the silvery mirrors lining the walls of the room; it was easier for her to believe in the illusion of her youth if she could not see her thickened waist and hips or the unruly white strands of hair spreading among the darker ones.

Johnny felt strange, almost foreign, in her arms. Her husband, Len, was such a tough, leathery, box-shaped little man. She was so used to touching him, brushing lint off his jacket, buttoning a shirt on his barrel chest, smoothing his Brillo-y hair. Now she was touching a body composed of new planes, different densities. It was curious. She wondered how Johnny's hair would feel—smooth and white blond, greased with brilliantine. His smell was different, too. Where Len smelled of cigar smoke, Johnny had a cigarette-whiskey smell about him. Len's smell reminded her of old Jewish men, whereas Johnny's smell had a sense of danger about it—of wild living, of irresponsibility. But that suited her. She was irresponsible, too! She had been here with him at Coney Island all day, and now it was late into the night. She had called Len, her heart in her mouth, to say she had met an old girlfriend in the city and was going to have dinner with her. She had prepared the name of a girl who had worked with her at the clothing factory around the time she'd met Len—but he didn't ask whom she'd met. He'd just told her to be careful coming home late on the train.

It was easy to lie. She had always thought it would be impossible, but it was easy. She was new at it and scared, but she could see that it could become a way of life. Maybe many women had lives lived in layers—the surface layer, or the "proper" layer, and then the lower layer beneath that, where the real life surged and roiled. How often did she tell Len what she was really thinking and feeling? Never! Almost never! Only sometimes, in real anger, did she cry out some thought she could no longer contain. But mainly she did her daily chores, made her proper appearances as a mother and wife, and lived her se-crets: her fantasies about her lost Papa (who had nothing to do with Nathan, that old man who wandered around the house with Mama trailing behind him); her dreams of glory for Richard, her beautiful son; her memories of Shmuel, her beloved lost brother, whom she prayed would find her again—if there were a heaven. One day, she and Shmuel and Mama and Papa might be together again, as they had been at the beginning.

What nonsense! What childish nonsense to think such a thing, that they would all meet one day in heaven. Life was life the way it was! This was what she had now. If Len and she could hardly talk to each other, that was her life! If war came, that was also her life. If Richard wanted to fly in a war, that was her life. Only Sammy was no worry—her darling boy, Sammy, who just grew and flourished and didn't give her worries. For his sake she was ashamed to be here, dancing with Johnny Quinn, her old flame and a little drunk now, more than a little drunk.

But he was a comfort! And who could say no to comfort when there was so little of it, day after day, year after year? Johnny tightened his arm around her waist and spun her around the dance floor. He had always been such a good dancer. In his arms she felt like a feather. Why was it that goyim were so light on their feet? Why was it they wore shiny black shoes, so shiny she imagined she could see her face reflected in them? But they were also unreli-able and drank too much—she had heard the warnings all her life. Did the two go together? Being light on your feet and irresponsible?

The dance was now ending. Johnny dipped her dramatically to the floor, so far that she felt her spine crackle. "It's so late, Johnny, so late," she whispered when he had righted her and drawn her close to him. "Don't you think it's time . . . time for us to go home?"

"You don't like it?" Johnny said. "Here, with me . . . ?"

"Oh, I like it, yes, I like it."

"You're getting tired?"

"Not that tired."

"Then why not one more dance?"

"Why not?" she considered. She had already done the deed; she had let another man take her in his arms, a man not Len, and it was not a matter of measuring her guilt in time spent. An hour, an eternity—it hardly mattered. She had conspired with Johnny and had destroyed that pure white kernel of loyalty that had lived in her heart since the day she had first met Len so long ago. It crumbled to powder, like a white candy almond stepped upon and ground into the carpet.

"Yes," she said. "One more dance. Why not?"

1938

NINETY-SEVEN

Like a Catholic taking communion, Musetta let the soda cracker melt on her tongue. She lay in bed in the rooming house, her hands resting lightly on top of her rounded stomach, listening to the sounds downstairs: Mrs. Schmidt banging pots in the kitchen, boarders' feet on the stairs, the shrill buzz of the doorbell (a delivery boy or the mailman with a package).

The cracker helped reduce her nausea. Meyer always left a few on a plate within her reach beside the bed before he left to fill his claw machines with toys and empty them of money. The wafer seemed to liquefy in the heat of her mouth, leaving a reassuring salty taste on her tongue.

When Musetta was a child, her father had told her that the Catholics believed the wafer they ate was the body of Christ and the wine they drank was his blood. She had imagined all the Catholic girls (who passed the Sauerbachs' house on the way to church Easter morning) biting down hard on their wafers (they were not supposed to bite them, only to let them melt) and then Christ's blood running out of their mouths and over their lips to stain their yellow organdy three-tiered dresses.

Musetta had long hours in bed these days. Her mind did strange things. She played games with herself every morning to keep the nausea under control. The sickness quivered in her throat as she imagined sacramental wine must quiver in the goblet held by the priest. The body and blood of Christ. Each baby could be a new Messiah. The Jews were also, she'd heard, waiting for a Messiah. What of this baby growing within her? Perhaps it would be ordained for greatness.

She attended to a movement under her skin. The baby tapped against her belly with its tiny elbow or knee, making its secret communion with her.

Its promised coming brought her so much joy—enough even to offset the vulgar way its life was started, in such heated muscular convulsions, in blind embrace, in the beating of Meyer's pelvis against her own.

She tried not to think much of the fetus's development in the deep cave of her womb, but thought instead of its beauty and intelligence and the way it would gladden her life.

When she thought of this baby, she felt none of her usual anger or jealousy or bitterness; she did not experience that common unnamable feeling that always flung her into a swamp of complaints—complaints so confused and passionate that she felt she must blame everyone but herself for what was not good in her life.

She breathed deeply, grateful to be alone here, in this tiny private room, with the secret joy burgeoning within her. It was a continual blessing to be away from Brooklyn and to be alone with Meyer, without the constant pressure of Mama and Nathan and the thorny presence of her sister, Gilda. She felt proud of herself, too—going through her pregnancy alone here, without Mama and Gilda hovering over her and clucking, picking apart her symptoms, analyzing them, predicting the length and ordeal of her labor, the sex of her baby.

She and Meyer had already made a list of names. They planned to visit the hospital soon and make the necessary arrangements for when her time would come. The baby would be born in March, the perfect time, at the start of spring. She thought of the day it would happen: she would be filled with light like a star. Then she would explode, and her baby would be her reward for all the troubles of her life.

"Mrs. Berger, you in there?"

There was a rude knocking at the door, loud and irregular.

The vibrations shook the room.

"Who is it?" Musetta called out.

"You got a telegram here, I'm holding it."

She sat up quickly, throwing back the warm, heavy bed covers. The impulse to gag rose in her throat as she put on her robe and slippers. "I'm coming," she whispered into the sudden chill of the room. She noticed a cloud of frost on the window glass. She saw, with surprise, that it was snowing outside, that the sky was slate gray without light. It was a shock to come out of the brightness of her mind.

Musetta opened the door, and Mrs. Schmidt handed her a yellow envelope. "Should I wait? In case you got bad news? I don't want you should faint
in my room, and then I'll have a lawsuit on my hands."

"Don't worry," Musetta said. "You don't have to worry." She closed the
door. She got back under the covers before she opened the telegram. Already
her teeth were chattering with cold.

MAMA NOT WELL STOP HEART ATTACK STOP

WE NEED YOU BOTH AT HOME STOP CAN YOU HURRY STOP

GILDA

NINETY-EIGHT

February 10, 1938

Secret Heart

I have my wish and they are home. How ironic it is that no amount of my own
pain and emotional suffering would ever justify the sending of a telegram,
whereas the merest clutching pain in Mama's chest warrants and receives
great life changes. (Not that I would minimize Mama's chest pains—but, in
fact, they have been going on for some time, and only because the doctor
called her last episode "a mild heart attack" were we able to act on it and call
Musetta and Meyer home.) And so I have them back. Musetta with her great
swollen belly, looking like a twig who has swallowed a boulder, and Meyer,
the dearest man on earth (who greeted me with a warm, shy, hard hug).

Musetta is in her bed already, suffering nervous tremors from the long
ride home and from the strain of seeing Mama in bed herself (and not scrubbing floors for once). I am so relieved they are here, despite my mixed feelings. Now, if Mama dies (which Dr. Zucker promises she won't), at least I
will not be left alone here to live with Nathan. What would I do with him? I
doubt Ava would take him to live with her. And if Mama died and if Ava did
take Nathan and if Meyer and Musetta hadn't come back —if worst came to
worst, I would have to live all alone here in this house. (Nathan is scared to
death these days. He sits at Mama's bedside holding her hand and pestering
her: "Rachel, you want tea? You want a cool cloth on your head? You want

me to rub your feet?") He breathes like a steam engine. I know his lungs are
failing him.

Only Bingo is sane, loving, clear-headed. She knows what she wants, no
pussyfooting around. (Lately she has been in heat and wants to go outside
where the male dogs are hanging around. I have to watch her every minute.)
How easy it is for animals to answer the calls of nature, to be unselfconscious
about their drives and needs. And they don't live with fear, as I do, because
they have no knowledge of the future, of loss, of their own deaths.

At night I often have dreams about Musetta's baby. I think it will be a girl.
I think she will be like my own child. She will have the soul of Papá and of
Meyer, but none of Musetta's anger and meanness. She will have the patience
of Shmuel and the beauty of Mama when she was a young woman. I will allow
her one thing of Musetta's (I speak as if I am God!)—her smooth white skin.

She should be blessed with an outside like Musetta's, an inside like mine!

Go to bed, Gilda, and stop this dreaming. You have work to do tomorrow—at least five haircuts and five manicures, and a promise to help with the
rummage sale at the shul. Milton Raspman called three times, Mama told me,
to invite me to the Young Jewish Socialites' dance. I don't understand his interest; he is so handsome, so eligible (a doctor!), so sweet and kind in his own
way that I know his interest in me is a combination of guilt for that terrible
letter he wrote me about the care of my skin and a favor to his aunt, who must
have painted me as this pathetic, lonely, handicapped little beautician who
is in dire need of male attention! It's just too embarrassing and complicated,
and I'm just so tired of wishing it would all come out right. I'm beginning to
believe I will have to live out my natural life without a man. Well, I won't die
if I have to. I'll go on living to a lonely old age, and I'll survive. Now that I
understand that, my panic is less. The thought of the baby living here calms
my fears. If I have to love only dogs and babies, perhaps that will do for me. It
may have to do.

NINETY-NINE

The ocean rolled and rocked, it roared in her ears. Fish were swimming in
her veins; sharks plunged upward through her arteries, flailing their razor fins

against the thin filament that kept the baby safe within her. In the blue-black depths Shmuel's face floated like the round body of an octopus, his eyes inky black, his mouth pulsing in and out on its drawstring.

"Ugh," Musetta grunted, gasped. She struggled out of her dream. She thought she heard Papa using the old treadle sewing machine, clicking and snapping the black metal grill beneath his feet. She rolled on her side to reach for Meyer, but she could not roll; she was held on her back, pinned flat by the leaden ocean, a million tons of water crushed against her spine, seizing her breath, zigzagging down her thighs. Her eyes flew open. She was not Musetta now, but a sea creature, writhing and twisting, astonished to be trapped, along with her baby, in this swollen, unwieldy object that was her body, feeling it pour fluid (without her consent!) out onto the bedsheets, juices leaking from her as if she were cracked and was now ruined.

"I can't do it," she moaned. She willed herself back to sleep, back into the dream, even though she knew she might meet her brother's drowning face again. But the tapping became louder, the ticking became a banging, then a thunderous hammering.

God, she'd forgotten those awful radiator pipes.

"Meyer, call Mama. Everything is wet."

"You've been moaning. Are you in labor? I can't call Mama. She's not well enough to help you with this baby. If it's your time, I'll call Gilda. She'll call Dr. Zucker."

"I don't want them. I want Mama." She heard herself whine while the radiator pipes boomed forth. "I think I'm dying, Meyer," she sang to him. "Good-bye, Meyer." She went under water again and concentrated on breathing. Let them do the rest; she had to breathe and swim, breathe and swim. She closed her eyes to their frantic faces. Gilda's eyes were hard and bright; she had to protect herself from them. Meyer's eyes were caverns of concern. Somewhere she saw Nathan, scratching his head with two hands. Forget them all. How stupid for them to take the car into the ocean. She felt the motor hum beneath her whale's hips. Someone stuffed a towel between her thighs.

They stopped at endless red lights on the way. In a long white corridor a witch dressed in white said to her, "Screaming will get you nowhere, honey."

She swam onward, away from them all. Her belly was like a beach ball now, buoyant. They did things to her, shaved the hair between her legs, administered an enema. She turned her face away and thought her own thoughts. She suddenly remembered Miss McGinley, elegant and slim, with her feathered hats. Soon Musetta would be slim again—and not only that, she would shortly fulfill her promise, so Miss McGinley need not be disappointed. This baby would be the precious gift, her way to fulfillment. She would try to locate Miss McGinley and show the baby to her. Would Miss McGinley be very old now? Or dead? She might even have children herself by now. Or maybe she was still as young as she had been. It didn't seem to matter, time was not important. Musetta was no special age either, she was just a woman becoming a mother, as women had done from the beginning of time. She didn't use to think motherhood would suit her, but now she felt it would. If only she could live through this, through the needles she felt, the rubber cup over her nose, the clamps on her arms and legs. They were pulling her in two like the halves of a peach, and inside lay curled this baby, this whale, this monolith.

"Screaming will get you nowhere, honey," they shouted at her. "Nowhere, nowhere! Shut up, will you? God, she's bellowing like a cow, can't you give her another shot?"

She did not bellow; she was a human being, not an animal. She folded her arms peacefully over her breast and let herself float slowly out of her body. Let someone else do this.

ONE HUNDRED

March 15, 1938

Secret Heart

She's born! On the very same date that Ava's Richard was born, twenty years ago. They named her Issa Marsha and will call her Issa, for Papa!

Issa! What a strange and beautiful name! It's spring! The sky is finally blue out there. The bees are dancing on the flowers. The world is going to bloom, and a new life has come to us. I want to spin like a whirling dervish!

ONE HUNDRED ONE

Musetta reclined in bed on soft pillows like a queen in the sunshine, receiving guests, delicately unraveling the pink silken ribbons on gifts laid at her feet, and accepting with modest murmurs the praise heaped upon the exquisite child she had created.

Issa, her beautiful, tiny daughter, slept in a cradle beside Musetta's bed. Gilda's customers and some neighbors came up to the bedroom, tiptoed past the cradle and crooned their approval.

Musetta accepted the adoration; it was her due. She felt she had been on a stage forever, in the dark, and finally now the curtains had parted, and her waiting audience was at last able to receive her gifted performance.

She was in exquisite pain; her breasts were cracked and oozing, her private parts had been lacerated and stitched. Great silver forceps had been plunged into her body to retrieve the infant (she was told), and she imagined she could still feel the cold, curved, spoon-shaped machinery within her. (The baby's head had been born misshapen, and cloverlike bruises still discolored her tiny nose and mouth.)

There was a hush in the house; even Mama rocked silently at the foot of Musetta's bed, keeping watch over her, her serious gaze indicating they both had passed through dangerous portals recently and miraculously survived. Mama carried tiny white pills in her apron pocket now, her weapons against the enemy within her. Her stiff and knotty fingers lay protectively over her pocket, keeping guard. Now and then, when there was a lull in the parade of visitors, she confided to Musetta stories of dangerous confinements she had witnessed as a midwife, tales she never would have told before, when Musetta was still uninitiated.

Musetta felt her heart open with sympathy; Mama had had a hard life, Mama had suffered. Musetta had never before felt this sense of kindness in herself toward her mother. Even toward Gilda she felt some sweetness.

"Come and sit on the edge of the bed, if you like," she invited her sister. "Come closer, you may hold Issa if you want to. Just support her head carefully."

Gilda stepped forward, then back, like a frightened rabbit. "You may feed her a bottle if you like," Musetta offered grandly.

She was of course not going to nurse the child. She had heard it stretched the breasts and made them sag. She had heard it wasn't hygienic.

Her nipples were already ugly, dark, rubber thimbles straining outward with a life of their own. She kept them hidden from Meyer under a quilted bed jacket—her swollen breasts and those thrusting nipples. She feared he would want to look at them, touch them, even put his mouth to them. Now that she had the precious infant, she felt she must keep Meyer away, discourage him, distract him. Her body had had all the attention she could stand, enough to last her all her life. Now she wanted to cover it, forget it, and get on with more important matters. It was essential that she lose no time. As soon as Issa was ready to be taught, trained, disciplined, Musetta would be ready. Refinement and culture took years to develop; there was no such thing as starting too soon.

She already had lists in her mind of things she would need: books, of course, to begin with. Nursery rhymes and fairy tales and stories of children who were ballet dancers and concert pianists and quiz kids.

But first there was her convalescence to accomplish. She would be patient, she would cooperate with the nurse. She had found the nurse there upon her arrival home from the hospital.

Mama and Meyer together had hired her, a six-foot-tall woman with a back as broad as the stove, who shouted orders and shook the beams of the house with the weight of her terrifying footsteps. Her name was Smitty. She required that Gilda follow her about and take down dictation in a notebook; every activity required a set of rules to be followed in an accurate progression. The ceremony surrounding the baby's bath partook of more pomp and circumstance than an affair of state. Musetta consulted the "Bath Notebook" that Gilda had left for her to study. Smitty would quiz her on it at the end of the week; if Musetta failed the test, Smitty would stay on for a second week!

Musetta read:

BABY'S BATH

Arrange my bed for feeding bottle after bath.

Time: 5:00 P.M.

Procedure:

See that bathroom is warm and windows closed.

Bring in bathinette. Fill with a comfortable temperature of water.(Test temperature with your elbow.) Put top down and bring in following things: Baby's clothes:

1 shirt.

2 diapers.

1 receiving blanket.

1 nightgown.

1 bath towel.

1 washcloth.

soap.

Required:

cotton, calamine, cornstarch.

alcohol.

Mennen's antiseptic oil.

Place oil in hot water (not running water).

Look around and check up on all things before bringing baby in. Bring in baby with diaper on. Remove nightgown with open back first. Take baby's arms out of sleeve and pull gown down. Remove receiving blanket baby is wearing and put on hamper. Open shirt. Remove shirt and lastly diaper.

Take diaper from crib. Put baby on it and wrap corners under arm. Leave arms out. Pick baby up into arms. Then lift top of bathinette. Put baby in slowly, holding baby's head with left arm, with right arm under her buttocks. Put baby in slowly. Then release right arm and adjust left hand under baby's armpit. See that you hold baby in a slide position with head always up high and feet down. Take washcloth. Wash baby's face with plain water. Soap cloth and wash baby's head with an off-the-face stroke to the water. Rinse head well and wash body with soap and water.

Baby is all bathed. Put washcloth in pocket, still holding baby under armpit with left arm. With right hand take corner of towel. Place under chin, still holding baby. Fold corners under each arm. Place foot on bathinette rail. Take right hand and pick up baby with her back against your stomach. Let towel drop from under chin on baby's head. Take ends and wrap around body and place baby into your arms. Then release bathinette top down and place baby on it. Do not rub baby, just pat till dry. Then if skin is in a prickly condition, do not use as much oil, but sponge with oiled cotton tightly squeezed and go over prickly parts, then calamine body. When thoroughly dry, powder with cornstarch. Pick up baby. Fold towel and start dressing baby, same as you did when undressing her. When putting on receiving blanket, be sure and open bathroom door. Finish dressing *baby, and last put oil on head. Put diaper around head and before leaving bathroom release water.*

Bring baby into bedroom and nurse for twenty minutes. If baby is twisting and doesn't seem to eat well after first ten minutes, stop and try to belch baby. After giving bottle, put baby immediately on stomach in crib. By all means avoid unnecessary noise after this feeding. Close door. Clean bathroom up and then have your dinner.

Musetta finished reading the bath instructions and felt herself smiling. After that ordeal, who could have an appetite left for dinner! She could hardly understand a word of what she had just read. Was she to put the oil on her head or the baby's head? Between chins and armpits she would never pass Smitty's test! And yet Smitty was the expert; she had cared for hundreds of children. If this was the way to bathe Issa, it must be done.

Now she heard footsteps thundering down the hallway toward her bedroom. Smitty's huge head popped in the doorway. "You are ten minutes past feeding time!" she called loudly, coming around to the cradle and swooping down on the sleeping infant.

"Oh—must you wake her?" Musetta said. "Can't we wait till she's hungry?"

"Do you want her to survive?" Smitty demanded. "Do you want her to be raised sloppily?"

"Oh no," Musetta said. "Not sloppily. That's the last thing I have in mind."

"Well, what did I tell you about feeding times? They must be exact, or the child's metabolism will be ruined!"

"I'll be more alert," Musetta promised.

"Have you memorized the rules about juice yet?"

"I'm still reading about the preparation of the milk formula," Musetta said.

"Juice is fed first in the mornings, so juice must be memorized first."

"I don't have the juice rules here," Musetta said.

"Well—I will have to find your sister and give her a piece of my mind!" Smitty said. "I told her to make sure you knew the juice rules by this afternoon. I'm going to send her up right now, and the two of you work on it! I'll feed the baby and be back to test you."

With a plunge and a snort Smitty flung the baby against her ample bosom and went pounding away down the stairs.

ONE HUNDRED TWO

April 15, 1938

Secret Heart

These are the "Juice Rules." I am copying here everything that that foghorn Smitty is teaching Musetta, in case at some future time I have a child of my own. It crosses my mind that Smitty has never had a child, and, considering what she's like, she probably never will. I quiver when she comes near me; Nathan told Mama she is like Hitler. Shouting orders all the time.

I asked Milton Raspman (he is a doctor, he should know!) if the oranges had to be absolutely fresh and with no blemishes on their skins, and he just shrugged his shoulders. What does he know, he's only a man! So, here are the rules:

1. Buy fresh oranges, watch out for thick skins, pulpy insides, soft places. Buy none with scars. Be sure they are round.

2. Take from refrigerator two full hours before squeezing for baby's juice. Set in pan of room temperature water. Since baby must have juice exactly at 6:00 A.M. and milk at 8:00 A.M. the oranges must be set in water at 4:00 A.M. Set alarm to be sure you do not oversleep.

3. Slice in half.

4. Examine.

5. Place on squeezer and rotate clockwise with slight pressure with fingers, not palm of hand. Palm will cause bitter oils. Don't go to the edge. Better too little than sorry.

6. Sterilize strainer for twenty minutes in boiling water. Do not touch.

7. Pour juice through. Save pulp for mother to chew. (This is good for stretch marks.)

8. Give baby one ounce and belch. Second ounce follows. All juice must be taken in the first hour. If any taken after 7:00, it will mix with milk at 8:00 A.M. feeding and curdle, causing colic. TAKE NO CHANCES. YOUR BABY IS A GIFT FROM GOD!

Poor Mama, Smitty is Irish and has no understanding of pots for milk, pots for meat; she eats what she likes when she likes and smears butter on a meat sandwich if Mama is not right there to stop her! Her rules are important to her. Our rules she ignores. That's the way it is with tyrants. But when she leaves, it will all be up to me; Musetta is still sick, she walks like an invalid, limping and shuffling. Smitty has bound her breasts tight and makes her keep ice on them. The milk keeps dripping out no matter what. Musetta must feel like a cow! I know how she hates that! But even so, she is a changed woman. That baby is her jewel. The baby could melt a heart of stone. Those tiny dimpled fingers! Issa's serious dark eyes opening slowly and then closing from the shock of light. The little pink knobs of her knees.

She is so delicate, so fragile, so valuable. A whole human life in so small a container. All the promise of her future! All she will learn and know! All she will suffer! All she will delight in! Little do we know, as we hold her in our arms, what may be in store for her.

ONE HUNDRED THREE

Richard, having just come home from a flying lesson, wore his flight suit to take Ava to Avenue O to deliver the present for the new baby. Ava sat beside him as he drove Len's black Buick. Six cases of Gerber's baby food were in the trunk. He was such a strong young man—he could lift the boxes with hardly a tremor of his muscles. She examined his profile as he drove: his nose not wide, like Len's, or long, like hers. He had dimples in his cheeks. He was handsomer than anyone in his family. He was kinder, wiser, and sweeter than any of them. His blue eyes expressed such purity and decency that she sometimes had to look away from their innocence and trust.

There was no one who didn't love him. If she ever saw Len look soft, it was when he stood beside Richard and clapped him on the shoulder. Sammy adored him and looked up to him without question. He was good to Sammy; he had patience for his insistent curiosity, was willing to teach him about how things worked, willing to explain to him whatever he wanted to know. A twelve-year-old boy has much to learn from a twenty-year-old brother.

Sometimes Richard rocked on his heels in amusement as Sammy demanded to know this or that, but he never showed impatience or annoyance. Seeing him so tall and manly made Ava wonder how it was possible that she had created this full-grown person, that he had come out of her and now was the kind of man she would have fallen in love with as a young woman. She had daydreams about being a girl again and meeting a boy such as her own son. Sometimes she had dreams at night about Richard, too wild and shameful even to think about.

Never mind, she thought. Everything in her brain was mixed up these days, so many men in her thoughts—Johnny Quinn, Richard, Len, Sammy—and from the past, Shmuel, her brother, and Nathan, her father.

She could hardly keep her mind on making a pot roast; all she wanted to do was wipe her hands on her apron and run upstairs and bury her head in her pillow. There was so much turmoil in her mind she hardly had the strength to keep her body moving, functioning, cooking, cleaning.

Once a month, because Johnny Quinn begged her to do it, she met him in Coney Island, and they would eat together, walk on the boardwalk, and dance in a café.

One day he asked her if he could rent a room for them, but she burst into tears. Then never mind, he said, it was enough to see her sweet face, enough to lift his heart and bring him through the dull days of his life till he could see her again.

She knew she shouldn't see him, meet him that way, but something drove her each month to tell the necessary lies, arrange the day around her faithless act. The day with Johnny seemed like a kernel of privacy, hard and small, but inviolable, totally her own. She needed this one special private thing that was her own, that no one knew about, that she could dream about when she was alone, with her head buried in her pillow.

It was not that she adored Johnny Quinn—he was too worn out, by drink, by tiredness, by no special luck in life. But she was ruined, too—by her losses, by her sadness, by too much flesh and too many years. They had a bond; what they remembered was a time when they weren't ruined, when they were young and hopeful together, light-hearted, a time when they were still physically beautiful and had waltzed till the warm gray dawn came creeping over the ocean.

She glanced at Richard, grateful that he was not a mind reader. Seeing his manly thighs moving on the car seat as he shifted gears and pressed on the accelerator, she suddenly thanked God also that she did not know what went on in his mind. A son could have thoughts that would surely astonish a mother, embarrass her. It was better she did not know them.

"So—Mom," Richard said, turning off Ocean Parkway onto Avenue O. "How do you think Aunt Gilda will feel about the new baby?"

"How should she feel?" Ava asked. "A baby is beautiful."

"I just meant—well, you know how she and Aunt Musetta don't get along. I wondered, that's all."

"I think Gilda adores the baby," Ava said.

"I hope Aunt Musetta is nice to her," Richard said. "You know how she is."

"Sisters always have difficulties, don't imagine it to be more serious than it is."

"I just wish Aunt Gilda had more fun in her life. I think she counts too much on Bingo. A dog is only a dog."

"Mama tells me she's going out sometimes with a nice young doctor."

"Aunt Gilda is so sweet," Richard said. "She's such a good person."

"And what about your aunt Musetta?"

"She's beautiful," Richard said. "When you're that beautiful, you don't need to be sweet."

"A philosopher I have for a son," Ava said.

All Ava had to do was mention to Len that she was worried about choosing a suitable present for the new baby, and before she knew it, he had made a phone call. The next morning the six cases of baby food had been delivered to the back porch. Len and his connections. His power frightened her; he could move mountains with a phone call. She had long ago stopped trying to understand what went on in his head; it was dense in there, dark and convoluted, filled with thoughts that didn't interest her—schemes about making money, about maneuvers. In her mind she had constant thoughts about people and feelings and memories. Len thought about making her happy with purchases, possessions, while she thought about how sad it was that he could never make her happy.

Gilda opened the front door. "Aah, my beautiful Richard," she said, standing on tiptoes to receive the full pressure of his embrace. "A kiss from you is like sunshine, like raisins, like vitamins."

Richard laughed sweetly, a little embarrassed. "I have some boxes in the trunk of the car, Aunt Gilda," he said. "I'll bring them in." Gilda and Ava watched him walk toward the car.

"Such a mensch," Gilda said. "Such a gorgeous boy. There should only be no war."

"From your mouth to God's ears," Ava said.

"Airplanes are so dangerous," Gilda said. "I worry . . . "

"Don't worry," Ava said. "Does worry change anything?"

They held open the door as Richard came up to them carrying a case of baby food on his shoulder.

"Come and see Issa," Gilda said. "I think Musetta has just finished feeding her."

Ava followed Gilda into the house. She flinched at the name "Issa"—it sounded so much like "Isaac" to her. She had a flash of his yellow face and hard black eyes, of his fury when he demanded that she return the coat Mr. Berk had given her at the clothing factory. She thought of Isaac's coldness to her (and, by contrast, his warmth to his own little girls). It was a pity you could never forget those things or forgive them. Isaac was dead almost ten years now. His "little girls" were grown women, Gilda twenty-eight and Musetta thirty-one. Ava herself, almost forty-two, still had the heart and feelings of that ten-year-old child whom Isaac punished, resented, and abused.

But of course Musetta had not been abused by him. Why should she not wish to honor his memory by calling her daughter "Issa"?

A great white creature blocked their way at the foot of the staircase. It took Ava a moment to realize this mountain of white must be the nurse, Smitty.

"If you please," the nurse said to Ava, wrinkling her nose in disgust. "Do you intend to enter the room where the newborn is sleeping?"

"Why, yes, I've come to visit," Ava said, stepping back. The nurse had her arms crossed over her immense breasts.

"Does the young man expect to hold the infant?" the nurse asked.

"Well, I don't know."

"It is expected, for hygienic reasons, that you wash your hands for a full three minutes, up to the elbow, before you visit the infant."

"Fine, I will," Ava said. "And I know where the bathroom is. The new mother is my sister."

"I don't care who you are," the nurse said, turning on her heel to go back up the stairs. "God himself would have to wash his hands in this house."

1939

ONE HUNDRED FOUR

"Look at me, I'm just as slim as before the baby," Musetta said to Meyer, spinning in front of the bedroom mirror in a full white silk skirt. "Meyer! Look at me, you're not listening! I said, don't you think I'm just as slim as before the baby?"

Meyer's dark curls shone in the sunlight coming in the front windows. His head was bent over the pages of the *Brooklyn Eagle.* "Hmm?" He was marking something with a pencil.

"I'm so glad it's springtime. As soon as we get Issa her first pair of baby shoes, we can take her to Prospect Park and walk along the lake and show her the ducks. I love springtime; I love spring clothes." She spun again before the mirror. "Issa can wear her white lace bonnet that Gilda made for her. We'll take pictures. Do we have film, Meyer?"

"Here's a job," Meyer said. "Man needed to drive bakery delivery truck, Klein's Bakery, Avenue M. It's a new ad. I'll go right over there now."

"I thought we could get the baby shoes today," Musetta said.

"What will we buy the shoes with, Moo?" Meyer said, getting to his feet.

"Don't worry so much," Musetta said. "We're not down to our last penny yet. You could always go back to selling pajamas if you have to. And it wasn't your fault that Hartman's shoe store closed. You know you were a good sales-man; you'll find something interesting soon."

"I've been out of work for two months," Meyer said. "I keep thinking maybe I'll open some kind of business. It has to be right, though. It has to be the right thing. You know Leo Crookshank? He's inventing things and patenting them. One day, he says, one of them will make him rich. I've been writing down some of my ideas—I have good ideas all the time. Like a new kind of ride for Coney Island, something like a merry-go-round, but I would call my ride the merry-go-bob, a turning circle, but on it—instead of horses—would be little pie-shaped wedges, and each person would stand on a wedge, and a giant arrow would whirl around over their heads (like a roulette wheel), and wherever the arrow stops—that person would get a prize."

"You have prizes on your brain since you had the crane machines," Musetta said. "Why have prizes at all? I mean, the ride is the prize. You're always giving away more than you need to."

"I'm not giving away anything, Moo," Meyer said. "I'm just thinking about how to make a living." He waved the newspaper at her. "Look, I'm going over to see about this job. I'll be back later."

"You don't want that job, Meyer. A delivery boy! Something better has to come along soon."

"Good-bye, Moo—I'll see you later. I'll be home by dinnertime. I may go into the city and see what I can turn up there."

"Just be careful," she said. "Please be careful." When his car had driven away, Musetta went to sit beside Issa's crib to watch her sleeping. Sometimes she had a fear that Meyer would die in a car accident or by some sudden illness. Then Issa would be a fatherless child. Fatherless children were such pitiable things. Their mothers had to go off to work and leave them with unsatisfactory caretakers. They always had runny noses and stretched-out socks. If Meyer died and Musetta had to leave Issa in order to work, who could possibly take care of her? Mama was getting too old; she had to stop what she was doing several times a day to put a nitroglycerin tablet under her tongue to relieve the pains in her chest. Nathan was out of the question—he was a cipher. He shuffled around the house all day clearing his throat, trying to fill his tired lungs with enough air. He was always drinking tea and leaving crumbs on the table. He had even stopped telling stories about his life as a brilliant young man in Vienna. No one believed he had ever been brilliant. He was dull as a rock, dependent on Mama for everything.

It would have to be Gilda who would take care of the baby! Of course, if it came to that, she'd have to give up her little job at Cindy Lee's beauty parlor since Musetta could earn ten times as much being a secretary. Gilda would be forced to give up her job if Meyer were killed. Gilda would have to take care of Issa, and Musetta would become a secretary to an important lawyer.

But of course Meyer was not going to die. He'd better not! Gilda would be a terrible influence on Issa. She was far too nervous, too hysterical about every little thing. And how she spoiled the baby. Even now, when she could spend her time in better, more practical ways, she would sit outside by the baby's carriage for hours, study the baby's face, and run her fingers over the baby's tiny features. The baby was gorgeous, it was true, but how long could anyone stare at a sleeping baby? Even now, looking at Issa's restful, delicate face on the pink satin crib sheet, Musetta felt impatience. It took so long for children to grow up and learn things! She wanted to get busy and teach Issa how to play the piano, how to read, how to speak! The child could not even walk yet. She was anxious for her to walk, so they could buy tiny white leather baby shoes and go walking, like a handsome perfect family, in Prospect Park.

Issa could just stand up now, clinging to some piece of furniture, but she'd always sit back down at once, not even thinking about walking.

Well, Gilda could stare at her all she wanted, but Issa knew who her mother was! Gilda could croon to her, make little wool dolls for her, and make faces at her, but Issa was Musetta's child, and no one was ever going to forget that for one minute. If Gilda wanted a baby, she ought to be out in the world working on finding a man, not sitting around mooning at someone else's baby or rushing off to Cindy Lee's, where, day after day, there were only women customers, women needing hair cuts and manicures and facials. If Gilda weren't so wrapped up in that messy, filthy dog Bingo, maybe she'd have some time for the doctor, Milton whatever his name was.

Mama was so baffled that Gilda turned down Milton's calls and invitations. She and Gilda argued all the time: "Why don't you go to the movies with him? He's a nice young man, he's a doctor!" And Gilda would say, "He just wants to study my face, for God's sake, Mama! I'm an exhibit for him! He wants to use me for medical experiments!"

Mama would say, "Your face isn't even so bad these days, maybe you're imagining things."

"Imagining things! I don't think so. And he's also calling me because he wants to be nice to his aunt Gertie, my customer. She tells him what a sad life I have, what a sad girl I am. I don't need charity like that!"

Well, Gilda managed to dig her own grave, time after time. She just didn't have what it took. But she wasn't going to take what Musetta had. No! Musetta resolved to keep Issa forever from Gilda's negative influence.

There—she heard Gilda coming up the stairs now. She must be home from Cindy Lee's for lunch. She could hear her delicate footsteps pattering down the hall. And right behind her, the pitter of Bingo's animal claws on the floor of the hallway. "Come here, Poochkala," she heard Gilda say. Hearing her talk that way turned Musetta's stomach. Gilda let Bingo up on her bed, even on her pillow. How could she allow that?

Now there was a gentle knock on the door. "Musetta? Are you awake? Could I come in and look at the baby, please?"

ONE HUNDRED FIVE

December 2, 1939

Secret Heart

The police came last night and arrested Meyer! We were having Shabbos dinner, and I had just given Issa the wishbone from the chicken and was teaching her how to make a wish when we heard a loud knock on the front door. Meyer went to the door and stayed there a long time, talking in a low voice. Then he came back to the table with a strange embarrassed smile on his face, looked directly at Musetta, and said, "The police want to talk to me about the papers I found in the trunk. I'm going with them now. I don't know if I will be back tonight."

He was already getting his coat out of the closet before Musetta said in a strangled, fierce voice, "I told you not to tell them about the papers. I told you not to be a fool."

"Don't worry," he said, giving us all a weak apologetic smile. He patted Mama on the shoulder as he went out. I got up at once and looked out of the front window and saw Meyer getting into the police car with two policemen. His shoulders were hunched forward and his head bowed just before he got into the car. I felt a pang of such love for him!

Musetta threw down her napkin and ran upstairs to their bedroom. I hated to see her that way, with her face white and the tendons in her neck tight and ugly. Meyer had only done the right thing. I understand why he had to turn in the papers.

Last week he was in the city, following some ads in the classifieds for jobs, when he passed the Mills Hotel and saw that they were having an auction on unclaimed items, lost luggage, things left behind by guests over the years. He's been talking about going into some kind of business for himself, maybe the secondhand junk business, and when he saw the auction going on, he took a chance and bought several cartons and a trunk for six dollars apiece. He brought them home and lugged them into the house, and we all stood around as he cut the twine on the cartons, opened the boxes, and pried open the lock on the trunk.

I was excited, thinking he might really find treasure, but Musetta stood back with the baby on her shoulder, her face wrinkled in disgust, as if she expected Meyer to pull out a dead rat and wave it at her. Well—it was mostly junk. There were old pajamas and a broken alarm clock and someone's torn raincoat and a dented flashlight and a bag of old comic books.

But then Meyer pulled out a little marble-based lamp that was quite nice. He looked so pleased; it was obviously an antique, made of a smooth pink marble with white veins running through it. Mama was anxious for him to look in the trunk. When he raised the lid, she sighed in disappointment: we saw it was filled with papers. Meyer got down on his knees and began to look at them. His smile disappeared, and his brow became tense and furrowed. There were pamphlets, tied together with rope, and letters and various other publications. Meyer was looking at a sheet of paper that had columns of names on it.

"What does it say?" Musetta asked.

"I don't know," Meyer said. "It's in German."

"In German!" Musetta said.

Nathan spoke up from where he stood behind Mama.

"Give it here," he said. "I can read it and tell you what it is."

Meyer handed him the list of names, and Nathan's face turned pale. "I think it's a list of Nazis in this country," he said.

"Does it say anything else?"

"It has addresses here of meeting places; look, here's an address in Brooklyn!"

"I'll have to turn this into the police," Meyer said, his face as serious as I have ever seen it.

"You can't do that, Meyer," Musetta said, stepping into the light of the standing lamp. "They will think *you* are a Nazi. Or a spy."

"Oh—but he has to turn it in, Musetta!" I told her.

"This is very important."

"We have to worry about ourselves," Musetta said. "We can't get involved."

Well, of course, Meyer, being the man he is, took the trunk down to the police station the next morning. He said they thanked him, but then—last night! They came to arrest him! Maybe Musetta was right! Oh God, Meyer, a Nazi! The most ridiculous thought in the world!

ONE HUNDRED SIX

"Little Bo Peep has lost her _____"

"Seep!"

" . . . and can't tell where to find _____"

"Dem!"

"Leave them alone and they'll come _____"

"Home!"

" . . . wagging their tails behind _____"

"Dem!"

"Very good, Issa! Very, very good. You are brilliant!" said Musetta, taking her daughter by the hand and kissing the top of her head. Issa clapped her hands gleefully and shook her blonde curls in delight. "Dost her seep," she said for her mother's benefit.

"Yes, yes, now come with me and we'll work on the blackboard. Here—sit on my lap. Now—what letter is Mommy making?"

"A!" cried Issa.

"And this one?"

"B!"

"Now here, you take the chalk. You try to make the next one. It's hard, I know. Well, let me make it then. What letter is this?"

"C!" said Issa, hissing the letter delightedly through her tiny front teeth. "And the next one?"

A car door slammed in the street and Issa slid from her mother's lap. "Daddy!" she said. "Daddy!"

"Come back here," Musetta said. "We're not done with our lesson."

"Daddy—balloon," the child said.

Musetta heard Meyer's heavy step on the stairs. He had been out again looking into some business deals. He'd given up the idea, for the time being, of buying old suitcases and trunks at auction. He'd turned over the trunk to the police, who, after questioning him about its contents, had let him go for lack of evidence that he was in any way involved.

"I don't think Daddy has a balloon for you today," she said to Issa.

Meyer came into the bedroom with his coat over his arm.

"Why didn't you hang your coat downstairs?" Musetta asked sharply.

"I didn't realize . . . I wasn't thinking," Meyer said.

"So—what happened today?"

"I decided to go in with Leo Crookshank on his new invention. I'm going to have to ask your brother-in-law for five hundred dollars."

"How do you know if Leo knows what he's doing?"

"Well—he's done research. He thinks the chin rest will go over big. He showed me a model today. It's made of elastic and gauze, and he claims that if a woman sleeps with it on her chin for a week, it will smooth out her wrinkles and reduce fat on her neck and chin."

"Neck!" Issa cried, pointing to her delicate throat.

Meyer picked her up in his arms and nuzzled her cheek, then blew on her neck. She giggled in delight.

"I'd rather you found a job," Musetta said. "Any job."

"You know what will happen," Meyer said. "You know what has happened already. If I answer truthfully about a police record and say I have one, they will check it out and find the stuff about the crane machines and the Nazi lists."

"But those were nothing. You were just an innocent victim in both cases. The crane machines weren't illegal when you went into the business, and the Nazi lists were checked out, and the police finally agreed that you had no connection to any Nazis."

"But it's on my record. Employers can't take any chances these days with what's going on in Europe now."

"I don't know if Len will lend you five hundred dollars."

"You know I would never ask him if this wasn't really important, Moo. I've tried everything. I can't seem to get started here in any business since we left Cleveland."

"But do you think a chin rest would sell? I mean, it sounds so silly!"

"Maybe Gilda can try to sell them at the beauty shop once we start producing them."

"See Gilda!" Issa cried. "Want Gilda!"

Musetta made a face. "The child is always running to see if Gilda is home from work. I'm getting tired of it. Gilda makes so much of her. She rolls curlers in her hair! That beautiful curly hair—can you imagine, curlers!"

"It's just for fun," Meyer said.

" . . . And she sits with her and cuts doilies out of napkins, and she makes wire flowers from the milk-bottle wires. I wish she'd get off her bottom and help Mama with the cooking when she comes home from Cindy Lee's."

"Mama likes to cook," Meyer said, "and thank God she's well enough to still enjoy it. Gilda is on her feet all day. If she wants to sit down with the baby when she comes home from work, why do you mind so much?"

"Oh—you just don't understand Gilda's ways, you never have," Musetta said. "She's so manipulative . . . I just don't want her to teach any of that to Issa."

"I think Gilda is very patient with Issa," Meyer said. "You should be glad she's willing to spend so much time with her. It gives you a rest."

"I don't want Issa getting confused, thinking she has two mothers, you know."

"I don't think there will be any doubt, ever, in her mind, about who her mother is."

"—and that dog!" Musetta said, with a shudder. "The way she feeds Bingo scraps from the table and lets her up on the couch, and then I have to sit there, put my body where that animal, who rubs her behind outside in the dirt, has been sitting!"

"Don't you think it's nice for Issa to be comfortable with a dog so she won't ever be afraid of dogs?"

"I hate for her to touch that animal," Musetta said. "When Issa's outside in her playpen, all the male dogs come around looking for Bingo or smelling her scent, or whatever, and they come right up to the playpen. If I didn't chase them away, well—they'd pee right on it, Meyer."

She stopped speaking, feeling that she had gone too far. Meyer looked upset, even shocked, at her anger and her language. She tried to calm herself.

"Well, forget the dog," she said. "I'll call Ava tonight and see when the best time would be for you to see Len about a loan."

ONE HUNDRED SEVEN

"Len will be home tonight, but I can't be here," Ava said to Musetta on the phone. "I have my meeting of the Noble League. Would you like to come with me some night, Musetta? We have twelve women now. It's such a mitzvah, Musetta, to help those orphan boys."

"Ava, you know I have Issa to take care of!"

"Oh, but Mama could watch her one evening a week, or Gilda. If you could just see how grateful the boys are . . . they have no parents, they have no family. You know that Shmuel was in an orphanage when Mama had to work. We owe it to those poor boys to help them."

"I have no time to work for charity, Ava. If Meyer doesn't earn money soon, we'll have to start asking for charity ourselves. Listen, do you think Len will lend Meyer the money? They have such good ideas, Meyer and Leo Crookshank. First the chin strap, to take away wrinkles. And they've been working on a hockey game, with some kind of twirling handles to hit the ball back and forth across the box, and after that an invention to stand up dinner plates in a cabinet so they don't touch each other. They're going to call it 'Stand-A-Plate' and try to sell it to Sears. Please, encourage Len to help him Ava. With all his police trouble, Meyer can't get any kind of job at all."

"I'll talk to Len," Ava said. "He knows Meyer is sensible, I can't imagine he'd turn him down. Tell Meyer to come over here after dinner, when Len is in a good mood and relaxed. I'm leaving a pot roast warming for him and a honey cake on the table. I'm sorry I won't be here."

"You're so busy these days, Ava. How come you're doing so much all the time?"

"I like to keep myself occupied, it's good for me," Ava said. When she hung up the phone, she hurried upstairs to get dressed for her appointment with Johnny Quinn at Coney Island. One day, when she had run out of good reasons to leave the house for her secret meeting with him, it had hit her like a lightning bolt—she ought to do something legitimate that would give her reasons to leave home and that Len would understand and could even check on!

Talking with some women in the bakery one day, she had heard about the Hebrew National Orphan Home in Westchester, a place that housed three hundred boys and was always in dire need of food and clothing for them. When she heard the words *orphan home*, a coiled snail of pain in her heart unwound itself and slowly traveled through her body. She remembered the cement floors, the metal stairways, the cold factory that was Shmuel's home for the years Mama had to work as a midwife. She could see the barred windows in her mind's eye, hear the clank of the metal dishes in the vast, impersonal kitchen.

"Look, if the boys need food, why can't we collect food for them?" Ava had said suddenly. She turned to the woman behind the counter who was putting Ava's rye bread into a paper bag. "Millie," she said. "How about here? At the end of the week, couldn't you spare some leftover bagels, cakes, breads, before they go stale?"

"You want them? We always have leftovers."

"I want them," Ava said. "For the orphanage for Jewish boys. If it's okay with you and your husband, from now on, on Fridays just before you close, I'll come and pick up whatever you can give me."

Several of the other women in the bakery had ideas—one of them knew the owner of the fish store; one's husband was a clothing wholesaler who knew where to get discards of out-of-style clothing. Another woman offered to knit socks—she was always running out of people for whom to make socks. Soon after that, the women named themselves the Noble League and met in one another's homes. They elected Ava the president, and once a month they went by train to Westchester to deliver clothing and games and toys. The perishables—the food—they sent by the fish-market delivery truck.

Now whenever Ava wanted to leave the house, she said, "I'm going to my league," and Len and the boys would nod. Though the work had started as a ruse to ensure her privacy and give her more freedom with Johnny Quinn, Ava found that she really began to enjoy it, to get a great unexpected satisfaction from it, a sense of something like real joy when she went to the orphanage and felt the arms of the little boys thrown around her neck in gratitude. The president of the home, Judge Aaron J. Levy, suggested one day that she make a plea on the radio asking for donations of food and money for the home. Judge Levy then found a sponsor for her, Consolidated Edison of New York, and every Saturday morning she spoke from station WEVD in New York, sometimes taking one or several of the boys from the home with her, to make her plea.

She was often a little surprised at herself—at her sailing around the city on her own, at her newfound confidence, at the forceful sound of her own voice when she was asking or sometimes begging for goods that "her" orphanage could use.

Now she turned the flame under the pot roast to a bare blue shimmer, left Len a note that Meyer would be visiting him in the evening, took Sammy's shoes with her to drop off at the shoemaker's for new heels, and went to take the train to go dancing with Johnny Quinn.

1941

ONE HUNDRED EIGHT

April 26, 1941

Secret Heart

Another spring. The peach tree in the backyard is blooming, the lilies of the valley are creeping along the base of the fence like tiny rolling pearls, and Bingo is in heat again. She becomes another creature entirely at this time of year, stretching out her hind legs and rubbing her belly on the floor, making weird sirenlike moans, speeding in a wild dash to get outside if Mama only opens the door to stick her mop outside and shake it. We must keep her in, or she will have mongrel puppies. There are always five or six male dogs near the front stoop; they must smell her scent from blocks away. Musetta is always kicking them out of her way and telling them to "drop dead." She claims that Issa will be eaten alive by one of them, though of course we all are careful never to leave Issa outside of the fenced backyard unattended.

Issa is the joy of my life. What sweetness, what beauty. She awakes from her nap with a smile on her face. She doesn't seem to have an ounce of her mother's vengeance and spleen in her! But what she has is all of Musetta's intelligence and perfect pink complexion and flirtatiousness. From Meyer she has an easy-going nature, a sense of humor, and just plain goodness. And from me—I think she has got something of me in her, I pray to God she does—she has an appreciation of small things, a patience and a firmness, a tolerance of all the stupid things she has to endure. Of course, she is only three, but she is so wise nevertheless. On March 15, her third birthday, a neighbor passed by and said to her, "Issa, my, what a big girl you are!" and Issa, wearing a little red plaid dress, opened wide her blue eyes and said, "I'm not big at all. I'm just a very small girl." The child has spirit and wisdom at the same time.

But Musetta is so possessive of her! If she sees me reading to Issa when I haven't first asked her Royal Highness's permission, she always invents some excuse to take Issa away from me. "We have to go to the playground now" or "Issa must have a nap now or a bath or a full course dinner at three in the afternoon"!

Once Issa just clung to me, yelling, refusing to be interrupted in the reading of a fairy tale, and Musetta fairly pulled her arm off to disentangle her from me. Well, Issa is hers. I know it. There is no contest, even if Musetta seems to think there is. She has what she has—she always has had exactly what she wants. Her sweet handsome husband, her child, her luck. And I have the spillover. A little time with Meyer in the living room now and then while Musetta is somewhere else pouting. A little time with Issa, whom I adore. I have given up hoping for a family of my own. I am almost thirty-one now; it is too late, or soon will be. Maybe I should consider myself blessed to live with my sister and her husband so that I have the chance to help raise Issa. All things work out for the best. Or so the saying goes. Or so it seems very occasionally.

Meyer is finally having some success with Leo Crookshank and their genius inventions. They borrowed some money from Len and took out a patent on an invention called a "Stand-A-Plate," which they are manufacturing in plastic from molds they hired someone to design. Meyer gave me one the other night—a little yellow square with bars set across the bottom that are supposed to hold your dinner plates upright in your cabinet. I tried to use it, but it toppled over, and Mama started to *shrie* about breaking her good dinner set. (Nothing broke.) But maybe I wasn't using it right.

I frankly don't mind piling up the dishes in the usual way. But Meyer thinks it's a more elegant way of storing dishes, and it keeps them from scraping on one another. The big news is that Woolworth's has agreed to stock the Stand-A-Plates as soon as they are manufactured, and that's a good sign. If they sell like hotcakes in Woolworth's, then our future is assured!

It's funny how I think of my future as being the same as "their" future. I suppose it isn't. I could still have a separate, different life, but I can't imagine how. The days I spend at Cindy Lee's are not my real life. All my old friends, my sorority sisters, have babies. They almost never call me or stop by anymore. I don't go to the movies much either—Mama is too weak to walk to Avenue P, and at night (when Meyer could drive her) she's too tired to stay awake. On the weekends I'm too busy washing my clothes and ironing and bathing Bingo and clipping her nails—the time just flies. And of course what I love best is sitting in the yard with Issa, teaching her about lilies of the valley and mulberries and peaches and butterflies and tiny lady bugs.

I live and breathe to see her every morning. What a gift it is, to give birth to a child . . . to be in charge of such a conscious, intelligent, feeling person. Musetta is in her glory, strolling along on Ocean Parkway with Issa, people stopping to admire Issa's beautiful curls or her beautiful little feet as she skips along in patent leather shoes. Well, life is at least peaceful here for the moment. But there is no peace in Europe; there is danger and talk of world war, and terrible things are happening. I don't understand much of it, speeches on the radio every day, and Hitler taking over countries, but thank God it is far away, and I pray that President Roosevelt keeps us out of it.

I must live in the small pleasures of life. The warmth of the sun, the smell of a baby's skin. I tell myself this for strength, since I know I will never have the big pleasures of life.

ONE HUNDRED NINE

"When I was seventeen," Johnny Quinn said, "I almost drowned, right there. . . ." He pointed out over the ocean toward a spot between two rock jetties, then he brought his arm back over Ava's head and rested his hand on her bare upper arm. The hot August wind lifted her hair gently over her ears and tickled the back of her neck. She breathed deeply, of ocean spray, of hot sun, of the musky smell of sand and body oils and rank seaweed rotting high on the beach, left by the tide that carried it there during the night. In the distance she heard the drone of an airplane; she closed her eyes and let the sun filter through her lids, seeing broad bands of purple and green seep under them.

"Tell me what happened," she whispered. She licked the taste of salt off her lips.

"Well—you know how a boy is at seventeen . . . he thinks he can do anything. It was in the days when I had big beautiful muscles in my back and arms—I was like a cocky lion, you know?"

"I know—" Ava said. "I met you just a few years later. You were pretty cocky then; you could dance like an angel."

"—but could only swim like a lamppost and sank like a trunkful of lead right to the bottom."

Ava laughed. "Tell me about it . . . "

"So I came down here alone. It seems like dawn was just breaking—no, no, now I remember, I had been here with buddies the night before, and we drank too much, and we slept on the beach for a few hours, and when I woke up, I saw that they had left me there alone. So to clear my head I just charged into the ocean. And swam like a bat out of hell, puffing and blowing and spouting like a whale."

"A lion! A bat! A whale! Make up your mind," Ava said, leaning her head on Johnny Quinn's shoulder. She could feel the vibration of his voice coming through the slatted wooden boards of the bench.

"Well, in a nutshell, I went too far. Couldn't get back. Was flailing around out there, one stroke toward shore, two pulls back by the rip tide. It was farewell and time to meet my maker; I could already see my mother in a black veil, lighting candles in church."

"And . . . ?"

"To tell you the truth, Ava, my girl, she lit them for me anyway, before her stroke, as if I were dead, because I hadn't given her any grandchildren. But on that fine day, God sent a savior to me. A fat boy, with eyeglasses and a stomach hanging over his trunks. But a heart of gold. He was an angel to me. He was out on the beach looking for treasure, I suppose—I never found out a thing about him—but he saw me taking my last breaths, and he dived in and dragged me out, inch by inch, till I could feel the sand come up suddenly under my feet. I remember that exact feeling, that exact moment. First, there was nothing solid, just that gray-green water pulling me under, and then, like I was Jesus himself coming to life, the ground pushed itself under my feet and got firm and hard and promised me life in the world to come. I couldn't talk for maybe an hour. The fat boy dragged me—stumbling—high up on the beach, and we both collapsed, and after a while the sun came up and started warming my back. I could hear him panting beside me. I could see a jellyfish out of the corner of my eye, a white limp thready thing, and before the drops dried on my eyelashes, I could see rainbows coming into my head. I still bless that boy in my prayers."

"You remember all that?"

"And more," Johnny Quinn said. "You know how certain times in your life are sort of circled in white chalk and stand out, brilliant somehow, from everything else?"

"Oh yes," Ava said. "I know that."

"It's like when you and I went dancing with Tony Angeloni and his girl; something about those nights, and you sitting out there in the smoky dark watching me do my number, and those long rides home on the subway. Do you remember, Ava?"

"It's like from another lifetime, Johnny," she said. "None of life seems real, when you think about it that way. What used to matter so much, like all the fights I was having with Isaac, just vanishes, and then different things matter, like now I worry about the war and Richard going to fight in it, and about the boys in the Hebrew National Orphan Home, and my broadcast appeal on WEVD every Saturday. The things I thought about all the time when I was young, finding my father, hating Isaac, are like dreams. Vanished."

"But here we are—you and me. We're not vanished."

"No," Ava said. "That's why I come here to be with you. I feel real here. It's like my real life goes on here, when we talk like this. I never talk with Len about what he remembers from his early life. His mind is so crowded with business, he probably doesn't even know he once was a boy with feelings. And I can't talk this way to my children—the way we talk—because you have to keep secrets from your children, don't you? They can't know how scared you sometimes are, or how miserable."

"You can tell me if you're scared, Ava. I know what it's like to be scared." He leaned forward and kissed her cheek. "Oh, you're my good girl, Ava."

"No so good," she said, staring out to sea where the sun rolled like a golden coin on the waves. "Not so good if I'm here secretly with a man not my husband."

"We're not sinning, Ava," Johnny Quinn said. "I'd like to be, you know, but we only talk. I wish we were sinning."

"Talk like this is even more personal than sins of the flesh," Ava said. "This is just as much a sin."

"If one sin is just like another," Johnny Quinn said, "maybe someday we can rent a room and I can hold you against me. What would be the harm in it? I dream of it."

"Johnny, it's hard enough for me, just doing this."
"But maybe someday, Ava? Please, *please* consider it."

ONE HUNDRED TEN

August 16, 1941

Secret Heart

Three weeks ago I had chills and fever. Pain in my back. My scalp was electric. I was at Cindy Lee's doing Mrs. Raspman's hair when I started to shiver so hard I stuck her in the scalp with a hair pin. I just kept going, though, rolling those pin curls, biting hard to keep my teeth from chattering. I remember she was telling me how bad Milton felt that I wouldn't go out with him. That was her speech every week when I did her hair. She never let it die. Milton and I were so good for each other, why was I so stubborn?

She simply will never understand that I feel he's not attracted to me in any way, but somehow pretends he is (out of obligation to her or out of some kind of misplaced admiration for me or out of medical curiosity about my face or out of a lack of being able to find some girl he really likes).

Anyhow: I was sick as a dog. I was slow. I dropped hair pins on the floor. Cindy Lee kept checking on me. She was doing a perm, and the smell of the chemicals was worse than ammonia, worse than peroxide. I could feel myself getting sick to my stomach. Then all of a sudden I had to make a run for the bathroom, and she was right on my heels, even as I was retching into the sink.

I felt the scissors fall out of my apron pocket and into the sink, right under the stream of water I had just turned on. She stood at my shoulder, saying didn't I know how expensive those cutting shears were and now they were wet and would rust. I tried to dry them off on my apron. I was so weak, leaning back against the wall, and there she was, shaking that brassy blond head at me, yapping like a parrot.

Finally she said, "You really look sick." (She knew I always came in even if I had just an ordinary cold or an allergy attack.) "You better go home. It must be flu. You'll probably be out a week, don't you think?"

I nodded; it felt like I would be sick for a year. "So—" she added, "let this week be your vacation!"

"My vacation? What kind of a vacation will that be?"

"That's your problem," she said. "I can only spare you for a week, so it's got to be this week, not some other week."

"How can you call this my vacation?"

But now she was looking in the mirror, arranging her curls, making faces with her reddish purple lips.

"Never mind my vacation!" I said. "Just find yourself another beautician! I won't be back!"

"Hey, kid!" she cried, her mouth going as ugly as I'd ever seen it. "You make good tips here."

"I can't work here anymore," I said. "I won't ever work for you again." I took a deep breath and went back to my chair, where Gertie Raspman was sitting with her mouth open, her hair half-curled. I didn't say a word, just gathered up my purse and my coat and the special curling iron I'd bought with my own money to do little ringlets at the hairline and my tin of cookies (which I made at home and offered to my customers) and the little blue box—the *pushka*—in which I collected money for the Avenue N shul.

Cindy Lee was standing with her hands on her hips, watching me, chewing gum. As I walked out the door, I heard Gertie Raspman say, "What on earth is wrong?" and Cindy Lee answered, "The kid is having a nervous breakdown."

To make a long story short—last week I opened up my own beauty parlor right here in the house! As soon as I got over my sickness (it was influenza, the doctor said), the ladies I'd worked on at Cindy Lee's started calling and stopping by the house and begging me to go back there; they loved my work, my gentle touch.

The said they'd never find another girl to do their hair and nails the way I did them. I told them I could never go back, so they urged me to open up my own business, and they offered to chip in to buy me a shampoo tray, a dryer, a manicure table (which they said I could pay off by giving them half-price cuts and sets for the first few months I was in business)—and there I was, in my own business! No one was more surprised than I was! Even Musetta thought it was a good idea and urged me to start giving permanents as well. We made the sun porch into my "salon"—the only problem is that we have to go upstairs to use the bathroom for shampoos.

But it's certainly convenient, and now I don't have to give any of the money to Cindy Lee, and little Issa sits on the floor while I give haircuts and helps me sweep up the hair and squeeze the gluey green shampoo gel into smaller bottles and shake it up till it froths and bubbles like a mint ice cream soda.

I feel so pleased! I feel more important than I've ever felt in my life. "GILDA'S BEAUTY SALON." What do you know!

ONE HUNDRED ELEVEN

Issa rode high on her father's shoulders, bouncing slightly as he strode over the boardwalk, feeling the grip of his large strong hands around her ankles. On one side of her walked her mother, wearing a big straw hat and a white dress, and on the other walked her cousin Richard, who had a dimple in his cheek. Every so often he leaned toward her and said, "Kiss me right here," and pointed to his cheek. She loved to kiss him. He had such a nice smell. He must put something on his hair like Aunt Gilda put on the ladies' hair in her beauty parlor. But the smell was more on his cheek than on his hair. His hair was curly and blew in the wind that smelled a little fishy, like cod liver oil, which she hated.

Her father kept saying, "Take deep breaths, this is wonderful sea air," and her mother answered, "All I can smell is pizza cheese and candy apples and dead fish."

"Can I have some pizza?" Issa asked.

"That's not food for us," her mother said.

"Are you sure you have the stomach for this, Meyer?" her cousin Richard asked her father.

"Did I ever show a yellow streak?" her father replied. (She looked down at his hair to examine it for a streak of yellow. All she could find was the little tiny white bump that grew under his hair at the back of his scalp. He had told her he had an extra bump coming out of his head because his brain was too big and needed more space. Mommy had said he shouldn't confuse her and that the bump was just a thing growing there like a pimple. But pimples were what Aunt Gilda had all over her face, and they weren't white, but dark red.

"There it is," Richard said, pointing ahead. "What a beauty it is." He whistled. Issa could see what looked like a very tall wire mushroom, still quite far away. Her father hastened his steps, and his shoulders bumped her more forcefully, up and down.

"Not exactly the merry-go-round," Richard said.

"Oh! The merry . . . go-round!" Issa cried.

"Do you want to go on a horse that goes up and down?" her mother asked, looking strange to Issa because of her dark glasses.

"First Meyer has to go up and down," Richard said and laughed.

"It's easy for you to laugh," Meyer said. "You've been turning somersaults in a plane at Stewart's Technical School for over a year. Your stomach doesn't know up from down."

"That's why the U.S. Army Air Force needs this boy," Richard said. "That's why this boy enlisted to serve Uncle Sam. Pretty soon I'll be learning how to solo on those babies."

"Thank God Issa was born," her mother said. "Or Meyer would be joining up under my nose."

"I'll do enough for both of us," Richard reassured her. "You stay here and hold the fort," he said to Meyer. "And I'll keep evil from our shores."

"There's Aunt Ava!" Issa cried, pointing vaguely toward some distant benches near the boardwalk railings. They all looked to where a woman and a tall man were sitting close together on a bench, looking out over the ocean.

"It does look a little like Mom," Richard said. "But it can't be her—she's at a meeting of the Noble League. She's doing such great things for those little guys. Every weekend she takes two orphan boys home to spend a night in our house. Sammy is real good about it—he teaches them to play handball at the park and how to ride a two-wheeler. Imagine—kids of ten or twelve who've never been on a bike. Mom is really great, doing that kind of work."

"Let's go to Aunt Ava," Issa cried, pointing back as they moved along the boardwalk.

"It's not Aunt Ava," her mother said. "It just looks a little like her."

They continued to stride along. Richard glanced back once or twice toward the backs of the man and woman who were looking out to sea.

"Do you really like it, Richard, being up in the sky—aren't you afraid?" Mommy asked him.

"Oh yes, sometimes I'm afraid. But I'm exhilarated, too! There's nothing like it, Aunt Moo. I mean, to be a man and to fly! To be up there in the clouds. To be out there among the stars!"

"Birds fly," Issa said. "They flap their wings." She flapped her arms to demonstrate.

"Hey, hold onto my head," her father said. "I don't want you flying off my shoulders just now."

"Here we are," Richard said. "The great and glorious Parachute Jump. For two bits, any ordinary civilian can know the thrills of jumping."

"Any crazy person," her mother said.

Issa could feel something tighten in her father's body; his shoulders got straighter, he squeezed her ankles harder. Issa heard the swish and click of machinery. There was a sound that reminded her of the sound of the clothesline as it slid on the pulleys and traveled across the backyard. She looked up. The wire mushroom towered above her, reaching far into the blue sky. It went up straight, like a tree, and then ballooned out at the top. Hanging from the top—no, not hanging, but falling down at her, were people, little tiny high-up people, hanging onto their seats, and bumping, bouncing down along the sides of the wire tree, falling, falling, right toward her!

"Run away, Daddy!" she screamed. She covered her head with her hands.

"They won't hit us," Richard said, sliding her from her father's shoulders and hugging her very tight against him, kissing her face many times. "It's only a ride, Issa sweetheart. Those chairs are on heavy wires, they're not really falling down, they just look like they're falling down. They give the people the feeling of falling down, as if they were jumping out of an airplane, wearing a parachute."

But Issa could only stare upward, her hands protecting her head, and watch the fast-falling seats come hurtling downward, toward her. Then she heard an awful thud, and a blast of air went rushing by her face; the chairs stopped just in time above her head and hung there, dangling like quivery worms.

"Anchors aweigh," Richard said, thumping her father on the back as he went up to a little gate, his fingers jangling the money in the pocket of his pants. "Or rather, off you go, Meyer, into the wild blue yonder . . . "

Then Richard lifted Issa to sit on his shoulders, higher even than her father's; she wobbled and clung to him tightly.

"He's a fool; he has a weak stomach," her mother said.

"Let him have this thrill, Aunt Moo," Richard said. "You know he'll never get overseas because he's got a wife and a kid."

"It's bad enough you're going."

"I'm only doing what has to be done."

"Hey—look up here," her father called out, and there he was, in one of those little seats, hanging up above her head. "Uh-oh, here—I—go—" and with a sudden jerk he was pulled away from Issa, upward, into the sky, climbing slowly, a dot of color growing smaller against the blue empty space above him, his feet hanging and swinging like her own when she was on the swing at the playground.

"Daddy!" She reached up for him, tears rolling down her face, but he was gone, just a dot of nothing, not even her father anymore, just a speck of black, then a colorless invisible vein of white on blue. She could not follow him anymore with her eyes.

"Don't be afraid," Richard said. "Daddy will be right back. Just keep watching. Soon you'll see him coming down. It's just a ride, for fun. Your Daddy's having fun, just like you have fun on the merry-go-round."

Her mother, tilting her head back too far, lost her straw hat, and a man standing behind her stumbled on it accidentally, stepping heavily on it and crushing it.

He apologized and handed the hat to Mommy.

"There he comes," Richard cried. "See him, up there, he's coming down, wow, he's coming down fast!"

Issa watched with horror. The falling thing was her father, hurtling down to the ground like a ball coming down from the branches of a tree, fast, with no one there to catch him. Even her mother gasped as the speck grew larger, and the clackety sound got louder. It seemed he would smash into them all and crush them like the man had crushed her mother's hat. But then there was a huge clunk, a jolt, and he was pulled back up into the sky and fell down again, hanging there, swinging helplessly.

"Daddy," Issa cried. "Wave to me." But her father was sitting limp and motionless. Some man extended an arm to him, helped him onto a little platform. He disappeared and in a moment reappeared, coming out through the gate on unsteady legs, not smiling, only trying to smile, his face yellow. It must be the yellow streak they were talking about, having come out on him, like measles.

"You just lost ten years of your life," Richard said, laughing.

"Better ten years lost in Coney Island," her mother said, "than a whole life lost in the war."

ONE HUNDRED TWELVE

Ava read:

AVIATION CADET, Richard Rabinowitz Squadron "D"

REPLACEMENT CENTER

MAXWELL FIELD, ALABAMA

November 8, 1941

Dear Mom, Dad, and Sammy—

It's just five minutes before lights out. The first five minutes I've had to myself since those army trucks pulled up to meet the train. Not a bad trip, not a bad camp either. Got most of our equipment today. They gave us everything from soup to nuts. Got a haircut. Haven't a hair left on my head more than one-eighth inch long, and I'm bald on the sides. What a mess. We'll be here five weeks, then on to primary to really fly those beauties. The idea here is to teach a man some-thing about being a soldier and an officer. We've already learned everything about marching and how to handle a rifle (though you know rifles don't interest me, only planes). We've got 750 British cadets here (they call them "Limeys") and 1,100 of our own flying cadets. All we do is drill and eat and hear lectures. I'm breaking in my new army-issue boots. Haven't had time to be homesick yet, but I feel it coming on. Don't worry about me, though. I'm tough, you folks made me that way. I'm doing a job that has to be done, just remember that!

Love, Richard

ONE HUNDRED THIRTEEN

December 7, 1941

Secret Heart

It's happening. War! Horrible war! I was setting Shirley Golden's hair when the news about Pearl Harbor came over the radio. She jumped up and we clutched each other, crying, "Oh God! Oh no!" Issa, who was playing at my feet, began to cry. Musetta and Mama ran in, hearing our moans. Our precious Richard—what will happen now? It feels as if the world has gone mad, and there is no safe place.

1942

Ava read:

AVIATION CADET, Richard Rabinowitz Squadron "D"

REPLACEMENT CENTER

MAXWELL FIELD, ALABAMA

December 9, 1941

Dear Folks—

I know that you're right beside me now, and love you all the more for it. To lighten any doubts in your mind, I still feel that I'm doing the right thing. Still want those wings very badly.

No definite orders have been issued yet, but it's uniforms twenty-four hours a day from now on out because of the war. So I packed up my "civvies," and they're on the way home. We're pulling out of here Monday. My destination will be Decatur, Alabama. This isn't the last word, though, because anything can happen in the army. We get all the war news. Newspapers, bulletins, and we've got a radio going under a blanket against regulations. If we get caught, we'll all be walking punishment tours until we leave here. Don't let those air-raid alarms scare you to death. We don't lose any sleep over them; we're so tired we're asleep before our heads hit our pillows. Thought you'd like this clipping from the newspaper.

Love, Richard

Ava unfolded the clipping. It showed a soldier wearing a gas mask, rifle pointed forward, rushing through a cloud of gas. The headline said: WAR GIVES WINGS TO ARMY MORALE. She read the article slowly:

"War and treachery came out of the skies—and now it's an All-American team with all bets off. Also, the actual outbreak of hostilities has sent a shot of electricity through every soldier in Uncle Sam's new army. Maybe they did grouse

a little before it happened—leaving that girl and job behind, turning out in the bite
of dawn to a bugler's sour notes, cleaning that rifle like a Dutch housewife and
slogging through mud and rain in make-believe battle.

"But now they are no longer training for something that might or might not
come off. The fight's on and the boys behind the guns are needed. And they're
ready and rarin' to go. Today, all Uncle Sam's 'chillins' got morale. The boys are
young and tough. They've got what it takes, and they're willing to give it, even if it
means giving their lives."

Ava pressed the letter to her lips. The man in the gas mask looked like a
monster, an alien, a blind elephant with a rubber trunk. She heard herself say
out loud, "Please God, let him come back to me."

ONE HUNDRED FIFTEEN

Ava read:

FLYING CADETS

AIR CORPS TRAINING DETACHMENT

DECATUR, ALABAMA

January 27, 1942

Dear Mom, Dad, and Sammy—

Got the cookies. Went over big. Lucky to get my share. Everyone I feed Indian
nuts to starts eating the shells and all. One fellow said the shells tasted better than
the nuts. My hillbilly friends just 'ain't never seen this stuff' before. Thanks, Mom.
I sure appreciated your best efforts. Have academic privileges this week. Can go
out tonight, but I won't. Need some sleep. Have a forty-hour progress check ride
coming up with the army sometime this week. Got to be in good shape. Got to give
the army my best ride. Already have thirty-nine hours to my credit. Going into
acrobatics. What fun. Never can figure out where I'm at. Just the thing to cure
a weak heart. I never get enough! My instructor tried to black me out yesterday
with an "Immelman." He was taken aback when he got the plane leveled off and
I was still smiling. He didn't know I was smiling because I was so glad to be alive
after that stunt. I bet Meyer would turn inside out at some of the tough ones. That
parachute jump at Coney Island was kid stuff. (Hey—Mom, did I ever tell you
that Issa thought she saw you at Coney Island with some big tall handsome man
the day we took Meyer up the 'chute? I miss that baby; I could eat her up.)

My shoulder is sore from the acrobatics yesterday. Flying upside down is not what God intended for man to do. I keep my shoulder wedged under the side of the cockpit so I can keep my feet on the controls. Otherwise you hang from the safety belt, and the altitude makes your ear drums crackle.

Sammy, my brother, still want to be a cadet?

Mom—don't shower me with too many luxuries. One bite into a herring might tempt me to swipe one of these ships and head for New York! Tell Grandma I miss her, and give Issa a big kiss for me. We leave here the twentieth of next month for flight school in Mississippi. Yoah boy is gettin' hisself a reaahl southern accent.

Love, Richard

ONE HUNDRED SIXTEEN

"Hickory dickory dock,
    The mouse ran up the _____ "
"Clock!"
"The clock struck one.
The mouse ran down,
Hickory dickory _____ "
"Mommy, sirens."
"What?"
"Listen. Sirens again. We're having the war again."

"Oh God—Daddy is out! He's always out with that stupid Leo Crookshank; he was out with him the last time we had an air raid."

"Close the curtains, Mommy."

"Gilda!" Musetta ran to the stairway and called again, "Gilda! Do you hear it? Get the blackout shades pulled. Tell Nathan to shut off the outside light! Hurry!"

Musetta rushed down the hall. She tripped on a soft mass and went sprawling on the rug, feeling her head smash hard against a banister post.

"Goddamn idiot dog! Gilda!!" she shrieked, pulling herself to all fours, struggling to get up. "Come and get your goddamn Bingo out of here. She almost killed me!"

"Don't kick Bingo, Mommy," Issa said. "She didn't mean to be there. Maybe the sirens scared her."

"Go lie down on your bed, Issa, I want you out of the way. We have to be in the dark now for the rest of the night. Just get into your bed and don't move."

"Daddy says not to worry. Daddy says the war is far away, across the ocean."

"Daddy is right, you shouldn't worry." Musetta could feel her heart thumping in her temples. She pulled herself up on the banister railing and heard the sirens rise and fall, rise and fall.

"Grandma says airplanes can fly over the ocean and drop bombs on our heads."

"That's why we have to shut off all the lights and pull the curtains, Issa. So the bad airplanes can't see where people live."

"Is Richard in an airplane?"

"He's in a good airplane. Not in a bad airplane." Having regained her balance, Musetta went downstairs. Her teeth were chattering with fear. What if the war went on and on, and Meyer was drafted? What if he were killed? God, she hated this war. Hated the fear, hated the rationing, the coupons, hated that she couldn't get nylons or sugar or good leather shoes! She had always loved having lots of fine shoes—now she had to wear her old ones down to nothing.

In the living room Gilda was calmly fastening the heavy curtains together with clothespins. Over them she drew the black shades. "There, now we can leave this one little bulb on, I think. Last time I checked from outside, and you couldn't see a thing, not even a splinter of light."

"Your dog almost killed me," Musetta hissed.

"She's just frightened of all the noise," Gilda said. "She likes to hide under my bed when the air-raid siren sounds."

"Mama could break a leg, tripping on her," Musetta said. "She ought to be kept in the cellar."

"It's damp down there."

"You ought to get rid of her. There's not enough meat now to give her scraps."

"Oh—the butcher still gives me scraps. The butcher likes me."

"The butcher likes you!" Musetta mimicked Gilda's tone. "And the druggist likes you. And the man in the fish market likes you. Aren't you the lucky one?"

"Calm down, Musetta. You don't need to carry on. We're all tense when this happens. Mama is making some tea for us. Go and get a cup of tea and sit down and try to relax. This isn't a real air raid. This afternoon when I was at the shul for my meeting of the Red Cross, Ellen Blitz said she thought there would be a test air raid soon—maybe even tonight. They want to keep us on our toes. It's not the real thing."

"What makes you think I think it is?" Musetta said.

"I didn't say that. I just said you look very worried."

"Why wouldn't I be worried? I have a husband! I have a child to worry about! Who do you have? No one! A dog!"

"Don't be nasty, Musetta," Gilda said in a low voice. "This is no time to have one of your hysterical arguments with me. Can't we all work together now? I mean—there's a war on. Why not use some of your nervous energy and come with me to the Red Cross meetings? You could roll bandages with us. You could knit socks for the soldiers. You could try to sell war bonds."

"I have my hands full," Musetta said. "I have a child to take care of."

"Mama and Nathan are perfectly able to watch Issa for a few hours. And I'd be happy to watch her when I'm working in the beauty parlor; she's an angel in there—she helps me pick up hair pins and hands me curlers. She's no trouble. You could have some free time to work for the war effort."

"You'd like that, wouldn't you?" Musetta said. "My leaving Issa in your charge! Do you think I want her to learn how to be a manicurist? I'm trying to educate her. I'm going to start her on the piano as soon as we get some peace in this house, without all your babbling women customers marching in and out."

"I earn money from those women," Gilda said. "Which puts less pressure on Meyer. I thought you liked my having the beauty shop in the house. I make better pay now than I did at Cindy Lee's."

"Well, we never had much privacy before, but now! Now! My bladder could be bursting, and I rush up to the bathroom, and there you are leisurely shampooing some dame's hair, and when I finally get in there, I could throw up from all the hairs left in the sink!"

"You do have a delicate stomach," Gilda admitted. "I'm sorry. I'll try to get all the hairs out, I'll be very careful. And if you must use the bathroom and can't wait, tell me and we'll get out of there if we have to."

The sirens had now quieted, and Musetta became aware of the harsh in and out grating of her breath. The fury of which she was capable sometimes astonished her! Words flew out of her mouth, even without her volition. She could continue the most fearsome harangue even when she felt it was no longer fair to argue. It often seemed to her as if a poison had been injected into her bloodstream—an involuntary flow of anger, grief, frustration, bitterness, and gall jetted forth from some dark pipe within her, flooding her ordinary rational mind and spilling itself out of her mouth as a fountain of bile and acid, staining and burning those she most cared about and loved. When such a stream was directed at Meyer, and he didn't walk out on her forever, she would—when her sanity returned—feel like kissing his shoes in gratitude.

But once she had started, she could not stop until pure exhaustion over-took her—or the target of her tirade ran away or crumpled in defeat. (If it were Meyer, he stood and listened, took it, waited it out.) Even as she ranted at Gilda now, a part of her recognized that, yes, Gilda's income was better now (and it was far better for Meyer to have less pressure on him, especially since all his and Leo's inventions had come to nothing, had not "caught on like wildfire.")

And yes, it was true that she could easily take some time off.

And yes, she should do some work at the shul for the war effort, and she could even . . . yes, even admit that Bingo was important for Gilda, was good for her, was no "filthier" than any other animal, and was, in fact, a gentle pet with whom Issa loved to play. But even as Gilda apologized for the hair in the sink, even as she became submissive before Musetta's wrath and righteous fury, even as she promised to try to keep Bingo out of Musetta's path, Musetta felt black poison shoot through her once again like octopus ink, and she began to rant about how "that promiscuous bitch, Bingo, attracts every male dog in the neighborhood, and they come with those red things hanging out of them, and they pee on Issa's rocking horse, and they leave dog shit in the yard, and I can't stand it anymore, Gilda, I can't, and I'm going to do something about it. You'll see! I'm going to do something before that dog is the death of my precious Issa, before some monster animal jumps the fence and tears her to pieces!"

ONE HUNDRED SEVENTEEN

February 17, 1942

Secret Heart

Bingo is dead. I write it, but don't believe it. Bingo, my precious Bingo. Is there such a thing as a devil? A witch? Is my sister's heart deformed, made of black pitch? Where in an ordinary human being do such depths of hatred lie, and why? Yesterday: I went to Kings Highway to the bank, to deposit money and to go to the vault to take out a tiny gold Jewish star I had as a child, which I want to give to Issa on her fourth birthday next month. When I got home, I asked Mama if there had been any calls, any appointments for haircuts or manicures, and Mama didn't answer me, just clapped her hand to her white head and said, "Oy, God in heaven." Then she just went upstairs, and I heard her bedroom door close.

How strange, I thought. Then I heard Issa in the backyard. I heard the springs of her rocking horse creaking, so I went out the back door and saw her, in her leggings and winter coat, crashing back and forth on her horse. There she was in the bare, wintry backyard, and standing under the peach tree, in a black coat, was Musetta. She had her hands crossed, almost entwined across her chest. And suddenly I said to her, my breath sinking out of me, "Where's Bingo?"

"In the cellar," she said, without hesitation.

"In the cellar? Why would you put her there?" Issa kept rocking, and Musetta turned away from me and I had a glimpse of her face, like white marble, icy cold. I ran into the house, down to the basement. I called for Bingo. She didn't come. I cried her name, begging her to appear. I looked near the furnace, under the washtubs, even in the green storage cabinets.

I raced upstairs. Musetta was just coming in the back door. Her cheeks, a moment ago white, seemed to be growing red.

"Where is Bingo?" I demanded. "She's not in the cellar! You know she's not in the cellar!"

"I gave her away," Musetta said.

"A truck came . . . " Issa said. She ran to me and threw her little arms around my legs. "A truck came, and a man threw Bingo inside, her legs were kicking."

I looked at Musetta. "What does she mean?"

"You know how dangerous it was for Issa," Musetta said. "Those huge male dogs, always wanting to mate." She spat out the word. "You yourself said it could be dangerous for Issa."

"But Bingo wasn't dangerous!"

"I didn't say she was, did I?" Musetta's eyes narrowed. "She was getting old anyway, Gilda."

"Where is she now? Right now?"

"She was taken to the pound."

"I'll call them!"

"It's over, Gilda. They did it this morning."

"Did what?"

"It's painless. She didn't feel a thing."

"My God, Musetta! You had her killed?"

"She didn't feel a thing."

"You had my dog killed? We could have found a good home for her! We could have kept her in the house and not let her in the yard at all. We could have worked something out."

"Her hairs were always getting on my clothes."

"But how could you sneak her away from me like this! How could you wait until I went away and then do it, how could you?"

"You knew it would have had to be done sooner or later."

Issa began to kiss my hands. "Don't cry, Aunt Gilda. Mommy says that Bingo will have lots of nice friends in dog heaven."

"You monster! You murderer!"

ONE HUNDRED EIGHTEEN

There was more commotion today than at her birthday party. Early in the morning Mommy dressed her in her best red plaid dress with red heart-shaped buttons and put on her patent leather Mary Janes. Then Mommy wet her hair with sugar water and made little curls that she was warned not to muss.

"Stay clean," Mommy cautioned her. "I'm dressing you early because I have lots to do—maybe you can help Grandma make *kreplach* for Richard. Or watch Daddy trim the hedges. I have to straighten our room and then wash my hair."

"Please could I watch Aunt Gilda cut hair?"

"What have I told you, Issa?"

"That I can't go in the beauty parlor anymore."

"And why, Issa?"

"Because the fumes from the chemicals are not good for me."

"And what other reason?"

"Hairs get in my socks and you can't get them out and then they feel sharp and stick my feet."

"That's right. You're a good girl; you remember what I told you."

"But I like the beauty parlor. It's nice there."

"It's not a place for a child."

"Aunt Gilda lets me play with the nail polish bottles."

"You have plenty of other things to play with. You have lots of books and dolls and toys."

"Well, then, can I help her in the victory garden? She says if we grow our own food, then the soldiers will have more to eat, and they'll be stronger and they'll win the war."

"I'm sure those marble-size potatoes are really going to win the war! Please, Issa—don't be foolish. I've told you that you are not to hang around Gilda so much—and just obey me. Don't question everything I tell you."

"I love it in the victory garden. Peas are coming up, and little green to-matoes are growing . . . "

"A garden will not win any war," Mommy said. "Rolling bandages does not win a war."

"Grandma is baking a cake," Issa said. "I smell it."

"Good—go downstairs and help her if you like."

"Will you put marshmallow bunnies on it?"

"You mean like at your birthday party? I don't think so, Issa. That would take too much time."

Issa remembered that at her birthday party, her cake was decorated with bunnies made out of fat white marshmallows connected with toothpicks and decorated with little colored candy buttons and with ears made out of colored paper.

"Just go now and keep yourself out of trouble. Aunt Ava and Uncle Len and Richard will be here very soon, and you will have lots to do then. Richard will tell us all about the army and about all the airplanes he has learned to fly."

"Why doesn't Daddy go in the army? Maybe he can help win the war."

"Because he has you," Mommy said. "That's why."

Issa went downstairs and out into the front yard where Daddy was trim-ming the hedges.

"Mommy says because you have me you can't fight in the war." Daddy had taken off his shirt and hung it on a branch; Issa could see the dark curly hairs on his chest and the droplets of sweat running in a little river down to his belly button.

"I want to fight in the war, Issa," Daddy said. "Your mother won't let go of me. I'd go in a minute, but she's too nervous."

"Why is she nervous?"

"It's the way she was born, sweetheart. Just like you were born with curly hair."

"Why won't she let me go in the beauty parlor anymore?" Issa asked.

"She thinks Gilda wants to be your mother. She's jealous."

Issa sat down on the brick stoop and thought about this. She loved Aunt Gilda very much. She loved how Aunt Gilda smiled when Issa gave her "raisins" and "vitamins"—really just her names for kisses. And now that Bingo was gone, Aunt Gilda was so sad. She kept Bingo's little blanket still folded at the foot of her bed as if Bingo might come back there someday to sleep.

The beauty parlor was the best room in the house. Because of the war, Aunt Gilda had a special box for collecting costume jewelry—the customers came and dropped into the box beads and strings of shells, bright-colored rings and bracelets, necklaces that jangled like little bells.

Aunt Gilda explained that some of our soldiers were fighting in the jungles, and the tribes that lived there loved bright-colored jewelry. The soldiers would give the natives necklaces, and the natives would give the soldiers food or a place to sleep. If customers remembered to bring a piece of jewelry, Aunt Gilda would reduce her prices for them.

She also had a box out in the alley for collecting empty tin cans that she told Issa were used to make guns and tanks and airplanes. When Mommy had allowed her to take walks with Aunt Gilda, the two of them would always keep their eyes open for tinfoil they could peel off gum wrappers and cigarette packet liners. Then when they got home, they would sit down together at the kitchen table and carefully smooth out all the creases in the silver paper. They would add it—leaf by leaf—to their beautiful silver ball. The ball was bigger than a giant grapefruit now, sparkly and magnificent as it sat in the glass fruit bowl on top of the radio cabinet. Just seeing it grow gave Issa the sense that she was helping fight the war. When she held it in her hands, she felt proud and grown up, part of all the excitement and commotion that had to do with "the war effort."

There was one thing they absolutely could not do: save bacon grease. Mommy and Aunt Gilda had a terrible fight about that. The radio told everyone to save bacon grease—the soldiers used it to oil guns.

When some of Aunt Gilda's customers from Cindy Lee's came for haircuts, mostly the Italian ladies, they brought bacon grease. Aunt Gilda wouldn't let them bring it in the house; she made them throw it away in the garbage can at the back of the alley.

Mommy had said, "If you're so patriotic, why don't you collect the grease, Gilda?"

Aunt Gilda had said a Jewish home was no place for bacon grease. She'd gladly collect jewelry and tinfoil and sell war bonds and knit socks and roll bandages, but the "goyim" could do what had to be done with bacon grease. Mommy had called her a hypocrite.

Aunt Gilda had called Mommy "a traitor to the Jews."

Mommy said how come Gilda liked to eat at the "Chinks," where they served pork and shrimp, and Gilda said her home was one place and a restaurant was another, but that she only ate chicken chow mein there, never pork or shrimp. Mommy said Aunt Gilda made her own stupid rules, and Aunt Gilda said, "At least I know what's important to me. At least I have some peace in my life. You're always looking for something better, the grass is always greener somewhere else for you. You always want to go, to run, to find happiness."

"I'd like to go right now, away from here," Mommy had said. "I can't stand your pitiful face."

Issa had thought it was wrong of Mommy to talk about Aunt Gilda's face. Aunt Gilda couldn't help her pimples—Issa had watched her try to scrub them away over the sink, with a sharp brush, with special terrible-smelling soap. She had seen Aunt Gilda try to cover them with some brown clay that squirted out of a tube like an eggy-smelling snake. Especially today, with Richard coming on a furlough from his flying school, Aunt Gilda was trying to hide her pimples. She had been in the bathroom all morning, and Mommy had been furious, waiting for a chance to wash her hair.

"Well, here they are!" Daddy said, as Uncle Len's car pulled up to the curb and parked in front of the wishbone tree. Daddy reached for his shirt. "They're early." There was some kind of quiver in his voice that Issa did not recognize. And then Richard unfolded his long body from the back seat of the car, stood tall in the sunshine, and sparks of gold glinted from the golden wings that shone from the top of his beautiful soldier hat.

"Hey! My gorgeous little princess!" he cried, holding out his arms to Issa, and into them she flew, running so fast she stumbled and then was swept up in a whirlwind, feeling herself swirl in the air above Richard's head, feeling the power of his hands under her arms.

Then she was perched on his shoulders, holding tightly to the circular top of his hat as he grasped her firmly around the waist. Finally he lowered her to his hip and kissed her with a "yummm" sound, kissed her on her cheeks, both of them. Oh—she was so happy! The gold on his belt buckle shone, and the tiny gold airplane on his collar glittered, and the great gold wings on his hat dazzled her eyes.

"Oh—did I miss you, you gorgeous little girl," he whispered in Issa's ear, and his breath tickled her, and she laughed in delight.

Then Richard was pumping Daddy's hand up and down, and then Grandma ran out, wiping her hands on her apron and crying. "Oh, such a handsome grandson, such a beautiful soldier you are, my Richala."

Nathan came slowly down the front steps and a little shyly shook Richard's hand, and then Aunt Gilda came out, her hair swept up and with a flower in it, and Richard hugged her, stepping accidentally on the toes of her white shoes, and then Mommy came out the front door, wearing sun glasses, in her aqua dress and her opened-toed matching shoes.

Richard said, "You look more glamorous than Betty Grable," and Mommy barely smiled, just let her dimple show for a second, and then coming down the steps like a queen, she gave Richard her hand, and he kissed it.

Uncle Len and Aunt Ava stood there on the sidewalk so proudly, and neighbors came out to smile and exclaim and to wish Richard good luck and to tell him what an important thing he was doing, fighting for our country.

Richard didn't look like someone who liked to fight; he looked like a young man who liked to hug and to laugh and to swing children around over his head. He liked to kiss his grandma and to give presents (he had promised

Issa he would send her a doll from Alabama, and he had, a little blue-eyed china doll with a blue silk dress), and he liked to hug Mommy and Aunt Gilda and to shake hands with men—Daddy and Nathan and the neighborhood men who came by and nodded their approval.

Whatever the war was, it was far away and had nothing to do with this wonderful party, with Richard smiling and laughing, with the *kreplach* simmering inside and a honey cake and a sponge cake cooling on the sink. The war was the color black in Issa's mind—the black of the blackout curtains, the black of the smoke of bombs and guns, the black fear in the eyes of the beauty shop women who didn't want their sons to fight in it, the black dreams she herself had on air-raid nights.

But today was sunny and golden. Richard was as bright as the lilacs exploding on the tree in the garden, his laughter was as full of song as all the birds' voices in all of Brooklyn.

"Show me your victory garden," he said to Issa, and she took his hand, and together they skipped up the alley and into the backyard.

There Issa showed him the little rows of green peas and tomatoes and squash, separated by rows of string, that she and Gilda were growing to help Richard win the war.

Richard picked one long green sweet pea pod from its stem and cracked it open, kneeling down so he and Issa could eat from the little boat-shaped cocoon in which the peas snuggled.

"Sweet and delicious," he said to Issa. "Just like you, Sweetie."

ONE HUNDRED NINETEEN

Ava read:

SQUADRON "D"

AIR CORPS BASIC FLYING SCHOOL

GREENVILLE, MISSISSIPPI

April 27, 1942

Dear Folks:

Flew like an angel yesterday. Things are getting tougher; I'm really learning how to twist that plane around the skies. It takes time before you can do all

those acrobatics real well. Practice every day and it's sure hard work. I like fly-ing upside down best of all. It's hard, though, since all the controls are reversed when the ship is on its back. What a job to keep your feet on the rubber pedals. You just hang by your safety belt. One of these days, Mom darling, I'm gonna take you up for a few "snap rolls." Our new instructor is a temperamental guy. Always afraid of getting himself killed when he's riding with a student. Grounded one of the boys today. Four fellows from Decatur have washed out already. This is a crazy army. First they make us ship all our civilian clothes back home, and then they issue this memo to all Aviation Cadets (enclosed so you can see firsthand):
Effective immediately!

Each Aviation Cadet at this station will secure and keep in his posses-sion one complete outfit of civilian clothing. Due to existing regulations it is impossible to permit a discharged Aviation Cadet to retain any of his issued clothing; therefore, in the event of a discharge of an Aviation Cadet, civilian clothing is necessary.

By order of Lieutenant Cooke.

So now, Mom, you can ship me back my nifty suitcase full of my civvies. I'll be able to use it on my next move, wherever that may be. Here's what to put in the bag: my precious blue sport jacket. Oh! It's gonna be swell having it back with me. Two white shirts. My blue knitted tie. Then, too, my fancy imported socks. Let me not forget my blue gabardine slacks. A belt, too. My tan pullover. That's all I need if they ever decide to ship me back home. Otherwise, I can just sit around and admiringly gaze upon all those pretty vestments (clothes to you). Pack them into my bag and get them down here by express as quickly as possible. Never can tell—a few critical mistakes and that could be it. It seems they aren't transferring the washouts to Navigation any more, but giving them discharges. One of my buddies asked to be eliminated. They brought in some new planes, AT-9s, built by Curtis; they look just like grasshoppers. I don't blame my buddy. Like him, my first love will always be those primary planes.

Throw a well-packed salami and some cornbread into the suitcase if you have time; make sure it's packed in wax paper to kill the smell. Hugs to everyone. Bought Issa a small set of wings just like the one I gave you for Grandma. Will send first chance.

Love, Richard

ONE HUNDRED TWENTY

July 7, 1942

Secret Heart

A parade down Avenue P on Sunday! I had the pip all the week before, and my face showed it! It was as red as the red cross on my white gauze hat! As I got into my uniform, I felt perhaps the way a nun feels as she puts on her habit—that I was to be a bride, not of Christ, but of the war. Hardly, however, a bride of Hitler! But the war has become my dedication. I am wedded to the cause. I live and breathe the war. If I get tired rolling bandages or sending jewelry overseas or baking cookies for Richard and Milton Raspman (yes, his aunt has begged me to write to him, to send him cookies, he is a doctor in the army now!), if I get tired ringing bells to sell war bonds, all I have to do is remember what sacrifices the young men of our country are making, and I have double the energy to go on. David Danzig, the dentist, has been wounded by shrapnel and is blind in one eye, his mother tells me. She says it with such courage! "He still has one eye, Gilda. It's all right." It's all right. We have to do what has to be done. I am just a small woman, but I can work as hard as any man. My old sorority sister, Sonia Kovitsky, has joined the WACS. All she writes about is how her permanent is holding up; she thinks that's what I want to hear. But I'm so proud of her. I'd never have the guts to do that, to go and be a woman soldier.

And Rozzie Dubin is working in an airplane factory, putting rivets in the wings! Rozzie the riveter! And she was always such a big one for fancy heels and lace dresses. Now she climbs into her overalls and puts her hair in a kerchief and gets filth under her nails. It's amazing what we women are capable of.

On Sunday I was a flag bearer; all of Brooklyn turned out to watch me go by—first my captain, heading the parade, her scarf waving proudly in the wind as she marched, and then me and the two other women who sold the most bonds. The shul on Avenue N has raised more than two million dollars in the sale of war bonds. I personally got a commendation for selling more than one hundred bonds myself! And guess what? A B-17 bomber has been named after the Jewish Center. Can you see it now? A B-17 bomber with the words *Avenue N Jewish Center* on its side! And instead of a pinup girl on the fuselage, what would they have? A picture of the rabbi?

I'm feeling so good about my work. I stay up late every night, writing to the boys in training or overseas, and then I bake hundreds of cookies every week. Business is good in the beauty shop. My shampoo company sent me a big poster showing a cartoon featuring a husband and wife. She's looking at him and imagining that he's got long hair and a beard. The caption reads:

She: "I'll gladly give up MY P. G. (Personal Grooming) if you give up yours, dear!"

Then the poster says: *Why is it that men get their hair cut regularly, but pooh-pooh the need of beauty shops for women during this emergency? Personal Grooming is certainly just as essential for women right now as it is for men. Next time the "big executive" husband makes the general statement that Beauty Service (Personal Grooming) is unnecessary today, ask him why he doesn't stop shaving and getting his hair cut for the duration. When American men are bewhiskered to help win the war, they will find their wives willing—eager—to be bedraggled, too. Until then, "sauce-for-the-goose" treatment will jolt "mere man" into realization that Personal Grooming is important for men AND FOR WOMEN!*

Well, I put up the poster, and the women all agree; they have to keep their morale up, too. So I have more sets and cuts and manicures and permanents than I can keep track of. I am always having to interrupt something to answer the phone to take appointments. Lately, Nathan has been acting as my secretary. I really appreciate him, slow and sickly as he is. He does his best. He tries to help. He has a good heart. Sometimes I'm tempted to ask him what happened between him and Mama so many years ago, but it's really not possible to start that conversation. Whatever happened is between them forever.

Of course, Musetta never answers the phone, never helps, never lets Issa walk with me or talk with me. It's always "she's busy doing this—or that." Well, we have our secret times, Issa and I. We manage to get together. That sweet child knows it's wrong for her mother to keep her from me, so she sneaks in to see me whenever she can. Bless her *pupick*. Whenever she sees a stray dog on the street, she wants to catch it and give it to me to cheer me up. I told her not to worry—that I am too busy these days to miss Bingo very much. (Of course that isn't true. But you can't always tell a child the truth.) Between Musetta and me, though, it's poison. I need a gas mask to pass her in the hall. My poor sister. Why is she so wretched? I try to get the hairs out of the sink. Meyer tries to cheer her up (but he has lost most of Len's money in these failed inventions). She has begun to give Issa piano lessons, but Issa shows no signs of being a child prodigy, at least not that way. What Issa likes to do is make rhymes. She made one up last week about Sadie Finklestein:

"My aunt has a customer
Her name is Sadie
I like her very very much
For she is a nice lady."

When I told Sadie the poem, she was so thrilled she made a little sweater for Issa as a present. Musetta said it smelled of eggs. (Sadie's husband owns a chicken farm!), and she wouldn't let Issa wear it. Maybe she is jealous. She never really learned to knit herself (though once when she was in Cleveland I think she tried).

Well—I'm too tired to go on. Much to do, will canvass Avenue P tomorrow to sell war bonds again. I'll win this war yet myself, single-handed!

ONE HUNDRED TWENTY-ONE

On her hands and knees, on all fours like an animal, Musetta hacked at the packed earth with a small trowel, hacked and smashed at it, attacked it with all her strength. Sweat was running in a river between her breasts. She felt dirt in her mouth, drawn in by her breath. She was alone for the day. Meyer had taken the whole bunch of them to Rockaway Beach to visit Aunt Rose, who had taken rooms there for the summer.

Meyer felt that Rachel was getting old and needed to get out now and then, see some new sights, breathe the fresh sea air. So all of them, Gilda and Mama and Nathan and Issa and Meyer, had piled into the car and driven off without her.

She told them she had no interest in going. She had a migraine headache again. The vein in her right temple pulsed and beat, and with every beat she saw colors, rainbows, ragged jagged lines of light shimmer across her vision. She was furious. Why? It was a summer day, a Sunday, her family was well, her daughter was a joy. And yet she felt something eating at her, not just her headache; that was a consequence, not a cause, of her anger.

Nothing in her life ever worked out. Meyer never got rich. Issa was not going to be a great pianist—she showed no special talent for music. Her own music had fallen to nothing—she had lost her desire to play. Now that she had frequent headaches, she had also stopped reading. She thought of Miss McGinley and felt ashamed. She had planned to do so much and had done nothing. All her great promise had resulted in nothing achieved. She was nobody. She had married a nobody. None of them would ever be a somebody.

And yet on Friday night at the shul, her sister, Gilda, that pathetic, weak, fearful, blighted girl, had been celebrated, applauded, awarded, praised!

Then, this morning, in the *Brooklyn Eagle*, there had been a picture of Gilda! The headline had read "PETITE GIRL RECEIVES AMERICANISM AWARD." Phrases from the article burned in Musetta's mind: "How could such a small girl have the energy to accomplish all she has done . . . ?" "In addition to her war work, she runs a beauty parlor at her Avenue O address . . . "; "really puts some of us 'larger' people to shame." Then they had listed all Gilda had done: sending more than two thousand pieces of old jewelry and trinkets to boys in the Pacific, who traded them with natives; sent sheet music and records to the USO, comic books to wounded veterans in hospitals, clothing to the war-relief organization. "This delicate woman who has been rolling bandages ever since Pearl Harbor has personally sold thousands of dollars worth of war bonds."

Musetta screwed her shovel into the earth! Little, tiny petty things— Gilda and her little ways, dainty fingers, cookies and embroidery needles, silly little poems and valentines! And yet—she was making a name for herself. She had become somebody.

Musetta felt her impatience must be her own fatal flaw. A little timid thing like Gilda, going her own slow dull way, could accomplish so much! And she, Musetta, talented, intelligent, beautiful, energetic—she felt she was always on the wrong line somehow, waiting for it to move, to get someplace. And it never moved! So she switched to some other line, and then that one barely moved. (If only she had stayed on that first line, it would slowly be inching forward, and she might have got someplace! If she had stayed a secretary, she might be manager of an office now. If she had gone to law school, she might now be a famous lawyer, even a judge. If she had married Arthur Eslick, she might be a society wife, rich, well dressed. If she had devoted herself to her piano playing, she might now be . . .

Well, it was hopeless. She felt tears start out of her eyes and let them drip into the dirt, heedlessly. Who was to blame for her nature, her constant unhappiness? Issa had said to her one day, "Smile, Mommy, I never see you smile." She knew how sour she was, how possessive of her time. She was always too busy to help out with anything.

Up till now, till this very moment, she had done nothing for the war effort. She had made a point to throw away tinfoil, not to keep it. She had purposely avoided buying savings bonds and had forbidden Meyer to spend his small earnings on them. When Meyer expressed a wish to enlist in the army, she had leapt on him like a madwoman! *"Do you want to leave me a widow?"* she had accused him. But she knew it was a shame, a humiliation of his, to be healthy and strong and not be in the war. When Richard came to visit, dressed in his uniform, looking so proud and beautiful, she could see Meyer's shoulders sink, feel his disappointment that he could not just go off and fight with the other American soldiers.

She hung her head even as her headache raged. She was not a good person. She knew it. She understood it. It was her fate. She would never be in the newspaper for her good works.

Well, at least she had dug up a plot of dirt. Here it was, her little private "victory garden." She had an envelope of seeds, tomato seeds, that she would plant now (though Gilda had told Mama that it was too late in the summer to plant, too close to the cold fall weather). Musetta was determined to grow round red tomatoes and eat them and thus not take food away from the soldiers. She would also stop buying leather shoes with Meyer's ration coupons and wear all her old shoes till their soles were paper thin. She would save old tin cans; she would save bacon grease!

But, of course, she could not cook bacon in this house! She was a married woman with a family, and she could not cook what she pleased because of Gilda! Musetta liked bacon. She liked pork chops! The only time she had had the freedom to cook those foods was when she and Meyer had been in Cleveland—and even then, she had had to deceive Meyer! How she hated being controlled by the wishes of other people! How she hated having no privacy! How she hated the fact that Issa was so anxious to watch Gilda in the beauty parlor and to imitate her in the ways of sewing and knitting and doing little dainty things. How jealous she was that Issa was so full of admiration for Gilda. And Gilda had so much patience—it was true. She could sit with Issa for hours, painstakingly showing her one crochet stitch till the child had mastered it. Musetta had to do things fast or not do them at all. She must have instant results! She must have success as soon as she put her mind to anything, or she wouldn't do it!

Even now she doubted that her present effort at making a garden would come to anything. It would be weeks, months, before she saw any results! The ground was made of dirt, and now the dirt was under her nails and had discolored her seersucker skirt. This was no way to produce food for humans to eat—growing it in the ground! Digging in the dirt!

The headache was pounding a madness through her brain. There was no one home; she could not even go inside and lash out at anyone, blame anyone for her misery! They all were to blame, of course! Mama and Gilda and their meaningless Jewish rules, their respect for old babbling rabbis who spoke gibberish! And Meyer was too genial, too easy-going, too happy and relaxed. The world could pass him by in an instant, and he didn't care. Not as long as he could sit in the sun and bounce Issa on his knees. A man without ambition! It was his fault! Her sitting here, alone in the dirt, crying, was his fault! He should have made her come with them! If he loved her enough, he would have insisted that she come to Rockaway. Then she could be sitting at the shore, instead of here, wilting in the miserable humid heat!

She had to get away, move away from here. Go someplace where she could start all over, think new thoughts. She hated the war and not having sugar or nylons! She hated victory gardens!

She stood and began stomping on her little patch of earth, grinding it down under her shoes till it was hard packed, like a block of granite. There! That's how much she cared about victory gardens! Let everyone starve. Let the world go to hell!

ONE HUNDRED TWENTY-TWO

Ava read:

THE COLUMBUS ARMY FLYING SCHOOL

KAYE FIELD

COLUMBUS, MISSISSIPPI

August 20, 1942

Dear Mom, Dad, and Sammy—

It was a tough battle, but thank the Lord I am almost through. Did I sweat! Took my forty-hour check the other day, rode with our squadron commander. What a prince. He really taught me how our maneuvers should be done. (Did I write you we did formation flying? That's the stuff! You get close enough to spot the gold fillings in the teeth of the fellow flying on your wing. Three feet between you and the next guy! You hold that formation on turns and on everything.) Only one more test to go now, which is all instrument. Went on our night cross country Tuesday. Flew over the base, didn't land. Dark night. Was flying my own ship in a three-ship formation. Tough flying formation at night. Easy getting lost. We didn't fly the beam. We used the light lines, which are flashing beacons that mark our arrival route. Each beacon is ten miles apart. You can always see the one ahead, so you follow the lights in. It isn't as easy as it sounds.

Lights on the ground are very confusing at night. When they are off in the distance, they look like stars. Couldn't see well, so I kept my canopy open, and it was really cold. My heater just barely kept my feet warm. Took us two hours. Made my first formation landing yesterday. Not bad. Went chasing around and through the clouds. For the first time you realize how fast you are traveling when you ride by a cloud in formation. Next stop Mitchell Field, Milwaukee. They sure move us around. After that, who knows? The Big Beyond. I'm sure ready. Don't worry about me. You know I'll always be careful.

And Mom—this is the life I was made for. I feel it every time I step up into one of those babies. So don't fret—your boy knows what he's doing. Hugs and kisses to all, an extra dozen for Grandma and Issa.

Love, Richard

ONE HUNDRED TWENTY-THREE

"Cream of Wheat is so good to eat,
Yes, we eat it every day,
We sing this song,
It will make us strong,

It will make us shout "Hooray!"
It's good for growing babies
And grownups, too, to eat,
For all your family's breakfast
You can't beat Cream of Wheat!"

Issa sang along with the radio and waited happily for the next installment of *The White Rabbit Bus.* To keep her hands busy, she was peeling the layers off a tiny green coconut she had found on the beach. Outside the window of the Mar Vista Hotel she could see soldiers marching in the street.

"Hup, two, three, four," she recited along with them. She liked to watch their brown legs open and close like a thousand scissors. She loved their marching songs. *"Left my wife and forty-eight kids, sick in bed without any bread, think I did right, right, right by my country, I had a good job, think I was wrong when I left, left, left my wife and forty-eight kids. . . . "*

Her very favorite song began, *"Off we go into the wild blue yonder, flying high into the sun. . . . "* She shook with a thrill when the soldiers sang that; it made her want to join them, to fly with them, to feel that speed and strength and bravery. She was so glad her family had come to Florida, where the world was so warm and smelled of flowers.

Between two buildings across the street, Issa saw the ocean like a blue-green chimney at the end of an alley. As soon as Mommy stopped feeling so nauseated, they would go for a walk on the beach. Mommy was having a baby, and whatever it was doing inside her, tiny as it was (no bigger than a hard-boiled egg, Mommy said), it made her want to throw up all the time. All she could eat was cold sliced tomatoes sprinkled with salt. Issa loved to eat coconut.

Daddy found big coconuts in the streets under the palm trees, and in the evenings, when the soldiers were eating their mess (a strange word, Issa thought, for dinner), Daddy would take Issa to the alley behind the hotel and let her watch him crack the coconut shell. He smashed it against the sidewalk, over and over, and then used a hammer and screwdriver to pry out the hairy monkey-faced nut inside. Coconut milk was watery and sweet. She loved it, but the smell of it made Mommy throw up. How different from Brooklyn it was in Miami Beach. It was snowy winter in Brooklyn, but it was hot all the time here. Issa's entire body was brown, and only the soles of her feet stayed white. Aunt Gilda had said, when they left, "How can you do this to me? How can you take away my sweet child?" and Mommy had said, "Because you have to learn she isn't your child! She's ours!" Issa thought it strange that either of them thought she belonged to them or anyone else. She belonged only to herself, and she knew it just as a tiny coconut knew it was a coconut and was itself, not a thing that belonged to a palm tree or to the ocean (even if it was floating on a wave).

The coconut meat was white and crisp and crumbled like a sweet carrot when she chewed on it. Everything tasted good here, everything smelled wonderful. The heat made her ears hot; she had never before thought her ears had feelings in them. When it rained suddenly, the sand gave off a sharp smell.

She loved to watch the rain make dimples in the sand, turning it darker brown in little circles, polka-dotting the beach with flat wet marks.

She had felt thrilled from the moment they arrived at the train station, with Mommy wearing her fur coat, and Issa wearing her leggings and winter coat. It had been snowing when they left Brooklyn, the air so cold she hadn't been able to inhale. But when they had arrived in Miami, all bundled up, and stepped off the train, the heat came up like a fire and blasted their faces and dried their eyes.

Daddy had laughed, and Mommy had said, "I never imagined it would be this hot." Right then, Daddy had stopped walking, peeled off Mommy's fur coat, untied Issa's wool hat and unbuttoned her coat, and shaken off his own heavy topcoat. And there they had stood in the middle of December in their bare arms in the beautiful clear, burning air.

"In no time, Moo, we'll be on easy street," Daddy had said. Days later, when Issa knew that their hotel was on Collins Avenue, she asked how come they had never moved to Easy Street. Daddy had laughed. Mommy had said, meanly, because she was already feeling nauseated by then, "Your father thinks Easy Street is always right around the corner. God knows where he got his map."

Collins Avenue seemed fine to Issa. All you had to do was walk out the front door of the Mar Vista, cross the street, walk one short block, and there was the entire Atlantic Ocean!

"Mommy," Issa said. "Please, let's go down to the beach."

"I thought you wanted to listen to *The White Rabbit Bus*," Mommy said. She was sucking an ice cube so that her words came out all garbled. The kitchen was in the same room as the bedroom, which was also the living room. Only the bathroom was separate. Mommy was leaning over the sink, gagging and sucking an ice cube.

"If we take a walk, maybe you'll feel better," Issa suggested.

"Okay," Mommy said suddenly. "Go to the bathroom first, and we'll go. I want to get a newspaper."

"To read about soldiers who were killed?"

"Who told you that?" Mommy asked. "Is that the only reason I read the newspaper?"

"You always read to Daddy how many soldiers were killed," Issa said. "If it makes you so sad to read the newspaper, you shouldn't read it."

"Go—" Mommy said, "wash your face. In this heat you need to wash your face a lot if you want to have nice skin when you grow up."

"Not be like Aunt Gilda," Issa said.

"Right—if you want skin like mine, you have to take care of it." She began to gag and retch over the sink. She waved Issa away.

In the bathroom a green segmented alligator lay slyly at the bottom of the bathtub. Its mouth was painted open. It was there that Issa went fishing. Daddy had made her a fishing rod of a stick, a string, and a wafer cookie for bait. Issa was happy to perch there on the cool rim of the bathtub and pretend-fish for an hour or two every afternoon while Mommy was napping. She would poke the alligator with her stick to make him swerve and slide down the length of the tub, and she would tempt him with the wafer cookie. Sometimes the cookie would get wet from a drop or two of water left in the tub, and then it would fall off the stick. Issa was allowed to use as many cookies as she wanted; she could poke holes in them to use them for bait, or she could eat them out of the box. As long as she didn't bother Mommy, she could do anything.

"I'm ready," she called. "I'm going to wear my butterfly pinafore." Aunt Gilda had made her a special dress, white with a blue butterfly that spread its wings across her chest. "Would you button the back?" Issa asked her mother.

"I wish I weren't so green in the face," her mother said, fastening the dress. "Green is not my best color."

Issa examined her mother's face. It looked perfectly brown, sun-tanned and smooth. Her mother was so pretty. Her mother's lips were delicate, "rosebud" lips, Aunt Gilda had once called them. Maybe Mommy never smiled because rosebuds never smiled. Flowers didn't have to smile; they were beautiful just as they were.

They locked the door, walked through the lobby that smelled musty and dark, and then were out in the sunshine.

Issa and her mother stepped in opposite directions.

"This way!" Issa said, tugging on her mother's hand. "To the beach."

"Let's stop in to see Daddy for a minute," Mommy said. "And then I can buy a newspaper, too—and leave it with Daddy."

They strolled down Collins Avenue. In Miami Beach everyone walked slowly except the soldiers. It was too hot to do anything quickly. The sun lay on Issa's hair like the steel rod from the measuring pole on the doctor's scale, pressing down, almost hurting. She imagined it, hard and straight and silvery, gleaming and shining on the crown of her head. They walked under the awning of a store, and she felt the steel rod lift up and float away.

Her toes in their white sandals looked brown, almost as brown as a colored person's toes, and the soles of her feet were white, also like a colored person's. Once Grandma had had a cleaning lady come in to scrub the walls and floors of the house on Avenue O, and her soles and palms had been white, though the rest of her skin was brown. Issa was glad to be all white; then she wouldn't have to be a cleaning lady and eat tuna fish from a cracked dish that Grandma kept in a separate cupboard from the regular dishes.

They stopped at the corner to buy a newspaper. The old man at the little stand said to Mommy, "Another long list. They're dying like flies over there." Mommy rattled the papers about her face as she tried to find the page she wanted to read.

"Thank God again," she said. "Richard's not on here."

"Richard won't let them get him," Issa assured her mother. "He promised me."

"Did he?" Mommy asked. She hurried on toward Daddy's store. Issa could already see the sign: SEND YOUR VOICE HOME TO YOUR MOM, YOUR BEST GIRL, YOUR WIFE. . . .

The little booth had its brown curtain drawn, which meant a soldier was recording; they would have to be very quiet. Now she could see her father standing at the back of the long narrow store, holding his stopwatch to check the time remaining on the record. He always stood far enough away from the soldier to give him privacy. He had explained to Issa that he tried not to listen, although occasionally when a soldier was really stuck and asked for help, he would suggest that the soldier sing a song, Frank Sinatra style, or read from a book of poems Daddy kept in the store.

The recording machine was outside the booth—a heavy metal box that stood on the floor, spinning out black flax as the needle cut the record. Issa left her mother's side and tiptoed into the store to collect the springy strands of warm black plastic as they came off the record. She heard the soldier behind the curtain clear his throat and begin speaking: *"Dearest Caroline Honey, Here I am in Miami Beach, where it's the middle of winter and I'm sweating like the devil. If you were here with me, we could really have another great honeymoon. I don't know yet when we're going over, but it'll be pretty soon. Don't worry about me. Before you know it, we'll finish this war up the way it should be finished, and I'll be home and we'll be together again. . . . We're camped out in a big hotel. I'm not lucky enough to be in a room, so I sleep in the cocktail bar with a hundred other guys. One of these days maybe you and me can settle down here in Florida, which is a Paradise on Earth. It's always summer, and when it rains, it only rains on one side of the street. Keep your chin up, kiddo, and keep that victory garden growing."*

(Issa heard the soldier drop his voice very low and whisper: *"I love you, babe, I'm missing you like crazy."*)

"Hi, sweetheart," Daddy said, switching off the machine as the soldier stepped out of the booth. "What are my two favorite girls doing today?"

"Mommy already vomited, so she feels better, and now we're going to the beach," Issa explained. The soldier looked from Daddy to Issa to Mommy, who was now standing in the shaded entrance of the store. He stood awkwardly, leaning on the counter, addressing the mailing envelope Meyer had handed him.

"Good luck over there," Daddy said.

"Good luck to you," the soldier said. "Over here." When he had left, Musetta handed Meyer the newspaper. "Issa and I are going to the beach," she said.

"Don't let a coconut hit you on the head," Daddy said. But his eyes were not twinkling; it was just a thing he was saying. He didn't laugh much anymore, and every time he saw a soldier, he bit down hard, grinding his teeth.

Issa knew it had something to do with her and with the new growing baby; because of them her father could not be a soldier. Because of them, he could not go across the ocean and fight the terrible enemy. Because of them, the muscles in his jaw got tight and strange when the army marched by.

"Looks like rain," Daddy said. "Don't let her get chilled. That butterfly on her pinafore doesn't even cover her chest."

"This is Florida, Meyer," Mommy said. "You said yourself, its always sunny in Florida."

When they got to the beach, the soldiers were just lining up in front of the mess hall for lunch. Mommy looked in her handbag and took out the square box camera she and Daddy had found on their honeymoon at Niagara Falls.

"I promised Grandma and Aunt Gilda I'd send them a picture of you soon. So run out there on the sand and pose for me, Issa, and I'll take a snapshot."

Issa pretended she was a butterfly, dipping and flitting over the sand in her butterfly pinafore. She felt the cloth blowing against her chest.

"Now stop right there . . . " Mommy called. "That's pretty." Issa stood on her toes and stretched her hands toward the sky, feeling them open like wings.

"Hold it," her mother said, and at that moment there was a thunderclap of applause coming from every direction, spinning over the sand like a tidal wave, the clapping hands of a thousand soldiers!

The soldiers were all on line in front of the mess hall. They applauded fiercely, louder and harder as Issa sank into the sand, then ran to her mother and hid her burning face in her mother's skirt.

The sound seemed never to stop. She was humiliated, yet terribly excited. All the army had been watching her in her pretend game, in her butterfly body. But the noise in her ears changed, became sinister and different. Lifting her head she saw that a huge thundercloud had moved in above the beach and was rumbling and growling in the darkened sky.

A dart hit her back, hot and sharp as a bee bite. Then another and another. "Hurry," Mommy said. "I don't want to get chilled. That's all I need, to catch pneumonia now." Her mother pulled her by the hand across the sand toward the mess hall. They cowered against its outer wall. All the soldiers had gone inside now, all but one, a very tall, handsome soldier who came over to where they stood hiding from the rain. He smiled at Issa; he had a dimple in his cheek like Richard.

"Would you like a Hershey bar?" he asked, pulling one from his pocket. He kneeled in front of Issa, but he was looking up at Mommy. "I'm getting in practice for what I'll be doing over there," he said.

"Do you know for sure that you're going?"

"We're shipping out in two days," he said. Then he touched the top of Issa's head and said, "Is your Daddy over there too, honey?"

"He isn't in the army," Issa said. "My Mommy doesn't want him to go because he might get killed."

The soldier stopped smiling. "No price is too high to protect our precious shores," he said. He motioned to the great dark ocean, rough looking and black now. The rain fell on it, into it, fiercely.

"Could we come inside till the rain stops?" my mother asked the soldier. "I'm having a baby," she added.

"I'm sorry," the soldier said. "No one is allowed in the mess hall except military personnel."

"You'd let a woman and a child catch their death of cold?"

"You'd keep an able-bodied man home for your own purposes?" the soldier replied.

"Oh, go to hell," Mommy murmured under her breath, tugging Issa by the arm and pulling her along in the downpour until they staggered, soaked and cold, into the doorway of the Mar Vista Hotel.

1943

Ava read Richard's letter to Sammy:

337TH TROOP CARRIER SQUADRON

APO 979 c/o POSTMASTER

SAN FRANCISCO, CALIF.

January 8, 1943

Dear Kid Brother:

The papers went through for my promotion to first lieutenant. Maybe I'll bring you back a Captain's Bars. Or a couple of dead Japs. If Mom and Dad let you join up, keep shooting for those shoulder bars. Then you've got a good chance to do the big jobs you're suited for. You've got the makings of a great officer and I expect you to get there. This war is too big for you to stay out of it. If you like life the way you live it in America, you'll have to go out and keep it that way. I'm looking forward to action. Tired of just sitting around. I can't tell you where we are, but I'll tell you this. No sarongs around here, only grass skirts. They say there are some nurses on this Island, but I haven't found them yet. A visit with my Red Cross gal wouldn't do me any harm—I could smell those steaks as we flew over camp, and here we are, putting another can of beans on the fire.

Say, my dear brother Sammy—how would you like to invest my money for me? Could you double it in a year? Maybe Dad could give you a few pointers. Also—if you want Dad to let you join up, tell him how proud he'd be to have two sons in the Army Air Corps. That might swing it. Or if you have to, just wait till you're eighteen—it won't be long. I'm very busy today—flew four missions. Only cool plane was at 12,000 feet. Sure can get warm down here. Have eighteen missions to date. Our transports can get stuff anywhere on God's green earth. It's

really amazing where we can get to, what we can get through. They're never gonna
touch me, brother. I lead a charmed life.

So: I wish you all the luck in the world. Be a careful kid and I will be seeing
you before long. Here's to a happy victory. A fellow never had a better brother.

Love, Richard

ONE HUNDRED TWENTY-FIVE

It was too hot to sleep. The cot was too hard. Issa threw off the sheet. The
colored lights attached to the palm tree just outside the Mar Vista shone in
her eyes. On the studio couch her mother and father were whispering angrily.
She heard her father say, "I just wish you'd let me go." She heard her mother
say, "Do you want me to have a tragic life?"

They made Issa go to bed too early, and then—because the three of
them were living in one room—they had to try to be quiet. She would rather
they talked in normal voices—if she were tired, she would fall asleep no
matter how noisy they were. She could sleep through anything except the
sounds of her mother's vomiting. That sound made something ugly happen
in her chest and in her throat, something turned upside down in her and
made her want to vomit, also. Now her parents had become quiet. Each
one had gone to bed on one of the studio couches. But they weren't sleeping—she knew by the sound of their fast breathing that they were still angry. After a long time, she heard her mother sit up and cry out. "Meyer! Go
out and get the paper!"

"At this hour?"

"Just go. I have a feeling in my chest. I must see the paper."

"You read it already today."

"But the night edition. I need to see it." She sounded wild, very strange.
"I have this feeling, Meyer . . . "

Issa heard her father putting on his shoes. She got out of bed and said,
"Let me go with you, Daddy. I can't sleep."

Mommy said nothing, did not protest. Issa felt alarmed that her mother did
not notice her. Daddy said, "All right, put on your dress and your sandals."

In the darkness she dressed for a walk. She took her father's hand, and
they went down the carpeted, musty-smelling hall. Her father's hand was

huge, calloused. It completely enclosed her own hand. They walked in silence out the door, down the alley—taking a shortcut toward the newsstand.

"Halt! Who goes there?"

A solder stepped in front of them. He had a rifle pointed at Daddy's heart.

"A civilian," Daddy said. "A civilian walking."

The soldier, wearing a military police band around his arm, looked at Daddy and said, "You here on vacation?"

"No, I have a business here."

"Your business is over there," the soldier said.

"I have a wife and a child," my father told him as if he were sorry about it. He pushed Issa forward as if to prove he had a child.

"It doesn't take talent to have a child," the soldier said. "You look able to heft a rifle. Here—want to see if you can lift this one?"

"No thank you," Daddy said. "May we go on?"

The soldier stood back and let them pass. Daddy walked on with his head bowed. He walked on, right past the newsstand, and turned down the street that went to the beach. Issa had to run to keep up with him—his hand pulled her along, and her feet had to take three steps to every one long stride of his.

"Where are we going?" she whispered.

They stepped off the cement onto the sand, and the world went quiet. It was like walking in a dream—hushed and strange, the sand sliding and falling away beneath her feet. The moon came over the ocean in a silver pathway, swimming toward them on the waves like little mercury fish. A gentle wind fanned the palm branches, striking one against another, soft swords rubbing together.

Daddy's head was bowed. She heard him draw in his breath suddenly and had the shocked understanding that he was crying. Did men cry? What could he need to cry about?

"Daddy?" She felt afraid.

Near the water's edge he sat down, bringing Issa down beside him. They both stared out over the shimmering black water.

"You said they can't get me," Issa reminded her father. "You said the bad people can't get over the ocean. The war can't get me."

Daddy looked at her.

"So don't worry so much," Issa said. "They can't get you either."

Daddy put his arm around her and brought her close to him. "I want to go there and make sure they can't get any of us," he whispered to her. "But I can't go."

"Someday maybe you can," Issa said and kissed her father's hand. She let her lips stay against his skin and felt the coarse hairs, wiry and comforting, under her lips.

"Well—we'd better go back, or Mommy will have the military police after us." He took a handkerchief from his pocket and blew his nose loudly. Then he lifted Issa in his arms and made his way quickly across the sand, back to the little side street, up to Collins Avenue and the newsstand, where he bought the evening edition of the newspaper.

When they got back to the Mar Vista, Mommy was waiting in the hallway with her arm outstretched.

"Oh God, hurry," she said, grabbing the paper from Daddy. "I just know . . ."

She flung open the paper on the kitchen table and ripped through the pages till she found what she was looking for. Her face looked hollow, her eye sockets empty, as she searched down the long list of names.

She screamed.

"He's there! Oh God, I knew it. He's there. Missing in action. Richard Rabinowitz. Oh no. Oh no, Meyer. Ava's beautiful boy. I can't live anymore."

Mommy sank to the floor, clutching the leg of the kitchen table. Daddy ran to lift her up, carry her to the couch.

She murmured, over and over, "I knew it, I felt it. It was in my heart. I just had a sudden feeling." She looked up and moaned. "Goddamn Hitler. I hate this war! I hate it!"

Issa felt her teeth chattering. She had never known this kind of fear. She came close to her mother and father and touched them, but they did not respond, did not try to hold her.

They had gone to some other place, both of them, a place she had never been and could not come into. Whatever it was they saw or felt terrified her. She tried to think of Richard, who was missing, whatever that meant, and she remembered his beautiful starched uniform, the creases in his pants, the gleaming wings pinned to his air force hat. She remembered his wonderful smile and his dimples.

"Mommy," Issa said, stroking her mother's calf. "If Richard is missing, maybe they will find him."

ONE HUNDRED TWENTY-SIX

Words, thought Ava. What are words? Bits of black scratching on white paper. Several words in a row create bits of information. Information can make the heart stop.

If Richard were far away, far away and healthy and alive, she could peacefully live out her life without ever seeing him again. But to know almost certainly that he was dead! Shmuel also—missing forever. Words had told her about Shmuel; now they told her about her own son. Both boys, first missing, then forever missing, the terrible word: *dead.* But maybe she had to believe the word. *Missing.* Maybe Richard was really missing, only missing, and he would return to her.

The letters told her to have hope. More words. Letters and more letters. In three of her dresser drawers she had all of Richard's letters. Now, beside her bed, were all the other letters: from Richard's captain, from his buddies, from the War Department, from Mrs. Karlsen in Wichita, Kansas, whose boy had been copilot with Richard when their transport plane went down. Over and over she read the words. What did they mean—what did they really mean? Could words be real?

From Richard's captain came these words:

My dear Mrs. Rabinowitz:

How it pains me to write you this, the saddest duty of my life. Your son was a fine young man, a good friend of mine. I knew of his devotion to you. Whenever I visited him in his quarters, I saw your picture beside his bed. All I can do now is tell you what we know happened on the 6th of February, 1943. On that day we took a flight of our ships to Wau, New Guinea. Six in all. Over the Wau airport we were attacked by about forty Zeros and some Bombers. Richard was flying a ship called Early Delivery *with Lt. Robert Karlsen. The Zeros came in fast and four were diving at Richard's ship. He went near the port—I believe he planned to land and unload ammunition—and from then on no one is sure. It's not anything to help your feelings, but the Japs lost twenty-six in this fight to (I am sorry to say) our one.*

In this land of thousands of miles of jungles, mountains, and God knows what, anything is possible. But all we can do is look and try to find his ship. This so far we have failed to do.

And it's not from any lack of search. It was not any lack of flying skill—it's just war and luck. These letters are harder to write than to live the war. Richard was my dear friend and buddy, and if there is any way to find him, we will do it. You can rest assured on that. I would like to write that I have lots of hope. But I can't and tell the truth. And I know that is what you want. As long as we are in New Guinea we'll be looking. That we may be successful is all of our hopes.

God bless you,

Captain Robert L. Wood,

33rd Troop Carrier Squadron

Tears ran from Ava's eyes like snakes, curling down her cheeks, spilling down her neck, burning into her breast. Words and more words. Words had pierced her heart, and only words could heal her. *He's been found, he's well, he's alive.* Those were the words she needed. Any second the doorbell could ring with the delivery of another telegram; the first telegram was wrong, this one is the real one, it was all a mistake, all is well, your son is alive.

Len didn't care about words. Ava knew he wanted no words in his mind. Every night he went out into the darkness, and hours later Sammy had to go and find him, drag him home, drunk and sick. He fell asleep in bars, in dark stinking places, and Sammy had to hunt for him and physically drag him home. He was like a rotting animal, foul, bedraggled, putrid. She couldn't look at him or touch him. Not one time had they cried together.

No one could share this with her—no one! Only she had carried Richard in her body, only she had his mouth at her breast, had held his precious living body against her body, had taken him into herself. There was no grief worse than this, no pain worse than this. More words came from his best buddy:

Dear Mr. and Mrs. Rabinowitz,

This is the most difficult letter I have ever attempted to write. No one was closer to Richard than I; we were inseparable—just like brothers. Please let nothing I say quell any hopes you may have of Richard's turning up safe and sound because we have had two crews who were lost in the jungles turn up five to six weeks later. At any rate, there are several possibilities, and I am giving them all to you because I sincerely feel Richard is not lost. I have never given up hope, and I look daily for Richard or news of him. Firstly, he may have been attacked by enemy planes as he was leaving the base; secondly, he may have had engine failure due to ack-ack from the ground; thirdly, he may have crash-landed behind the enemy lines and been taken prisoner; and fourthly, he may have landed out of sight of other aircraft and is trekking home, which would take quite a while. It is only five weeks now since he is lost—that is not very long ago.

I was in the flight that day—in fact my ship was just behind Richard's when the bombs were dropped from above us. Luckily I was at the closest point to home—for which I headed. I believe Richard managed to land and unload tons of ammunition in order to hold the air base, which saved many lives. When we met at the coast, however, one ship was missing. It was Richard's.

There isn't much else to say except that all hope should not be given up. I want you to keep hoping and praying just as I am. Jungle warfare is not similar to any other type of warfare where men are clearly determined lost. Richard's belongings are intact and every bit of it is waiting for his return here, just as he left it.

Keep your fortitude,

Respectfully yours,

Monroe Ackerman

Ava opened the picture album that contained the photos Richard had sent her since he had joined the air force. She was looking for a picture of Monroe Ackerman. Here was Richard holding a rifle, here was Richard in a gas mask, here was Richard in a great puffy flying suit.

Here was an airplane called the *Flying Jeep—Curtiss AT-9* that looked to Ava like a silver vacuum bottle with a red-striped tail. Here was Richard with Mama (his grandmother smiling proudly), here with Issa, the child fingering the wings on his hat, here with Meyer (the two men grinning, a little embarrassed, their arms about each other's shoulders). Here was her precious son sleeping on his bunk, then eating in the mess hall, then leaning against the side of a convertible.

In the last one he was holding a girl in his arms! What was her name again? Ah yes, Rita with the flaming red hair, Rita—a cross between Betty Grable and Rita Hayworth. And there she was again, this time with a blond, genial-looking boy, and at the bottom of the picture, in Richard's hand, were the words "Monroe and Rita." So, that was Monroe, Richard's dear friend. And Rita—Richard had met her at a USO dance in Georgia, during training. How did Ava know her hair was red? It was not red in the picture. It must have been because Richard had written about her. And what a beautiful girl she was. Perhaps Richard would have married her—perhaps they would have had children!

More tears came bursting from the endless fountain of her grief. Had Richard ever been with a woman? Had he ever experienced that, exercised his manhood, bucked and roared as Len used to do in the days when he and Ava did such things?

What was she feeling in her heart? Did she hope he had felt that passion, experienced passion and relief? Or was she jealous? Did she want him only to have known her love, her total adoration and no one else's? She hoped at least he did not experience it cheaply, with bought women, in an atmosphere of tawdry wantonness.

There was one more letter she had to read again, a letter from a bereaved mother, a mother whose son had gone down at the same time, in the same jungle, in the same plane as Richard had. She read:

Dear Mrs. Rabinowitz—

I have your address from Captain Wood, the good man who was like a father to our boys, and who grieves for them much as we do. I had intended to write you much sooner, but I have been so blue and discouraged that it is all I can do to get to my job at the Cessna factory. I work here on the night shift, twelve midnight until eight in the morning. I have tried to stay hopeful, but I am so sad today. This is the first wedding anniversary for my lost boy, Robert, and his wife, June. On Wednesday will be Robert's twenty-second birthday. Oh my dear friend, each day is so hard to live, and the special ones are heartbreaking. Our eldest son is in a camp only two hundred miles from Wichita, and his wife is living with us. He is flying a B-24 four motor bomber and expects to go over in a few weeks.

He will be a pilot on a heavy bomber, at least this is what he has trained for. He is twenty-six. Then we have William, twenty-four and the father of our precious granddaughter, one year old. He has asked for voluntary induction. Next Robert, who is now gone, and then Howard, nineteen in July and en route to camp somewhere now. The youngest, Justin, is not yet eighteen, but is clamoring to enlist with our consent. Can we tell him not to go? And yet, could I bear the loss of one more beloved child? When I think that all five might be taken from me, I ask myself—can any war be worth this pain? All I can say is my heart is with you. We all are hoping and praying for good news each day. Many friends have said that time makes things easier to bear, but it seems to me in our case each day is harder to live.

Your sister in grief,
Mrs. Bess Karlsen

There was a knock on Ava's bedroom door.

"Come in," she said, wiping her eyes on the hem of her dress.

"Mom—" Sammy said. "There's a man on the phone for you."

"Who?"

"I don't know."

"Sammy—" Ava said. "Go and find your father."

"He won't come home with me this early in the evening. He's too strong for me to pull him home if he's not really drunk. I have to wait a little longer."

"Sammy—" Ava said, getting up to go downstairs to the phone. "Promise me you won't go to war."

"I can't promise. You know Richard wanted me to go. You've read his letters to me."

"I would die if anything happened to you."

Sammy came to her and hugged her. "If I go, I'll be so careful—I can run between the bullets, Mom—you know me."

"Go!" She pushed him away. "Go find your father. Maybe this once he will come home early."

She went downstairs and took the phone in her hand. Sammy went out the door with a wave.

"Yes? Hello?" More words—like in letters, words came over telephones. Any word could be the one she waited for.

"Ava, it's me, Johnny Quinn."

"I told you, Johnny, never to call me at home. And how can I think of such things now with my broken heart. I'm like a dead thing, a stone."

"I don't ask anything of you, Ava. Just a time to sit and talk. Maybe I could help you."

"Are you God? Only God can help me."

"I'm just your friend."

"So be my friend. Leave me alone. I have nothing to give. I can't talk. I can't listen. I only look at his pictures and read his letters. Hell can't be worse than this."

"You know where I am, Ava. Call me, and I'll be there. When the time comes that you need a friend, I'll be waiting."

"When my son rises from the jungle like your precious Jesus was raised up, I'll call you then," Ava said. "Good-bye, Johnny."

ONE HUNDRED TWENTY-SEVEN

March 30, 1943

Secret Heart

In such strange ways do dreams come true. Through the grief of others I come close my heart's desire: a man may marry me, and Meyer has to bring his family home from Florida or he will be drafted. Thus I will get Issa back!

Milton is in a wheelchair. Milton Raspman, the kind doctor, now crippled by a bomb and in a wheelchair. His hands like a little boy's, useless, innocent, shaking in ruin. Gertie Raspman with her hearty voice—"Go, please, Gilda, go and wheel him on Ocean Parkway so the two of you can talk and be alone."

Mama thinks it's a good idea for me to consider marrying Milton. She's afraid she will die soon (she will, she has to, she's not well) and I'll be left a lonely spinster. And Milton, sweet frightened man, shrapnel in his spine, bloody screams in his dreams, thinks it would be a fair exchange. He won't be a burden, he promises; there are jobs for men like him.

When the war ends, a job will be found for him. He still has his mind, his training, his knowledge. In some veterans' hospital, perhaps, they will put him to work, a place where there are others more crippled than he, where he won't be a terrible fright to others.

So picture it—a stroll in springtime, Gilda (a sprig of lilac behind her ear) and her fiancé on Ocean Parkway. Everything I've always wanted: my customers recognizing me and greeting me, smiling their surprised secretive little smiles: there goes that skinny Gilda, the beautician, with a man. I never thought she'd catch one. And a doctor yet!

And Milton, the top of his head just below my breasts, his head bowed with embarrassment as I rolled his wheelchair along the promenade. Cyclists passed us on the bicycle path, horseback riders gallop by across the street on the bridle path, and I rolled Milton along, the smell of spring in the air almost unbearable.

He reached his arm back, blindly, behind his head.

"Gilda?" He was fishing for my hand. I bent low.

"What is it?"

"Let's not walk anymore. Pull me over to a bench, and you sit down, and we'll talk."

I was full of fear. He was going to press me for an answer. It was no secret what he wanted; his aunt put it straight to me before the walk. He didn't have the strength or courage to face me if I didn't know something about it. I can understand that. I have been afraid in my life. But why didn't I have the courage to say *No, I won't! I can't!* Instead I agreed to take him for that walk, to consider the offer.

And so I am still considering it. It isn't lightly that at my age, thirty-three, one can turn away the only and possibly last offer of marriage of one's life.

Besides, who since Bingo ever looked at me with eyes so liquid in their need, with need so desperate and so humble? My skin, my wretched life-long handicap, is as nothing beside Milton's devastating life-long handicap. I felt I almost glowed with beauty, sitting on that bench, my violet-dotted white skirt spread on the bench, my sprig of lilac giving forth its scent.

Ah, Milton—will you ever be so cocky to give advice as you once gave me advice in your arrogant letter? I have often wondered if being married to a doctor would provide a margin of safety in life. After all, if a fishbone stuck in my throat, would you not be there to remove it for me? And if I choked on a piece of gristle, would you not rescue me from instant death? And not only me! Mama—could you save her life if her heart began to clutch and close? If you lived with us, an ambulance on wheels, could you keep us from that most feared monster, death?

If Issa had a fever of 105 degrees, would you cool her, save her life? And even Musetta, with her retching and vomiting, with her headaches and fits, with her melodrama and her sufferings—could you give her pills to bring her back to sanity and calm? What a priceless husband you might be! Not a man to turn my heart over, not Clark Gable to thrill me, but a man nevertheless, to put a ring on my finger, to give me the respectable name of Mrs. Milton Raspman, to love, honor, and protect me as long as I shall live . . .

from the limits of your wheelchair! Oh God, I might yet accept! Help me to figure this out!

I am full of private thoughts when my mind and energy should be turned to the war effort. I have dreams nearly every night in which Richard, in the shape of an airplane, hovers over my body, buzzing and vibrating, begging me to relieve him of his burden. He wants to land, he wants to land safely, and it is up to me to direct. And I can't! I don't know how to bring him in. And soon he buzzes away like a fatally injured dragonfly and sinks to his death somewhere in the garden.

If I have such dreams, what must my poor sister Ava dream? To lose a son! Richard, a young god, so beautiful, so warm and loving! What if he is lost in the jungle, starving? What is war about? Why is there war?

There are days I would put on a uniform and personally take up a rifle. I would shoot the enemy. I would gladly kill. And other times, when I think of the meaning of war, I am horrified. If life is all we have, and if life is the most precious gift we have, what on earth could drive us to choose death (for ourselves or others), to choose it as an activity? Why do we train doctors to learn about disease and aging and accidents and to save lives, but at the same time send men to snuff out life in a single violent burst of metal? Here I am, raising money daily for war bonds, for the manufacture of bombs and weapons, and at the same time I want to stop it all, stop the ugliness and terror.

One night—the night I had to call Musetta with the news about Meyer's having to return to Brooklyn—I spoke to Issa on the phone, and she said to me, "Don't worry, Aunt Gilda, the bad people can't get to us, they're all the way across the ocean."

To think that Issa will be home in just a week! Great luck for me, misery for Meyer (who finally is making good money in his recording studio), misery for Musetta, who is vomiting her guts out and now has to make the long trip home.

But for me—joy, that sweet curly-haired child in my lap again, turning pages of a book with me, helping me to make *hamentashen, kreplach.*

Meyer didn't at first seem to take seriously the letter that came here for him. But it said he must take a defense job within two weeks or he will be drafted. Manpower is short in the war. Uncle Sam doesn't care that Meyer is married and a father. Even the coming baby won't make any difference. He must work for the war effort, or they will take him!

ONE HUNDRED TWENTY-EIGHT

The train shuddered over the tracks as if the rails were made of shattered stone. Musetta felt her guts smash against themselves with each jolt. Issa whimpered at the window that she hadn't seen a single cow. Meyer had told her she must take one bite of her banana every time she saw a cow. The banana had gone soft and mushy in her hand; she was bored, and the trip seemed endless to a child. Soldiers were everywhere on the train, a single field of dull brown, and here and there the glint of eyeglasses or a mouth thrown open in sleep, showing white teeth. One man had saliva running down his chin. Musetta retched at the sight. Meyer stood up and offered his hand to guide her to the tiny bathroom between the train's cars.

She shook her head. There was no more to vomit. She waved him away and covered her sour mouth with her handkerchief. She could have flown home to Brooklyn on an army plane. She had got special permission with the help of a note from her Miami Beach doctor to ride a troop plane back to New York. He said her condition demanded it. A two-day train ride would be too dangerous in her condition.

Musetta knew it, and yet she disregarded the facts. She had tried to insist: she wanted and needed her husband and child to fly with her on the plane. The army was adamant—they simply had no room for an entire family on a troop plane; however, under the circumstances, they would make room for a single passenger, the pregnant woman. But some fear was in Musetta, some dependency that alarmed her. She wanted Meyer and the child with her. She felt too vulnerable to be alone, at the mercy of her unpredictable and hostile body. She saw herself lurching up the aisle of the plane, her mouth filling with burning poison. She saw herself bleeding suddenly, the child she carried breaking loose, and the soldiers all gathering round and watching her humiliation.

Why couldn't Meyer be the one to bear the children, to have this unspeakable thing happen inside him? Let him blow up into a huge and grotesque form, let him be pressed out of shape, distorted, invaded! Why should he and Issa take the train alone, lighthearted, fancy free, a pleasure trip for the two of them. No—she would take the train with them, make them share her experience, her pain, her embarrassment.

She could tell Meyer was tense and grim; she felt a weighty satisfaction that for once he was not amiable or playful or relaxed. He ought not to be able to sail through life in his usual hopeful, generous way without occasionally sharing her vision, her conviction that life was an ordeal, that human beings were victims of an ill-conceived arrangement for living and dying.

Oh, what she would give to have him acknowledge, finally, that life wasn't this lovely gift everyone got, that everyone alive wasn't lucky to have been born . . . for him to see that life was a big nothing.

Sometimes she wanted to kick him, bite him, and say, "Look, *now* you have to admit that life is a tragic ordeal, a burden with a brutal conclusion, and that in the end we'd all be better off not having been born."

But no—he would debate this with her, show her starlight and moonlight and flowers; show her Issa asleep, with her curls sticking damply to her brow and her long lashes casting delicate shadows on her cheeks. He would kiss her and tickle her and make her laugh (against her will!), and then he would say, "See? Isn't life fun?"

What could you do with a man like that? Well, certainly you could take the train home to New York with him, prod him with his disappointment, the loss of his business, the loss of his joy in the balmy air of Miami Beach.

"It's a pity," Musetta said as the train crashed and rattled through the swamps of Georgia, "that finally, when you *finally* get into a business that promises to make money, you have to give it up."

"Oh well," Meyer said (he was now holding Issa's blackening banana), "our good luck couldn't have lasted. Others were catching on to the idea. Like the fellow who opened right next door to me, with the same sign— 'Send your picture home to your mother, your wife, your girl'—just imitating my sign that said, 'Send your voice home to your mother, your wife, your girl.' In another week there might have been ten other recording studios. We did fine while we were there. And someday we'll move back to Florida, Moo. I think we'll settle there someday, when the war is over, and the world is more peaceful."

"When will the world ever be peaceful?" Musetta asked darkly.

"Don't worry, Moo. Everything will work out," he said reassuringly, touching her hand. She drew it away, scowling. Even the scenery was unpleasant—nothing but gray trees and revolting Spanish moss hanging from them, like the beards of smelly old men. At that very moment Meyer said to their daughter, "Look, Issa—look at the Spanish moss hanging from the trees. Isn't it graceful? It's like lace, blowing so gently in the wind. Maybe I can get you some when the train stops at the next station. Then we can bring some home as a present to Aunt Gilda and Grandma."

Musetta shuddered. "Ugh, who would want that stuff as a souvenir? I can just imagine it on the hall table in a glass jar, looking me in the face for the rest of my life."

"I could put it on my doll for hair," Issa said, with interest. In some ways the child was just like her father. Although it was Musetta who spent hours with her, teaching her words, rhymes, facts; although it was Musetta who bathed her and fed her and taught her how to fasten the buttons on her clothes and the laces on her shoes; although it was Musetta who had made her—her flesh and heartbeat and blue eyes—Meyer seemed to have an unmistakable claim on her, his presence existing in her mind and body, and all he had done was his manly job of huffing and puffing and squirting, what any man could do, and what all of them did, leaving the work and the responsibility and the worry to the woman. It was so easy for men! If only she did not have this unbearable job of bearing children. How she dreaded the inescapable conclusion to all this retching and distension—those hours on the table, screaming, mooing and moaning like an animal, feeling she was being torn in half.

The train jolted to a halt. The soldiers stirred, stretched. She could see their knees unbending in their sharply creased khaki pants. All of them with their legs, their V-shaped legs coming together at the place where . . .

Never mind. She was feeling nauseated again. Why did she get on a subject that was bad for her and keep gnawing at it, never letting it go? When she went too far, she was sorry, sick. It took her hours to calm down, cool off, to stop hating or resenting or fuming. Yet it was some kind of spiral ride—she could get on it and spin for hours, entertaining herself, passing time that was heavy and dead and dull.

"We're going out to see if we can find some Spanish moss," Meyer said to her. "Do you want to come?"

"Of course not."

He began to walk down the aisle, holding Issa's hand.

"Don't stay long!" Musetta cried in panic. "Don't miss the train. My God, what if it left without you . . . "

"Well, we'd get the next train." Meyer smiled. His smile was so beautiful; that was the trouble. Half the time she believed he could figure everything out. "But we won't stay long. We'll be right back." He threw her a kiss. Issa followed suit. They loved her. She leaned back and covered her eyes. Meyer never failed her. She was so lucky to have him. If only she could make herself believe—in all ways—how really lucky she was. She understood this luck, but a part of her was out of control, it acted without her permission. It wanted miracles, new rules for life, a way out of all the nonnegotiable conditions of life.

ONE HUNDRED TWENTY-NINE

Ava read:

May 2, 1943

My dear Mrs. Rabinowitz:

This newspaper clipping that we are sending you gives us all the hope in the world that our boys are still alive somewhere. It was clipped from the New York Sunday News *by my sister and says quite clearly that Colonel Charles Lindbergh flew over a mountain top high in the jungles of New Guinea and saw three United States C-47 transports that appeared to have made forced landings there. Since it would have been impossible for the planes to take off from that spot, it is most likely that our sons are still living in a village known to be in that area. I advise you to write to Colonel Lindbergh immediately and ask him, as I have, for a reply. I have no idea if our letters will reach him, but the poor man knows what it is like to lose a son, and I am sure, if he gets our letters, he will answer them.*

We shall continue to pray for your son as well as ours. Remember that God is a loving, merciful father, and he has been very close and dear to us, and we know that he knows and hears our prayers.

Yours, Bess Karlsen

Words and more words. Prayers were words, letters were words. The Jewish God was not the same as Mrs. Karlsen's God. A "loving and merciful father" called up no images in Ava's mind. Her own father, the young Nathan, had, in the end, been neither loving nor merciful (he had harmed her, deserted her!), and the old Nathan was a useless shuffling old man. He could be any old man—not the handsome, special father of her childhood.

There was another letter, also, from the army.

Dear Mrs. Rabinowitz:

I wish to assure you that our squadron has made extensive searches since February 6th and have not given up hope yet. It is possible in this country of countless miles of jungles and forests that the boys could be doing the same as other crews have done, namely, walking to some outpost. Understand me that I don't wish to raise false hopes, although the above is entirely possible as it has happened before. However, I must tell you, as brutally frank as it seems, that this is wishful thinking on my part, and while it is possible, the chances are very slim. All of Richard's things are being taken care of and sent through channels so that eventually they will reach you intact. While it is very little consolation to you in your grief, I wish to advise you that Richard was recommended for the Distinguished Flying Cross before the last action took place. I can assure you it will be awarded regardless of what has happened.

Again extending my heartfelt sympathy, I am,

Yours truly,

Captain R. Wood,

33rd Troop Carrier Squadron

This meant that Richard's trunk would arrive at the door, and she would have to see his sweaters and his shirts, and her heart would stop. Would her heart stop? Could it? She thought she would like to die. It would hardly be a loss, her life, at this time. What was there to live for? To see Len dragged home, stinking and drunk, every night? To wait for news. To imagine—without hope—Richard tramping out of the jungle with a healthy growth of beard and a big wave and a smile to rescuers, when in fact his precious flesh was already rotted off his bones in the hot steamy jungle of that foreign place?

Better to die. What was there to live for? she asked herself again. To wear the Distinguished Flying Cross on her dress and parade around Brooklyn, looking for sympathy? Who could comfort her? Len was like an animal, mute, dense, and secretive. She saw him as a gorilla, his arms hanging, his knuckles scraping the floor. She could no longer bear to share his bed. For weeks she had been sleeping in Richard's room, in his bed, her face buried in the pillow where his head had lain. She knew she was ill; grief was what they called it, but it was a sickness unto death.

She was too unwell to write the letter to Lindbergh. It was another hook of hope upon which she could not hang herself. She would call Gilda and ask her to write the letter. Maybe Mrs. Karlsen was right. Maybe the boys were safe. Maybe the world was a place in which she could hope to live.

Maybe.

ONE HUNDRED THIRTY

Mama had lost a son, Ava had lost a son, and now Musetta had lost a son. She had become a woman, like her mother and her sister, who had a tragic life.

She felt still and peaceful as she sat at her bedroom window looking out at the summer dark falling heavily on Avenue O, watching it dim the houses across the street, blur the outlines of the leaves on the maple tree in front of their stoop. She should never have taken the train, of course. The guilt was hers; she took full responsibility for the death of her infant son, although the doctor said it could have happened on the plane or even in bed. But she had bled like a torn water main. It began there among the hundreds of soldiers, somewhere on the outskirts of Virginia. The barren landscape was jarring across her dulled vision when she felt the jet of liquid heat scald her thighs. She knew at once how great her humiliation would be—how Meyer would have to help her to the bathroom, how towels would have to be summoned with great urgency, how Issa would be frightened and stunned till it all could be explained days later. She saw it in her mind's eye before she even cried out: her agony, her shame, her blood, her weakness as a woman displayed before all those bloodless men.

And it came to pass exactly as she had imagined it in that instant before she cried for help. If she could have died right then, she would have chosen to do so rather than go through the experiences she had to live through to get to this moment, sitting here at the window, the grief understood, the bit of flesh and bone that was to have been her baby boy disposed of, the basins flushed of her blood, the towels burned, the proper reassurances made to her daughter, all condolences received, all tears (for the time being) shed.

The peace she felt was strange, as if, having just survived something so great and hideous, nothing bad could happen again for a hundred years. Her life had become calm once again. Her body was her own, empty and still. Issa did not clamor for attention and storytelling now that she could be with

Gilda in the beauty shop for most of the day or sitting on the footrest of Milton Raspman's wheelchair, listening to him tell her about the wonders of medicine. The child now often spoke of becoming a doctor. It was good that she was occupied, for Musetta had no patience for her. And Meyer—he was also off her hands, working twelve-hour shifts at a defense plant, making airplane wings. He felt less shamed now that he was working for the war effort. He seemed proud to be grinding away in the machine shop every day, coming home filthy and exhausted.

One day he had got a bad cut on his finger from a sliver of metal that pierced his skin—and he had been so proud. He'd shown it around like a medal of honor when he had come home from work. Mama made much of it—getting a little packet of ice for him, murmuring about the dangers of his job, patting his shoulder in approval.

At last everyone was satisfied in this small, immediate way. No changes were anticipated. No big events, except the war, colored their horizons. Musetta stood and walked slowly to her bed, where she blissfully lay down and went to sleep.

ONE HUNDRED THIRTY-ONE

Ava read:

June 6, 1943

My dear Mrs. Rabinowitz:

At the time of the writing of my last letter I was able to give you a small amount of hope concerning Richard. It is with the deepest regret that I must tell you at this time that we are forced to give up our efforts to find the plane and its occupants. We cannot determine whether he was shot down by the Zeros; the only evidence gained was from several Australians who reported seeing a transport followed by some Jap planes.

There were no Japanese forces in the area over which he was flying; therefore it would be impossible for him to be a prisoner of the Japs if he survived the crash. If anyone had survived the crash or the landing, they most certainly would have used their flare guns to attract the attention of natives.

Since it has been four months since that unfortunate day and we have been unable to find the plane or any clue as to what happened, we are compelled to place your son and his crew in the status of "lost in action" in place of "missing in action."

We all remember Richard as the most cheerful, energetic boy in our squadron, who was always willing to do more than his share. His record certainly speaks for him. He will be awarded the Distinguished Flying Cross, Air Medal, and Purple Heart posthumously, and he has been recommended for the Silver Star for gallantry in action.

Richard was the perfect type of young man who represents American manhood against the Axis. Please accept the deepest sympathies and regrets from myself and the boys.

Captain R. Wood
33rd Troop Carrier Squadron

ONE HUNDRED THIRTY-TWO

July 14, 1943

Secret Heart

I have been thinking about the death of babies. Musetta's baby, that tiny waxen thing with his tiny genitals visible and clear, and Charles Lindbergh's baby, that golden, curly-haired angel with the dimpled chin. They were to have been men, both of them. Men with strong bodies, good minds, loving hearts—and men who could be called to war. Like Richard, those babies, had they lived, might have died someday in war. Or like Milton, they might have come back half-men, parts of them shrunken, paralyzed, useless.

We must make it up to those who survive. We must support them. *I will marry Milton.* What a nervous tremor the thought gives me, yet also pleasure. He cannot father children, so that matter is settled. Thus, in the end I will be a kind of spinster after all, shining though my wedding ring may be. I will not be loved physically by a man. Will all the world know? What does it matter? Milton will be my child.

Issa is growing up, and she will be in school in the fall. She is not mine forever. Who knows where Musetta and Meyer will take her next? (There are troubles with Meyer, I will get to them.)

But Milton needs to be bathed, needs nursing, needs gentle, soothing care. And I am a gentle woman. If I am anything, I am gentle. Milton has a heart of gold. He gives me every chance to refuse him, encourages my refusal, recites to me long lists of reasons I should not commit myself to him. Yet he would wither and die if I refused. This way, he will have hope and will use his medical skills to help other men so damaged, even more damaged.

In truth, it is in my nature to serve. Just as it is in my sister Musetta's nature to be served. And Milton was somehow assigned to me by fate, placed in my care. Who knows if there is a Grand Plan? Somehow I was led to this, and it's time, in my thirty-third year, to use all the powers I have. I will no longer save them for some Prince Charming.

So it will be. Tomorrow I will tell Milton that I will marry him. I know his sweet, hopeful face will light up like the moon. He is so thin! I will fatten him up! Meyer has said he will build a wheelchair ramp up to the front door! But it will have to wait till Meyer's arm is healed. (And can Milton and I live here, with Mama and Nathan, with Musetta and Meyer and Issa? The house is bursting! We are too many people living too close together. But one thing at a time. Life is so various these days.)

There is some bad news: one is a piece of news about Richard from the great Colonel Lindbergh, and another is about Meyer's arm. Last week, poor clumsy Meyer, with his long limbs and his awkward ways, ground to pieces the wing of an airplane. He told us he doesn't know what happened: the gears went backwards, the machine went crazy, and the wing was ruined, went flying off the table, bits of metal shooting like stars through the room, one hitting Meyer in the eye (it was removed, no real damage) and one tearing through his wrist. The foreman at the defense plant (who didn't like Meyer from the first day) immediately cried "Sabotage!" and called the police to arrest Meyer. Such troubles! Musetta was beside herself with panic that Meyer would be put away behind bars till the end of the war. Of course, they then found Meyer already had a police record: those dumb crane machines and then the business with the Nazi names in the trunk. So for a while they thought Meyer was a German spy, infiltrating our aircraft factories to do damage!

He was in jail overnight. Musetta gave the police the full treatment, tears, posturing, melodrama, her miscarriage, her nephew missing in New Guinea, Meyer's own injuries—so that finally, getting sick of her hysteria and finding no real evidence that he was a saboteur, they agreed to let him go home. Now she is afraid the factory won't take him back, and the army will draft him. There is no end to the troubles, both real and imagined, in her life.

We all have terrible troubles. But would any of us want to change with the other? Would Musetta want to change places with Ava? With me, about to marry a paralyzed man? Even with Mama, who bravely faces what comes her way? At least when we have our own troubles, we know what we have. Now Ava's troubles are heavier than ever, with Colonel Lindbergh's reply. I wrote to him care of *The News* after they published the article that Lindbergh had seen an American transport plane that had crash-landed on a mountain in New Guinea. They were kind enough to suggest I write him at the Ford Motor Company in Detroit, Michigan. To my astonishment, I received this personal reply just a week later:

The Tompkins House

Long Lots Road Westport, Conn. Miss Gilda Sauerbach

405 Avenue "O"

Brooklyn 30

New York, New York

Dear Miss Sauerbach:

I am extremely sorry to have to tell you in reply to your letter that the newspaper report about my seeing an isolated place in New Guinea, cut off from communications, where several planes had made forced landings is untrue, as are so many similar stories printed these days.

I want you to know that you have my deepest sympathy in your great concern for your nephew who has been reported missing. I wish I had information which might be of value to you.

Sincerely,

Charles A. Lindbergh

I was so touched to have his personal answer—the man is so busy, and so hard-working—and so famous. Of course, there are some who think he has too much respect for the Germans, but all you have to do is look at his picture, at his serious, decent face, at his intelligent eyes, and you know he is a good and fine man. His wife reminds me of myself—she's petite, like I am, and she loves to write, as I do, and she has a certain steely courage, which I also have.

When I think of what he and his wife have been through, the impossible loss of their little boy, I know he can understand all the suffering in the world. I feel that his sympathy somehow makes the loss of Richard a little easier to bear.

Ava's answer, when I read her the letter over the phone, was: "Well, maybe Richard's plane was there, and he just didn't see it." She can't accept this. She can't and won't, and will probably live the rest of her life waiting for Richard to walk out of the jungle and back to Brooklyn and in her front door.

ONE HUNDRED THIRTY-THREE

"You're making me crazy! All you do is cry!" Len banged his fist on the dining-room table. "I say 'hello' and you cry. I wake up in the morning and you cry."

"And you—what do you do? You get drunk and slobber like an animal."

"I like to be drunk!" Len shouted. "I like it because then I don't have to be here watching you cry."

"You could cry with me," Ava begged. "We have something to cry about, don't we? And now Sammy is gone to war, too. Another flier! God knows, we could have two gold stars in the window. Won't that make you proud?"

"What did you want, that Sammy should stay home and be a sissy-boy when all he's been wanting to do is join up?"

"I want him alive, Len."

"Alive and ashamed, like your brother-in-law, Meyer, or a hero, like Richard?"

"Alive, any way he can be alive. What do I care about a hero? The army writes me letters and promises me medals. What do I want with medals? I want my boy alive, with his bright eyes, and his smile. I don't want words."

"Words!" Len said. "All you do is talk."

"Oh shut up," Ava said. "You—gorilla. You bum!"

"You crazy bitch!" Len lunged out of his chair, staggering heavily toward her. He was no better than a drunk on skid row; in spite of her disgust, she felt pity, grief. This was the man she had married. Did all marriages sooner or later come to this, this indifference worse than hate? She didn't care about him. He was like a stranger.

"You dumb crazy bitch," he mumbled. "You shrew."

He came at her and punched her on the side of the head with his boxer's punch before he lost his balance and banged into the wall.

"You touched me?" she screamed, incredulous. "Now you're beating me?" The pain in her head was nothing to the fury and astonishment she felt. Her husband had punched her!

"Get out of here, you filthy dog," she sobbed. "Get out. Drown in your whiskey. Don't ever come home. Get out! Get out!"

She picked up a brass candlestick from the side cabinet and held it in the air. "If I can live without Richard, I can live without you! You disgusting pig."

Len staggered out the front door, grizzled and uncoordinated, his mouth ugly and babbling terrible words. Ava ran up the stairs. Each day was worse than the last, pulling her lower into despair, a wish for death. On her bed was the letter that had come yesterday from the Adjutant General's Office, more words, with the message meaner, crueler, and more final than any previous letter had been. She read it again:

Dear Mrs. Rabinowitz:

Since your son, First Lieutenant Richard Rabinowitz, 0790598, Air Corps, was reported missing in action 7 February 1943, the War Department has entertained the hope that he survived and that information would be revealed dispelling the uncertainty surrounding his absence. However, as in many cases, the conditions of warfare deny us such information. Public Law 490, 77th Congress, as amended, provides for a review and determination of the status of each person who has been missing in action. Upon such a review the making of a finding of death is authorized. Information in the hands of the War Department indicates that your son was a crew member of a C-47 (Skytrain) transport aircraft of the 33rd Troop Carrier Squadron, 347th Troop Carrier Group, which was in a flight of three planes engaged in a routine flight to Wau, New Guinea, on 7 February 1943. The three planes departed from Jackson, New Guinea, near Port Moresby, at 9:20 A.M. and arrived in the vicinity of Wau at 10:45 A.M. As the flight was circling Wau, preparing to land, it was attacked by enemy aircraft consisting of bombers, dive bombers, and fighter planes. Two planes of the flight succeeded in getting away and returned to Jackson at 12:20. Your son's plane may or may not have landed at Wau, but it did not return to its base. A search of the surrounding area did not reveal any trace of the plane or the crew members. Since no information has been received that would support a presumption of his continued survival, the War Department must now terminate your son's absence by a presumptive finding of death. Accordingly, an official finding of death has been recorded. The finding does not establish an actual or probable date of death; however, as required by law, it includes a presumptive date of death for the purpose of termination of pay and allowances, settlement of accounts, and payment of death gratuities.

I regret the necessity for this message but trust that the ending of a long period of uncertainty may give at least some small measure of consolation. An appraisal of the sacrifice made by your son in the service of his country compels in us feelings of humility and respect. May Providence grant a measure of relief from the anguish and anxiety you have experienced during these many months.

Sincerely yours,

Edward Whitehall

Major General

Acting Adjutant General of the Army

"Oh you bastards!" Ava cried, throwing the letter to the floor. "All of you with your apologies and your fake sympathy, damn you all!" Whoever Mr. Edward Whitehall was, he was probably right now enjoying a good dinner and not imagining his son rotted to bones in the jungle, or alive, with a leg blown off, trying to crawl toward civilization, or impaled on a tree branch, starving, starved, dying, dead. These images flooded Ava's head when she was unguarded—when she was stirring Richard's favorite flanken-barley soup, when she was pulling on her stockings, when she was stepping into the bathtub. They would rise up like scenes on the stage in Radio City Music Hall, and she would see all the details in floodlights: the expression on Richard's face, of pain and fear and terror, the high grasses in which the plane had come to rest, the snakes in the underbrush, the vultures and insects ready to feast on her son's flesh.

"Oh, I'm sorry, I'm sorry, my Richard, my Richard." The flood overtook her again, the tears sour and hot. "I'm sorry," she whispered, "I'm sorry that I gave birth to you."

And suddenly she felt something turn in her, close down, a valve suddenly being turned off. She felt her face harden, as if concrete had been poured into her cheeks. Her eyes grew cold as marbles. The flood ceased and froze in her veins. The nausea that had begun to close her throat backed down, drained away. A column of energy came up, like a steel rod, and raised her head. The thing in her that had given birth to Richard shriveled to the size of a pea, turned black, and hung at her center like a drop of lead. Her teeth had become magnets, held together, tip to tip, in a smile. She felt herself hold the smile; she watched herself smiling in the dresser mirror as she searched through her jewel box for Johnny Quinn's phone number.

ONE HUNDRED THIRTY-FOUR

They entered a room so white, so sun crazed, so blinding in its whiteness, that Ava hid her eyes behind her arm. She could feel the rumble of the roller coaster under the polished floorboards of the rooming house. When Johnny locked the door of the small slant-ceilinged room, she uncovered her eyes and walked to the window, moving aside the white window shade.

The brilliance of the beach came up at her, the sun flashing mirror signals from the whitecaps of the ocean and sparks of fire from the windshields of the cars passing below on the street. The heat rose up from the pavement in a burning column and opened like a flower outside the third-floor window, waiting in a shimmery haze to be let in.

She hadn't enough strength to pull up the window, so stood aside to let Johnny do it. He snapped at the frayed white cords till they released the white-painted window frame from its runner. The window rose up.

"Well, here we are," Johnny said.

"I know," Ava said. "That I know."

"The air smells good."

The boardwalk below was nearly empty; the Labor Day weekend had just ended, giving the closing signal for most of the pizza stands, cotton-candy concessions, and game booths. The rides still rattled vigorously through their motions for the few remaining summer vacationers.

Johnny Quinn had rented this room for two days, telling the landlady that he and his wife needed a peaceful undisturbed time in which to recover from a recent grief; a nephew of theirs had been killed in the war, he'd said, and they required privacy and no interruptions. The landlady had pressed her hand to her heart and sworn she would see that they were not bothered.

Ava had left home with no explanations for Len. He would be too drunk to read a note or even notice her absence. However, she had called Gilda and told her that she was going to visit the orphanage for two days and wouldn't be home till Thursday. She had given no further details. She owed nothing to anyone. Now she began to unbutton her dress. She stopped, letting her handbag slide from her arm onto the bedspread. The bed glowed white; the bedspread had little cottony white knobs on it, like little white heads bobbing in a white sea.

"Do you want to go for a swim first?" Johnny asked. "Shall I get on my bathing suit?"

"No," Ava said abruptly. "I just want to get into the bed." She pulled down the zipper, let her dress slip over her hips. "Johnny," she said. "Take off your clothes."

He seemed embarrassed, shy.

"It's fine, Johnny," Ava said. "Neither of us is a bathing beauty. Just do it. It doesn't matter how we are now. We know how we used to be. We both used to be beautiful. That's why we love each other."

There—she had said the unsayable. She did love Johnny Quinn, in a way she loved no one else or ever had. She went to him, touched the slack pale skin of his cheek, smoothed back the gray-blond hair on his head. He was so tall—she had to reach up to touch his brow.

"Hurry," she said.

He looked puzzled.

"I just need to lie down," she said. She pulled back the tight white cover and entered the bed as if it were an ocean. She let it wash up over her skin, feeling a kind of shock, as she inched her way to the far side, against the wall, the place where the attic roof came down so low she could reach up and stroke it with her fingers.

When Johnny came into the bed, the mattress rolled and shivered, and his weight pulled her down toward the middle. This meeting was a sin. In Johnny's church it was a sin, and in the church of her mind it was a sin. A man other than her husband was now encircling her with his arms, was burying his head against her breasts.

She gasped at the need that washed over her like a flood. She thought that Johnny Quinn's arms were like the arms of God, like the arms of the father that were to have protected her and taken care of her, like the arms of her husband, who was to have loved and honored her, and like the arms of her son Richard, who was to have grown up to revere her and adore her and care for her in her feeble old age.

"Don't cry," Johnny whispered into her hair. "Here—raise your arms, I'll take off your slip." She saw him above her in the bed, just an ordinary man, a man nearly fifty years old, a man who had no special powers, who could not keep her safe from harm, who could not stop himself from dying.

The light came into the room like a prayer, blinding and piercing her. She opened her arms to Johnny Quinn, and as he came over her like a cloud, she felt the air go black and heard the demented cackle of the Fun House lady rising on the wind. She began to laugh herself. "Come into the Fun House, Johnny," she said to him. "Come with me to the end of the world."

ONE HUNDRED THIRTY-FIVE

The tables were tiny, the chairs were tinier. Just as the baby bear's chair had been too small for Goldilocks in the three bears' house, everything in kindergarten was too small for Issa. In actual size the furniture accommodated her body quite well, but she was used to larger furniture at home and liked for her feet to swing from the couch, enjoyed having to hold her arms out to reach the armrests, was glad to have room to grow.

Another thing she noticed on this first day of school was that she was more brave and more calm than the other children. Of those other five at her table, the girl named Paula was now crying quite miserably, the girl named Rose had wet her pants and was now waiting for her mother to come and pick her up, and the girl named Arlene was holding her dress up over her face. The two boys at the table, Billy and Jimmy, twin brothers, wore white shirts and blue ties and sat stiffly, not talking or looking anywhere but straight ahead. They reminded Issa of the businessmen who walked past her house on the way to the Culver Line subway every morning.

So this was school. When were they going to get to the rhymes and spelling games Mommy had promised her? When would she be able to demonstrate that she could tell time, knew how to read, could count to ten in Spanish (as far as Mommy could teach her) and to a hundred in English, and was going to be brilliant? That was exactly what Mommy had told her as she kissed her good-bye at the schoolyard gate of P. S. 238 this morning. "You, my darling daughter, are going to be brilliant."

Issa hoped she would be. It sounded like a very happy idea, sparkling and full of promise. She had the feeling that from now on everything would get nicer as she got older. She would have more freedom—by fourth grade, her mother had promised her, she would know how to cross streets and might even walk to school, all fourteen blocks, by herself.

She had a tricycle now, but someday would have a two-wheeler. They had no pets, but someday she might have one. She had no brother or sister yet, but someday, maybe very soon, she would have a little baby boy or girl in the house. All these things seemed marvelous and worth waiting for. She could write quite nicely now, but someday she would know how to type. Mommy had been the best typist in her office and assured Issa she would be even better, even faster.

Gilda was teaching her how to knit and purl, how to embroider, and how to hemstitch, although Mommy had no interest in those things. Aunt Gilda had given Issa a very old and precious book, from her own years in elementary school, which had sample stitches, from the longest, loosest basting stitch to the tiniest invisible hemstitch. She was also learning to cook all of Gilda's and Grandma's favorite dishes: *kreplach* and matzo balls and chicken soup, stuffed cabbage and potted brisket and *tzimmes*. Mommy was annoyed at this, but less than she used to be, and she now allowed Issa to spend hours in the kitchen with Grandma or in the beauty shop with Gilda. Mommy seemed much calmer these days. She even smiled sometimes.

"Attention, class." Issa looked up expectantly. "May I have your attention?" The teacher was a very thin woman with gray hair. She was Miss Anderson. She held her hands together over the front of her purple dress.

"Shh, shh, shh," she said.

Issa wanted to get on with things, and yet the room was full of noise and strangers, full of shuffling sounds and whimpers. She hoped she would not always have to wait so long for everyone to get ready to listen; it would be very boring at school if that were the case.

"May I have a volunteer?" Miss Anderson said. "I need someone to accompany Rose to the office, where her mother will be coming to pick her up. Is there anyone here who knows where the office is?"

Issa raised her hand. She didn't exactly know where it was, but she had been sitting a long time and felt she would like to take a walk around the school.

"Let me see," the teacher said. "Issa Berger, are you sure you know where the office is?"

"Yes," she said, "I do."

"Then will you accompany Rose there?"

Issa smiled and held out her hand to Rose. "That's very nice," Miss Anderson said. "During the course of the year many of you children will be able to help me like Issa is helping me. If you are quiet and attentive the way Issa has been this morning, you may get to be a monitor also."

The little girl named Rose walked with her head down; Issa knew how ashamed she must feel.

"Don't worry," she said to Rose. "It could happen to anyone. Don't be sad." They walked down the long quiet hall in the direction where Issa thought the office might be found. A white-faced clock hung from the wall like a ticking moon. "Look," Issa said. "It's ten o'clock." To accent her statement, the clock made a little clicking sound.

"How do you know that?" Rose asked.

"I learned it," Issa said proudly. "You'll learn it, too. Learning is going to be fun."

They passed a room that smelled of tomato soup.

"Ugh," Rose said. "That's the hot-lunch room. Everyone vomits there, my brother told me."

"We don't eat lunch at school yet," Issa assured her. "In kindergarten you go home for lunch." They passed a room in which there was a high desk and grown-up-size chairs. "This is the office," Issa said. They turned into the room, and Rose saw her mother sitting on a bench. She began to cry.

"Good-bye, see you tomorrow," Issa said. "She's all right," she assured Rose's mother. "She's just nervous on the first day."

"Well, you certainly are a confident young lady, aren't you?" the woman behind the desk said to Issa.

"I hope so," Issa said. She waved good-bye to Rose. She walked back into the hall and had no idea in which direction her classroom might be. Every door looked the same. She walked and walked till she knew she must be lost. Her teacher would wonder what had happened to her. Her mother would come at noon and wait outside at the schoolyard fence and be frightened when Issa did not come out with her class. All the children would learn how to read and write and find out where China was and what geography was, and Issa would still be wandering in the long, empty halls. She felt she might cry. She knew this was a moment when all those other five children who sat at her table might very well cry, even the stiff little shirt-and-tie twins. But no; even though her heart was pounding and the fear was in her throat, she knew this was some kind of test. Her father sometimes got lost when he was driving them somewhere, and he never cried. She was not going to cry either. She would just use her brains and be tough. She had a feeling that was a good thing to do for the rest of her life, use her brains and be tough.

Boldly she opened a blank door and walked into a room full of strange children, much bigger than she was. She tried to make her voice loud and steady. "Can you please tell me where to find Miss Anderson's room?" she asked.

"Oh, it's right down the hall. Room 105," the young woman answered.

"Thank you," Issa said and delicately closed the door. She was not safe yet, but in a minute she would be. She felt triumphant and knew she had passed some kind of a test. She also knew she would not tell her mother about this adventure, or Aunt Gilda, or Daddy. It would be a kind of private secret, something to belong to her, to make her feel proud of herself. When she came to Room 105, she threw open the door and held her breath till she saw it was indeed her room. There was her teacher; there was her little baby-bear chair. Miss Anderson looked up from a story she was reading to the class. "Everything all right?" she asked Issa.

"Just fine," Issa said, taking her seat and smoothing out her skirt. "I took care of everything."

1944

ONE HUNDRED THIRTY-SIX

Curls of sawdust crunched underfoot. Musetta breathed in the aroma of newly sawn wood as she walked slowly up the stairs. Mr. Schneider, the carpenter, was on his hands and knees at the top of the staircase.

"We're comink along gut, Mrs. Berger," he said, " . . . and we got pipes for the bathroom. We are lucky to get pipes, with the war."

"Very good, Mr. Schneider," Musetta said, stepping carefully around him. "You're doing a fine job."

The conversion of the house was going beautifully, although Gilda had warned Musetta that the smell of glue and sawdust would doubtless make her sick to her stomach. The fact was that Musetta had hardly vomited at all so far in this pregnancy, and the smell of wood was like perfume to her. Gilda was against the project for a hundred reasons: the carpenter was German, how could Musetta have hired a German?! And what was the point of spending all that money to make the one-family house into a two-family house? Where was the thrift in having two separate kitchens, two separate full bathrooms, two separate households!

Thrift?! Musetta was buying privacy, peace, the right never to have to see hair in the sink after Gilda had shampooed one of her customers. She cared about having locked doors, separateness, division. For years she had lived with too many people, too many diverse opinions as to how she and Meyer and their child should live. Now she was going to get what she wanted. There was enough money—at last. Meyer was making a living. The government had finally let him go—admitting he was no spy, no saboteur, but just a man who was not adept at cutting metal. He had opened a little antique store, Berger's Antiques, on Hansen Place in downtown Brooklyn. In the mornings he went around on calls, buying old furniture and antique objects, and in the afternoon he sat in his store, selling them. It suited him. He could move around, could drive places, talk to people, kibitz, and not ever have to worry about reporting to a boss.

Gilda was making money, too. Her beauty shop was busier than ever, and, in addition to that, she would soon have a doctor supporting her! She and Milton were engaged. He had bought her a diamond ring "big enough to choke a horse" was the way Mama proudly put it. And he had opened an office on East Fifth Street, just off Avenue P. Wheelchair or not, he had customers right away. His aunt, Gertie Raspman, rounded them up for him like a policeman. He was looking better all the time. Since Gilda had accepted the engagement ring, his face had new color in it. He seemed to be gaining weight, too. It was luck all around—for him, a crippled man, and for Gilda, an old maid. Musetta was always amazed at how often the unfortunate had good luck. But maybe the tilt of the world was changing—she was having better luck now, too. Another pregnancy, but without terrible nausea. Her husband making money. Issa blossoming and glowing like a little sun.

"Are you ready, sweetheart?" Musetta called. "Did you find your tap shoes? We have to be at Madame Lalique's in a half-hour, and you know we have to walk slowly."

Issa opened the door of the bedroom and ran to Musetta, pushing her head against her mother's stomach. "Careful, careful of the new baby," Musetta cautioned her.

"Do I look like a teapot today?" Issa asked, showing her delicate and sweet smile to her mother. "Madame Lalique told me to think hard till I believed I was a teapot."

"A teapot? You look like an angel," Musetta answered.

Mr. Schneider, still on the floor, raised his carpenter's cap at them as they passed him. "Good-bye, dance beautiful, little dahlink," he said. Issa stopped and stared at him. "How come—" she said, "if Germans are so bad, you're so nice?"

"Shh, Issa!" Musetta whispered.

"Dat's fine, Missus," the carpenter said. "Children are smarter then we are. Honest is okay." He smiled at Issa. "I'm a German who's a good German," he explained.

They left the house by the front door, saying good-bye to Mama and Nathan, who were drinking tea and listening to the radio, and passed through the front porch where Gilda was giving a permanent. The smells of chemicals were fierce and sour. It would be such a relief when the conversion was done. Enough room for all of them, finally—Musetta and Meyer and the two children downstairs, and upstairs, over the new back porch, two extra rooms and a bath for Mama and Nathan, and eventually plenty of room for Gilda and Milton and the beauty parlor.

Gilda had wanted the downstairs of the house because of Milton and his wheelchair, but Musetta had insisted that she needed it more: with Issa needing to play in the backyard, and the new baby needing to be wheeled in and out in its carriage many times a day. If Milton was going to be rich, they could build some sort of elevator on the staircase eventually. Or—Musetta had said pointedly—Gilda and Milton could just move somewhere else.

"Oh—I could never leave Issa," Gilda had said. As if Issa was hers, as if Issa belonged to her as much as she belonged to Musetta and Meyer.

Issa swung her mother's hand as they walked down East Fourth Street toward Avenue P. The summer heat rose off the sidewalk and blasted their faces. Here and there a heavy overhang of leafy trees shaded their way. Musetta felt the swift relief of coolness as they passed under the branches. In the windows of many houses were gold stars—sons lost in the war. How could anyone bear to lose one son, two sons? One house had four gold stars in the window!

Musetta prayed she would have a girl baby. And then she corrected herself. Prayer was for superstitious old people. She wished for a baby girl.

She wondered if Ava ever prayed that Richard would somehow still appear. She wondered if Mama ever prayed that Shmuel would one day walk out of the ocean and come up the steps of the house. It was so easy to pray, like the Italians did who lived on East Fourth Street and went running to church every Sunday, dressed in big hats with ribbons and tiers of lace on their dresses. Anyone could pray, just turn everything over to God—God having a reason for everything, God testing you in your suffering, God taking a baby's life because He wants the baby at His side to do His work. It made her sick. It was no God who made her bleed away her tiny son; no God who shot Richard's plane down in the jungle; no God who drowned Shmuel. It was the aimless randomness of life.

Once you understood that, you could just go on and do the things you had to do—squeeze orange juice for breakfast, sew buttons on a shirt, take a child to a dancing lesson.

"Oh, I think we're late," Musetta said. "They're playing the music already." Madame Lalique's studio was in a basement store near the Claridge Theater. She had two pink ballet slippers hanging in the window. Issa took ballet on Monday and tap on Thursday. Madame Lalique had said, "She has a grace beyond her years." On Tuesday and Friday of each week Musetta gave Issa a piano lesson. If nothing else, she would be a cultured child. She could read with ease and write beautifully. She had filled a little notebook with poems. She was able to play simple pieces on the piano and now, this summer, had learned the basics of tap and ballet dancing.

In the fall Musetta was going to give her voice lessons. There was a young woman who lived on East Third street, Goldie Haverman, who had once given a concert at Carnegie Hall and was now offering singing lessons to talented children in Brooklyn. Issa already had a clear, vibrant voice. She could hold a note long and true and was always on key. Musetta hoped she had inherited Isaac's fine singing voice and his love for song. It made her happy to think that Issa might carry on his talent and his devotion to music.

But to become important and famous, Issa would have to work hard, concentrate, and practice! If only she did not spend so much valuable time doing little crochet stitches and mending doilies for Gilda. If only she spent less time in the kitchen pressing out cookies and rolling *lukshen* dough. She would have servants for that when she grew up; servants could not play the piano for you, but they could certainly cook and sew.

"Come, come!" Madame Lalique cried, clapping her hands together. "Get on your teapot hat, the cups and saucers are waiting!"

ONE HUNDRED THIRTY-SEVEN

Richard's trunk, which was brought to the door, was shaped like a coffin. Ava, who was ironing a dress when the doorbell rang, laid the iron down heavily on the metal wedge-shaped rest and went to the door. When she saw the trunk in the arms of the delivery man, her first thought was that her son Richard was inside it. She lost her balance suddenly and reached out wildly for the closest thing, a brass lamp, to keep herself from falling. She heard the thuds of Len's footsteps coming down the stairs.

"What the hell is going on?" he shouted.

The delivery man stood helpless, the heavy trunk straining his arms. "This is addressed to Mr. and Mrs. L. Rabinowitz," he said.

"Just put it down, for God's sake," Len said. "Right there on the rug. Fine, fine." He fumbled in his pocket, then handed the man some coins. "You can go now."

Ava, with her eyes open and unblinking, saw the man look uncertainly in her direction and then leave. She was aware of the trunk waiting there to snap open its lid and devour her. She heard Len begin to walk up the stairs.

"Oh please!" she cried. "Don't go, Len!"

She felt the floor stop moving, knew he had paused on the steps. Finally he said, "How come you're talking to me? Almost like I'm a human being."

"Please, Len," she said. "Don't walk away right now. I can't open that trunk all alone."

"So finally you need me enough to talk to me? How long is it you haven't talked to me?"

"Let's not argue now."

"For a year, maybe more, you refuse to talk to me," he said. "There's your dinner. Lock the door. You sleep by yourself in Richie's room. Now—you want to talk?"

"I don't want to talk," she said. "I just want you to open the trunk with me. He's your boy, too. I can't do it alone."

"I'm a no-good drunk, right?" Len said. "How come you want me near your precious boy's trunk?"

"Because . . . it's right that you should open it with me. He belonged to us, only to us."

"Yes," Len said softly. "He belonged to us." He sat down on the bottom step and buried his head in his hands. Ava came to him and sat slowly beside him.

"That is what is left of him," she said.

"And what is left of me," Len said. "Rags in a box, that's what I am."

His hair was nearly white. His heavy head seemed lighter to Ava, who had not looked at him in months, perhaps in years. He was weary and old. They sat for a long time on the step. Finally, Ava touched his shoulder very lightly, almost afraid to touch him at all. "We have to look inside, Len. Would you untie the ropes?"

He grunted assent. He went and stood before the trunk bravely, and she was reminded of the time Richard had had a pet rabbit and it had died. She had found it in its cage, on its side, stiff and hard, ants crawling in its eyes. She knew what had to be done but could not do it, so she had called Len, and Len had come and stood before the cage in just this same posture, girding himself to do the hard thing. Without protection, without gloves, he had pulled out the rabbit by its feet. She had cringed as Len carried it to the trash can. He had looked at her, once, as if to say, "Look, this is what happens, this is a fact of life, this is death." Her admiration for his bravery had been boundless then.

Now, kneeling on the rug, he gently unwound the ropes from Richard's trunk. The clasp had long been broken; he lifted the latch and motioned for Ava to join him. As he raised the lid, she shuddered violently. Len, without looking at her, reached for her hand and squeezed it.

"Look," he said. "It's only his clothes. They can't hurt you. The ghost isn't in there, Ava. It's here." He struck his heart. "The ghost lives here."

Tentatively, she touched a thing in the trunk, a sweater. Then she lifted a few things out: their son's favorite blue sports jacket, the blue tie Gilda had knitted for him, his gabardine slacks. She tried to see them as they were, innocent cloth, and not as they had been, the coverings of her boy's living flesh. Together, on their knees, the parents circled themselves with their boy's possessions: his camera, his radio, his air force wings. When the trunk was empty, they were ringed with the artifacts of a lost life.

Len turned the golden wings over and over in his hands. "Ava," he said, looking down, "I'm sorry for what I've done to you. All I could do is run away—to the bars. My heart hurt too much to stay here and look at your face, a face with such torture on it."

"So did going to the bars make you happy?"

"Going made me unconscious."

"And I was left alone."

"I know . . . so I'm telling you this. I'm sorry."

"All right," she said. They sat without speaking, touching their son's clothing. "Tonight," Len said, "maybe tonight you could sleep in the big bed."

"Yes, maybe I can," Ava said. "Maybe I will. Yes, I will." She stood uncertainly, unsteadily, like an old woman. "I was ironing when the bell rang. You have any shirts that need ironing? Maybe I could do some of your shirts."

"That would be good. The laundry, they put in too much starch, the collars cut my neck."

"I'll do your shirts. Why not? I always used to do them, so I'll do them again. I'm doing the ironing anyway."

1945

ONE HUNDRED THIRTY-EIGHT

February 17, 1945

Secret Heart

Musetta had a baby girl tonight, eight pounds, nine ounces. She says she didn't suffer—which is God's miracle! She was smiling when I saw her, also a miracle, not complaining about her stitches or her breasts, just smiling like a queen. The baby is fat, fat and red. Her cheeks like rose petals, her hair straight and black. (Who did she get that from?) Meyer is dancing with joy, Issa is acting as if she arranged the whole thing herself. The hospital—with their rules—wouldn't let Meyer bring Issa up to see Musetta, but he's a wily one, my brother-in-law. He buttoned Issa inside his big winter coat and went sneaking up the stairs with his two long legs and her two little skinny ones sticking out of the coat. Mama and I were there visiting Musetta when they walked in as this four-legged creature, and Issa was laughing so hard when he unbuttoned his coat that we all burst out laughing.

What a precious child she is. I call her "Iskala," which annoys Musetta, but Issa knows it is a love-name. Everyone is feeling some happiness. The war may soon be over, which is the biggest blessing. Sammy wrote to Mama, "Don't go worrying about me. Leave the worrying to the Germans and the Japs. They haven't got a single thing in the world to look forward to."

He's such a dear boy; he's somewhere in Belgium now, and he heard from Ava that Mama was worried about him, so he wrote her a wonderful letter. He said (I have the letter right here):

"Gram, I'm in a little danger, but so is every soldier whether he's sitting behind a desk or up front with the infantry. I'm not trying to be a hero or anything. All I know is that I want to go home and see the end of this war and never see another. I want to come home and play a game of Ping-Pong with Meyer and eat all that good food you cook and water the lawn for you and play with Issa. I want to do a million things that have to do with Mom and Dad and you and everybody.

"To do all that, Gram, I have to help finish things up here. I don't want to be sitting around in your parlor in a few years and hear the same thing that the world heard that 7th of December in 1941. I'm going to be okay. Someday soon Richard and I and all us soldiers will be marching home, and then we can all go back to those things I talked about. Let's have a little cooperation. I want no tears shed for me — I'm so anxious to get home and see the new addition to the family that I won't let anyone take a shot at me. You tell Musetta to have a good strong baby. Send me a picture of you smiling so I can say, 'Fellows, that's my Gram with hair as white as fresh snow and my best gal next to Mom.' That's all for now, Gram, I'm going to be a very good boy, so you be a very good girl for Richard and myself. Take care of everybody. You're the best bubbeh in the world.

Your grandson, Sammy."

What's amazing to me is that even now, even after the army has declared Richard legally dead, even after they've sent his things home to Ava and Len, Sammy still talks about them both coming home at the end of the war. Please, God, let Sammy come safely through this. Ava couldn't survive another loss—I know it. She looks suddenly much older. She's stopped running to the orphanage, to the city, or wherever it was she was always going. She stays home nearly all the time now. And she's getting white hair, just like Mama. And she's wearing big ugly black shoes, like Mama, with laces and squat heels. Old lady shoes. But she seems calmer, somehow. She's less frantic and less hopeful. She reminds me of women who sit on the benches on Ocean Parkway and watch the cars and the bicycles and the lovers go by. They all have the same expressions on their faces—a kind of knowingness, as if they've seen it all, and here it is, going by again, and there's nothing better to do, so they sit and watch it happen.

Even when I go by them with Milton, pushing him in his wheelchair, the women on the benches look at us as if to say, "Well, yes, that happens, too—young men get maimed, and young women lose their chance for having a normal life and children. Well, yes—we all know that happens, and what can we do about it?"

Even I have come to see it that way. What can I do about it? Nothing. So I do what I can—I work for the war, and I tend to Mama's needs, and I plan for the time Milton and I will be married, probably at the end of this year. By then the house will be perfect. The conversion was finished just in time for the birth of the new baby (not a minute too soon). Mr. Schneider was slow, but very thorough, and his carpentry was magnificent. Just last weekend Meyer did the necessary things to make us, finally, into two separate households. The front room upstairs, which used to be his and Musetta's bedroom, is now a beautiful living-room, dining-room, and kitchen combination.

The middle small bedroom will be my beauty parlor, and at the back of the house are the big bedrooms, one for Mama and Nathan, and one (I blush!) for me and Milton. Someday Milton and I may want to move to our own house, but with apartments so scarce now, this is the best arrangement. We've talked to Mr. Schneider, and he says he can build a special seat on electric pulleys for Milton to use to get up the stairs. There can be a storage place for one wheelchair downstairs, and then he can have a second one for use upstairs. These are all details, but they are exciting and wonderful to think about.

My one burning sorrow is that I shall never know the beauty of physical love. I should not even write about it here; it's private and personal. But even so—is it not one of life's great experiences? As childbirth is? Well—God has been good to me, letting me live with Issa and now with the new infant. Musetta wants to name her Iris Fern. Mama has already said that's no name for a Jewish baby, but Musetta's answer is that Musetta was no name for a Jewish baby either!

ONE HUNDRED THIRTY-NINE

Musetta lay on her new down comforter in her newly built bedroom with her new baby cradled in her arms. She watched as her little Iris Fern sucked hungrily from the bottle. There was no tyrannical nurse this time—Issa was old enough to be helpful, and Meyer took care of the baby's night feedings. If there should be an emergency, there were always the "upstairs people"—but Musetta never called on them. She preferred to pretend they were not there. She made a point of locking the stairway door to make it clear, especially to Mama, that they were now living in two households, and if the upstairs household wanted to visit the downstairs household, the members had to do what anyone else would have to do: ring the front doorbell. The door at the bottom of the staircase between the two households had only a skeleton-key lock, but for Musetta it was the symbol of what she had always wanted: privacy with her family. That was why they had paid to have a separate side entrance built for the upstairs apartment— to give both families their own entrance and even separate mailboxes. Never again would anyone march into her bedroom—as Mama had always done—to collect her and Meyer's under-wear for the wash or to dust under the bed!

Something in her had relaxed—she didn't feel angry when Meyer walked around in his undershorts or stopped her in the kitchen for a lengthy bear hug. Even if Issa were there, watching, smiling shyly, Musetta didn't feel that old rush of tension and resentment. This was the way it should have been from the beginning: just them—husband and wife and, later, as was normal, their children. A pity they had wasted so many years of their marriage with-out privacy, without freedom from constant interruptions.

She could see the lilac tree from the window, just budding, and could feel and smell the coming of spring in the air. Issa was in the next room (the old dining room, now their living room) listening to her programs on the General Electric radio; she loved those fifteen-minute adventures—Captain Midnight and the Lone Ranger. She would often sit on the armchair, trans-fixed, her back straight, her eyes unseeing, her feet not quite touching the rug, listening intently to her heroes' adventures.

These days the radio seemed to control their lives. The news promised the war would soon be over. Terrible news had come recently about how many Jews had died, been starved, tortured, in the concentration camps in Germany. Musetta realized that if she'd lived in Europe, she would have been counted as a Jew no matter how little she followed Jewish law. She would probably have been sent to a concentration camp and killed there. It was really beyond belief—that Hitler hated Jews because they were Jewish. That he wanted to kill every Jew. That he would have killed Musetta and her entire family.

She would be so glad when the war was over, when the victory garden could be dug under and flowers planted in the backyard, when Gilda could stop selling war bonds and playing some kind of heroine, when sugar and nylons and soap powder—and soft shoe leather!—would be available again. Musetta hardly had a decent pair of shoes to her name. The war had interfered with her life for years. The sooner she could be done thinking about it, the better.

She tapped the bottom of Iris Fern's little feet to wake her, to hurry her with her feeding. It was time to get dinner started, Meyer would be home soon. Every night he brought home a box of delights for Issa. They never knew what treasures he would find in any ordinary workday, when he went on calls to buy antiques. Last night he had brought home a chewing gum machine—of the kind that were usually placed in subway stations. And the night before he had brought her a clown costume, probably once used in a circus. What Issa loved most were the books he brought her—cartons of books bought at estate sales. Her goal was to read them all—whatever they were: dog stories or history books or comic books or Nancy Drew mysteries. She'd pile them beside her bed in great towers and explain to Musetta that she put "the best" books on the bottom, an arrangement that would force her to read the harder books first so she would be on her way to being rewarded with the fun books. In that way, she told her mother, she'd get a good education on all subjects.

Musetta smiled, feeling great pride in Issa. The new baby was a great joy, also. She seemed to have a fiery temperament. Even at two months, if she was waked from a nap, she would cry for an hour before she could be distracted and calmed. She was passionate about things, and, like her mother, she was not easily pacified. Musetta looked up at the sound of a little whimper.

Issa stood at the foot of the bed with a complaint.

" . . . and right at the best part of my program, Mommy," Issa said, "they interrupted to say that President Roosevelt had died, and now I won't know what happened . . . "

"What? Turn the radio up, hurry!" Musetta said, putting Iris Fern in her crib. "Make it loud!" There was a rattling at the stairway door. Musetta usually called out, "Go to the front door," but this time she ran and jiggled the skeleton key till the door opened.

Mama stumbled into the living room, her eyes wide with panic. "Did you hear it, did you hear?" she cried. "The president! A blood clot in his head! What will happen to us?"

Gilda's heels clattered down the stairs. She was followed by her customer, a woman with half her hair rolled in pin curls.

"Oh God, Musetta—did you hear?" Gilda said. "He was like a father to us all. What will we do without him?"

Issa began to cry, Iris Fern began to scream from her crib, Mama began to sob, and Gilda and her customer embraced each other. For some reason, which was a mystery to Musetta, she felt her own eyes fill with tears—hot, burning, violent tears—and she began to sob. Gilda held out her arms to her, and Musetta came into them, and the two sisters clung to one another, crying.

She felt Gilda's frail shoulders shaking in her arms, felt how small and delicate and vulnerable Gilda was, felt how easy it would be for her to die, also, and the flood of tears renewed itself. "We have all had so much grief," Gilda sobbed against Musetta's shoulder. "So much."

"I know," Musetta said, holding her tight. "I know."

"I love you so much," Gilda cried. "I love you, Musetta."

"I love you, too," Musetta said gently. "It's true. I do."

ONE HUNDRED FORTY

Ava heard a knock on the front door. In the early morning light Len groaned sleepily in bed beside her. Ava threw on her robe and raced down the stairs.

God, please God, let it not be a telegram. Sammy was supposed to be home in just a week. Please! No more bad news! "Who is it?" she asked, hearing her voice crack.

"Ava," a man whispered. "Open the door, just for a minute. It's Johnny Quinn."

She opened the door. "Are you crazy? Coming here?"

"I need to talk to you, Ava. You haven't called me in so long, not for months."

"I told you, things are different now. I can't get away."

"But I need to talk to you."

"All right," she said. "Go—go away right now, go to Avenue P. I'll meet you in front of the Chinks. I'll tell Len I'm going to get some bagels for breakfast. Good-bye." She closed the door in his face, her heart shuddering. Upstairs again, she dressed in a housedress and her black oxfords. In the mirror she looked so much like Mama, with her ample breasts and her hair going white.

She felt it a relief to be getting old, to be asked less of, to be able to rest. The war was ending, a peace was settling on her and the world. She and Len had somehow restored their connection; the chains of their marriage had been resoldered by their pain. It was no fairy-tale romance, but an acknowledgment that what they had shared was theirs, and only they could understand what it had been. Len had given up going out to drink at bars. He stayed home at night now.

Could she ever show Johnny Quinn the baby pictures of Richard and feel his heart move the way she knew Len's heart moved? Could she ever tell him how it had been with her in childbirth? Len had been there, had felt her pains, had promised her it would soon be over.

Perhaps it would have been different if she'd been a passionate woman, someone who cared about sex—but with Len or with Johnny Quinn, all she wanted was for it to be over, for the man to take his need of her and be done, let her be, let her sleep.

She went quietly downstairs and left a note on the kitchen table: *Gone to bakery for rolls and bagels. Home soon.*

As she approached the Chinese restaurant, she saw Johnny leaning against the glass-plate window, shifting his weight from one long leg to another.

She saw her reflection in the window and wanted to say, "Look, look at that dumpy old woman in the window. You don't want her."

Johnny seemed nervous. It was not like him, with his easy Irish ways, to look so serious. Something was wrong. "Come inside, we can have some tea," he said. "No one is in there. They're making egg rolls for lunchtime." He held the door for her, and she entered the dark place. The white tablecloths gleamed in the dimness like tombstones. There was a smell of strong spice, gingerroot, garlic. The gaunt Chinese waiter brought them a steaming pot of tea. Johnny took her hand. "I have something to say, Ava. You keep putting me off. I've been waiting for you to call. You've warned me never to call you, so I don't. But you promise to call me, and you never do."

Ava withdrew her hand. Some afternoon Musetta and Meyer might come here for lunch, as they sometimes did, and the Chinese waiter might say to them, "Your sister was here with the blond man, her lover."

"I don't know how to begin," Johnny said. "You've meant more to me than anyone ever has, in my whole life . . . "

"Please, Johnny. It can't be. I've tried to tell you. My life with Len is my only possible life. We still have a son who is ours and who needs us to be his parents. God willing, he will be home from the front in a week. His only injury was that he took some pieces of shrapnel in his body. He went to war for me, for all of us. Do you think when he comes home I can tell him I ran away with an Irishman?"

Johnny buried his face in his hands. Ava wanted to leave the restaurant. He was going to make it hard for her. But then he raised his head, and she saw he was smiling. It was a guilty, confused, pleased smile. It was the strangest smile she had ever seen.

"Oh, Ava," he said. "No, no, no—that isn't what I mean, oh, no, no, no." He was almost laughing now. He took her hand again and held it tight. "It's something altogether different. I was worried to tell you about it, but I see now you will truly be relieved."

"Tell me what?"

"There is a woman I know . . . she's thirty-five years old, she works in the Automat, she weighs nickels in her hand . . . "

"And?"

"She never makes a mistake."

"So is that a miracle?"

"Her name is Annie O'Meara."

"So?"

"So every time I go there, and she's there, she gives me twenty-two nickels for a dollar."

"And you get rich? What are you saying, Johnny?"

"And she smiles at me."

"So she smiles, so what?"

"She lives with her old mother."

"Johnny, this is making me crazy."

"She's in love with me, Ava. She wants from me what you used to want from me. A little walking, a little talking. And maybe other things. We haven't done anything yet."

"So what are you telling me for?"

"I want your permission. Only if you don't want me—if you really don't want me—will I start to see Annie."

"Oh my, of course, go, go. You have my blessing, Johnny. You know I have hidden myself from you for months and months. There is nothing here for you—I'm tired and old, and I want no more trouble, no more excitement."

"I'll see this girl only if you swear you mean that."

"I mean it with all my heart. Go, Johnny, be happy if you can. I just want to live in peace. Len is good to me now. He is going to take me to South America on a cruise someday. On a banana boat. That's enough excitement for the rest of my life."

"You are an angel, Ava."

"Only an angel and not a saint?" She felt unusually lighthearted, almost cheerful. Johnny was going to leave her alone and not be angry, not be miserable, not drink himself to death.

Just then the waiter emerged from the dim back of the restaurant. "Cookies come with tea," he said, setting down a plate of fortune cookies.

"This is just what we need, Johnny. Something to start us on our new lives."

"You first."

Ava cracked open the cookie. She laughed and read her fortune aloud to Johnny: THE SUN WILL ALWAYS SHINE THROUGH YOUR HEART, LIGHT UP YOUR SMILE AND WARM YOUR SOUL.

ONE HUNDRED FORTY-ONE

Rachel and her sister, Rose, were sitting on the new couch in the living room upstairs at 405 Avenue O. New wallpaper, light green, with white roses twining among vines, brightened the walls. A hand-painted plate of a castle on a mountain, overlooking a river, hung on the wall. Rachel had kept it for years in a drawer; it came from the old country just like the jewelry that sat on Rose's lap, a few things that had belonged to their mother in Poland. They were talking about what to do with them.

Hymie and Nathan were playing pinochle on the dining-room table. Hymie was not allowed to smoke his cigar in the house, not with the new baby and Issa downstairs, so instead he was cracking peanuts between his teeth.

"Watch that the shells don't fall on the floor—or else!" Rose instructed him.

"Or else what?" Hymie challenged her. "You'll make me snort them up like I'm a vacuum cleaner?"

"Oh shut up," Rose said.

Rachel and Nathan exchanged glances.

"What?" Rose said to Rachel. "You and your husband never snap at each other?"

"We don't," Rachel said. "We like to have peace together. We have no strength to fight."

"Peace is in the grave," Rose said. "What is a life, anyway? Nothing but struggle, battle, tears, pain, and then it's all over."

"Nathan and I had our struggle. Now we are old and grateful. We have a good life now, without tears."

Rose lowered her voice. "I still don't know why you took him back."

"And I still don't know how you stayed with Hymie," Rachel whispered. "He's hard as nails."

"You didn't complain about him when he was supporting you and your children, when Ava lived with us."

"I had no choice," Rachel said quietly.

She looked at Nathan again, and he gave her a quick smile. She smiled back. She felt her good fortune all around her. She appreciated the new kitchen upstairs in the big front room, her new stove and sink, the space they all had gained from converting the house to a two-family place.

For once, the sense of struggle within her was quiet; her daughters were alive and well—Gilda would soon be married, Musetta was happy with her new baby, Meyer had a business that was working out, and Issa was a pleasure to see every day. Ava, too, was more calm these days. She and Len were planning trips, they were enjoying their money.

"So what should we do with Mama's jewelry?" Rose said. "We're getting old, Rachel, we should decide who should have what."

"Like these are the queen's jewels?" Rachel said, laughing. "Look at the little pile in your lap. The same jewels you had in the cigar box for years: Mama's pearls, Mama's little diamond earrings, Mama's wedding ring."

"They're not all mine. I kept them safe for you till right this minute."

"So who should have them? I don't need them now."

"And I don't need them either. Let's offer Gilda Mama's wedding ring. Maybe she'd want it for her wedding."

"And let's give each of Musetta's girls one of the diamond earrings. When they grow up, each one can wear a diamond on a chain."

"And the pearls?"

"You take them."

"No, you take them."

"I'll take them," Hymie said. "I'll pawn them and buy a good cigar."

"Shut up," Rose told her husband.

"Let's go in my bedroom," Rachel suggested. "Leave the men here in peace."

They gathered up the little lapful of jewels and went down the hall to Rachel and Nathan's bedroom.

Rose said, in Yiddish, as soon as they had closed the door, "Did you ever think we would live this long, Rachel?"

"Who could know what life would bring? We got to the *goldena medina*, didn't we?"

"It wasn't so gold," Rose said.

"But look at us—we have a house in Brooklyn, your Hymie made money. Who could have guessed what would happen to us?"

"We're still two greenhorns," Rose said. "You and me, we're still chicken pluckers."

"But we made a life here, Rose. I had my children. You nearly forced me to marry Isaac, but from him I have my precious daughters."

"And from them your gorgeous Issa and your Iris. I will never have grand-children, Rachel. God didn't grant me children."

"Musetta says there is no God. Do you think there's a God, Rose?"

"We're here, what else can we know? We're here, we have a life, we suffer, we love. What's the difference if there is God?"

"If there was God, we wouldn't have lost Shmuel and Richard."

"Who knows if they're lost? They could be together in heaven, playing pinochle right now."

Rachel, sitting on the bed next to her sister, put her arms around her. "Rose, you and I together here, right now. We're counting our blessings right now. Our men are eating peanuts in the next room. Maybe that's enough. Maybe we can't ask for more."

"I always could ask for more," Rose said. She embraced Rachel. They rocked their white heads together. "But for once I'll shut my mouth."

ONE HUNDRED FORTY-TWO

Issa could hear her father singing to Iris Fern all the way from where she stood on Aunt Gilda's kitchen table. He was out in the front garden with the baby, rocking her in her carriage and singing:

> *"Praise the Lord and pass the ammunition,*
> *Praise the Lord, my baby's going pishin',*
> *Praise the Lord and hurry with the diapers*
> *Or we'll all get wet!"*

"Meyer!" Mommy called to him from the front door. "Don't sing that song so the whole neighborhood can hear you! Do you want them to think you're vulgar?"

"Turn this way," Aunt Gilda said to Issa. "You're coming apart back here." Aunt Gilda looked just like a bride, dressed in her white dress and wearing a white crown on her head. Only the red border of her sleeves, the red cross on the top of her crown, and the red streamers down her back gave away the truth: that she was a Red Cross woman and not a bride at all.

"Oh my Iskala," she said. "I've got to run in one minute. The parade starts at Ocean Parkway at noon, and I can't be late. I should have started on you sooner. I never knew it took so long to make a star."

Issa was sandwiched between two pieces of cardboard each shaped like a star, and Aunt Gilda was smoothing silver foil—bit by bit—over the cardboard. She was carefully unraveling the silver from Issa's newest silver-foil ball. Now that the war was over, they no longer needed the silver for weapons, and Aunt Gilda said they might just as well use it for the star as to buy some. They had done most of the silvering last night, but this morning they'd found a whole blank area of cardboard they'd overlooked.

"How do I look, Aunt Gilda?" Issa asked. "Am I beautiful?"

"You are the most exquisite child in the world," Aunt Gilda said. "I could eat you up."

"No, no!" Issa cried as Aunt Gilda bent to bite her bare leg. "Then I can't dance at the block party. I'll be in your intestines."

"Oh don't be such a smarty," Gilda said. "You and your big words."

Issa laughed. Today was going to be the most wonderful day of her life. She had never seen everyone so happy. The war was over! That's all anyone talked about! It's over, it's over, the boys are coming home! Their boy, Uncle Sammy, was already home, and he would be at the parade today. Aunt Gilda and Nathan had this morning set up a big table in front of their house and covered it with a red-white-and-blue tablecloth. On it they had laid platters of food from their victory garden: long crisp slices of cucumber, crunchy fresh carrots, sweet ripe tomatoes, wonderful baby peas.

Daddy had picked a basket of fresh peaches from the peach tree and had piled them up in a big glass bowl. All the neighbors were doing the same— bringing out tables, setting out food from their gardens.

"Do you two need some help?" Mommy had come upstairs (today the stairway door between their apartments was going to be open all day!).

"You take over," Gilda said. "I've got to run. Milton will be waiting for me out front by now. Oh my God, did I put on my face? Is my lipstick on?"

"You look wonderful," Mommy said. "You look perfect. You look as if you won the war single-handedly."

"I almost did," Gilda said.

In a blur of red and white gauze she spun around and rushed away.

"Listen to my tap shoes," Issa said to her mother. "Do you think everyone will hear them clicking all the way down the street?"

"I'm sure they'll hear you all the way in Canarsie," Mommy answered, laughing. She looked beautiful, too. She wore an aqua linen dress and had a bright pink snowball flower pinned behind her ear.

It would be marvelous, Issa thought, if wars could end every day.

"There, you're all done," Mommy said. "The brightest star in all of Brooklyn." She lifted Issa off the table. "Now go downstairs and wait with Daddy in the garden. In a few minutes you should hear the band, and then Aunt Gilda will be marching by in the parade."

Issa raced down the stairs and out through the new side entrance. Grandma and Nathan were sitting in the alley, fanning themselves with fans.

"Don't rush so fast," Grandma said. "Rest, you'll live longer."

Issa flew to the front of the house, feeling the hot summer sun fly off her silver body like jets of fire.

"Mmm," her father said, standing in the garden, bending to kiss her cheek. "You look just as glamorous as Betty Grable." The new baby, Iris Fern, lay in her carriage in a yellow sun suit, kicking her fat little legs in the air.

"It's too bad she doesn't know anything important yet," Issa said. "Not anything. Not even who Hitler is."

"She'll grow up soon enough." Proudly, he rocked the carriage. "And then you two can be best friends. But listen, I think I hear them!" he said, puffing on his pipe. "This is it."

"Oh pick me up, please, Daddy," Issa cried.

"How can I?" her father said. "The points of your stars will pierce my heart."

"Well, then, never mind! Uncle Sammy will pick me up. There he is now, with Aunt Ava and Uncle Len." She dashed away, her tap shoes ticking like a crazy clock. Uncle Sammy was not as tall as Uncle Richard, but he was just as strong. "Will you pick me up?" cried Issa, and he swung her way up, careful not to bend the points of her silver star. Then he held her on his shoulder so she could have a good view of the parade.

First came the marching band from Midwood High School and right behind them came the Avenue N shul's Red Cross team, rows and rows of women dressed just like Aunt Gilda, marching briskly in their white shoes, their red banners flowing from their white hats. And there was Aunt Gilda, right at the front in the center, carrying the American flag! It was taller by far than she was, and she held the end of the flag in her hand so it would not blow and flap in the faces of the women on either side of her.

She marched proudly, taking big strong steps, smiling beautifully as she passed their house at 405 Avenue O, smiling a special loving smile at Milton, who sat in the wheelchair beside the wishbone-shaped tree right at the curb. She seemed to be smiling at everyone, at Mommy and Daddy, at the new baby Iris Fern, at Grandma and Nathan, at Uncle Len and Aunt Ava, at Sammy the soldier, and most of all she seemed to be smiling at Issa.

Everyone was roaring and cheering and clapping. All the neighbors were yelling and whistling and screaming. When the parade had passed by, the people at the block party gathered at the tables, which were brimming with food. It was a better party, by far, than Issa's last birthday party. There were more cookies and cakes, more balloons and banners, more crepe paper streamers and tissue flowers. There were noisemakers and popguns; there were yo-yos and kites with smiling faces on them.

After a while Aunt Gilda came back, breathless and flushed, and went to stand behind Milton's wheelchair; he reached for her hand and kissed it. With her other hand she gently stroked his hair. Shyly, Issa came forward and stood before them. When she looked down at her tinfoil star, she saw them reflected in it in a hundred little shining images.

"I think it's time," Aunt Gilda said, nodding firmly.

"It's time," Issa called to her father. He came forward and cleared a place on the table. Then he swung Issa in the air and set her down where the bowl of peaches had been. "Ready?" Her father cleared his throat and began singing:

> *"You're a grand old flag,*
> *You're a high-flying flag,*
> *And forever inpeace may you wave.*
> *You're the emblem of*
> *The land I love.*
> *The home of the free and the brave . . . "*

Issa did her tap dance. She danced with all her strength and all her heart; she danced for everyone on Avenue O and in Brooklyn and in all America; she danced for all the lost soldiers like Richard who couldn't be there to see her. She danced so fast she felt she would fly off into the wild blue yonder.